T0198915

MAD ADDIE

A New Woman Before There Was One

S. JOSEPH KRAUSE

Order this book online at www.trafford.com
or email orders@trafford.com

Most Trafford titles are also available at major online book retailers.

Print information available on the last page.

ISBN: 978-1-4907-5699-8 (sc)
ISBN: 978-1-4907-5698-1 (hc)
ISBN: 978-1-4907-5697-4 (e)

Library of Congress Control Number: 2015903730

Trafford rev. 03/09/2015

 www.trafford.com

North America & international
toll-free: 1 888 232 4444 (USA & Canada)
fax: 812 355 4082

CONTENTS

PART IV
New Love and Beyond

PART V
Impulse Will Have its Way

PART VI
Whimpy in Chains: Riots

PART VII
A Bombshell Letter

PART VIII
Politics & Johnny

PART IX
Dealings With Dunny

PART X
The Life Beyond Johnny

PART XI
History, Fire, Murders Resolved

PART XII
Climax

PART XIII
Explosion and Showdown

PART I

THE BARON AND HIS CASTLE

CHAPTER I

"The Baron and His Castle"

His turreted castle loomed over the city from its perch on the crest of North Hill, the highest point in a five-county area. This flamboyant textile baron had had it built as a tribute to his success in the 1920s heyday of luxury silk cloth. After doing a heady business deal in Germany, he had a notion one rainy afternoon to trudge up the zigzag path leading to the famed Hohenzollern Castle. He had vaguely heard about it while consummating a deal with a leading fashion house, and he wanted to know if it was worth a look. His guide said something under his breath in German.

Nonetheless, neck arched, the baron had his look and was so impressed by the massive grandeur of it that he thought he saw a noble pile piercing the clouds on almost every distant hill from there to Lake Constance. His castle—which took all of five years to build, sandstone slab by meticulously chipped slab—was familiarly known in town as Sam Farber's Folly.

What did he care? He had started out with a little three-vat die shop in a garage down by the river and got flooded out and fined for dumping, which poisoned the carp; and he vowed he'd never stain his hands again. A partnership, a crucial loan to bid on a foreclosed mill, economies (his shops were "scab heaven") and he was shortly on his way up. The jobbers that he'd once had to haggle with over piecework were crowding his outer office.

Besides, dying rather quickly became a small part of his total business. He'd branched out into woven fabric and installed Jacquard looms, and his biggest moneymaker became fine silk brocade. Buyers reported that their moneyed trade simply loved the novel designs and, even more, the feel of it: it was great against a woman's skin.

As he prospered, the baron had crowed, *Why not put a castle on a hill built for myself?* Not fully three years after its much-heralded completion, the castle/mansion was thought to have been suddenly abandoned when the baron overextended himself. Galloping inflation in Germany resulted in the cancellation of his big contracts there, and his own bulging inventory helped to grease the price slide that did him in. His loans were called; and the biggest of his mills, counterpart of famed Henry Doherty's, closed about the time that he disappeared.

The banks immediately had their lawyers assess the value of his assets so they could slap a lien on whatever they could lay hands on and much else that they couldn't (anything to get themselves first in line among creditors—forefeet in the trough). When the baron failed to show up in court, the lawyers got a warrant to snoop around in the mansion itself and found him half-sitting and slumped against the wall of an upstairs bedroom with a bullet in his head. His wife lay face down on the bathroom floor, half-naked, with the hair on the back of her head soaked in blood.

CHAPTER 2

"The Baron and His Italian Wife"

As reported by his former aide, Domo, the Terrible Turk, when things were going well, the couple neatly complemented one another. His favorite sport was making money; hers, spending it. They'd been known to have arguments when business turned south, but as was known so far, there was nothing that might induce violence—though money <u>would</u> become a sore spot. Known for his silence, Domo was in on most personal matters and, to all intents and purposes, out as well; he knew when to get lost, and in the heat of one of their arguments, that's what he did. Detectives who finally got the chance to question him drew a blank.

Some rookie cop, who was not the sharpest pencil in the box, said that Domo had always wanted to hook up with the Dillinger gang. Actually, it turned out that Domo's son was the one who had the gangster fantasies: As a kid, he ran around the house yelling *"Bang, bang,* Bank. Gotsha!" Using graduation money, he bought a genuine Buster Brown belt with horsehair inlay. It got him into some fights, winning more than he lost. A replica of the old man, he sported a brush cut and a stubble beard. He told people that the baron should have gone after the banks instead of letting them come after him, which netted him a laugh.

Young Domo followed Dillinger's antics in the newspaper, got himself a fat 45 pistol, and decided to have a try. He scared the teller and walking out with his pockets stuffed, he bumped into a cop, was jailed, and, like his hero, escaped. Gone and nowhere to be found. But he briefly showed for the double funeral as he'd had a crush on the baron's wife, one of a number he was sweet on.

Gina, the quick-witted wife, said her husband could have used the kid. Until the baron's abrupt skid, regarding business, she didn't ask and he didn't tell. But once she did start asking, she asked a lot. *What made him think he could trust the Germans when he couldn't even speak their language? And what stupidity was it for him, a business genius, to sink good money into this gothic monstrosity?*

"Pure ego," he admitted—which, from her (palm to forehead) evoked an "Oy vey!" And now he wants into her *trust*!

"Okay already," she ranted, arms akimbo and eyebrows arched, "but now we're talkin' cash, are we? Mine included?" When upset, she'd imitate a Jewish intonation. He'd joke that she was his "Italianische Yenta." She liked the fact that he was lavishly generous with her and made nothing of it. Despite which, she nagged enough about his spending on other stuff that one day he was willing to grant that things were getting . . . "well, a bit troublesome."

Just like the activist that he was, after their disagreement, he was on the phone all day; and the following morning, he snatched up the financial page of the paper and tore it to shreds. His wife was even more taken aback when he swung himself into a brisk-legged dance only he could call a buck and wing—which, with spread arms, he ended with a lurch and a "Huzzah!" She met his pursed lips but wanted to know what the ruptured tap was all about. *He was celebrating going broke?*

"Not to worry, honey. I've been in touch with the Big Boys. They did some financial maneuvers that would protect profits. In fact, they were shorting the market and making big bucks. Meanwhile, with the rest of their holdings in Treasuries and Munis, they were gonna be able to ride this thing out. We did the same."

"Yeah, but they don't tell you how much they'd lost already."

She wanted to know how much <u>he</u> had lost. After all, there was the matter of her trust. Well, like he'd told her before, it takes money to make money (just ask that young Domo), and just like the sweetheart that she was, she wouldn't charge like a bank.

"You <u>mean</u>?"

CHAPTER 3

"She Kept Her Family Out"

What family friction there was, was between Gina and her family—particularly involving her brothers, who thought she had been obliged to bring them into the business. They were angered at her telling them that, for their information, business was Sam's business, his plaything; and hers was shopping. If he happened to ask why she needed a new dress, the latest fashion in shoes—whatever—she'd model them for him. When he asked how much, she'd lowball it, lying no more than was necessary. With her family, she lied even when it wasn't.

She was the daughter of the baron's top competitor, Angie Guipeletti—who had a proud Roman nose and an ancestry that he claimed had come down from Augustus Caesar, the real successful one. Word had it that when the baron bought Angie out, the guy wanted his daughter to be part of the package. Headstrong about having things her way, she insisted on keeping her family apart from her husband's money; she wouldn't let Papa Angie get his covetous foot in the business door. Jealous of the baron's Midas touch, Angie liked to rib his in-law Boss-man.

"Hey, Sam, Jews don't build castles."

And Sam liked to josh back. "Papa Angie, you forget that, for the wedding, Gina made me convert!"

"Okay, but in your heart, Sam?"

"Is Gina."

He was sincere. Despite their spats, he did love her and knew how to smother her complaints: there were hugs, love pats, endearments on bended knee, and a diamond ring bigger than the last (which got him a throaty "Oh, yee-ah!"). She bended both knees, and there was peace.

CHAPTER 4

"A Perfect Match"

They were a perfect match: she had a temper, and he had charm. She said she fell for him because he was always well-groomed, looked and was a gentleman. He was a touch bigger than medium build, wide at the shoulders, and had wavy black hair, with a tinge of gray at the temples signifying the affluence that women found attractive. As fond of sailing as he was of doing a business deal, he had the look of a bronzed sea captain who would squint at the least hint of trouble, which was often enough. A-ship or a-shore, he enjoyed sailing close to the wind and was flattered when people took him for a goy.

He said he liked a spunky broad; and in Gina, he had one, who also happened to have a fleshy nature that hinted at a racy bedroom. Knowing how attractive he was to other women, she enrolled in a fitness class wanting to cultivate the hourglass figure that kept eluding her. Always fashionably dressed, she wore tight dresses that accented her ample bosom. She had a preference for stiletto heels and blonde frosting for her hair. She liked to brush her squeezable butt against him.

Whatever she said or did, like it or not, he'd mostly go with it, which even extended to Christianity. Church attendance was practical; it broadened his acceptance in the social circles where he'd been snubbed. But when chided by the priest for being a Christer, Sam kindly asked whether those two key dates didn't outweigh all the others. The priest smiled indulgently as if he were dealing with a naïve child.

Sam smiled back and spoke of endowing a family pew as he pressed a five-digit check into the priest's limp palm, an unheard-of sum in that day but heard of from the pulpit in the upcoming Christmas service. Thereafter attendance became a nonissue.

Close to retirement, the elderly priest was all congeniality; and so was Sam. But not so much his treatment of competitors, among whom there were some who hated to be beaten by a Jew. People who were around when the baron got mad wished they weren't: they said his ears got so red they looked like they might burst into flames, prompting his contemporary father-in-law to concede that in this world the devil does get his due.

Gina understood he was tough; and she'd heard stories from her father about the baron's underselling and breaking once-flourishing rivals, leaving grown men in tears. But not wanting to know the particulars, she said she found such things hard to believe and fluffed them off, never having seen a wisp of anger herself in those ice-gray eyes.

She did get the lowdown from her father about the "Big Boys" connection. Sam apparently had done business with wily Joe K, who had enriched himself first on booze and then on commodities, last resort of the Chicago Irish and, having moved on, knew where to place his stash. In financial circles, Joe was known as the Wall Street seismologist. The way friends quaintly put it, aside from his kinesthetic sensitivity, he could smell trouble in the market like the polar bear could smell a seal miles away. One of his few envies, Sam wished his smeller carried to Chicago.

CHAPTER 5

"Papa Angie"

When questioned about what happened up at the castle, Papa Angie tartly replied, "How da hell should I know?" He wanted it observed that he was in prolonged mourning over the loss of a daughter, and, somewhat more (people said), over what would become of the spoils, so annoyingly tied up. Angie was a rather beefy guy who, because of his heft, looked taller than he was. Habitually nervous—especially when pressured as he was by the police—he had a habit of giving short answers, spoken out of the corner of his mouth. He repeated that he deserved to left alone. *Didn't he have enough grief?*

He occasionally wore loud sports coats (mostly checked) like he'd been at the racetrack, where he was often enough. It was hard to believe from the looks of him, but Angie was said to be a lady's man. Sam had asked whether or not they went for that rascally twinkle in his eye. Angie went on to brag that since he had to work harder at it than a guy as "well set up" as his son-in-law, he did okay for himself. Sam congratulated him, and when Angie mentioned the latest wealthy widow he was in touch with, Sam smiled. "They say modesty doesn't become a dago."

Unlike Papa, his twin sons were somewhat on the long and lean side in looks—pretty much resembling their recently deceased mother, a rail-thin and ulcer-prone woman who was thought to have been done in by what passed for ptomaine poison. She had been a wealthy widow herself, the original one in the family. After suspicion passed, (Mama's estate went to the twin sons) Angie had to endure additional sessions with the police regarding the deceased son-in-law and could only venture that Sam had made enemies enough—some from suspicious husbands. *Didn't his former secretary say the women called him drop-dead handsome?*

Knowing Angie liked to showboat, especially when talking to the press, reporters wanted to know about those false friends Angie had mentioned when he was interviewed by detectives just back from the crime scene at the castle. The detectives wanted him to tell whether he knew of any suspicious people, and they wanted answers this time. No more "I dunno."

With arms across his chest, Angie said, "You, dicks, want suspects, huh? Well, lemme think. There were those salesmen who didn't get a bonus because they kept shining up to Sam. He didn't like 'em. Thought they made freelance deals behind his back. When he caught 'em, "*boom!*" Out da door dey went."

Number One detective was annoyed and pressed for <u>real</u> suspects. "Come on, fella. We're not here for fun and games. Da people who threatened him. Names!"

"Okay. There was also that secretary he fired for listening in on long distance calls. Gave her a check and threw <u>her</u> out da door." Beyond that, Angie said he knew "nuttin'." Grieving over the loss of his daughter and increasingly saddened that she didn't leave him anything, he repeated the refrain that he wanted some peace.

Asked about his sons, he declared they were out of town. Where didn't matter; they also knew nuttin'.

Detective One said they were taking him down to headquarters. After he was charged with obstruction and was booked, Angie called his lawyer—who bailed him out and drove him home, where first thing he did was to call his bookie and yank the cord off his listed phone.

CHAPTER 6

"A Classic Cold Case"

The *Morning Messenger*, paper of The Party out of office, was daily riding the police for spinning their wheels. People were incensed. Sam Farber had been an economic boon to the community. Editorials pointed out what a prince he'd been. When he closed the firm's centerpiece mill—the one running jacquard looms, said to be biggest in the entire woven garment industry—Sam set up a self-liquidating foundation that kept his unemployed workers paid for up to three months.

People insisted they wanted to know who would want to kill Sam, and this evoked the knowing response from city hall. "The way this dude did business, who wouldn't?"

The police had to confront angry citizens who gathered outside headquarters. Stung by cries of incompetence and puzzled that they could no more find a true suspect than the weapon that did Farber in, they were determined to find <u>something</u>. So they decided they'd save themselves a pack of trouble if they came out with the finding substantiated by their one-eyed coroner, that in lieu of contrary findings, it had to have been a murder-suicide.

The supposed motive was that the wife found out he had emptied the money in her trust and lost it in the stock market. So she was going to retaliate by disclosing his connection to the financier of a Chicago crime syndicate.

It sure made a lot of sense to the inquiring reporter, who treated it sardonically in his editorial column. The baron bludgeoned his wife from behind when she went to run water for her bath (perhaps she'd threatened one time too many?); then he took himself back to the bedroom, stuck a gun in his ear, pulled the trigger, got up (strong guy that he was), cranked out a casement window, tossed the gun over the cliff, and calmly sat himself down to die.

With people still mystified as to <u>why</u>, the police chief snidely asked, "How come those guys jumping out of windows in New York didn't have wings?" After a to-do, he shrugged, put the case into the unsolved file—a classic cold case—and after getting his cozy coroner to close the good eye and certify the cause of death as unknown, he told his men to get on with their work.

Since everybody's patience was wearing thin, the jokesters took over and told stories of the one-eyed coroner at a masquerade party bringing his monocle up close to compare the bullet in the baron's head to the one in the chief's regulation 45, which had strangely showed up at the crime scene in place of the one thrown out the window. Detective One piped up and said it actually was his. He'd been looking for it in the bushes at the foot of the cliff.

After a while, it was difficult to distinguish fact from parody. In any event, One thought they ought to be looking for Domo— who supposedly knew about those late-night, long distance calls on the private line. They shared the same bookie, the guy that One secretly called a living Fright.

When the reporter doggedly noted that one of the headbangers who had lately traveled with the baron—a certain ex-cop, Billy-club Bill—was still around, the police considering he was one of theirs said he'd been questioned and released. The guy had plainly been at the hospital watching out for his ailing mother, <u>or</u> as he said, "This thing could never have happened in the first place."

That shifted the focus back to Papa Angie for a while as it was recalled that he had wanted to have his wife cremated before an autopsy could be performed; however, the sons objected to setting Mother on fire—it was bad enough she died.

When the ptomaine poisoning was chemically dismissed, there had been rumors of arsenic oxide as the lady had died very suddenly after a seizure of vomiting. Angie said he'd had no objection to the coroner's exhuming his wife, but his lawyer tied that up. *What need was there for it, anyway?*

He observed that he never cooked dinner, but his wife did. Since the arsenic was odorless and tasteless, and a dose the size of a penny was enough to do the job and get it done quickly, the coroner noted he would have needed a tissue sample to make a determination. Ignoring the consent of the husband, he said that for an inquest, he'd need a ruling from the judge—who, pointing to his calendar, was signaling one case at a time.

When people cried for action, the judge languidly pointed to his docket.

CHAPTER 7

"A Magnificent Eyesore"

So things got stalemated for a while, and it became a lasting while.

As far as was known, there was but one heir, a young epileptic daughter tied to her bed in the insane asylum down state. She had been a bone of contention between her parents. According to the wife's friends, this produced their one real argument, with Sam attributing the falling sickness to her Italian side of the family (Didn't it go back to Caesar?) and Gina accusing him of being a bastard of a father for consenting to have their poor child confined.

It didn't matter that the daughter had made off with the family car one night and slammed it into a tree, almost killing herself. Sam conceded that he was probably wrong to give in to the doctors, and it bothered him. Over that, he would go through fits of guilt and vowed he'd somehow make it up to the girl, leaving the "somehow" for his lawyer to work out. And he could begin to make it up with financial goodies.

The son of poor Russian immigrants, Sam Faber at twelve was a floor boy in a Rhode Island textile mill and grew up never having had a toy of his own, a sense that never left him. So despite having the intuitive business smarts, he liked the feel of having possessions, which when crunch time came would make him loath to outright liquidate low-risk holdings.

But as that would to some extent be done for him, the baron, having courtesy of the Chicago Irishman anticipated the market, still died a rich man as fate—plus shrewd legal planning—enabled him to hide a tidy pack of assets for the daughter and another pack for an obscure heir that everyone was curious about. Regarding which, inquiries got nowhere.

His castle, on the other hand, did not fare very well. It was, to begin with, a gloomy Tudor affair with narrow casement windows—some were of stained glass—and affixed to its far end was an ivy-covered tower capped with battlements that overlooked the monopoly-sized houses far below. Accenting the isolated hilltop spread was its setting. Occasionally enveloped by storm clouds, the tower looked down on a sandy saucer carved out by the river meandering its way to the signature waterfall—which, on the recommendation of none other than Alexander Hamilton, inspired the founding of a city. Cheap power was always available. Just the thing to enchant a penny-pincher turned national treasurer.

From down below, the castle looked grotesque. People at first had greeted it with bewilderment, then amusement, and eventually indifference until the sensations occurred.

Years after Sam and Gina had passed, the hulking presence would remain empty, its former magnificence an eyesore. Prior to the great inferno that engulfed it, like it or hate it, it had a presence: The sandstone façade had darkened and was streaked by rusting gutters, green copper stains, and bird droppings. The broad plaza fronting it had been skillfully laid out with glazed brick, which had weathered and disappeared under a sea of weeds. Rumor had it that, when the famed Viennese architect Joseph Urban came over to have a look, he shook his head and put a hand over his eyes.

CHAPTER 8

"The Cousins"

What originally put the place in limbo was the dispute over ownership that broke out when two second cousins showed up several months after the funeral. *What were they thinking, what wanting?* Word got out they figured that, as relatives, they could do an end-run around the banks, sell the damned castle to whomever, maybe even lay claim to a remaining derelict mill or two, sell those, and walk away with a settlement that would fit their status.

They seemed to have credentials, producing a copy of their mother's birth certificate that showed her maiden name was Evelyn W. Farber. She—like the rest of the clan—had also craved power, tried a risky deal, gone broke, and had a nervous breakdown which did her in. Pity. She was a good mother. She remembered Uncle Sam, admired his ambition—which was limitless—and said he'd be unhappy unless he had worlds to conquer.

Upon the advice of counsel, before these newly emerging cousins went for the Henry Doherty–type mill, they figured that if they played it right, why not go to court and demand that the banks cough up their booty to legitimate heirs? The one cousin with the bald head and mustache talked a lot while the other—a short, pudgy guy—puffed on his cigar and nodded a lot.

This ambitious lawyer they'd gotten for themselves tried to nudge them back to reality. What he could do, he said, was show that the baron died intestate and draw up papers declaring the daughter incompetent, which went nowhere in court as there were conflicting medical evaluations of the daughter's condition, plus that business of an unidentified mystery heir.

The cousins soon got to be known as Curly and Moe, but before Billy-club Bill could drive them to the train station, their lawyer came up with a telegram that the asylum doctor had tried an experimental drug on the daughter, which produced a pretty bad seizure. So that seemed to settle the matter of competence.

"Not so fast," said Papa Angie as he moved his fat way in front of the cousins who were holding court in Mama Perez's backroom, burgers on account. As chief mourner, Angie held that any claims had first to be cleared with the probate court and, frankly, with him. Just as he'd raised hell about the poisoned carp, he had a habit of wanting to get his two cents in before anything was done relative to the inheritance. He claimed that if they examined his daughter's trust, they would likely find that the castle belonged in it. For starters, that much he should certainly have.

The banks had told him to take a hike; they'd already been there. Angie insisted "Not so fast," his standard brake when all else failed. There had to be other documents somewhere; his daughter did keep records. He was told to come back when he found them.

What he learned from the Yale-educated lawyer—in whose prestigious hands the baron's various trusts had been placed—was that on Gina's passing, the remainder of her trust got folded into that of the epileptic daughter; and provision was made for the entire package to fall into yet another trust set up for the obscure beneficiary should the epileptic predecease that party. All of this the Yale lawyer had, of course, successfully excluded from that part of the estate under dispute by the banks and cousins.

Papa Angie listened to the legalistic explanation and groaned. In other words, just now, there was really "nuttin'" for him! And here he thought the marriage had bought him insurance. He cursed the day he had sold out but got little sympathy from his sons—who thought he should have fought his way back in, at which he scowled. "Oh yeah, easy for them to say. What help they were! The one namely Angie Jr. had a hobby of chasin' skirts."

Meanwhile, Curly and Moe weren't exactly improving their popularity. While casing the mill property, Curly kept pumping the cabby for information. Question piled on question; and with his head swinging back and forth like a weather vane, the cabby missed a red light and rear-ended Klagemann, the town grouch, who gave him a blue earful and made out a police report.

Given his clients, the cousins' lawyer preferred anonymity. He got with the inquiring reporter and gave him background— hoping to soften hard feelings if people knew that these fellows were deserving, community-minded gentlemen (regulars at the Red Cross blood mobile) who had fallen on bad times (swindled by a tent preacher they gave their savings to).

They were even willing to give the city a cut of proceeds from the sale of the castle; and the devil takes the banks that had already glutted themselves on securities, two of the mills, and the lingering piece of a Cuban casino. Like moles spreading out under a lawn, the banks had their own lawyers digging around for more offshore properties. The cousins' lawyer claimed the baron's estate had been bleeding properties. He just wanted a modest piece of them for his clients so they could pay his fee.

When the banks made noise (saying any sale had to go through them), the cousins' lawyer proceeded to get the city interested in turning the castle into a museum. The fee advanced to the cousins for a ten-year lease would be coverable by a bond issue. With fix-up contracts being offered in places where they would do the most good, things were beginning to look up for the cousins, but salivating at the prospect of real money, they fell to quarreling; and their deal blew out the window.

The one cousin blocked the other from getting clear title, but with that settled, neither would agree to the lawyer's cut unless they first got theirs *in full*. The lawyer told them to kiss his, the city washed its hands, the daughter recovered, and the status of the castle that nobody wanted got filed away like the case of its last occupants; and it continued to molder like the ancient relic the baron had wanted it to resemble in the first place.

Taking a good look at the thing, the cousins, brandishing Aunt Evelyn's letter, shook their fists and promised they'd get a New York lawyer and be back.

CHAPTER 9

"Angie's Sons, Plus Another Dual Homicide"

Everyone had pretty much accepted the police version of what happened, except for one lone detective: Angie's son Mario or "one somber Dago" as the chief remarked. He was also a persistent one, who would dedicate his life to finding out what happened to his sister and her husband. Wrinkle-browed Mario was the twin of girl-crazy Angie Jr.—who liked to go by his middle name, Rocco, so as not to be confused with his Lothario father, who didn't like to have a son as a competitor.

As for the twins themselves, beyond their physical resemblance, they were as different as night and day. Rocco was the debonair man about town. He titillated the women by posing as a retired prizefighter (just consider the name). Three months after marrying, he found himself afflicted with the roving eye and came to the conclusion it was impossible for him to make love to just one woman.

Mario, on the other hand, was a quiet, good-natured fellow. At the desk, he was a dull plodder, which was why he was given cold cases to work on. He was drawn around the eyes from dawn to dusk looking at photocopies of evidence and, where necessary, applying case law cited to impress skeptics. He was chafed by his father's drumming "Chicago, Chicago" at him. Surely the underworld connection would unveil the source of the baron's murder (no longer a suicide?) thereby giving their family an in on *that* part of the inheritance, which was said to include a Chicago bank, target of Domo Jr.

Mario murmured, "This baron guy must have been a business octopus who had to put certain enterprises in his wife's name. Makes it tough to find out who got him the pistol and who bashed in his wife's skull, assuming it couldn't have been the baron himself. Well, okay, I never got an easy one." Fact is, as Papa said, he liked it that way: it kept him busy. With there being a reward this time around, the snail in him might accelerate.

Meanwhile, brotherly Rocco liked to tease Mario for his sobriety, and on occasion when he was reported to have been found dead drunk and passed out in an alleyway, Rocco would say it was actually Mario. Untroubled by scandal, once his wife filed for divorce, a thankful Rocco was so absorbed by his pursuit of the latest wealthy widow—the one who had rejected his dad—that he failed to show up at his sister's funeral, having booked a flight for two to Miami.

Duly chastised by Mario upon his return in the midst of the hullabaloo over the cousins, Rocco, ever the agile prankster, retaliated by replacing the service revolver in Mario's holster with a water pistol; and when Mario let him have it for that, Rocco misidentified the fingerprint data Mario had gotten from the FBI lab, switching Cousin A with Cousin B. Undeterred, Mario plodded ahead with his investigation. Suspicious of the cousins from the beginning, he thought that given a separate session with each, he could expose them as phonies and probably connect them to the murders. Having already picked up a couple of clues—their alibis for the night of the murders didn't check out, and the family names they'd given (Pfaule and Fisch) couldn't be found anywhere in the Farber genealogy—Mario was ready to tell the chief that the case he had built was practically a lock. Time to alert the DA.

Meanwhile, failing to get a response when he knocked on the door of the cousins' motel room, Mario took a runner and shouldered it in only to find them dead in their bloody beds, each with a bullet to the back of the head. It looked as if someone had taken a ball-peen hammer to them while they slept and then applied the coup de grâce.

For all of a week, the town was in an uproar. In addition to the slaying of their most honored citizen and his wife, now there are execution-style killings in their midst! *What's going on?* "Hey, this town is a good-folks place to live!" the Mayor crowed. The police chief asked for the people to calm themselves down. This was a case of outsiders doing in the outsiders who had perpetrated those heinous murders at the castle.

Through diligent police work, the chief assured the people that his detectives were on track to solving the crime at the castle. People could rest easy knowing they were well protected. Two double murders had been quickly and efficiently solved. ("Mirabile dictu," the *Morning Messenger* reporter wrote.) The chief called in the press and said that hereafter, dammit, criminals wouldn't dare challenge his vigilant cohorts.

In truth, few townspeople believed those two stumblebums had it in them to commit a double murder. Nonetheless, they were willing to go along with the chief as, like him, they wanted the whole nasty business shoved under the rug. Actually, Mario himself was not fully convinced; and he embarrassed himself by talking to the DA about his case.

"Case?" DA Magowan roared on the phone to the Yale lawyer—who, since he represented the baron's interests, volunteered that one day he might have to look into his murder, if not a suicide. "Slow-mo Mario wouldn't know a case if it came up and bit him in the ass!" "Says he was hot onto the cousins. Hot as a two-dick dog. But of course, our chief says, 'Don't put him down. He's the best we got. Think about it.'"

Magowan had to be painfully blunt with his friend Mario, pointing out that suspicions don't make a case. *Did he have even circumstantial evidence, anything to place these cousins at the crime scene? A weapon? A witness? A motive?* Anybody adequately scared could manufacture an alibi. *As for their being impostors, what did that prove?* A couple of two-bit crooks trying to get away with a

23

con. *Moreover, if the cousins did in the baron and his wife, <u>who</u> did them in? And why?*

The bulldog in Mario wouldn't let it go. He'd show that whiskey-cheeked DA something yet. So on the qt, he asked that he be allowed to find out who whacked the cousins. At first, the chief said "Who the hell cares!" When Mario reminded him of Magowan's ridicule—adding that if they found the guy with the hammer, they'd have the one behind the murders at the castle too—the chief gave him a grudging okay, so long as no one knew what he was up to and so long as <u>he</u> did.

CHAPTER 10

"Ghosts at the Castle"

As the years rolled by, the baron's folly got a reputation for being haunted—especially among the kids, who claimed that they heard voices upstairs when the wind whistled through broken windows. For the fun of it, people played along with the idea that it was haunted until one murky fall morning when they awoke to learn that a ghost had come to life; then, hallelujah, another jumped up. Police were asked to check it out, and their knock on the door was answered from the upstairs bedroom window by a woman's husky voice asking them to try later.

In time and generations later, there would be three of those ghosts come to life with yet a fourth to come, a regular parcel of them. Prior to their arrival, the only visitors had been the chimney swifts which came up from the river and circled till their leader suddenly dropped down the central chimney, giving a signal for the others to follow—which, one by one, they did.

The first ghost sighting was at the sturdy oak door, with its weathered crest showing a lion couchant above an F fashioned into something like a left-handed fleur-de-lis. Smiling as she ran a dust cloth over it, the ghost lady suddenly sensed she was being watched from beyond the fence and turned to give the kids a cheerful little kiddy wave that however sent them scurrying down the hill. Anything but ghastly, she was a broad-beamed woman draped in a purple moo-moo. More frightening yet was the glimpse they later got of her pale, moonlit face, round as the moon itself, peering out over the tower battlements.

But what people remembered most after Moonface died was the face of the other one, the mystery woman (MW), who after an absence unexpectedly reappeared and soon had guests. The police got an idea that there might be a warrant out for the thin fellow among those guests; however when they came for a look, they discovered that the clever dude, thin as the air, was long gone by the time they decided to be going for him.

Meanwhile, the mystery woman occasionally could be seen at the third floor window hovering in chiaroscuro over a lone candle for the knight who hadn't come. People weren't used to that kind of carrying on. They invented all sorts of strange tales for what was happening up there (she was hiding a secret lover?), and the seclusion became a daily conversation piece—sad as it was to the few who knew her. Assuming there'd be a time when she would have to come out of seclusion, the police said they would just as soon wait until they were needed. In the meantime, they settled for just doing routine surveillance.

One day things went really quiet at the castle. MW had disappeared. The kids tried the big oak door and found it was bolted shut, so they had their fun throwing rocks through the windows. Empty, the dark hulk was as spooky as it had been with Moonface and friends. The Yale lawyer had apparently contacted the police and put up a "No Trespassing" sign. A patrol car would swing by from time to time.

The kids grew up and ignored it, like everybody else. And for a while, that was it. But the town knew it wasn't. The MW was still out there, and although the lawyer wouldn't be telling anything, it was understood that he knew a lot—in the first place, presumably who she was. Evidently, she had left word with the reporter that she hoped he wouldn't give up finding the culprit who had murdered the baron. Otherwise, there was all-around silence.

From time to time, people were rankled that there had been two double murders in their midst, and no one—least of all, the police—had a clue as to who might have been responsible for either. Except for ongoing curiosity about MW, futility finally gave way to complacency. After all, there must be a fat list of unsolved murders in New York.

PART II

PHYSICAL EDUCATION

CHAPTER 11

"Back to the Beginning"

The MW story reached back a ways. Its beginnings came to light by indirection as a result of the reporter Tom's pressing his uncle Bob for more information about the baron. Bob, in the long years that he did the City Beat for the *Morning Messenger,* came to know just about everybody in town and more about the baron than anybody else. So when—for all his prodding and cajoling—he was still stymied in his investigation of who was behind the double demise in the castle, Bob went back in time to look for clues and wound up putting together a rough chronicle of the baron's life. After his retirement, Bob passed this on to Tom when he brought him on the paper as a cub.

Tom's interest shifted to the asylum daughter and from her, when she gave him a bad time, to none other than the mystery woman—who, from secret information Bob had unearthed, might have had more to do with the baron than she knew. Moreover, Bob held that to find a solution to the castle murders, one had to start precisely with that mystery woman, who disclosed nothing.

She laughed at Tom's idea that she knew more than anybody else—that, in fact, she was the product of an inside story. "All dark to me," she asserted in a way that made one suspicious. The situation might take some time to unfold, but Bob challenged Tom to go for it.

A number of years before financial chaos descended on the baron, there had been a freak March snowstorm that closed the city down under three feet of snow, a meteorological landmark. The sandblasting wind that came up drifted the snow into barricades, a huge one at the juncture of Main Street and awesome North Hill Road. No one could get up or down it for three whole days.

Gina, in high dudgeon, was stranded downtown at the Centre Hotel while the German housekeeper was marooned with the baron at the castle. When she slipped out of her duster and changed back into a close-fitting top and slacks, suddenly she was a woman ten years younger than she'd looked before, with a well-rounded chest and a tight waste that suddenly made for the hourglass figure. A lady whose marble-smooth cheeks had him taking a second look, as of discovery.

When things returned to normal, Gina moved to dispel rumors before they got properly started, telling her friends "Don't think bad things. Sam's a gentleman." One of the friends breathed behind her hand, "She ought to know." Gina's involvement with Sam had started with a stayover after the office Christmas party. In the New Year, she became his very private secretary. Likewise, it was said that in a snowstorm, a new life was begun. The rumor outraced Gina's effort to squelch it.

It was not quite by accident that Tom settled on the mystery woman with the strange name Addie. He'd known her before he seriously wanted to know <u>about</u> her. They had in fact become personal, a situation he sort of slid into—as he put it, not unhappily—that gave him a sense of obligation initially unneeded from her point of view but, in time, appreciated.

In her former role, she had been a great favorite with the nursery school kids and, later on, with the kindergartners as well. The little ones would circle round her on the floor while she, with exaggerated spooky gestures, acted out the fairy tales she read them. Spellbound, the kids kept asking for more. These were kids of the former rock throwers, so Addie felt an ironic connection to them.

She was herself a kid among them, playing blind man's bluff, hide and seek, and whatnot. When it was her turn to tie the handkerchief on, the kids let out shrieks of delight as she went through her stumbling act. "'N' Affentheater," (sheer chaos) her father called it the time he visited. At day's end, the kids didn't want to go home.

She loved taking her charges to the petting zoo—where, when they became curious about the lonely burro with the big club, she kept them back by saying "Poor thing! He'd probably been petted too much."

That didn't quite satisfy a smart little guy who said the burro needed a girlfriend, upon hearing which she put a finger to his lips. She talked to her charges about friendship, and asked, "Hey, kids, we're all going to be good friends to one another, aren't we?"

"Oh yeah!" they came back in chorus.

CHAPTER 12

"Mr. Elliot Her Hero"

That was the contented side of her story, often interrupted. The other side she would treat as mostly a chronicle of misadventures. For early on, she had acquired a kind of innocent indifference, an attitude of letting things happen and moving on. Not everything was supposed to work out, but sometimes she would find herself in a reflective mood and would come away feeling bad. All of that and the story of what follows she sedulously recorded in a journal that she left in a conspicuous place for Tom to pick up as if wanting to have it properly recorded, which is the basis for much that follows.

She remembered talking to her English teacher, Mr. Elliott, about being disappointed with herself. He said, "Listen to your heart instead of what people try to put in your head. It only counts as disappointment when you go against the heart. Disappointing the head can be a good thing." Mr. Elliott was considered troublesome and, particularly so, when pupils who broke the dress code pointed to his slovenliness—he being noted for coming to class in a food-stained flannel shirt and worn-at-the-knee jeans. He was full-bearded and could use a haircut and on hot days some deodorant.

A shoe-in as the school weirdo, Elliot was continually trying the principal's patience. He finally gave the principal the grounds he wanted for dismissal. Some parents had a complaint over his telling his class he wasn't very keen on the idea of commandment when asked about *the sacred ten*. Doesn't believe in them? In *them*, he does but, in commandment, doesn't. And as a matter of fact, he was more interested in *shalt* than *shalt not*. Easy to get balled up.

He had stuck up for some of the unconventional kids who dressed like him, but when he was about to get the boot, none of them came to his defense. Ruefully, neither did she. She wanted to but was intimidated into silence by the fact that no one seemed to care, and she didn't want others to think poorly of her. She hated herself for that.

When Mr. Elliott saw a lawyer about getting his job back, she circulated a petition asking that he be reinstated. But she got few signatures and a reprimand from the principal, who warned that something like that could be put on her school record. She said she hoped it would be. But she was angrier at the kids who wouldn't sign and said she was a weirdo herself for sticking up for Mr. E. Good enough she'd just go her own way.

There was, however, one thing she kept very dark about: her more than fascination with the baron and her dedication—mainly evanescent—to finding out who did him in. In retrospect, she—for no good reason—thought Mr. E. might have somehow been involved. He had been called to the station house by Mario when it was learned that he had no good words for the man "atop the money pyramid," as he put it. Rather attached to the baron, Addie filed that one away with other suspicions. She kept them from trustful Tom; and overall, they didn't interfere with the amorous side of her life, which was rich and was soon enough to get richer.

CHAPTER 13

"A Cold Winter Train-ride"

It began rather casually, as Tom fondly recalled it, with him in his easygoing college days and becoming a participant in her string of early misadventures. In high school, she had been a freshman when he was a senior; and they'd had a nodding acquaintance when she worked at the church nursery school, and he did odd jobs for the priest. They had taken one another in physically, and when he caught her looking (seemingly by inadvertence), he thought he detected more than a flicker of interest.

But she, for her part, had thought Tom was rather snooty back then since they came from opposite ends of the social spectrum. Tom's father, whose ancestry could be traced back to the early Dutch settlers, was the prominent Yale attorney who had deigned to do work for this new- money, low-class baron. Her immigrant father had been a humble warper working in one of the baron's textile mills where he had met her mother, who worked in the same mill, on a floor rented out to a shirt manufacturer.

After taking up ABA (Bachelor of Arts) in journalism at the University of Missouri, Tom had switched to psychology and switched schools. He wanted to work with people, particularly those in distress. He was headed back to Washington University in St. Louis to finish work on his master's degree when, to his surprise, he saw her on the train.

36

She had taken a job as children's librarian in a suburban St. Louis branch library, hoping to get back with a boyfriend whose wandering she thought would run its course, an idea that seemed crazier with each passing week—also more desperate, she realized. Yet the crazier it became, the greater the yearning; and sadly, the more she found herself sticking it out—that is, until unable to get rid of the rock in her chest, she decided to give the library notice. But she worked on anyway, needing the money despite knowing she was kidding herself. She'd been there going on three months and was returning after a Christmas visit back east with her folks, as was the case with Tom.

It was well past eleven when they changed trains in frosty Chicago. He had moved across the aisle and taken the seat next to hers as the train trundled southward through the stubbled cornfields that flew by in the icy moonlight. They hadn't said much, but when the conductor turned off the lights, they instinctively moved close and soon were snuggling together under the overcoats they were using as blankets.

He could sense that she appreciated the warmth of his body, and he was fascinated by the marble smoothness of her skin set off by dark hair and moist gray eyes. As he took her in, it came over him for the first time that he was looking at a pretty good-looking face; and he brushed his lips against her cheek.

She came back from the bathroom rubbing her arms to chase away the chills. He lifted the coats, and she moved in tight against him. He'd noticed how daintily her hips had swayed with the rocking of the train as she made her way down the aisle. It was such a sweet rhythmic movement. The image of it lingered, and he found himself navigating his hand over to circle her trim little belly.

When she responded with something like a low purr, he pulled his coat over both their heads; and he could feel the heat coming up between them. At first, she returned his kisses with trembling lips, her clenched teeth chattering ever so slightly; then when she suddenly thrust her tongue full into his mouth, he slid his hand under her skirt, softly stroking the inside of her thigh before moving gently on to where she pushed herself onto his palm.

Meanwhile, with him kissing her on the neck and ear, she slanted a hand inside his zipper. Not a word passed between them.

They awoke from their sleep to the conductor's singing out the indecipherable name of a town they were approaching. Apparently running behind schedule, the conductor was more interested in getting their bags off than in examining their tickets.

"Goodness, where are we?"

He shrugged, looking around at the strange rural scene. Across the tracks was a scrubby cow pasture. Just up from the station was a dirt road that ran by a row of tar paper shacks—each with a large, black cauldron in the backyard facing the tracks. The other way was downtown—a fire station with a sow warming her back against the chimney, the local cafe, a barber's pole, a wagon backed up to the feed store dock, an upstairs dentist's office over the post office, and (in front of the station) a cabbie with a fedora sitting down on his nose stretched out on the backseat of his hack.

A black couple was getting off and, when they did, said their part of town was Pokeville.

"Where's that?

"Here, Arkansas, ma'am."

"Oh boy."

So there they were a little before seven in the morning, numbly huddled together on a clammy bench in the waiting room—red-eyed, dry in the mouth, and none too clear in the head—wondering when, and if, the ticket agent would appear. Noticing a schedule posted next to the window, he roused himself; and finding it would be evening before a train came the other way, he suggested they wake the cabbie and have him take them to a decent hotel.

"What?" She wasn't going to any hotel however decent. She wanted to go back to her apartment—as if it were just around the corner.

"Don't you want some breakfast?"

"No. Let's rent a car and go back to St. Louis."

He talked to the cabbie, who said, "Glad t'oblige," and dropped them off at the local U-Haul—attached to a gas station where they were presented with a rattly little, two-ton Chevy truck and a map north. He was skeptical, but she rather liked the old thing.

She found it quaint, and he scratched his head.

"She's a good un. Moved lotsa folks," the attendant said.

Tom said he believed it had, and while he was paying, she hopped up into the cab and honked the horn.

"Hey, y'all comin?"

Once they pulled out onto the main highway, she curled up on the seat and laid her head on his lap.

"I forget your name. It ain't John, is it?"

"No. Tom." Laughing, he ruffled her hair and gave her earlobe a little nip.

"Tom-John, huh? I once knew a guy by that name. Tom-John Jones he said it was until I found out he didn't have any of those names but kept them in case. He told me he sold cemetery lots. He could be real affectionate, but he told strange stories. Had a tongue like a car alarm. You couldn't turn it off. We didn't have a whole lot in common. Or well . . . what we did have didn't go very far."

They made just one pit stop on the way, pulling into a small town where they had biscuits and gravy—the typical Southern breakfast special—at a storefront restaurant. As he drove the two hundred and fifty plus miles to her place, he could feel by the way they were bounced around that this thing had next to nothing for shocks.

With the tight grip he kept on the wheel, he didn't realize till they arrived how really tense he'd been. His legs went rubbery on him as he carried the bags up the front steps to the elevator. Once unpacked, she fixed him a bourbon and soda; and pulling out the sofa bed, she motioned for him to rest a bit.

He said he was okay, so they showered separately; and after their early evening lunch of omelet and salad, she said she had better go down to the square for some shopping before the stores closed—especially as that was the last of the bourbon. She said there were nights it helped smooth out the rough spots.

Her street was flanked by rows of brick apartment buildings, many showing signs of random maintenance; and running down the center of the street was a grass island shaded by knobby old sycamores, where people walked their dogs. There was a rusting bench at the corner bus stop and beside it a grocery store displaying baskets of polished red apples, rows of wet lettuce, and a pile of cantaloupes.

Nestled in the square at the end of the street was a small plaza containing a liquor store, a launderette, a beauty salon, a drugstore, and a good old-fashioned German bakery where she got the morning's warm bread and ate it right out of the bag as she walked back to her apartment. The neighborhood had a comfortably lived-in feel that allowed people to enjoy their isolated togetherness as much as they pleased. *Too bad*, she thought, *it couldn't be moved to the pushy east, where people seemed to get on one another's nerves.*

He offered to go with her and help—he'd buy the whiskey—but she put up a hand, telling him he really ought to rest. She threw a blanket and sheets on the sofa bed, accepted the bills he stuffed into her fist, and was quickly out the door. Hearing a key turn in the lock, he tried to turn the rigid knob.

"Hey, come on! What's this?"

She chuckled. Evidently, she'd paused to catch his response.

"Okay, but don't lose the key, huh."

CHAPTER 14

"She Was Strange"

He instinctively went to the window (all of three flights up) and, looking down at the ambling residential traffic, smiled. *Well, they said she was strange.* When told about it, she would give him a look. Strange were those who called her that, she said. Pulling back, he insisted that <u>he</u> <u>had</u> found <u>her</u> intriguing.

"Never mind me," she said folding her arms across her chest. "Tell me what you know about the baron."

"Tell me what <u>you</u> know," he replied, and she went silent. "What Uncle Bob tells me is that you're closer than you'll admit. Indeed, Bob said there probably was a blood relationship. True? . . . Anyway, some people get it in their head that your folks are somehow involved—independently. Know anything about that?"

Tom volunteered that his killer was probably in plain sight. As that fell flat, he asked her about the life of the heart that Mr. Elliott had talked about. Yes, she was a believer; but she had to admit, with a smile, that along the way, the heart thing got mixed up with the body thing—which, when they became synonymous . . .

"Well, no need to go into that."

"You'd be vulnerable and get stung?"

She went silent. He'd heard rumors about her, and though it seemed pointless to go into anything personal, he was about to ask her something when she read him.

"Yeah, there were girls who didn't like me and said I was for free love."

"You weren't?"

"They don't know what it means. As for love, wouldn't you say *we* oughta have the kind that's as free as it is for men?—I take that back. If you talk about a dream, you kill it."

As he'd recently studied dreams, his psychological interest was piqued.

"Being in love is a dream state? Did you ever have strangely impish dreams . . . the kind where you were doing things you didn't want to?"

"Are there any others?" she asked. "Actually, after some of the stuff I've been through, I don't need to <u>dream</u> that kind of thing. Anyway, one day maybe I can tell you why I'm here."

He liked to think he could handle the unpredictable, but he also knew it would take a certain kind of man to swim with her. *Me?* Unaware of how she would grow into his psyche, he thought it would be enough to watch her from the shore as she struck out for the current where the river ran dark and deep, and where downstream there were rapids.

One thing that did emerge from their talk that would fit her subsequent history was her hair-trigger sense of justice, and particularly her sensitivity to the injustice visited on women. She would in time develop a good old-fashioned shit detector, which could pick up stuff that others—usually men—wouldn't. But she said women were dumb too for going along with it. It irked her to be called a "feminist." She hated being labeled and hated the idea but didn't mind being hated.

"Whom the Lord loveth, he chasteneth."

When he got to know her a little better, his photographer friend, Deleste, would ask what she was like; and Tom had to think for a minute. *How was he supposed to describe a woman like that?*

"Well, like the lady used to say, when she was good, she was very, very good. And when she was bad, she was better."

However, as her adventures began, she was primal innocence personified. She didn't even know she was in the midst of an adventure when it first took place. Things just happened, and she liked to cultivate a little distance even as she was part of them. Hell was when she let herself fall in love, and she hated being vulnerable afterwards.

CHAPTER 15

"Her Folks"

For much of the rest of her story, except for events that involved him himself, Tom relied on the previously mentioned journal he came upon among the private papers she entrusted him with. As she put it, she was offering him her "odyssey of love"—said with her typically wry smile.

First, there were her folks and the matter of her name. Otto, her father, was a tight-fisted German who was cynical about everything in sight: taxes, landlords, factory bosses, Puerto Ricans and Blacks, the too numerous children of both, noisy neighbors, thieving doctors (all, actually), cheating banks, and—particularly—wasteful Americans and their white bread that was more air than flour. Outside of that, he was content. Content to complain, which was outdone only by his best friend, George Klagemann, to whom Addie as a kid, had once crawled under the table to give a hot foot in the midst of their litany; another time, she hid his hat. He was a heavyset man, wide in the gut, bowlegged, and not too fast on his feet. She liked to hear him spew out those low-throated German cusswords punctuated by *ach* as he stomped around looking for her, only to break out into a coughing laugh. He was "a sweet man with a sour name" as Otto put it.

Not so funny was Father Otto himself—who groused about the bargains that Hannah, his dutiful young wife, failed to find and, when found, complained she'd picked too expensive a brand.

He wanted no birthday presents: he'd buy all he needed on his own—for less— and above all, he wanted no additional children. Hadn't their frail daughter, who never found a sickness she couldn't embrace, run up the doctors' bills, which they were only recently paying off with the money Hannah earned by doing housekeeping for the baron? Weary Hannah let Otto's sulfur and smoke slide off her back though she had her limits, like the time he frowned at the sight of a blouse she'd bought for a dollar at The Salvation Army. Before he could tell her they should have given it to her for free, she spat out at him, "For you, <u>life</u> is too expensive!"

His face aflame, he barely restrained himself from hitting her. But when told one cold night that she was three months late and had to see a doctor, that hand flashed out and sent her reeling against the kitchen cabinet. *What was wrong with her? Couldn't she for Chrissake count!* He went into an even bigger rage when, trying to accommodate his money worries as well as her own, she said she knew of a midwife who could help her miscarry.

"<u>Abortion</u>!" he shouted. "Gott in Himmel! Didn't the priest say God cried every time a baby was killed?"

He shook her like a rag doll until it suddenly occurred to him he might be doing what he didn't want <u>her</u> to do. She dared not say any more and, in that moment, vowed to take her secret to the grave. But there were times when she wondered about Otto's fits of irritation, his trembling lip, and his head-shaking rage. *Could he have been having some vague suspicion that he couldn't bring himself to accept? Had <u>he</u> done the count?*

There was the night that things suddenly changed. He and Klagemann got themselves howling drunk, with Otts (as he was called by family and friends) treating to celebrate his forthcoming fatherhood. The thought evidently intrigued him that, like the doctor said, it looked like he was going to have a boy; and he was out of his head about that. His young wife was equipped to nurse the kid.

The baron's prize mill having closed down for the introduction of additional high-speed looms, and with a strike in the offing—over one weaver to four looms—Otts said "To hell with it!" and sailed into a weeklong binge, nightly lasting into the wee hours.

Hannah was glad he was happy; but she worried that, lacking restraint, he might at any night come back at her with suspicions. Anyway, she tried to stay out of his way; for at week's end, he came looking for her with that intense fire-eating stare that made her fear for her life. She said she had to go and see Iris Klagemann as she eased her way out the door. The Ks' apartment was just one story below theirs.

Finally sobered up, Otto spent all of a morning with the priest, which was quite unusual. The sermon that week became "Do Not Sin against the Child" (Gen. 42:22). With his head down, Otto's lips moved in silent prayer. Hannah prayed with him. He even went to Saturday night mass and stayed for yet another closed-door talk with the priest. While he had been brought up Catholic, he had said if he was true to God's law, he didn't have to go to church any more than he wanted to beyond Christmas and Easter—which, he noted was good enough for the baron.

"Whenever you show up, they keep reminding you that you gotta give more money when the church is so rich already." This was a gripe" he shared with Klagemann, who was quick to chime in, "And still they pull the last cent out of the noses of the poor! I don't like them to tell me if I suffer here, all I gotta do is give them the little I got, and they'll send me to the good place later when—excuse me—it ain't gonna matter."

As the time of delivery approached, the tension grew so thick that she couldn't keep her food down. It was like a walnut got lodged in her craw; then shortly before she was due, Otto surprised her with an unexpected—for him—lightness of mood. He even gave her a kiss and apologized for his whisky breath. Extravagantly, he wanted to have some cigars on hand to show his pride like he didn't want people to think otherwise. She understood and was relieved.

Of course, when the baby arrived, his first impulse was to blame Hannah for its being a girl, which was just fine with her as it showed that the Old Otts had suddenly returned. (Okay then, the doctor's fault.) He'd been telling them all along it was sure to be a boy, which Otto admitted had reconciled him to having another mouth to feed. And here he'd had a good German name picked out—August, after the great old Saxon king seated on a golden horse in Dresden who (stud that he was) had fathered over three hundred children. The kid was to be his little "Gustl."

However, reminding himself that even a girl could have a good German name, he told the nurse to put Ulrika on the birth certificate. Hannah, reverting to <u>her</u> former self, felt the old bitterness at the back of her tongue. Tired of being blamed for everything, she told the nurse to make that her middle name and to place Adelaide—her personal joke—in front of Ulrika and let him wonder how it got there on the birth certificate.

CHAPTER 16

"She Breaks a Leg"

Once the child was in their midst, Otto became extremely protective. A fatherly instinct took over, and with those cute little-girl ways of hers and her being so loving to him, he grew to love that child as he loved no one else. When he came home from work, she'd call out "Der Papa Otto kommt!" and run to give him a big bear hug. She became the light of his life. Seeing how endearingly she looked at him, Otto confided to George Klagemann that he'd thought of what the lonely black girl had said when asked why she wanted a child. "Why I wanna have a keed? I wanna have somebody to luv me."

As George Klagemann liked to tell it, Otto Heiss had a soft side and a hard side, making him in the little caricature that George sketched of Otto Heiss *oder Eis*—in one hand a warm heart, in the other a cake of ice. George recalled that when an old codger in their club had asked a second time if his name was really Heiss, Otto abruptly yelled, "Ja, Heiss, wie kalt!"

The softness was mostly reserved for this younger daughter, the hardness for almost everything else, particularly for those that had to do with money (which is not to say there weren't times when he could be hard on the little one too). The older daughter—she who had racked up those big medical bills—considered herself the *stiefkind* (stepchild) though both parents were aware of the unspoken mystery as to who the literal stepchild was. When people commented on his favoritism—"Hat 'n Herz für die Kleine" (Had a heart for the Little One)—Hannah couldn't help feeling slightly jealous, but she was also glad for both father and daughter.

Otto's feeling for Little One unfortunately also had its downside: <u>his</u> little Rika (never Addie) was not going to have roller skates or a bicycle; she'd surely fall off and break a leg. (Look at all they'd had to go through with their daughter Eva.) But Addie, having inherited by age seven some of her mother's willfulness, managed to sneak rides on the twenty-six-inch bike her girlfriend Betsy had taken over from her brother.

They lowered the seat and found it such fun that they got on together one night and rode wildly down the lower stretch of curvy North Hill Road. The thrill of defiance, add to that the wind in their faces, brought out the daredevil in them, which had them swaying as they picked up speed (one on the seat and the other on the crossbar). The third time down, the wheel turned when they hit a rise in the pavement; and off they flew with a crushing impact. Addie's left leg got tangled around the crossbar, which had crunched it over like she had two knees.

When Otto had her about lectured out though still shaking his fist in her face, she was able to bring his attention back to the throbbing in her leg. The pain wouldn't let up. He had Hannah fetch a retired German doctor—who, looking over his spectacles at it a second time, agreed he would set the bones for less. This was different from the earlier time when Father had found the money to get a private doctor for her tonsillectomy.

Somehow the old German either set the bones wrongly or didn't do a secure enough job of splinting, for within a month, a painful blue lump appeared on Addie's shin. Otto got her into the hospital as a charity patient—pointing out he was about to be laid off from work, which meant that she had to wait most of the day for the bone doctor to look at the leg; then, they were told it might be a while before he could attend to it.

"Yeah, maybe a week" Otto groused.

Meanwhile, he persuaded a nurse to give the girl something for the pain. Disgruntled over the shabby treatment, he urged the girl to wait till tomorrow. He knew of a person who would lend him the money to get her to a specialist.

He returned late at night so completely agitated that Hannah thought they'd need a doctor for him. With him sitting there on the couch with his head back and his hands over his eyes, she knew better than to ask him anything and was even less inclined to do so when he said to tell the specialist they could pay cash. She had an idea of where that kind of money came from and surmised it would have been as difficult to part with as it had been tough to obtain. Both knew the unmentionable source of this strange largesse, a mystery they shared but of which they didn't disclose their knowledge.

Before he could change his mind, Hannah proceeded to get an immediate appointment with a specialist who did osteotomies. He had to break and reset both bones with the result that once they healed, Addie came away with her left leg being a trifle shortened. The hurt was easier to overcome than the embarrassment as kids made fun of her in the school yard, some imitating her slightly up-down walk.

Otto was sympathetic; but he was also guilty and, more than that, angry. His kid was being teased! No way was he going to let that happen to his Little Bear. So talking to members of the local German clan, he found himself a crabbed, old-country shoemaker who didn't charge too much for making her an insert and afterward a special shoe.

When she was fully healed, she got herself a paper route, wanting to help pay for the shoe, which Otto appreciated; but it didn't last more than a couple of weeks as all that walking became too much of a strain on the leg. So she was at outs with her father again. (It wouldn't have come to this in the first place if she hadn't disobeyed him.) When she turned to her mother, all Hannah could do was to raise her weary arms and let them fall back in despair and say "Your father is not a happy man."

CHAPTER 17

"The Recess Brawl and Beyond"

For a while, things began to get better for Addie in high school. With a fitted shoe, her walk straightened; and with the combination of her mother's raven hair and those haunting gray eyes (which would sadden Hannah), she suddenly blossomed into a fair young lady who the boys were quick to discover, particularly when she started using dark cherry lipstick. Her finely developing breasts and hips gave her an inviting outline that got her noticed by the most popular boy in class, the son of a well-known physician; and that made her unpopular with the girls—who spread rumors about their spending after-school time in the cloak room, which she brazenly defied. "So what!"

Marie Dimallo, the one who had imitated her gimpy walk, said her skin was so pale she looked like a week-old corpse. If that was what the boys wanted, they could <u>have</u> it. Addie stuck her tongue out, and down they went—fists full of hair, screeching as they rolled over, and finally landing on the cinder track. At first, Marie got the better of it because of Addie's awkwardness. She had her straddled and sat on her head.

Incensed, Addie let out animal growl; and with her unguarded adversary declaring victory, Addie summoned every ounce of strength in those wiry arms of hers and, thrusting up, bumped her off. When they gained their feet and faced off, Addie backed up with her cheeks flushed and her ears burning; and with her

S. Joseph Krause

head down, she took a runner at Marie, butting her full in the stomach, which bounced her down on the prickly cinders. As she arose, Addie followed up with a swift kick that sent her adversary home in a trot—crying that Addie didn't fight fair, which Addie was glad to have advertised. It meant she'd no longer have to fear lunchtime in the playground and could eat her baloney sandwich in peace. Or so she thought.

Next day during recess, Marie's brother slipped a foot under Addie's bad leg and gave her a nasty tumble. On all fours, she turned on him in a fury and sank her teeth into his bare calf. He howled like he'd backed into a bear trap and banged a fist on her head, which made her clamp down all the harder. Her face was tomato-red, her ears on fire. Somebody said they twitched.

"Leggo my leg, you mad dog!"

He bashed her again; and with that, the teeth really cut in, producing an agonized "ow!" that brought the teacher over to separate them. She scolded Addie and led hobbling Nicky to the infirmary with him clutching the wound. The kids screamed "Eeh!" upon seeing blood ooze through his fingers; and Marie snapped a scarf at Addie, chanting "Mad Addie! Mad Addie!"

Addie chased her off with a throaty rumble and showed a pair of bloody incisors to those who chimed in. The kids couldn't tell whether she meant to bite someone else or was just being funny. Either way, it scared them; and they gave her a chorus of "Mad Addie," a tag that would echo behind her from the back of the classroom, out of a crowd, down a hallway pretty much throughout her high school days.

Marie and Nicky were the kids of a well-known Italian family that was politically well connected with thriving businesses thought to have been fronts for ill-gotten gain. They were also benefactors of the Catholic Church, as well as the Protestant clergy who had led the charge for dismissal of blasphemous Mr. Elliott. Since the Dimallo kids cultivated a lot of followers by bringing candy to school, Addie wound up being pretty much of a loner. The petition for Mr. Elliott further isolated her. Resigned to being lonely—the enthusiasm of the doctor's son having evaporated—she buried herself in her books and became an honor student.

As a senior, her favorite course was the Bible. It struck her that those old Israelites were a lot like the rest of us, some a lot worse. Herod massacres all of those children of Bethlehem in an effort to get little Jesus, to say nothing of his putting away a wife and his own kids. *Nobody cares for old Herod, but what about good guy David—who, it turns out, was no better?* He goes after another man's wife and schemes to have the guy killed in battle. And come on! Didn't he kill a bunch of Saul's kids? He's a king, so not much gets said about the dirt he did.

Abraham, the great patriarch, thinks nothing of having a child with the maid because he can't have one with his wife, except that he does manage to have one with her when he becomes an old man. Oh boy, it sure must have been fun for her since he was all of ninety years old! Still horny at that age.

Then there were those clever Moabites. They were not very good at fighting the Hebrews, so they had their women go to work on them. They also had a nasty habit of sacrificing their children until Solomon put a stop to it. *Okay, then what was all this talk about keeping bad books away from the kids?*

Mr. Burrow, who taught the course, thought that Addie was simply joshing.

She said, "No, I wasn't at all."

"Haven't you read the Bible before?"

"Parts, yes."

But it used to be that she didn't pay all that much attention to what she read; then along comes Mr. Elliott, and he tells her to look for the meaning of what she reads. So now reading's different.

"Oh, that so?"

Mr. Burrow found himself intrigued. He started looking at Addie in a certain way, like he was wondering if she just might not be that innocent. He found it attractive, indeed, and engaging. He said he liked her curiosity and added that he liked her for herself too.

Patting her on the head, he quoted from Matt. 6:22 (King James Version), "The light of the body is the eye . . ."

He got her a job helping his elderly aunt with the nursery school class at St. Thomas's, which had been getting to be a little more than Aunty could handle. It was there that Addie really found herself—and people found her. She told the little ones tales from the Bible though not particularly for purposes of religion—which was what the priest, in his praise, thought she was doing. Rather, she treated the Bible selections as stories about people, which she made interesting, like the excitement of the story of Mary and Joseph escaping in the night with baby Jesus to save him from being done in by Herod.

"Close call, wasn't it?"

She went on to tell them how cleverly Jesus dealt with the tempting devil, repeatedly putting him off with answers that left him no comeback. *Didn't he know how to deal with a pest, also with people who got mad!* Like a soft answer turneth away wrath. Looking for the meaning, Addie did the same sort of thing with the nursery rhymes. After they'd do the sing-song "Jack and Jill," she'd ask, "What about poor Jack with that broken crown? Oh, yeah, that hurts, huh?

"Okay, but doesn't it look like Mother Goose wants to make it funny, like it's not for real? Well . . . Yeah. He's supposed to mend his head with vinegar and brown paper. Supposed to be silly, huh?"

There's a ripple of laughter and they clap hands. The kids were entranced, as was Aunty—who, instead of merely using Addie as a helper, was glad to have her take over the class.

Addie was soon getting the attention of appreciative parents. Word got around; and Uncle Bob did a feature piece on her for the *Morning Messenger* complete with photo spread (Deleste, ace photog at his patient best), which brought the newly elected president of the board of education over to see her. He said he was there on business, which made her nervous.

After watching her in action, he said he really marveled at how she got to the kids. She said that it surprised her too. He asked, "Did you happen to know how come you went over so well with them? . . . No? Did you realize that these are not the usual nursery school kids? They are mainly five- and six-year-olds who should have been in kindergarten."

If she'd been reading the paper at all, she'd know that the outgoing head of the board had become so angry with the voters for turning down a school levy for the umpteenth time that he canceled kindergarten on them. He, the new head, on the other hand, had campaigned on a promise to bring it back and save money elsewhere. So he had a lot riding on making a success of it—and not just an okay success but an attraction, a showcase, in fact. *Would she be interested?* Yes, but she was happy where she was.

He asked, "Would you like to have lunch? Did you know you have pretty eyes?"

Growing shy with all the attention, Addie offered the excuse that Mother wasn't well. He didn't know what to make of that but said to look after Mother, and he'd ask her another time. As he went for the door, she wanted to call out "Wait! I'll get my coat," but the words wouldn't come out.

There was a rugged handsomeness about this guy with his square features and blue eyes crowned by a blonde flattop. He was a real hunk with a ready smile that showed he wasn't stuck on himself. Known citywide, Johnny R. had been a star halfback on the high school football team and walked with a slight rotation of the shoulders as if he were still sloughing would-be tacklers. She had a romantic daydream about him.

Well, life was full of missed opportunities, wasn't it?

CHAPTER 18

"Attentive Mr. Burrow"

Mr. Burrow had become especially attentive. First off, he got her a substantial raise, covering it with an under-the-table stipend from the board of education. (Ah, so she'd impressed the right guy! That was good to know.) Public money going to a church wasn't something to concern oneself with. She was as green as the meadow and just as pure. In passing, Burrow would innocently put his nose to her hair and breathe in deeply. He taxied her to and from school and church and prepared hot lunches in the church's basement kitchen, which they ate together just down the corridor from the nursery school room.

He made one super luscious Spanish omelet with mushrooms, onions, ham, sharp cheddar, and green peppers, sprinkled with a touch of olive oil and garlic, which he spread over a pair of English muffins. The aroma had her salivating. She didn't know what to make of it all, but she was appreciative and told him so.

He was the deacon's lieutenant, a business-like type who strode around with his head erect like he was the floorwalker in a downtown department store. He gave people the feeling he was strict and maybe even a little prissy though behind that exterior, he also had a soft side, which was a pleasant surprise to the special few he was soft with.

The new priest, who was a college-educated man, used to tease Burrow about wearing tinted glasses, saying he mostly looked at things through a glass darkly anyway. But as Addie found out, there was actually more to him than that; he opened up to her, relating how he had mainly kept to himself after his wife died. She recalled that he became so absentminded he wore the same navy blue blazer every day for almost half a year thereafter.

The kids started calling him Blazer, and others picked it up—among them the priest, who was particularly amused at the incongruity. Though a number of widows had an eye on him, Burrow took no notice. Addie could tell that he was trying to stifle his loneliness by immersing himself in school and church and that it wasn't always working.

He was extra busy around the church at Christmastime, having been put in charge of decorations. He held Addie at the ankles when she went up the ladder to put the angel on the peak of the tree. She had the feeling that he might have been looking under her dress, which she thought was rather funny.

Hmm, shame on Blazer. What to say? In a perverse kind of way, it flattered her to think she was getting him aroused—and hopefully, frustrated too as punishment for doing that. Pretending to lose her balance, she thought she'd send him a message by landing a shoe hard on his foot as she came down; however, he was too absorbed to notice.

In fact, there was a contrary effect. She could tell it got to him that she didn't <u>say</u> anything. He put on the Santa suit and made Addie sit on his lap and tell Daddy Klaws what she wanted for Christmas, a paw on her thigh. As she slipped off, his breath quickened like he'd just raced up a flight of stairs.

When he drove her home after the priest's little party, he lunged over to give her a kiss. But she slanted her head just enough that he missed her mouth and planted a wet one on her ear.

"Do you know what you are doing to me?" he breathed.

Unsure of what to say—as she valued her job—she came back with "Well, I always wanted to do good things" and gave him a wispy smile.

Next day, he asked her to pray with him for dear Aunty, who was having an operation. They were sitting in the shadowy last pew just in from the choir loft, eyes closed, when she all of a sudden felt a python-like arm coil around her back and draw her close. His mouth enveloped hers, and his other hand roamed over her thighs. Ignoring her insistent "Please," he proceeded to explore her middle, which for a moment was not unpleasant.

However, when he started to position her on his lap, she let out a ferocious "Nooo!" that echoed through the empty church. He went limp; and releasing her, he was suddenly down on his knees before her in tears, kissing her hand and begging her for forgiveness.

"C-couldn't . . . C-couldn't . . . help myself . . . was uh-o-overwhelmed . . . a-a th-thousand pardons."

Adjusting her dress, she said she hoped Aunty was going to be okay.

She didn't know how to explain the roses that came next day, except to say that it was her boss's way of complementing her for the good work she'd been doing. Otto said it just went to show how the church was wasting parishioners' money. *On second thought, why didn't they just give her the cash? "Flowers? A couple o' days and they shrivel up!"*

Hannah, recalling past experience, was suspicious. Assuming the worst, she followed Addie to her bedroom and asked whether or not she knew anything about ovulation.

"Don't jump 'cause he's good to you. Might be a come-on. What did he look like? Handsome with a Glark Gable dimple?"

Hannah went on about money enough to have a nice house in an expensive neighborhood.

"Says he loves you? Aha! Men will talk love to get something else. You like him? Well, before you know it, he's in you. Anyway, what do you know about contraception?" . . . A child? Did you know? At your age!"

Perplexed by it all, Addie had only half listened. She said she appreciated Hannah's talking to her. She was left wondering how she was going to handle things with Blazer after she'd accepted his invitation to go to the Elk's Club New Year's Eve party. She couldn't afford to offend him, needing the pay to show Otto she fully intended to contribute to her keep.

And truth be said, despite the episode, she felt she could grow to like the man. On second thought, except for the deception, it wasn't that bad a thing. He was a good-looking man, and as she reminded herself "Yah wouldn't know it, but he's sensitive." Father would like the fact that he had a good income and a steady one though at what, she didn't know. Moreover, when she explained that she had to make more money, he indicated he knew someone who could offer her part-time work. It looked like Blazer just wanted to find ways to please her.

Being in a quandary about sex, she'd talked to her friend Betsy—who, having had a head start, said "What's to wonder? Just enjoy it! He's got money, hasn't he? Could be a big thing for you." She laughed at Addie's scruples. "Never mind about doing this to get that. It's time women got their heads straight and took their goodies both ways. Givin' 'n takin'." She laughed. "Men are stupid. They think it's all their game!"

Addie's interest was stimulated, but there was also the fear of getting obligated or, worse yet, entangled beyond what she wanted; and needing a way out, she asked Betsy what to do." She was told women should just use men for their pleasure. If a man became tiresome, it was time to discard him and catch another. Addie said Betsy was cynical, to which she replied, "No. Realistic. Let the men cry! The women have done their share."

In no mood to get into anything like that, Addie had more immediate things on her mind. So when Blazer came to pick her up, she made him know how she felt about the hands. She stopped him before he could get wound up with the apologies, saying it was enough for him to promise.

When they got back to his apartment, which was tastefully redecorated—with light blue walls and beige carpeting—with the wife's insurance money, she let him know she was impressed. She was also needing a rest and cast an eye on the bedroom with its king-size foam-rubber mattress.

Having downed strawberry daiquiris like they were soda pop, she'd gotten quite a buzz at the party and had danced with half the middle-aged men who had been crowding around her. Not knowing what else to do, Blazer came to the bedroom door. She had tugged her stockings down and, with a sigh of relief, plopped herself face down on the bed and called for him to massage her bad leg, which he lovingly did.

He shortly moved up with the same delicate motion, which felt nice; and she responded with the slightest wiggle. Overpowered by those milky thighs, he tongue-seamed them with the touch of a summer breeze, bringing forth an "Ooh" of delight. They french kissed; and he bathed her in tender caresses, rolling a supple tongue over her till as from a power beyond her control, she was arching toward him. And in one swift move, he was there. Startled she felt like he'd plunged a hot fist into her, and she let out a cry. She had grown curious, even a little anxious, to find out; but no one had told her anything about the pain.

She felt herself being nudged and awoke with a start to total blackness. *What time was it? Darn, too late to go home now!* He brought her close, reassuring her it would get better. His warm hand came up gently from below, and it felt good; but she held him off. *Where was the bathroom?*

As it turned out, Hannah had covered for her, telling Otto she had stayed over at Betsy's, who he never liked because he thought she was so totally unreliable—giving him somebody to take it out on. Hannah, however, now wanted to really know who the <u>he</u> was. *The one who sent the roses, no doubt. Was he serious, and shouldn't she bring him over so we could <u>see</u> him?* Otts would be sure to ask what German fathers always ask: "also, wass macht der Vater?" (What does his father do for a living?)

Without waiting for answers, Hannah said she hoped Addie would get married soon. The doctor had told her that she had a tumor. It might just go away, but if it didn't, he'd have to go in and cut. She said not to get alarmed; she was feeling fine, and she started to mention a letter written up by the lawyer that was to be opened afterward. But noticing Addie's impatient frown, she said no time to talk about such things now.

Hannah had this idea that having done wrong, she would die prematurely but—with God's forgiveness—not before this child of her sin had grown up and demonstrated that she could make it in life. For her part, Addie thought her mother was being paranoid and wished she wouldn't act like her death was imminent. *Didn't she say she was healthy?* Addie wanted to know more but just not then.

CHAPTER 19

"Next Time"

He was right about next time. She was back at his apartment that evening, and it felt much better (he'd used a lotion). Addie found herself thinking, *Hey, Betsy was right. A body could get hooked on this!* School was still out, so they had themselves a weeklong marathon. He was so gratified at how she accepted him that he became extremely considerate in his lovemaking—slow and, to keep up with her growing appetite, prolonged. She absolutely glowed—literally, with a blush in the cheeks—which made him want to please her all the more. So began her odyssey of the flesh, and she plunged into those wine-dark waters with exhausting joy.

When school resumed, she was amused at how straight-laced and proper he could look. *Surely a put-on for my benefit*, she thought. When she ran into him at the church, his glasses sparkling from the votive candles, he gave her the hint of a smile and a formal nod. It was fun to savor the secret. Who would have guessed? Not her nor, hopefully, anybody else.

The hiatus gave her a chance to think about it though; and she wondered, *Was he after all serious? Was I?* Now that she thought about it, Hannah had a point. She could almost see Father scowling at her with his infamous "<u>Also</u>?" (<u>Well</u>?) *Well, darn it, I want to know too! Good as it had been, where is it going?*

"<u>Where</u>?" was the inflected response. She could have hit him with a dishrag. *What did that mean? And what did he mean by, "typical of a woman"?* It was the first time she'd heard that tone of voice from him. So now she is just <u>a woman</u>. That was a bit of a shock. He had nothing more to say and said so.

She could see that anything more on the subject would more than raise the annoyance level. So it was a stupid question, was it? That cooled her. It took a person's breath away how fast things could get turned around. They got downright frosty when—not knowing how she could, for goodness' sake, bring it up after all that happened—she asked "Are you going to marry me?" as if her mother were talking through her. And before she could retract it, he comes out with an inflected "Shouldn't people be in love first?"

She swallowed hard and took the bus home. For a while, there were regrets. He had been a good lover, and it had gotten so she could hardly wait for the next time and could think of little else in the long hours in between. In fact, she later recalled that upon hearing the fire engines roar past one night, half asleep, she'd murmured "Blazer." So against her better judgment, she wondered for a while if they could somehow get back to where they were until pride came to her rescue. Along with a new boyfriend.

PART III

FORTUNE FAVORS THE BOLD

CHAPTER 20

"Part-Time Work"

She was one of the few people who knew that Burrow's first name was John, and unlike the chameleon friend that he'd introduce her to, it apparently was his real name though his public look discouraged people from addressing him on a first name basis. It wasn't long before she was once again seeing him as others did. Always on hand for holiday festivities, weddings, and funerals, he was at his floorwalker best with a clipboard in hand, turning his head this way and that to make sure that all the details had been taken care of and that people were where they were supposed to be, the priest included. As alternate deacon, there was no better head usher.

It was only in looking back after other experiences that she understood what, in her blind absorption, she had failed to realize. It seemed a lot like she had fallen into the hands of a wily operator, a crypto artist in fact who got his jollies from practicing his craft while passing himself off as a first-class bore, heavy-lidded, and pompous to a fault.

Of course, he had no interest in the widows who sought him out. Seeing him with Betsy later on, she wasn't entirely surprised. On the contrary, knowing how both disguised their respective smarts, she was curious to find out who would get the better of it. Betsy had been around the block more than once, she but retained the look of those sweet-scented maidens who were just his thing.

It amused her to recall what a sensuous novelty it had seemed on that first night when he once again had put his nose to her hair and breathed in ever so deeply. The guy disguised himself so well; no one would have guessed he was a pro, a professional Lothario. *Didn't he once say he went by the Spanish heritage on his mother's side? Fortune favors the bold! Ho-lay!*

She was initially grateful to Burrow for introducing her to the quick-smiling fellow with the jug ears and mirror sunglasses who wanted her over evenings to do his book work. That was the one whom Burrow had promised would be her part-time job guy, just the one she needed, lacking extra money from John the Blazer. She used to see this new fella in church consoling elderly people who had come to pray for ailing relatives and were not exactly specimens of health themselves.

As Blazer later told her, when he had originally met this guy, he wanted to know what his business was; and when a crisp twenty was crinkled in his palm, it didn't much matter—so long as the crinkles kept coming and nobody complained. On the side, Blazer introduced him to the well-off divorcées. The two of them became fast friends and were often seen together exchanging pleasantries on the church steps as they sized up the passing women (elderly for the one, youngish for the other).

He said his name was Ron but allowed that his middle name was John, which some people called him by. She elected for Ron-John, which got an easy smile out of him. She thought he was making it up anyway—like in giving himself Jones as a last name—but that was all right. In his milieu, an Italian could pass for Jones. Just looking at him, with those ears and slicked-down black hair, a stranger might think he belonged in the funny papers until he put those hypnotic eyes on you.

As he was always so neatly dressed and so deferential to women, there was not an inkling of what she later found out. *So what*, she thought, *looks aren't everything.* And he was exceptionally nice to her. He had her out for lunch to show her how he wanted the books done; and from the way he ordered (top of the menu steak) and what he offered to pay for pretty simple work, she saw right off that he was not cheap, which helped put the Blazer debacle behind her.

After a Sunday buffet at the roof garden of the ritzy Centre Hotel, she put in her first stint on the books right there in the plush booth, following which he looked around and said, "Let's go to the 'Orifice' and finish up." Once there, they fell into one another's arms and had themselves a matinee on the convenient inner office couch, close by his desk. She could see it coming, and it happened so naturally that they were right in sync with one another. *Was this guy ever good?* She recalled what Betsy had said about size. *Look at the feet.* She wouldn't know about ears. Anyway Ron-John was what she needed to get the sour taste of plain John out of her mouth. He was romantic and treated her admiringly—telling her directly how pretty she looked and, with a tilt of the head, what a great bod she had. *Hadn't Blazer done the same? Are these guys in a partnership?*

Wide-eyed, she really took in his expensive house—a newly built ranch in the better part of town, individually architected, with a cathedral ceiling in the living room and skylights in the bedroom and bathroom, plus original artwork on the newly papered walls. The carpeting was so thick she couldn't wait to go barefoot on it, so she instantly kicked her shoes off.

She was impressed at how easily he spent money on her— like the time they moseyed around in the exclusive suburban department store, and he bought her a gold bracelet studded with deep-red rubies (the real thing!). All he had to do was spy her lingering over those glimmering stones in the display case. When she said "No, that would be taking advantage," Friend Ron-John would, with a regal flick of the hand, wave the clerk to put it on her wrist. Didn't he know how to turn a girl's head!

He also got to her folks. When the toaster went out at home, he immediately turned up with a deluxe four slicer to replace it, which made a hit with Otto and slowed his curiosity. When she asked how he liked her new beau, Otto paused for a moment and said "It looks like he can hear good." He guessed a guy who gave her an orchid corsage just for taking her out to dinner couldn't be all bad. Hannah, on the other hand, told her to seize the opportunity to marry a generous man while he was interested. She said that if things didn't exactly work out, it was still better to be miserable with money.

For a while, he wouldn't tell her what he did for a living; but she finally got it out of him that he sold cemetery lots, which paid better than she might think. He made some pocket change running the crematory—having replaced the one set up by the inefficiently meticulous mortician, Ol' Man Bettler, who likewise served as mortuary cosmetologist. He was so good that widowers said their wives never looked so beautiful and wished Bettler could bring them back to life.

Of course, the real money was in commissions Ron-John got from the undertaker he was hustling for, Wolfgang Totenbett— who ran the most exclusive establishment in town, "Your Ideal Home Pre-Heaven."

For the deluxe package, her friend was netting $5,000 a "call" so named in the trade. Despised by rivals, they said he was becoming the local Rockefeller. Ron-John was such a smooth salesman; she learned that around town, he was known as "Bullshit Eddy," distinguishing him from his fast-talking cousin of the same name who ran a garden store and was called "Cowshit Eddy."

"So then, you're an Eddy too?" she asked. "My goodness!"

"My mother used to say a good boy has many names."

Nothing fazed this guy, she thought, looking him up and down. But for the time being, none of that bothered her as much as she thought it would; however, a certain uneasiness occurred in a goodnight clinch when she felt something hard against her thigh that wasn't him. She dropped a hand on it and quickly drew back as if from a snake. *Why did he carry a gun?* She wanted to know.

He offered several explanations ("Death is a dangerous business, you know"), none of which she believed though it seemed to go with the brass knuckles she found in his dresser drawer. *Well,* she rationalized, *there are lots of bothersome things that come up even with close friends and often with relatives.*

Far from being bothered by the guy, Otto, whose shop happened to be on strike, made the predictable remark "Remember, this fella will always have steady work." Besides, he had continued to show himself mindful of her folks, like when he brought over that bottle of Kümmel for Otto. "Your friend's a sport," he said. And it looked like he was very devoted to her. It was true enough— except that she had to bring him back to the other bulge, over which he had himself a rollicking laugh. All the more reason she felt that this guy was the type who liked to create problems she couldn't have anticipated, a way to keep her on edge if need be. She saw that her Ron-John-Eddy wanted to be regarded as full of surprises. Names were a starter.

Once they got fairly comfortable with one another, he began to get himself worked into a hankering for innovation (maybe the fetish for an appetizer). One time, after their good night kiss, he wished she could leave her panties with him so they could be rubbed on his pillow. She saw that she still had a lot to learn, but for kicks, she thought she'd play along. Since her mother had not yet done the week's laundry, she said she could do even better by him. *What? He was serious! Well,* she thought, *so long as it got him going in the right direction because once there, he really was an exciting lover.*

However, the time he had himself an orgy on her toes, she could swear he was frothing. Aroused to a nasal growl, he got his furnace stoked to the point that it looked like there'd be smoke coming out of those extraordinary ears. She finally reached down and tugged on an ear to urge him upward until all of a sudden, her spell was broken by the sensation of something sharp. *Holy Smokes! Teeth? Outrageous!* And with a reflex "yow!" she beat down on him with both fists. He looked up glaze-eyed and stunned. But after a moment's pause, the trance unbroken, he was about to go back when, quick as a whip, her hand flashed out and gave him a resounding slap. When he wouldn't back off, she knotted a fist and gave him a stinger right smack in the eye.

He arose as from a cold shower.

CHAPTER 21

"An Earful from the Earman"

Thinking it over in the light of day, she was at odds with herself on how to handle the situation. Distressed as she was by his kinky side, she nonetheless found that her hunger for the excitement only increased at the thought of having to part with it—and from a partner of his caliber. Maybe she could be a little more understanding; this guy had his needs like she had hers—for which, toes and teeth notwithstanding, she strangely wanted him back.

But that got her to thinking. Hadn't Betsy told her there was such a thing as addiction, and then you were at the mercy of it? It might be, from the way it took him over, that Eddy himself, she thought, could be the victim of such a thing. One never knew what deep down in his innards a person might need. Well, she was learning a lot; and so long as this thing could be kept within some kind of bounds, she wanted to have an open mind.

She half expected him not to show the following evening but more than half hoped he would. And sure enough, there he was—shiner and all—with a self-conscious smile and a huge orchid corsage made up of South American imports. After cocktails and hors d'oeuvres on his living room love seat, he turned on the soft music. Impatient to make up, they rushed to the bedroom, discarding clothes as they went. She held off long enough to wag a finger at him, making sure he got the point.

In the aftermath, she couldn't explain it; but good as it was to be back again, an uneasy feeling had come over her. The thought of those teeth still lingered, but it was more than that: she'd sensed he was detached. She put it to him that, as much as she thought of him, when he got carried away so big that he seemed to forget she was there . . . well, she might as well not be there. He said he was glad she mentioned that because he saw nothing wrong with indulging oneself and offered to have her do what she wanted, ignoring him.

"Go ahead, darling. Let the animal out."

"How so?"

"Yeah. Bite, scratch, twist it . . . Whatever. Ever hear of hurting good? Once you find yourself on the other side of that, you're in another world."

"I'm pleased with this one."

"I swear the pleasure's much bigger both for those that give and those that take, each imagining the other's—"

She clamped a hand over his mouth and said she didn't want to know any more. She wanted to be driven home. As if fearing he might lose her and wanting to impress her that nothing was to be denied, he instantly had her in the car and drove off with the abandon of a big city cabbie, tires screeching. She wasn't home, but half an hour when he called and asked when they were going to get together again, she said "never" and hung up.

Next day, she received a telegram. He had something important to tell her. Good. She had something important to tell him too. Father had inquired about her pay.

Eddy was humility personified when he picked her up, making wide-eyed compliments as he looked her over in the expensive tailored suit he had bought her. He took her to an exclusive hilltop restaurant, and over dessert, he said there were things he had to clarify.

"Ever hear of the Arabian Nights? It wasn't enough for the king to just have a virgin every night. As Big Man, he needed more than just doing it. A bore. His idea was you suffer good in the bad that you do. I know you find it hard to believe, but—"

"Please, enough of that stuff," she interrupted. "Stop it or I'm leaving!"

But he was irrepressible. "Listen. My people came from Egypt, a land of ancient tradition. I know all the secrets of eastern gratification. You'd be surprised at what those old mummified kings did in their heyday. That's why they died young. And talk about fetish . . . ever notice how big they were on cats?"

"I thought you had Cuban ancestry—No? I'm getting confused. That was the other John—er, excuse me—Eddy?"

"Doesn't matter. So long as you recognize *me*. In case not, just listen for a bit."

Lifting his wineglass, he paused to wet his throat, giving her the chance to ask about the important thing he wanted to tell her because she had a question of her own. He said later while and she said now. When he started up again, she stamped her foot. He said to go easy; people were looking over at their table.

"Patrons don't make a scene here." He asked the waiter to move them over to a private booth, and closing the drape, he went on. "Once you understand—"

She put out a restraining hand, but he smothered it with kisses.

"Addie, please listen. Afterwards, I'll do anything you want."

"Sorry, but I have to tell you all I want is <u>out</u>. And my father wants me to show up with the pay I told him I was getting."

His face sagged and he asked for her forgiveness; however in the next instant, his eyes brightened again. "Honey, you're gonna come into the business with me, and you won't have to worry about such a thing as <u>pay</u>. The money won't be yours or mine. It'll be ours! Besides, I feel like I'm fallin' in love with you."

How to find a decent way out? She indicated that they didn't seem to have much to talk about; besides, if it was the undertaker business . . .

"No go. What do you take me for?"

"Nothing to talk about?" he exclaimed. "My oh my, let me <u>tell</u> you what's to talk about! You won't believe the astonishing things you'll find out when we partner up. Ever think of writing a book?"

She realized she'd made a strategic mistake, converting that good tongue into a clattering Niagara, which made her sorry she hadn't settled for mood music.

He could go on for days at a time, he said, regaling her with stories about people's hidden lives. Human nature. That was their common interest, wasn't it? She said he had told her quite a lot of that already. She got up; but, hands to her shoulders, he gently sat her down while ordering another bottle of wine.

She would have no idea of what people were like when it came to death, the fantasies—the "final reality," as Totenbett piously liked to say. Before she could get in a "Thank you but the money please," he was off; and there was no stopping him.

"I mentioned cats. Just think of the old gent who wanted to be buried with two cats on his lap since in the sweet by-and-by, he'd miss the warmth they gave him for his arthritis. Hmm . . . warm cats. In his lap? Think about it.

"Then there was the case of the missing corpse. The hospital kept the anxious relatives sobbing for all of a week while they searched for Mama and finally gave them an urn of ashes, saying somebody must have given instructions for cremation.

"When the hospital heard from the family's lawyer, they double-checked and found that the old girl had been shipped out by mistake to a commercial biology lab, where they made haste to throw some missing organs back in and started sewing in double time. You'd never know the difference seeing how good she looked in the open casket. One of my morticians, Finsterherz, was a world-class artist. The grateful family gave back the ashes with thanks, glad it wasn't them that called for the tracing.

"And talk about interesting corpses, we got one in just the other week which was a woman who had died of a disease that turned people into stone. No joke! They call it systemic sclerosis. Anyway, she died with her arms held out in despair, poor thing, like she was saying 'Lordy, Lordy,' couldn't she just hug her kids? So we had to bring the stonecutter in to chip her off at the elbows. Otherwise, no sliding her into the coffin. Weighed a ton too. Had to charge extra. So much per overweight pound. Okay with the client, so long as . . ."

And on he went, bringing her back into the booth when she bolted and taking her purse when she got up for a second try—talking all the while he was reseating her at the table.

"No scene please."

Hadn't she read about the woman who killed her husband for subjecting her, as it said in the paper, to bizarre sex acts, including paraphernalia? Since that could go just so far, sure enough, when the gossips got finished with it. "Darned if he didn't fetch the dog!"

She told investigators her husband had been a good Christian man; and the only explanation he had was that he'd gotten bored with the same old, same old after reading pool hall magazines. Well, nothing changed so she took an ax to him; then, she cut it off and glued it in his mouth. Could Addie imagine the work Finsterherz has putting <u>him</u> back together again and making him look respectable? *Sure put ole Fin to the test!"*

He wanted to tell her about the guy who fell into a twenty-foot animal-rendering vat at the tallow works and wound up pulling his rescuer wife in after him. Addie shook her head, exclaiming "pity;" and waving a nervous hand in his face, she stopped him long enough to remind him of the money.

"For goodness sake!"

He told her to check her purse. Satisfied, she got up to leave; but he grabbed an arm and whispered in her ear, "Like I was going to tell you, there's a rumor the baron's daughter may get herself checked out of the loony bin."

"What's that got to do with me?"

"Dunno but maybe a lot. Big money, I hear. Kin tell yah more."

"Save it."

"Would you like to see the Frankenstein movie tomorrow night?"

CHAPTER 22

"Oh Say Can You See"

It wasn't easy for her to tell Betsy what had happened. She felt so foolish. Betsy leaned back and had herself a throaty laugh.

"Honey." she chortled. "You were prime naïveté up against prime deviousness. The rumor is that you're supposed to come into some money."

"Oh, sure. So you're saying that, that was courtship? Well, I may be naïve, but I ain't stupid. I knew—finally—why that creep wanted to get me hooked on his thing."

"Not what you think. Sex was his gambit. His friend probably gave you to him to see what could be done. Wherever they think there's easy money, they'll have a look. But he's an opportunist wanting to have something for himself first. And let's face it. He was not above having some fun while he was lookin' into a payoff. Meanwhile, milkin' it for what was available for him."

"Me, the subject of easy money, a payoff? Give me a break!"

"You didn't think he was going to tell you anything of importance, did you?"

"Of importance? This guy could talk yah to death."

"Sounded like his profession, of course. All I can say is there's some secret that you're destined to be taken care of. It's kept close. To get into it now might be hurtful to a person you won't want to hurt."

"What's the goddam mystery here? And how do <u>you</u> know this kind of stuff, anyway?"

"Rest assured for now your secret is in good hands—Van, the lawyer's—and he's obliged to keep it out of anybody else's."

"How come there are things you know—affecting me—that I'm not supposed to know?"

"I was Mr. Lawyer's secretary at the time of a disclosure that's not to be disclosed. You know all the law offices surrounding city hall plaza, don't you? Well, with me running back and forth between them, they used to call me 'Mayor of the Plaza.' I got to know quite a bit. Meanwhile, it's a good thing you blew Eddy off.

"Didn't think I did. He was very generous to me."

"Well, people think the Ear is a little . . . uh, deranged, and he wants 'em to think it. His protection. With all his contacts, it seems like he got himself in with the Connection. You know Fat Tony, don't you? That's how come he's supposed to keep you in contact while they figure how much you're worth. At the end of the day, he gets his cut and they theirs . . . Yah ever see that big Black guy makin' his rounds? It's the kind of organization that makes it easy for a person to slide in with them. You wake up one morning, and they're talking to you like you're one of them. That didn't mean Eddy couldn't freelance."

"Why are you scarin' me?"

"Well, just want you to be careful. If you scared Eddy off, that's a good start."

"I did? Why this wad of money? All I wanted was to show Father my pay."

Counting out all of fifteen twenties, Addie gasped and said she couldn't take all of that.

"Cost of doing business," Betsy assured her. "Peanuts. They expect to get more down the road. Among the baron's stashes, there's supposed to be a juicy one for you. He, above all, wanted it kept quiet. Somebody says so and everybody knows."

"I don't like what you're telling me."

"I always knew you were worth something. Maybe a lot. Awarded in time, they say. The sharks are in the water. All it takes is a little blood."

"What's this all about? What do you know, anyway? Listen, I can take just so much kidding."

"The lawyer ain't tellin'. And me? I plain don't know. Like I tell you about lovemakin'. For now, just let it happen."

Grabbing Betsy's arm before she left, Addie insisted she had to be more forthcoming.

"People know stuff about me that I don't know. I don't like it."

"Okay, then let me give you something to chew on. You have an interest in finding out who killed the baron and Gina, yes? Well, this picture plays right into that one. Remember, he made a lot of money. Also stashed a lot."

"Really?"

"Well, since you didn't know anything about it yesterday, you're not gonna know any more tomorrow. And by the way, don't you know who sings the "'Star Spangled Banner'" at high school football games?"

"Yeah. Does that too. Anything to keep in the public eye."

CHAPTER 23

"Halfback Has Her Back"

And never sung more lustily than when he was the halfback who made the all-state high school football team.

"Football? Who needs it?"

Betsy had put her head in a stir. She had the notion there was an immediate need for . . . well, more info but first *protection*. Money. Yes, money had exchanged hands—lots more than she had expected from that earful. *Not good*, she thought. Particularly if it meant owing somebody a payback.

But mercifully on came square back Johnny R, the all-state halfback himself, arriving at just the right time to have her back. Johnny used to be a Saturday night bouncer for the roughest bar in town. *Who knows? In dealing with that crowd, maybe he'd come across a hired gun.* She told him the latest from Betsy, and clenching his fists, he said "Addie, honey, I'll be your gun. And anything else you need."

Johnny instinctively hated Eddy—in fact, more like despised the guy. When he had caught Eddy hanging around the backdoor of the church about the time Addie left for the day, Johnny got in a grazing punch and chased him down three city blocks.

She had been hoping that this president of the board of education would find his way back, officially or otherwise. She wanted job security; hence, she'd been waiting for another invitation to lunch and eager to take it—contrary to the confusion last time. And on the next day, suddenly he's there. Looking in on her at the nursery school room, he said darned if he could remember what it was he had in mind; but he was glad to be there anyway to check things out. So was she, she told him.

He took out a legal pad and scratched down some notes. He ran a thumb down the wall and, talking half to himself, noted that the nursery school could use a coat of paint. Subtlety was not his strong point. Not to be too obvious about wanting to get with her, he prattled on about small-time politics.

"I'll bet the priest could get this place fixed up for a bingo room, and with the board taking its cut, why, maybe we could do business! Be a nice moneymaker for both. You know, even priests can be tempted." he chuckled.

She hoped he would, for goodness' sake, come to the point—first, about her teaching kindergarten (one up from nursery school), for which something extracurricular would help, like taking the kids to the zoo. The board would like that; it pleases the parents.

"Zoo?" she repeated with a slight chuckle, "I'll show 'em my job."

It was apparent from the way he looked her over while dabbing at the walls that he was indeed on the verge of asking her out, and it was no mystery that the look told her another chapter was going to unfold in her ongoing saga of salacity. Now let it be for a purpose and, hopefully, she sighed, with a little more pay and a little less complication. Above all, job security.

She didn't like to be scheming, but frankly she was curious. Didn't seem her type, *but yah never know unless you've tried it.* Just as he was smitten with her bod, so was she with his. Who knows? Maybe the bastard had some charm, a little more than she saw. She couldn't help laughing at herself. In circumstances like that, Betsy had taught her to check her pride at the bedroom door.

However, as she reflected, it was when she most looked forward to something that it often turned out to be something other than she expected. Her father had a German nostrum for that, which went something like "Erstens kommt es ein mal, tweitens als man will." She recalled her excitement the time Otto took her down to a hot spot on the river; and she caught a big, fat carp, a goldy at that. *Beautiful!* One minute, she had him in the net; and the next, there was a splash as he wriggled free. (Future's uncertain.)

As he turned for the door, it looked like this was to be another almost-landed fish. Having been spooked before by high expectations, she had her misgivings (a this-for-that?); but a date with Johnny R, hunk that he was, was simply too enticing.

As football hero, he was a rare one, having been the only white running back on the Northside High team in recent memory; and he'd carried them to a state championship. They'd called him "Bronco" at first for his crushing style, but he so hated the comparison that he told people he'd drown the next person to use it.

The goal posts in his day were set at the front of the end zone, and he thumped hard into an upright on a spectacular scoring run. He had shed one tackle after the other, and when asked who the toughest tackler was, he said the last one. "That son of a bitch really put a hurt on me. "Yeah, right here on the shoulder."

In any event, he got himself a sports scholarship to an Ivy League college—where he shone a little less brightly and, for want of speed, was converted to linebacker. Tutored, he did manage a law degree. No one found out who took the written exam for him, but the lady with the oversized glasses was careful not to make it look too good.

Back home he was still everybody's hero, likable Johnny. Even his former black teammates, who used to call him "The Great White Dope," acquired a better opinion of him when he promoted himself politically as a champion of the underclass. He was taken into the town's ethnic law firm and started his political career by running for a spot on the board of education. Once the powers that be had him tone down his talk about putting more money into schools in the poorer neighborhoods, he was a landslide winner; and the other members promptly voted him to be their president. He'd be the big shot, but council members assumed they'd call the shots.

In the hurly-burly of politics, he was nobody's fool, of course. He discovered that they could get federal funds for the city's nursery schools if they could just move the biggest one out of the Catholic Church. So he wanted to have a chat with the priest, thinking it was worth a try, even if he came away empty-handed—particularly after he'd checked out the nursery school itself, which was known to be a model of its kind, and saw Addie at her appealing best and leading the happy kiddies in their clap-clap version of "Ten Little Indians." It was so infectious that Johnny sat that big frame of his down on the floor and joined in. The kids couldn't stop laughing. He had one straddle his neck.

She kept expecting an invitation, and it looked like he wanted to extend one; but looking out the window, he said he just remembered he had some appointments. *What, no lunch?* She was also disappointed that after complimenting her on how good she was with the little ones, it looked like he forgot what he'd said about reviving kindergarten for them.

He seemed distracted as he edged out the door. Well, she'd heard about big guys who turned out to be rather shy with the girls. What else to expect from a clumsy football player? He'd left the game, but it never left him. She had to laugh at herself; she'd been involuntarily taking in his blocky build and wondering what it might be like with him.

She came out of her trance to hear him saying "Excuse me, you're gonna be leavin' in a half an hour, right? I've got some business to attend to. But there's always that. Gotta clear the coast for you."

Curious, she found herself running after him; and there he was in the parking lot, biting off his words as he approached a shadowy figure nonchalantly leaning on his car. It was none other than Eddy. (Jealous?) Removing his mirror sunglasses for eye-to-eye emphasis, Eddy evidently had some choice words for Johnny, who thrust his hands out as if to go for the throat. Eddy quickly edged his way behind the steering wheel and shouted a few choice words out the window that got a laugh from Johnny and a finger.

CHAPTER 24

"He Does a Runback"

However, the chairman came running back at week's weary end and, for happy hour, took her to the local version of the Downtown Athletic Club—so named, in fact, but called the DAC (pronounced "dack"). Seen from the outside, it was a seedy-looking bar where all the politicians and newspaper men hung out: it was neither a club nor the resort of an especially athletic crowd. It was not a place where a guy brought a woman. No objection, though, if she showed up with one of the unofficial members.

There was an abandoned workout room in the basement (with weights, treadmills, and stationary bikes), and while the rusting equipment was encrusting itself in dust and cobwebs, athletics of the day were practiced at the backroom poker tables run just about nightly by, it was said, the suddenly ubiquitous Eddy in that establishment called "A-rab."

As everyone knew, he would do anything for a buck though even he had his limits. When asked to set up a craps table for Tough Tony's youngest son, Eddy inventively sidestepped the matter by pointing out that he had nothing against the crap-shooting clientele so long as the boy didn't mind catering to guys from the Black neighborhood; however, Eddy dispensed with snobbery when the son made a believer of him as the kid—no longer a kid—swiftly turned that felt table into a solid moneymaker.

Another guy Johnny had no great fondness for, this Tony Jr., it seems, was a constant disappointment to his father, who had initially assigned him a couple of whorehouses only to have the kid alienate the cops by asking them to take their protection out in trade. Next, he botched a small–time pot operation at a nearby college by strong-arming an instructor-pusher who he thought was being too cautious, only to have the guy turn snitch on him.

Shaking his head, Papa had to buy his boy out of trouble and sit him down for a little "learnin'," like "How many times do I have to tell you? Nobody ever ran a successful business by starting out too cheap and too eager. You gotta show a little class, even if you ain't got any!"

As Johnny went on with stories about the DAC, Addie began to think she was getting stuck with another motormouth. The other one was a compulsive talker by design, this guy obviously from nerves. There being no way to reassure him, she went along with his tales about the mischief of others as it gave him some welcome Schadenfreude; and since she'd learned how to please men by laughing at their unfunny stories, he was relieved. He made a sign to the barkeeper, who knowingly delivered the double order of burgers and fries.

The whole place reeked of cigar smoke down to the lacquered oak tables—over one of which hard-faced men in worn fedoras were chewing on cigars locked, as they were, in serious considerations. They were leaning over and writing down figures, which they passed back and forth, while jawing at one another like it was a council of war.

"All the yak-yak over there . . . What are they up to?" she asked.

"The city's business."

"And what's that?"

"Carving up the budget."

"What about you?"

"That's what I want to know. They've been puttin' me off."

Johnny nodded at the two guys who came by their corner table, and he waved them away.

"Bookies," he said, "and deal makers. Hard to keep 'em apart."

From his bloodshot eyes, it looked like he'd had a good start on the evening when he picked her up. He hastily downed yet another shot and a beer and said, "C'mon, let's go."

They got onto the interstate, and watching him warily, she thankfully noticed he was able to steady himself at the wheel. He had driven a good way out of town when he took an obscure exit, and they came upon this rundown truckers' motel set in a grove of spindly locusts, calling itself "The Palms." Wrong motif for the setting, but they made up for it with a green neon palm beside the entrance and a potted plastic one coated with the dust of ages in the lobby. *My big shot football hero could do no better than this?*

She had all sorts of questions, but the one that kept nagging at her was "What was it with Eddy?" Poor timing or not, she had to ask.

"Oh, that. He wanted me to remember he packed a gun and to let me know he was connected. Might have been phony, might not, but above all, I didn't want to have him sighting on you because of me."

"Oh . . . Thanks, but what's with this business of being connected?"

"Ask me later, okay?"

The room was all aqua green plastic. It was as if the Giant Gila Monster float donated to the Easter parade had been overinflated and exploded its plastic hide over everything in sight: there were cracked plastic drapes, a plastic headboard, a cold plastic armchair, plastic curtains (one closing off the closet, the other the shower stall), warped vinyl tiles on the floor, plus matching wallpaper and polyester bedspread—all in nauseous aqua, which made the room that much chillier. Far from chilled himself, he was throwing off clothes like they were on fire.

But for her, there was no overcoming the atmosphere. So circumstanced, that alluringly muscled bod, sadly enough, didn't quite make it. Noticing the downer look on her face, his spirits dampened but revived when she began to roll down her stockings. Despite the shivers, having gone this far, she decided to go through with it. Slobbering over her in what passed for foreplay, he had all the finesse of a goat in rut; and he was rough but, fortunately, also quick.

She hopped into the bathroom, washed off, dressed, and went for the door. Still in bed, he had pulled a bottle out of his briefcase; and as she turned the knob, he asked her to get a bucket of ice and to hurry back. She shook her head.

Incredulous, he rasped, "You leavin'! Baby, come back. I can make it up to you. You'll see."

"Seen enough." She said she'd wait for him in the car.

On the drive back, with him sitting there in such grumpy silence, she did her best to stifle her own glum mood; and trying to lighten things, she came up with some cheerful chatter about his golf game (hadn't she read about a hole in one?), his little league team (a winner), his standing in the community (seen as a mover) . . . anything but what seemed to be plaguing him.

Evidently, the small talk was not doing the job; on the contrary, it only seemed to irritate him. It would be the easiest thing for her to just come out with it and say, it was a wholly forgettable thing for her, "Why should you be in such a funk about it?" But she thought better of it. His frown wouldn't go away.

"I swear I'll make it up to you." His eyes were flooded. "I swear. What you saw wasn't me."

From the slanted look he gave her, she thought—maybe wrongly—he was itching to lay it on her that any ten women in town would have busted their butts to be in her place. But it really wasn't that. Having a second glance at his hang-down look, she saw how genuinely hurting this guy was. The image of defeat, he sat there clutching a handkerchief.

He leaned over to give her a kiss as he was letting her off; but she was too swift for him, giving him a cheery "See yah!" as she spun out the door. The screech of tires could be heard for blocks. *So much for romance with the all-American stud.*

But again there were second thoughts. He did that to you.

CHAPTER 25

"The Halfback Is Back"

Next day, he was waiting at the basement door of the church with his shoulders hunched and his head down while puffing intensely on a cigarette. When she came out, he said he had to tell her how sorry he was. She was startled to see him there but noticed he was teary-eyed. Rather than get in his car, she guided him over to the picnic bench.

"I want you to know I'm not the idiot I was last night. There were things on my mind mixin' me up. And before I know it, it gets to be very disappointing. Er . . . I mean me, not you. I felt it wasn't right and still couldn't help myself. Like you got an achin' tooth you keep touchin' with your tongue. And my God, were you ever nice to me when you had every reason to get mad! I say to myself, 'This girl has class.'"

He paused and took a deep pull on the cigarette before mashing it underfoot. Still exhaling as he spoke, he went on.

"But I would like you to know I'm a serious person, and I wanna do good. Ever see those dilapidated schools where the Blacks and Puerto Ricans send their kids? They reminded me what I said when I went to them askin' fer votes. So the Connection Boys at city hall . . . They tell me, "'Okay. They'll vote for us. Now go and find the dough.'"

"Well, I made a deal with the bookies. For a percentage, they could work those neighborhoods, and we'd look the other way. The

Boys are madder 'n hell! How am I gonna keep it away from the stinkin' press? They say they'll cut me off at the knees if it gets out. Okay, I tell myself. I always bounce back. Done it all my life, and hey, I got the lumps to prove it."

He was rambling on about promises—political and personal—when she interrupted to let him know that time was a factor for her. School was going to be out a month early on account of the budget crunch, so she had to be looking for full-time work. She might as well have saved her breath. He sped right through the stop sign, harping on the budget worries and saying that nonetheless his assurances were good. She'd have a contract guaranteed. He may foul up from time to time, but she'd see that Johnny R. comes through.

"What's your last name, by the way? "Heiss? Honey, I'm one Polack who's Heiss all over for you." Meanwhile, would you do me the favor of putting on a nursery school demonstration?"

"A <u>what</u>?" *Good grief. Politics. He gives you something, and you're supposed to reciprocate!*

He was going to have some important people from the legislature coming in—people on the Finance Committee. In fact, he'd gotten in touch with the lieutenant governor. Says he wants to run for governor and puts some chips on the table—first off, talking big about education. As he blubbered on, she closed an ear. *To hell with political complications!*

But before she could ask what he expected her to do anyway, he was falling all over himself, thanking her for agreeing to do it and promising her a fat check besides. She could bet the house on it.

She was all for reminding him of the infamous bet he'd made as a kid to run through the neighborhood stark naked for five bucks, but she saw how once that politician tongue of his went clacking down the track; it would take a mightier wind than what she could muster to derail him. This guy was not going to get bogged down by particulars, and frankly neither was she.

"I told you more than I should, but I like you, Addie. I made you a promise, and I'll come through like I will with the people. Just a matter of time. Be a honey and hang in with me. Fact is I got even bigger plans. Like bringing you in as my executive assistant.

Lots more moola than you're gettin' now. How does that grab you? You're cut out for better things."

Half amused by her helplessness before this bewildering hustler, she broke a smile, at which he returned his own dimpled smile, his so-called lady crusher.

"And no demonstration is necessary unless you really want to do it. Of course, I'd like to have you in with me on the new deal for education. And I'm glad you heard me out about my bein' such a miserable jerk."

She detected his whiskey breath as he bore down. *Oh yeah, a new deal. Just my thing.* But the smile took such hold of her that she wanted to say something nice, like she was sorry if she didn't know what was on his mind but appreciated what he said about kindergarten; however before she could get a word out, he had his arms around her. Surprising herself, she instinctively hugged back.

Bungler that he was, she was convinced that like he said, he did mean well. *Innocent but damned if he wasn't a charmer!* Opening his car door, he volunteered to drive her home.

"No monkey business. Just want to tell you somethin' where nobody can hear."

"Enough BS! For goodness' sake."

"No, listen. These Connection folks have an idea you'll be comin' into money. And you know about the baron and Gina being whacked. Well, if you think about it, maybe that was a matter of money too. Count on it. I'll look out for yah."

"Idiot, are you makin' this up?"

She was shaking her clenched fists as she yelled at him. She didn't want to hear any more. He seemed crushed, and for all of two seconds, he was.

"Addie, honey, you have no idea how cute you look when you're mad. Ever notice the vigil lights in church? Your ears redden up like that, only they look like they're gonna pop." Flashing the lady-crushing smile she'd seen on his campaign posters, he added, "Hey, if I told you, you had a great bod—"

"I wouldn't hold it against you."

He chuckled all the way to the car.

PART IV

NEW LOVE
AND BEYOND

CHAPTER 26

"Ah, Doctor Boy"

She would remember it as the most promising spring of her young life, topped by a lush summer that was almost too full to be real. She would put it to herself afterward that she could have been better at reading omens. With such things totally out of mind, she glowed even in letters to her sister, needing to share her newfound life. Eva said she noticed an entirely different style of writing, to which Addie replied "No kiddin'."

The croci bravely thrust their purple heads up with the first touch of a March sun (pale as it was) only to be dusted by snow at nightfall, and to be shriveled by a hard frost within a day of blossoming. A cold spell had ensued that delayed the appearance of the daffodils and jonquils as well as the deep blue hyacinths—which, when they all did shoot up, were forced to bend over in the brisk wind. A host of yellow daffodils (narcissi that they were) had windswept heads bent eastward toward the pond, which suddenly became shaded by onrushing clouds. And not long afterward, the sturdy irises had their broad lips torn in a hailstorm also brought on by that raging west wind.

For a while, the gaudy May tulips seemed to have made up for it all with a defiant burst of reds, whites, and yellow-reds in their tightly packed beds, smiling back at the sun that had licked their fleshy petals apart to expose the shivering stamens and dark vaginal richness within. In a show of abandon, the cherry blossoms burst forth; however, they left themselves vulnerable to the icy fingers of a late spring frost (*die Drei Eismänner*, according to Otts) that threatened to close their petals.

Those were the beds Addie and Burrow had dug on either side of the church steps, planting premium Dutch bulbs donated by Tough Tony (legitimately the produce king), who had made cut flowers a profitable sideline of the garden store that Cowshit Eddy ran for him. Addie recalled going down on her knees to put her nose to the fresh earth and to breathe in its woodsy sweetness. *Ah, this all-embracing earth, mother of us all!*

The new, young priest, who had a habit of showing up when you least expected him, took note of her working the soil with her bare hands and remarked that she seemed a rather earthy girl. She blushed, wondering what the all-knowing padre might have meant. She wanted to say something about worship of the life-giving earth ('How about it, Daddyo'), but not knowing what he'd make of it (probably irreverence), she let it go.

She'd be the first to admit there were indeed lots she didn't know. She didn't know at first what to make of the unexpected renewal of a past friendship; nor could she know that once renewed, she would savor a blossoming that paralleled nature's.

They had passed one another as she rushed through the lobby of the hospital, retreating from its odor of stale disinfectant. She had been visiting Otts, who was recovering from what they thought must have been a mild heart attack. Her friend was the selfsame boy (now much changed), who had made nice to her in the cloakroom at school, the erstwhile boyfriend she'd had a crush on until he spinelessly went with those others who shunned her.

He called her name and, coming over, took her arm and asked with concern how come she was in the hospital. She told him about Otts. She said she wouldn't have recognized this friend from high school now sporting that mustache and scruffy beard (not that they were unbecoming). He'd taken an advanced placement test so he could graduate half a year early and had been away at college studying to be a doctor like his dad. He was back working as a nurse's aid to make some money for living expenses out there in the heart of Missouri.

Here was someone her own age and experience. The past was swiftly forgotten. They hit it off from the start, and that's what would make it such a heartache because she found that she had really fallen for him, which would burst forth like the short-lived splash of color that lit up the garden.

She saw that what was missing in her prior relationships was not so much about anything the other men lacked as opposed to what had been lacking in her—the secret something from within. From them, she'd learned basic lovemaking—what Eddy called gratification of the bod—which she didn't minimize; however when the inside feeling emerged, it made her blood tingle.

The phone messages she'd left for Joyride Johnny brought promises to be more distantly honored with the proviso that honored that they nonetheless would be. Still harping on much to make up for. She should count on him coming through. Because of her objection to the company he kept, he said he'd started to move away from the shadier element and was now running a thoroughly clean operation—which however was making it harder to squeeze out the money but, for her sake, was worth the doing. She shouldn't have sent that check back. He wanted her to have the wherewithal that could see her through the summer, an offer she resisted.

How long would it be, she wondered, *before the boy in him realizes he was chasing an illusion?* Of course, maybe that was taking it too far. There was something so sad about the guy that it evoked the sympathy she felt for a child: he belonged on the floor of the nursery school.

The priest, also concerned about her, had offered to put her in charge of Vacation Bible School; but she could well imagine him in apoplexy over what she would make of that. On her modestly declining, he said he'd see if he couldn't come up with something else for her. She was rather glad of his interest, but hers lay irreverently elsewhere. The future be damned, it took no great effort to shake herself free of everything but Doctor Boy.

Talk of reliability, the first thing he did upon learning she was at loose ends with nursery school being out was to get her a job in the hospital kitchen. It was not the place you'd want to be in the summertime—hence the opening—but it paid decently, and she got her meals for free.

For the cook, a cleanliness fiend Dutchman, it was a revelation to see how she threw herself into the scrubbing of pots and pans; and so he sent her around with the lunch cart to give her some relief from the steamy sink. He also trained her to cook so she could cover his Mondays off.

With some steady money coming in, she talked about getting herself an apartment. Her friend encouraged it and, once again, was there for her. He helped her move into the dingy studio apartment they would call "The Nest" and, without saying a word, paid the first month's rent. It was an elongated—though not very long— one-room affair with a kitchen and a bathroom at one end and a table, a chair, and a bed at the other. It made her think of Van Gogh's painting of his tight little bedroom.

They had fun painting the walls white, which made them pull back a bit; and he brought over some rugs to give the place a cozier feeling.

"Still more like a caboose," Hannah remarked, "than a railroad car apartment."

Otts scratched his head and said that if she ever went to a convent, she wouldn't be surprised. He was glad she was making enough money to support herself. She would not want for eats. Maybe someday she'd be a regular cook so she could marry a rich chef and bring her daddy lots of fat little grandsons.

Her friend was the quiet type. He was polite and a little on the modest side. On the first week, he'd go out in the hallway when she changed. His being restrained was something she saw as a sign of respect, and she liked him even more for that; but she also thought it was time he broke down and got a little closer. *Am I going to have to break him in?*

They'd scarcely done more than friendship huggies; nevertheless, it got so she just wanted to be with him all the time.

Every minute away, she was trying to picture what he was doing. *Likely at a bedside applying the stethoscope to an old codger's wrinkled chest.* When she told him this, he laughed and said he was probably doing bedpans.

It turned out he was pretty handy, and the night he installed a shower for her, he stayed late. Rigging the shower curtain around the tub involved drilling into the bath tiles, which split on him and had to be grouted back together. Overall, it took more time than he thought it would; and he had the same problem putting up the medicine cabinet. Having finally finished, he made a halfhearted swipe at picking up his things and stood there a moment in hesitancy; then he kicked the tools aside and, shirt off, plunked himself down on the bed.

She drew a cool washcloth across his face and chest and snuggled in beside him. Noticing the tense uncertainty written on his face, she didn't know whether to back off or to throw her arms around him.

"You're bushed. What can I do for you? . . . Got a cold beer in the fridge."

No sooner were the words out of her mouth than he started pulling her over to him, and they instantly found themselves afloat in wet kisses. The dam broke, and they went at it like young animals. Sweaty as they were, she liked the taste of him; he was such a clean guy. So *"appetitlich,"* as Hannah might put it. She sensed from his excitement—a case of the trembles—that maybe she was his first. *Oh my!* Considering what was real, that's how <u>she</u> felt. Ecstatic didn't do it justice.

Yet finding him asleep beside her when she awoke in the thin light of morning, she found it hard to convince herself that it wasn't unreal, that she wasn't making footprints that washed away in the surf. Amazed at the moods which came over her, she hastily shook it off and had to smile as she fixed coffee—thinking of how each night when he'd formerly gone home to sleep, she went to bed with a pillow between her legs. She so ached for his touch. Now it was like she had freshly awakened from the long sleep before birth and, looking around, bright-eyed, discovered that life had just begun.

It was a glorious summer but also an extremely hot one and particularly so in the hospital kitchen despite the rattly exhaust fan. The elderly lady who took the cleanup job had passed out one humid afternoon, so Addie had to do her job at the boiling dishwasher on top of her own. But she just toweled the sweat out of her eyes and hustled all the more so as not to keep Doctor Boy waiting. The cook was amazed at her spirit. She told him that so was she, considering how she'd always hated this kind of close heat.

Lots of things changed. After a full day in the kitchen, the food smell was so thick on her clothes that she couldn't eat her evening meal there, which worked out just fine since it meant she'd be preparing dinners at home for the two of them. Having picked up recipes from the cook, she made a great Italian meat loaf, which became his favorite; and when he bought her a wok, she also did some zesty stir-fries, which (with a wink) she steeped in fresh garlic.

He provided the wine, and after assorted sampling, she took a big liking to the after- dinner Port wine; so he made sure to pick up some on his way over. She acquired a yen for the heavy sweetness that lingered on the tongue; it helped to ease her out of momentary doubts. It got so they fell into a nice domestic routine—usually listening to soft music with their wine, which induced tenderness and shortly rolled them into urgent lovemaking. The hunger only grew. One prurient morning, they called off work, went back to bed, and exhausted themselves.

But above and beyond the passion, they simply enjoyed one another. They would snack on cookies she'd baked and talk about the day's doings before going to sleep. She asked if he knows Betsy LeBrun, who went to school with them, and laughably got herself a job in hospital security through a friend in the business. It seems her former employer, a slippery lawyer having taken one slip too many, was awaiting trial.

"Well, ol' Betsy said to say hello."

She had told Betsy about the apartment, and she wanted to drop by and have herself a look-see, at which news her Doc-boy seemed uneasy; then Addie realized what a boner she had pulled, recalling how ever-competitive Betsy had also been sweet on him.

Had she come over not to just see the apartment but to take him in, in his new digs? Jealous was she that her old flame was nighting it with a friend? Addie saw the danger of thinking any further and let it pass.

The weekends they got off together were fun times: she couldn't remember when she'd laughed so much over so little. The freer their intimacy became, the more frolicsome—particularly on her part. He said they ought to do something about those bare walls, so she cut off swatches of his pubic hair and taped them up in a suggestive outline.

On their way back from a concert in the park, she had a sudden impulse to unzip him as he drove; and ignoring his mild protest, she went after it. Coming up for air, she rolled down the window and called out, "Hey, Dad, you oughta see me now!"

It was so good that every now and again, the doubts would creep in; and she'd get the feeling it was too good. As the weeks sped by, rushing them toward the day when he'd have to go back to school, she kept pushing back the clouds that told her a storm was approaching that would bring down their nest. The first sign was not long in coming.

They had gone swimming out at Reservoir Park; and while she could waddle along well enough in the sand, shifting from leg to leg without looking too awkward, when they stepped onto the grass going to and from their blanket, she felt self-conscious about her shoeless gait with its dip to the left. Much as she tried to diminish it by going slow, she had the sense that though he had become accustomed to her little limp in private, out in public, it seemed to strike him as embarrassing.

He had her by the arm with a certain care, like he was escorting a cripple. And here he was going to be a doctor. Awful. She wanted to say something but didn't know what. It hung there between them, and it bothered her that he said nothing.

A couple of days later, he said he'd drop her off after work because he'd promised his mom to do some chores that he'd kept putting off and that she was depending on him to get done before he left for school. The more he apologized, the worse it became. She cried herself to sleep.

He came around again on the weekend before he had to leave, but it wasn't the same. He wasn't all that eager, and neither was she. It might have been less painful if he hadn't come. On Monday morning, he held her real tight when he said his goodbye. Herself, she was holding on for dear life, refusing to let go. His eyes were red and watery; hers overflowed while her lips quivered. He literally had to break her grip. She told him to write, and he was gone like a puff of smoke.

CHAPTER 27

"She Goes out to See Him"

She couldn't eat or sleep. She tore up his card that said "Goodbye. I love you." and flushed it down the toilet. After a week of sheer agony, she decided she was just going to have to go out there and see him at his college.

Her mother told her it was foolish and it was, but she couldn't help herself; besides, she had to tell him. Betsy was glad to take over her little apartment, and if it came to it, she thought the good priest would hold the nursery school job open for her. Hopefully, it wouldn't be necessary; but she really couldn't think about that or anything else.

She went by Greyhound. With stopovers in places like Harrisburg, Wheeling, and Indianapolis, it was a dragging two-and-a-half-day journey but made less so by her telling herself to buck up and imagine his baby-faced surprise when she threw herself into his arms. She knew she meant something to him, and when she told him what happened, he'd have no alternative but to take her in. She'd get a job, be his cook and housekeeper, set up a budget, and handle responsibilities while seeing him through college.

She had never been on a college campus before. To her it was like a big park with old museum buildings squared around a huge lawn. Bearded men with briefcases—some pretty shabby-looking— walked alongside milling students going from one building to another. Here and there, knots of kids sat around on the lawn and on the steps of buildings—talking, smoking, drinking Cokes, munching on a sandwich, reading.

It looked like a great life: nobody seemed worried about having to work for a living. (Papa Otts might have had a word or two about that.) *Wouldn't this be a nice place to settle down?* "Looks like easy livin'," she said to herself.

She got his address from the student directory she found in the big building at the far end of the square. A student gave her directions to the boardinghouse where he was staying. It wasn't but a block off campus, across the street from a girl's dormitory.

She sat on the porch rocker and waited for hours that stretched endlessly on. Her eyelids were becoming heavy when she shook herself and looked up to see . . . There! He was coming up the sidewalk. She was breathing so hard that she couldn't call out to him. Instead, she jumped off the porch and started to run down the walk but stopped in her tracks when he swiftly changed course.

He had run across the street and was vaulting over a low balustrade to reach the terrace in front of the dorm where a stately blonde in a cashmere turtleneck was rushing out to him, arms extended. It was obvious she came from money and, nose up, had the look of a snoot. They hugged, held on for a delicate kiss, and walked arm in arm into the dorm lobby.

"<u>Bastard!</u>" she yelled.

Her first impulse was to dash the box of cookies right there on the porch and charge off to the bus station. But choked as she was, she held on and calmed herself. What made her think that for her, daughter of a poor immigrant family, it would turn out any other way but this? Weren't the rich boys supposed to take advantage of the poor girls from a working class family? Screw 'em and leave 'em? What else?

Yet since he had to be told, how was she supposed to talk to him now? What awful words might come out of her mouth, giving him an excuse, putting him in the right? She left the cookies by the front door where he'd stumble over them, his chocolate chip favorites that she had baked for him on that dreadful last weekend when <u>she</u> was trying to cheer <u>him</u> up.

She had the presence of mind to call her mother from a rest stop to let her know she was coming home and then wished she hadn't: her mother's questions were no help. An awful heaviness came over her, and she sobbed softly to herself most of the way back. *What to do?* Her face got so puffed up that by the time she arrived, her mother scarcely recognized her.

Practical Betsy said the best way to get over it was to look elsewhere. Get with some good guy she could blame.

CHAPTER 28

"Back to Tom"

She was barely in the door, lugging groceries, when Tom stood there demanding "Where the hell are my shoes!"

"I thought you were going to lie down and rest. I was going to join you."

"First, I'm locked in then my shoes are gone. What's the game here?"

"Why don't you help me with these grocery bags?"

"What's with the locking?"

"Aren't you flattered? Look, I got us a new bottle of Jack Daniel's." She reached over and lifted his chin for a kiss.

"You're not telling me anything. You got secrets, have you? First of all, what brought you out here anyway?"

"There's lots I can tell if that's what you want. Fact is I'd like to know what a psychologist might think about my crazy life."

"Well, like I said, some people back home did think you were strange."

"I know. Better that than being the stranger like here. And even that is better than people being strangers to one another. I can vouch for that too. Hey, you're not leaving, are you?"

"Not yet. But I'd sure like to have my shoes. I'm going to have to get down to the university before too long."

"Oh, so you've got somebody waiting for you."

"Not what you're thinking. I'm working on case histories with another guy. It's our project for the Masters' Seminar."

"Case histories, huh? Well, I'm a case, and I've got a history to prove it. Interested? Here, take a sip. You will stay and keep me company, won't you? I can tell you a lot about being lonesome too."

"Sorry." His look changed. "Sure, I can stay. Fact is I intended to. Was hoping you'd ask."

She put their drinks down on the end table next to the overstuffed chair by the window, pushed him into the chair, plunked herself down on his lap, and covered his mouth with her ice-cubed lips.

"I just didn't want you to turn out to be one of those screw-'em-and-leave-'em types. Don't take it wrong. Not that you would have been."

Taking her head between his hands, he returned her kiss and held it. She soon had him out of his shirt and trousers and herself down to her panties and bra. As he eased his shorts off, he was startled to see her looking out the window and fluttering her tongue at a woman in a wheelchair watching them from her window one flight up in the close-in apartment house next door.

"For goodness' sake! What's this?"

"Haven't you ever been onstage—a high school play where you could do things you wouldn't in life?"

"Come on now. I'm dealin' with make-believe?"

"If for yourself, you've just made your debut."

She pulled down the shade and ran for the bed with him in close pursuit. She started by gently nipping at his pecs. He humorously returned the compliment. But—what with the bourbon and the sense of release at being close with a man again after the emptiness— a momentary giddiness came over her, which got swept away by a surge of raw desire. She took them on a wild ride that had him calling out her name. It emerged in a drawn-out manner, like he was asking for mercy. She grinned. It seemed like a vengeance screw on man-unkind.

As they caught their breath lying on their backs, she looked absently at the ceiling and couldn't help feeling strangely detached.

It made her wonder if the real feeling would ever come back. At any rate, it seemed that the tables had been turned: now she was using the man to satisfy a need, for which she didn't especially have to relate to him.

Apparently, it went undetected. What man would turn down a free screw? Whatever his prior confusion, he was charmed by her lovingly cuddling up to him afterward and running her sweet little hand over his chest.

She lit the candles and set out a platter of cold cuts and potato salad for a light supper. After he'd called his research partner to reschedule, she refilled their glasses; and they talked into the early hours. He said his research was on spousal abuse—not the obvious physical kind, rather the psychological type wherein people prey on one another's weaknesses.

They deny they're doing it, but if it's revealed to them, the men will put it on the women (they're asking for it); and the women themselves will still hang in with their abusers, thinking maybe it's deserved. It was perverse, but she said she understood it. As badly as she had been treated by a man she loved, if he were to show up tomorrow, she'd throw herself at him and forgive everything.

"She would?"

"In a heartbeat."

"Well, I guess so."

She told him about Doctor Boy, filling him in on how she'd resolved that she absolutely had to try again to see the guy. She had to let him know. Was she going to go full-term? It would sure mess things up. Yeah, for two lives. Certainly a third. She hated the thought, hated herself for having it.

Despite fearing the worst, she told Tom how she'd steeled herself and went out there a second time, planting herself as before in the porch rocker. The tension had worn her out to the point that she fell asleep and woke up at three in the morning, fogged over. *Had he seen me and quietly tiptoed in, hoping I wouldn't wake up? Could he be that low?* She left a note, giving her boardinghouse phone number and saying it was urgent.

A week passes. Then two. So she has to call, distasteful as it is. Maybe he was expecting the blonde, for after a cheerful "Hi there," his voice falls. When she tells him, he asks if she had been fitted with a dam and if she had the frog test. She tells him his tough little sperm didn't give a damn and that it must have swum right over one. And he said that there was no need to kill some creature, if that's what happened. (A doctor would know.) *He'd want that?*

He said that he doesn't think it's funny, and she said that neither does she.

"What're you going to do about it?"

Silence.

She said, "I feel like I've been used and discarded, but darn it, you've got a responsibility!"

He asked, "Haven't you been with other men?"

She hangs up.

"If he doesn't want me, I don't want his kid. But then, how can I take it out on this little innocent something living inside me? And where do I go? If I go home, I have to have it and put it up for adoption, which I can't do. Catholics have a placement service. Experienced too.

"If my father finds out, he'll raise holy hell. First with me, but he'd go after him too with the old-fashioned shotgun for sure! So there's no going home. And no solution out here either. I go to the free clinic, and it'll haunt me the rest of my life. I have the kid, I'm out of a job, and we sleep in the street."

"So?"

"So bullshit!"

"Why, if you were in love, wouldn't you find a way to have—"

"What? Have it and bring it out to him? Here's a present? As for having been in love and the kid our joint blessing . . . Well, yes, according to this future doctor, he had nothin' to do with it. The kid was all mine. I couldn't tell you what life was or wasn't gonna be like after that phone call, except desperate. I hoped I'd miscarry, but that would have been doing the kid in just the same. My own flesh and blood." She apologized for crying.

It being that bad, Tom suggested counseling.

"For what?"

He changed the subject. "What was all that about with the crippled girl at the window?"

"Ah, that. We became friendly. I felt for her. She wasn't ever taken out. Never would be. And cooped up as she was with that bitchy widowed mother of hers, they had some awful fights. In warm weather, you could hear the yelling all the way down the block. She'd spend much of her day at that window.

"Her only outside contact was with a guy in the army. She'd volunteered to become a pen pal. When he wrote that he wanted to visit, she told him they were moving. I used to wave to her and give her a smile, so we talked now and then. Her face hung down, and she was red-eyed. Had obviously done a lot of crying. I felt pretty isolated myself. Seeing her made it worse."

"Then why would you want to taunt her?"

"Can't you see? I don't like myself. We have something in common."

They had been smoking, and he went to open the window; but she swiftly angled in ahead of him. "You almost lost your shoes."

CHAPTER 29

"A Friend in Need"

He came to visit quite regularly, but it was not like before. The more he learned of her troubled psyche, the less amorous they became—particularly in light of the damage done by previous amours. She rather liked talking to him: he was a good listener. They became friends. He wanted to know more. She hoped he wasn't drawing her out for a case history. *Was he?* He said he didn't want to go professional on her; he thought she might just like to have a friend she could talk to. He'd fallen behind on his project, so it was two weeks since his last visit.

"What about the kid? What did you—"

"Please," she interrupted, "don't put it that way. Did I have a choice?"

She told him about the not-so-funny funny thing that happened when she rode her bike to the clinic.

"There were these three black kids standing around on the corner, joshing one another, and playing tag. They burst out laughing when I put the chain around my bike and locked it to a fence post. They knew it was going to be gone when I came out, and so did I.

"I guess I could have brought it in with me, but I didn't. Wouldn't have been able to ride it back anyway. If a loser, why not a total loser. You get to feeling that way and . . . well, you know how it is."

She said it was quick and it pained. More so afterward. It was a long walk to the bus stop. The people at the clinic couldn't have been nicer. They asked her twice—maybe more—if she really wanted to. She told them "No, and please no more questioning." The black doctor, a spindly old fellow with a shiny bald head and a kind eye, gave her a test that he said told him it didn't look like she had a viable fetus. She thought he was just trying to make it easy, but it didn't help much.

Sitting there alone in the examining room after the procedure, eyes closed, she told them she was cold; and they got her some heated blankets. She found herself in a nightmare of the soul, wandering the streets and calling out, against her will, why she wouldn't give the little one a chance. The only way she could stop the shivers was to get up and run from them. The police were chasing after her, blowing a whistle, and yelling "Stop her! She killed somebody. Yeah, her own kid too!"

Once home, she crawled under the covers and must have stayed there for at least two days. She dreamt the most perverse dream in which despite her wracking guilt, someone came over and stayed by her bedside, uttering comforting words and telling her she was a good person. She kept shaking her head. He fixed her toast and bouillon, which she brought right back up.

He cleaned up, fixed her a hot bath, and gave her a soothing back rub. She at first couldn't make out his face. When it finally came into focus and she saw the scruffy beard, she screamed.

"You! Go away. You are mocking me!"

She hit the floor with a thud and came to. At that moment, she resolved that if it ever happened again, she'd see it through with the kid no matter what—or whose.

"Be assured I'm well over it now. Remember, you asked me to bring it out, and I'm putting a lot of trust in you. I wouldn't have said a thing if I thought you might be using any of this stuff. Now I'm getting the feeling maybe you'd like to."

"Not at all. True, I was tempted. But from all the hurt, I'm hearing it's a lot more important that I try to do some good for you. What about other men? There were others?"

"Oh, weren't there?"

"None that <u>he</u> would know of," she said, piqued at the question. And truth be said, it was like there really weren't any others. "But," she concurred, "talking was healing."

So she told him about Burrow and Eddy and Johnny.

"Oh yeah." she gave a forced smile. "None really a relationship. Will there be more? A chance there might be. Of what kind? Who can tell? I do need to find work, you know."

At first, Tom was incredulous; but reading her sincerity, he was attentive and helped her sort out motives, not least of all her own. She began to loosen up. At last, as she wrote in the journal, she felt that here was a man who was interested in her for herself. *Ah, the sweet breath of kindness!* Not only had she found herself a friend, but the friend had also become a brother. Her confidence was coming back.

Tom wondered why she was staying in St. Louis: it seemed pointless now. She agreed, "Yeah, it's been a bad scene for me. Dunno. Was I gonna barge in on him and the snoot? Tell her to look at me, and she'll see herself a month from now? Pour a little vinegar on their love life? You know, chill their anticipation." One way or another, she felt like she was going to bust out and put it to him. Maybe through a discreetly sent telegram. Sent to the dorm with "Hold for the addressee" on the envelope. Something he was sure to look at—and she to ask about.

She recalled Tom telling her that spite might be a delight, but it wouldn't get her anywhere. She said she agreed and vowed to spite this "two-faced bastard" anyway.

"You did have an obligation to tell him, though. You did, didn't you?"

Since that had been duly taken care of—a red-ink note topped by an ice bag left at his boardinghouse—Tom suspected that the truth was that she stayed because he <u>had</u> been her one true love. *"And the thought of it lingered?"* *Was she subconsciously hoping against unrealistic hope? Like all she had to do was spoil it with Snoot, and then she'd catch him on the rebound? The imp complex right out of Poe."*

They agreed it was time—really past time—that she let go. She had to go home. He made some phone calls and was able to locate a good person to take over her job at the library, it being a condition of her leaving on short notice. She did need that last paycheck. After they got her place dusted and vacuumed, he arranged for the landlord to do his inspection and to return her deposit.

A week later, he was there to help her pack, to surprise her with a train ticket, and to drive her to the station. There were hugs, and she came back out on the platform for a kiss. He told her he expected to be back east with her before too long, degree in hand.

She had taken a window seat, where he could read her lips.

CHAPTER 30

"Chaos in the Classroom: Johnny's Rescue"

When Addie finally stuck a nose into her home apartment again, it took her all of three days to clean up after Betsy, who was no great shakes at housekeeping. It looked like she'd had one of her boyfriends in with her. He had left his own mess in the bathroom: a couple of dirty socks and balled–up jockey shorts, a pair of torn sneakers, a tin of roaches, and a twisted tube of toothpaste. There was also a lipstick imprint on the bathroom mirror. *Was this guy expecting to come back?*

She went on all fours trying to scrub a nasty grease spot out of the rug, and having assumed a "why bother" attitude, she was about to get up when in burst her mother with word that the board of education was authorizing a resumption of kindergarten. The paper said that they would shortly be interviewing teachers and that they were asking applicants to submit resumés. *Resumés? Where did that put me?*

Her mother noticed the puzzlement. "Aren't you excited? That's the job you've been hoping for, isn't it?"

"Yeah, badly. That's the problem."

"Problem?"

"If it's a formal process, that means you've got to have credentials. My credentials? I'd have to get down on my knees to remind somebody of a promise."

She called the board, and they told her to call his law office. The secretary reeled off three Polish-sounding names beginning with R and told her to leave a message. He was in a conference. In a way, she was relieved he didn't call back. To start all over with this Johnny boy didn't intrigue her.

At week's end, she thought, *What the hell! Maybe I should try again to make contact.* It was then that Betsy called, and before she could tell her to come over and help clean up (for goodness' sake), Betsy asked if she had seen the morning papers. It looked like they'd already hired the three kindergarten teachers they were after. Seems like it went pretty fast, and the one that got the school in their neighborhood was the Dimallo girl, Marie.

"Easy now. She's much nicer than she used to be. But I don't think she knows from apple butter about working with little kids. Addie, it for sure should have been you. But I don't think people knew you were back in town."

"Was I supposed to announce myself?"

She went to see the new priest, Father Jay (as Johannes was familiarly known). And he said he'd be glad to have her back, except that half the kids had departed for kindergarten; and for the rest, it wouldn't do to sack the nice elderly lady they'd brought in to replace her. He genuinely wished there was an opening. Knowing how good she was, he said he'd create one if he could. For himself, he had frankly missed her. She was pleasantly surprised by his cordiality, but wouldn't he then go on and ruin it!

"However, you burned the cozy little bridge you'd built here, didn't you?"

Acting the lower case father was he? What was it with this priest that he had to make a woman feel uncomfortable? She couldn't put her finger on it, but she had the feeling something was going on inside him. *Guess he has his problems,* she mused. Behind all that black, he is a man.

He was the well-groomed young priest who had replaced old Father Ambrose, her father's mentor. He had an athletic build, and guys at the gym who saw him work out said he'd do the most punishing kind of lifts on the Nautilus. When they kidded him about it, he said with a wink, that there was an old dictum that to workout is to pray.

At least the hospital cook was glad to have her back. Though she lacked her former enthusiasm, that was okay with him; she still never left a speck of grease on the pans.

Barely three weeks into the kindergarten experiment, all hell broke loose: The kids at their neighborhood school were becoming bored then surly. The noise got louder. There was bashing and the spit wads went flying. Young Marie, putting on her sweetest face, did what she could to appease them; but the strain was showing, and the kids picked it up.

The day she brought in a *home baked* cake, she took a hit on her snug little butt from a bean shooter; and that did it. Calling out names in a voice about to break, she grabbed a couple of the rowdies who had been making life miserable for her and let them have it with a ruler. When the ruler broke, she took a book to them. They wailed bloody murder, denying it was them; and the furious parents came pounding on the principal's door, whence they were referred to Johnny, who they threatened to besiege with lawyers. One wrathful mother stomped into his office with an ultimatum and the name of a lawyer.

"Physical violence against five- and six-year-olds! Horrible! How can you allow that? We'll see you recalled. Take you to court."

The newspaper was playing it up, and the other board members were ducking reporters. They said it was not their fault. The board VP cited a consensus neutrality. Members were laughing behind their hands. Johnny held the parents off by solemnly agreeing with them.

They asked, "But what are you going to do about it?"

"Not to worry. I'll see to it the situation is remedied. See to it personally.

But can't let kids spitball a teacher. Not anywhere."

Addie got the SOS after a long, sweaty day in the kitchen.

"Would you please take over?" he pleaded.

She shook her head. *The nerve! He needs me, but where was he when I needed him?*

"Can't, please, get into that."

It was out of his hands. People went over his head. Done before he knew it.

"Be a friend, huh."

"You're kidding. A lot friendship did for me."

"Look, I'll make it real good for you. You know what I've got invested here. This kindergarten thing is just getting off the ground. If it caves, hey, I'm in the deepest! Addie, please." His voice rising, he clasped both hands, pleading, "Come on, you gotta do it."

She said she would do it only if he came up with a contract that made the job real, as well as good.

"Like I said, it should be for the rest of the year and beyond."

"I want it to put me on civil service."

"Civil service?"

"Yes. Remember the guarantee thing?"

"Oh. Civil service. That would be . . . Not sure how to handle something like that. Complicated, but can give it a college try."

She had had some of these kids in nursery school. They cheered when she walked in. She was back in her element. The contract? It was just a paperwork problem: it was nothing to worry about. And truth be told, she was so delighted to be back with the kids that she didn't.

She worked her way out of a dark mood, and time went by quickly. But by the last week of class, there still was no hint of a contract; so she wrote and reminded him with a more-than-gentle prod. He called, apologizing that he hadn't gotten back to her and saying that she'd be amazed at all the fires he'd had to piss on lately; there could have been costly lawsuits.

She let him go on for a bit before putting a stop to it.

"Oh, for sure! A promise is a promise."

"What did it mean that the secretary said she never received a vita from me?"

"Ignore that for goodness' sake! I know nothing about that sort of thing. Hell, I am the vita. All the secretary needed to know was that we had made a deal, and I intend to make good on it. And by the way, you checked your bank account recently?"

"Yeah. Don't care to be bribed, but thanks. Don't care to be broke either. And out in the street. Bills . . . You say send 'em on to that bighearted donor, right? But please, we gotta be real."

Seeing him go pout face, she put an arm on his ample shoulder. On the job security front, she expected nothing; and come that fateful last day of class, she would in hindsight have preferred nothing. She had been saying good-bye to beaming parents, who showered her with compliments (several, with cookies), when, heavyhearted, she spots clownish Johnny at the curbside. He was giving her the big-dimpled smile and was waving a large manila envelope.

Slipping off the fender of his big, bad Buick, he shuffled into a slow jig to the whistled tune of "Happy Days Are Here Again." It looked a lot like a bear doing soft-shoe.

"I got it, baby, I got it! Wait'll you see."

"A song and a dance, huh?"

"Come <u>on</u>. Civil Service, like you wanted."

What she read brought her up short. "You're making me a <u>secretary</u> to the board? What's that?"

"I'm the board. Let me explain. What you want, we ain't got."

"Damn it! You just said that you did <u>got</u>."

"Hold on, please. Teachers don't get civil service appointments, so I was stumped. Whatta we do? Well, we got this lazy-ass mulatto secretary who spends half her time playin' the numbers, and she finally hits. Big Louey—Sonny, to his girlfriends—is giving her a fifty, something she's never seen. And she's so nervous a wind takes and blows the bill out into the street. She chases and, bending over, gets her broad one in the way of a delivery truck. So we got an opening."

"You fool! I can't take shorthand. No way I can be a secretary!"

"You ain't gonna be. I can assign a secretary anyway I wanna. We got three of 'em. Two of 'em do-nothins sittin' there, doin' their nails. I'm assigning you to kindergarten, where you do <u>do</u> somethin'. Okay?"

He went on to explain there was no way he could have outright appointed her to a teaching job since they were usually spoken for well in advance. Every Alderman had at least one big contributor with a college-educated daughter he wanted in the public school system—a nice, clean place to park her while she shopped for a husband.

"You know I'm always on the lookout for ways I can help somebody. Why, just last week, a teacher with a funny lisp comes in and says the kids are making fun of her. She's cryin, so I find her a guy who . . .

"Idiot," she breathed as he droned on. "All of this palaver. I have no idea what you've got me is legal."

He was getting her edgier by the minute. How distasteful to have to remind him it was she who had done him a crucial favor! She had to kiss his for him coming through with what he'd promised! But she let it go.

Presumably that's the way it was with politicians: nothing ever goes quite straight, which is why they make it seem like it does. Except that this guy appeared to be the most notoriously inept of politicians. And he's got all of these grandiose plans.

"What am I in for," she moaned, "workin' a job I'm not hired for?"

She had heard that he'd been dropped from his law firm not only for failing to pull his weight, but also because he had enlisted in the Public Defenders' Office and was spending company time doing a lot of free work for the poor. The "idiot" tag had been tossed around quite a bit—sometimes in his presence—but to look at him, you'd never know he was bothered by it.

She had words of her own but checked herself. *He was not stupid. And do I want to be siding with those who made small of him? Who wouldn't admit he had a heart for the little guy?* He was overboard pleasant to her. "We handle it calmly, baby, like it's for real."

She suppressed a laugh. And looking at his dimpled cheeks alone, she mused, *What woman could deny that he was ferociously handsome?*

She had a hard time figuring herself out: one minute she was berating him and, the next, going to his defense. When he told her how much she meant to him, she was about to tell him off but noticed he was moist-eyed. If the sidewalk was muddy, he wouldn't put down a cloak: he'd put himself down.

"Sorry. What was that?"

"I was saying how about us celebratin'." Unfolding the contract and pointing, he continued on, "I don't think I mentioned that the salary's a full fifteen percent more than what a teacher could make. Honest. Take a look."

He gave her a congratulatory peck and praised her work, her looks, and her chic clothes (of course!). He added, "Aren't you salvation itself for the kids, the parents, the Board—and *him*!"

She said, "Please, enough."

Nonetheless, he did make her feel better, considering what she'd been expecting. He'd never been accused of sophistication, but no matter. There would be a paycheck. She was tired and saw no need to fight it. *Never mind particulars if he was going out of his way to be nice!* Nicer yet was to be pulled in to that robust chest. Without knowing how it happened, she had her arms around his neck; and he pulled her in close. Those were real, bighearted tears.

CHAPTER 31

"His Idea of Fun"

As they drove off, out of nowhere, he asks, "Hey, why don't we start off by going over to the country club and hit some golf balls? They got a great drivin' range. You seem a little on edge. Good way to unwind."

She laughed. "Me? Hit golf balls? You're kidding."

"Okay. Come watch me. Been a hard week. Then, we'll have us cocktails and dinner."

"Only if you take me right home after dinner."

"Sure, sure. That's a good sport."

After watching him go *swish, swish* and crack a whole bucketful of balls out into the sky like so many soaring darts, she got up to go; but he wanted her to give it a try. She shook her head and told him she'd probably wind up facedown on the turf.

He said he'd show her how, and after demonstrating, he came up close behind her so she could feel his parts and took her arms through the swing. With the way it happened, she didn't think it was intentional; but it gave her an arousing jingle that made her wonder how far things might go. *He had to make it up to me, huh?* Aware of her weakness, she got herself out from under and said "Let's go eat."

He parked beside the marqueed entrance to the club, went in for a moment, and came out saying they'd have about an hour's wait for a table.

"How about we mosey over to the bar?" he asked.

Reminded of what had happened last time, she didn't particularly like the idea of drinking for all of an hour.

"Could we go someplace else?"

"Baby, do I ever know of a great place! Top cuisine."

"Really?"

"Yeah, my place. I'm some cook, you know, if I have to say so myself. Been gettin' quite a bit of practice lately, what with me and the wife separating. Not much fun eatin' alone."

"Wait a minute. You are married?" *Why, darn it, hadn't that occurred to me before?*

"Well, you couldn't call it a marriage."

"No wonder. You're gonna drive me home."

"No, you've got it wrong. Please. She's gone so much, she's no wife to me. It's been going on for some time now. She claims I started it, but she knows better. She's just trying to get an advantage in court—and more money. You don't want to hear all the crummy details, but—"

"True," she interjected. "Which is why you're drivin' me to my apartment."

Acting like he hadn't heard her, he continued, "After the honeymoon, she didn't much care for me in bed. Too conventional? When I found out she'd been passed around by the football team—she bein' a cheerleader—I didn't much care for takin' seconds—on my wife, mind you."

She kept interrupting, and he kept dispensing his marital history. "So you see, it was rotten from the beginning. She takes up with an older guy, that Guipiletti. They still call him Stud Angie. Maybe you heard of him, the ex-baron's brother-in-law."

"Yeah, heard about him. He could be her father. Sounds like incest."

"Just the point. Anything to embarrass me. Tells me he's a real lover. Far from old. 'Just distinguished,' she says. Fat as he is, I could strangle the guy with one hand, but why take it out on him? Next, she's sayin' I'm not a very good provider. Always tryin' to make small of me."

"You're telling me things I don't want to know. Drive me home please."

His eyes closed. He bowed his head and his face went dark. She'd peed on his parade. Reaching over, she gave his arm a reassuring squeeze. He covered the hand with his and squeezed back.

Shortly recovered, he said, "My wife told me she'd be in New York for a week visiting her cousin. I know what that was all about. She made no secret of it. Anything to rub it in."

"Enough. Give me the car keys, and I'll drive myself home."

"So we're gonna celebrate, aren't we?"

"What! You got a hearing problem?"

Looking him in the eye, she saw that he needed somebody to just listen for a bit. As he went on, however, she was about to tell him this was not something she wanted to get in the middle of; but she thought of the effect on his wounded psyche. And when he pleaded "Okay?" she gave him half a nod.

While he cooked, she looked around at the obviously too-expensive furnishings.

"My wife's doing," he called from the kitchen, noticing how she took in the decor. "'Can't make it look good on the cheap,' she says. I object. She says, 'Make more money.'"

There was this plush cream-colored carpeting throughout the downstairs, a deep-pillowed white camelback sofa with glass-end tables, antique Chippendale chairs and settee that had been reupholstered, a cherry dining table with French provincial chairs, a handcrafted walnut sideboard, and (framing a large picture window) pleated royal blue chintz drapes cinched with gold tassels.

The place didn't look like it had been much lived in: everything seemed newly bought. Since there hadn't been any sex to speak of, spending money was his wife's sublimation.

A guest bedroom ran off the living room. She had herself a peek and was taken aback by the gaudy red dust-ruffle around the bed. *Wouldn't that wake you up in the morning?* The living room–dining room "L" gave the place a feeling of spaciousness. She thought a person could be a lot lonelier here than in her little hovel. A satiny black cat slid out from behind the couch, and she absentmindedly ran a hand along its back. *Ah, company.* He said his wife couldn't stand it rubbing against her leg. She had taken little Schmutzy to the pound, and he'd rescued her in the nick of time.

Dinner was good—indeed gourmet: a bowl of crabmeat bisque, stuffed butterfly pork chops, wild rice, asparagus with hollandaise sauce, and chocolate mousse. After, he brought out an after-dinner stinger: brandy with creme de menthe.

"Good for the digestion," he said.

They had moved to the couch, and he turned on some music.

"Mmm . . . I like this stuff."

She took several sips then a nice, cooling long one. Head back, she asked for another; and by the third one, she was beginning to feel a buzz. She wondered if he happened to have any Port wine, a favorite of hers. He said that he did but cautioned her, "You don't take Port with anything else." She spread her fingers a liberal inch; and he gave her half that—which she downed at a gulp—and, holding up the empty glass, asked for "one teeny-weensy bit more."

"This is grrreat!"

She became woozy, and the last thing she recalled before everything went black was telling him she had to be getting on home.

She was awakened in a pool of total blackness. There were muffled voices angrily snapping back and forth then came a frantically shouted "Nooo!" followed by a piercing pop and loud "Oww!" There were more shoutings and a house-shaking slam of the front door.

"Oh my God, where am I?" she sighed. "What's going on?"

There was a steady throbbing in her temples. As her senses slowly turned on, she became aware of a chill on her arms, of cloth on her legs. She touched a hand under the sheet and gasped. She was naked! She felt further and was relieved. Nothing amiss—panty and bra in place. She flung an arm to the left, and it bounced off the empty bedding.

Groping to the right, she felt a lamp and switched it on. She sprang out of bed and ran for the bathroom. Next, looking about for her clothes, she picked up a nauseating odor. *Oh, no.* She'd tripped on her slippery blouse and kicked it away. Her feet toweled, she stepped nimbly into her shoes and, gripped by the shakes, snagged a huge sweater that she threw over her head for a shift.

He was jackknifed over an arm of the couch, clad only in jockey shorts that absorbed blood oozing from a smudge in his lower back and soaked those downy white cushions. His ruddy leather face had turned tallow white.

"Addie, Addie," he moaned. "She shot me. Please help me get around on the couch. And call a doctor. Oh, me."

"Bastard! You were trying to take advantage of me."

"Nooo! You got real sick. I cleaned you up and put you to bed. Didn't know what else to do. I treated you like a baby. Tenderly, I swear . . . Ow . . . please, please call a doctor."

"You, creep! You undressed me! What else did you do?"

"Nothing. Please understand. You were a mess. Had to get you out of your clothes and sponge you off. I couldn't have a bad thought and didn't."

"Couldn't because you couldn't. You pathetic son of a bitch! Didn't you realize she was setting you up?"

"Oh, Addie, not just couldn't. I wouldn't. Don't think that of me. I was glad I got you clean and gave you a hug. Nothin' more. 'Cause I tell you true, Addie. I love you. Believe it. But, baby, I'm hurtin' . . . real bad. Call, please call. Please!"

"What the hell are you telling me? Just a hug, huh? There was a moist place on my panty. You don't realize how pathetic you are."

"I do. I heard her come in and bolted out here to catch her. You're right. I shoulda known she was settin' me up. I tried to push her back out the door, but she slipped by me goin' for the bedroom. She had the pistol out, and I was runnin' to get there first and she shot me. The cat jumps out with a helluva meow like somebody stepped on its tail, and it scares her. She sees what she's done, and that scares her even more, so out she flies . . . Help me get on the couch, huh."

Drawing him by the wrists, she pivoted him around to where he could fall fully on the couch. He let out a screaming "Ow!" as he fell and a husky "God bless you." The ugliness of the wound, which was beginning to get to her, grew worse from the contact; and with the exertion, her stomach rose, and she gave him back the rest of his dinner on that creamy, rich carpeting.

She swished some water in her mouth, called for help, and told the operator to send an ambulance; then taking his car keys from the kitchen counter, she was looking to speed away in the Buick. The last thing she saw on a look back was the cat calmly licking milk from her bowl while Johnny, groaning on the couch, weakly called out "I love you, Addie, and I'm sorry—sorry as a poor son of a bitch can be."

She told him the medics were on their way. She would recall unaccountably taking in those great hairy legs of his before leaving.

It was hot news for over a month, with new developments that kept coming out almost daily. "Community Leader Shot in Domestic Quarrel," "May Be Paralyzed from Waist Down," "Wife Found in Motel with Lover," "Other Lovers Identified," "Wife Says She'll Name Names," "Football Hero in Game of His Life" "JR in Rehab, Will Get Legs Back," "Hero Takes First Steps, Promises More," "Wife Indicted on Variety of Charges," "Friends to Testify for Prosecution."

Word got around that his wife had been cheating on him for years and blamed it on him. Someone produced a photo of Angie and her in a big clinch, only it was Junior (horny Rocco). *She'd had both, did she?* Months later, the day she was to go on trial for assault with a deadly weapon, Johnny emerged from the rehab center able to take his first steps. Waving his cane for the cameras, he declared he was going to run for mayor—vowing to clean up corruption, wage a war on crime, and bring in new industry to provide jobs for the unemployed.

Contrary to all reason, she found herself rooting for him like everyone else, cheering his courageous comeback. Seeing the dinner episode a good deal differently, she felt somewhat guilty about how she treated him. She was above all thankful that his getter-offer lawyer, the suave and shady Edgar Allen, had been able to keep her out of it on the threat he was going to bring the Angies into it—which wouldn't sit well with the bow tie mafia that wanted to put Angie Senor on the clean house reform ticket for, of all things, DA.

When Allen came to pick up the car, he told her to get out of town for a while in case the wife's lawyer wanted to subpoena her for a deposition. Appearing at her door in an immaculately tailored suit and sporting a fat pinkie ring, Allen handed her an envelope and patted her on the shoulder. "Here's my card. In the event you have additional needs, call. Collect." She'd never seen such a clutch of hundred dollar bills.

"And Johnny sends his love."

"Tell him he has my understanding."

"He'll appreciate that. Sometimes he exasperates, but frankly, he amazes me."

"Me too!"

CHAPTER 32

"The Story of Brother-in-law Al"

If Addie was to have any future in the School System—or anywhere else in town, for that matter—her name had to be free of scandal or any hint thereof. She was told that as a necessary precaution, suave Edgar Allen had contacted Domo Jr. (DJ) to put out word that he would be keeping an eye on her. Since Papa Angie might want to use Addie's name to keep his clean, Allen wasted no time in getting her that one protection which would cover all. As Edgar crowed, "Nothing else need be said, if that much."

DJ's first step was to whisk her away to visit her sister Eva in upstate New York. Fearful Eva liked the idea of having him around and set him up in the guest bedroom, from which he could negotiate business while watching a story crucial to Addie's unfolding history.

Eva's husband, Al, worked for a business machine company. Otts said he was such a nice guy that you'd never know he was a Jew though that didn't mean he was sorry he hadn't attended the wedding. Nor, for that matter, was Eva sorry she had roundly chewed her father out for not coming. He'd never gotten over her having been the sickly kid who ran up doctor bills. At least, Al had a good job and earned a six-figure salary, which was quite big for his time.

Addie thought Eva took the risk of marrying an older guy and doing so right after high school. She couldn't wait to get out of the house and wasn't shy about saying how lucky she was.

It turned out Al was one peach of a guy: he was generous and awfully good to Eva. Flat out spoiled her, she admitted. There was a time when—thinking of her father's attitude toward Hannah—Addie saw that Al installed Eva as all-reigning, decision-making boss which he backed by giving her a private checking account at the local bank. "Good old Al," she insisted, "was that kind of a guy." Eva had to smile, pointing out that Addie had never seen him burning mad after his boss had given him a hard time.

Al was at the other end of the spectrum from the baron, humbled by the prejudice which had made the other bold. He was very hospitable to Addie. He took them to the movies, out to eat at a classy restaurant; and on her first weekend there, he packed a picnic lunch with his homemade chicken salad and drove them over to the famous glassworks museum. They had some great penny-ante poker games. After telling them to know when to hold 'em and when to fold 'em, he managed to blunder both ways, which got lots of laughs.

Eva said the whole house smiled when Al was around, and knowing how his wife felt about the out-of-town trips demanded by the company, Al usually found a way to get out of them. He pretended to be unruffled that the boss got on him about it.

"Did you say your wife sometimes got lonely out here? How old is she? Thought she was Catholic. Plenty of company there."

Al didn't make anything of it. The company byword was that you had to fit in. He, in fact, joked that Addie was a big city hick because she couldn't believe this was New York. The town was nestled in a rustic countryside with open fields where they actually raised corn, wheat, and what (for all she knew) might be hay. There were large wooded areas, hilly pastures, even farms with barns and real cows and chickens. It was a region known for its dairy products. When kids in her class were asked where the milk came from, they said the milkman.

Addie marveled. All that, in the midst of which they lived in a modern split-level brick house in a cul-de-sac where, in the woods out back, guys would hunt wild turkeys. They put on an annual turkey calling contest. Out of curiosity, Al had gone on one of the turkey shoots and gave the guys a laugh when a turkey they flushed out of a tree landed on his back and sent him sprawling. Somebody called out to shoot because it was best to hit them flying away, so the buckshot got under their feathers. But in pulling himself up, Al foiled the shot.

"Unbelievable, huh, Addie? Still, this is where America is."

"How come, with all these wild turkeys, the pilgrims never found this place?"

"The way people think out here, pilgrims would have been right at home in these woods."

He had to admit it was a lot more prosperous than their decaying hometown. A person could live quite comfortably in these surroundings if he didn't talk politics with the locals and didn't mind being bored by their small talk. There had been a big to-do over who plays first base when the company's big guy moved.

Addie got on Al for snobbery; and he said he had indeed corrected his first impression when, disgusted with the hometown TV station, he had said all local news was yokel news. He now listened more attentively; besides, he had been well rewarded working there.

It was a really fun visit with lots of kidding back and forth, and they had the lively neighbor couple over for Friday night poker. Addie cooked some of her dinner specialties and loved the way Al, a great eater, smacked his lips and asked for seconds on her meat loaf. He returned the favor by grilling some steaks for Addie's farewell dinner.

Time had gone by pretty fast. Eva wanted her to think about taking a job up there. But thankfully, Addie did have that contract from Johnny—supposedly fat—and had to get back to reality and work out some class plans for the kiddies.

She had put through a call to Edgar Allen to make sure DJ signaled that the coast was clear. He assured her the heat was all on Johnny's wife while he meanwhile was doing quite well at rehab and, thanks to The Party, getting excellent press. And he asked her if she, by the way, would like to have a cat.

It was a heavyhearted departure. Little did she realize how sad it would become a short month later. Al never let on how bitterly he was eating his heart out at work. The company he worked for was the upstart competitor of the industry giant and was nibbling away at the giant's market share and, to the giant's great annoyance, was doing surprisingly well in the international sector. Founded by two hotshot entrepreneurs, Kenston and Yee, who had formerly been with the giant—the latter from Hong Kong—the firm was vulgarly known as the KY, which didn't bother the hotshots, who countered that it was a good name to have because they sure were sticking it to the giant.

To gain its competitive edge, KY pushed middle managers to the limit: sixty-hour weeks were the norm. Al was a born workaholic, so he did seem to fit right in. He knew the workings of that business machine inside out, better in fact than some of the technicians. So he trained his sales force accordingly, had them demonstrate the thing, and also saw them outperforming all comers (which showed up in sales).

That caused a lot of jealousy, as did his bonuses. But for the third time in a row, he was the prime candidate for a promotion and got passed over. He hadn't complained before, but this time, he couldn't just sit there and take it. They had promoted one of his former trainees and made him a rising star. *But who had put the rise in his star?* This kid—a smart Chink—was to be Al's new boss!

Word got out, and the guys in the office started ribbing him.

"You want a promotion, do you? Well, there's an opening in Egypt. A big bonus just for going. Wasn't everybody told when they came on that just like with the giant, in time they'd be moved? Expenses paid. In your case, they'd provide a camel. Your wife could walk behind. A scarf would keep the sand out of her nose!"

Steamed up, Al went to see Nailson (aka Hard-ass), his divisional head honcho, who it turned out had gotten a lesser bonus (wrong guy to see). He tried to soft-soap Al, saying he understood his disappointment and that everyone up the line appreciated his value to the company. When pressed, he gave Al a silent long stare under those thin Anglo-Saxon eyebrows of his, as if to ask "Do you really want to know why?"

Finally, pulling some reports out of a file, Nailson slid a summary sheet across the desk, emphasizing those were not his views. Doing a quick scan, Al swallowed hard when he came upon a remark that said "an eager-for-the-money, bonus-happy Jew, the pushy kind that people wouldn't like to be working under." And there was more of the same put in other words.

Al fired back, "You don't believe that bag of shit, do you?"

He wanted to know who the hell was saying such things. As he went on, Nailson—never known to be big on patience—exploded on him, banged his fist on the desk, and said something about using that kind of language in his office. Considering what people thought (and remember, he never came down on him for it), Al ought to be grateful he still had a job.

Hardly listening, Al got up to leave—*what was the use?*—until Nailson, still grousing, let something that sounded like "whining Jews" slip out; and Al lost it. Before he realized what had happened, his hand had whipped across the guy's crooked mouth with a resounding slap, which was instantly followed by one the other way that sent the pile of papers flying.

Simultaneously stunned, they stood there face to face for a second. Alarmed at himself, Al was trying to blurt out an apology when he felt himself being gripped by the lapels and propelled back against the mirror with a force that broke it around his head and made him collapse in a heap of shards.

Scarcely aware of how he got there, he found himself in his car speeding on home with "money-grubber" this and "kike" that ringing in his ears. He told Eva he was feeling tired and needed to take the afternoon off.

"Tired? What about that cut on the back of your head?"

"Yeah," he explained, the tiredness made him dizzy and he fell against the bathroom mirror. "Nothing serious."

He was good at putting up a front, but this time, she knew something was wrong—and badly so.

He was up at the crack of dawn, and before Eva—half asleep—could tug at him for an explanation, he had grabbed his twelve-gauge shotgun out of the closet and said he was going turkey hunting. It would be a good way to work off what was troubling him. He'd tell her about it when he got back.

The "assassination" was a fiasco. After calmly driving over to the wide-lawned Nailson estate and, headlights out, finding his way up the winding driveway, Al parked in front of the garage. He took a deep breath, pushed the seat back, and within minutes was fast asleep, exhausted from a sleepless night. Next thing he knew, there was a rapping on the window and a familiar graveled voice dinning in his ear.

"Loony bastard. Yeah, you're fired. Now get the hell out of here before I call the cops!"

It was like ice water splashed in his face. Coming to, out he sprang, banging his shoulder against the doorframe—which jostled the gun out of his grasp and bounced it off Nailson's shin, sending him into a one-leg hop. Cowering under a torrent of curses, Al, short of breath, still managed to bring his gun back up and steady it; but when he squeezed the trigger, all it gave out was a dry click.

It wasn't till Nailson had bounded up the steps to the veranda that Al got his cartridges properly stuffed in the tubes. With his cheek against the stock of the gun, he sighted the man frozen a good ten paces from the front door, a hand to his chest, turning for a hopeless last look. His face was a death's-head image of openmouthed terror. Shaken, Al lowered his gun. A wrenching sense of futility came over him, and he began to sob.

"What, oh what, heaven help me . . . What am I doing!"

The gun dropped from his hands, and clattering on the pavement, it let out a startling *pow, pow* as both barrels peppered the garage door. He wanted to just go to the police and turn himself in. But for what? Well, he had threatened. Still, he didn't do anything; then, why go? Instead, he drove to a gas station and phoned his lawyer, wanting to know what in the world he should do. The lawyer, being late for court, was practically out the door.

"Tell me something, please," Al pleaded and was told to go home and to say nothing if the cops come calling until he was able to be there with him.

"Shouldn't I just tell them what happened? It would help, wouldn't it, if I showed them I was telling the truth?"

This brought a resounding "No way!" from the other end of the line.

Feeling wholly bereft of help and not wanting to alarm Eva (think of how she'd react to police coming to the door), he decided he would have to do it his own way—stupid or not. He'd go down to the station and lay it out before the desk sergeant. *Let him make what he wanted of it.*

He knew a couple of cops; they'd see he was no criminal. He would feel better and wouldn't have to wait in trembling anticipation of their coming for him. But the police meanwhile had learned everything from the honcho's frantic wife; so cops in a squad car, hearing that the murderer was armed and dangerous, pulled him over on a side street a block short of the station.

Since they were just sitting there in their car, the one cop having a radio to his ear, Al got out to approach them, saying he wanted to turn himself in, at which the other cop popped out brandishing a pistol and telling him "Don't make a move." The radio cop leaned out, saying what Al thought was something about a driver's license; and the next instant, both cops seeing him reach for his breast pocket, fired a joint volley that dropped him in his tracks.

The corporation put out a press release saying the man had simply gone berserk. He made a good living with the firm and had to know that pressure went with the job. After acknowledging his valuable contributions, upping production of the sales force, etc., they went on to paint Al as pretty much the company pariah.

He was known to be paranoid and a complainer who frequently shirked out-of-state assignments that others had to cover for him. He was very aggressive for the money, which made him unpopular with his colleagues. He was also known to have a violent reaction to criticism however justified. Proof all of this—if any were needed—was apparent in the fact that he was temperamentally unsuited for the promotion that the vice president, at nearly the cost of his life, had to deny him. "It's all here in his file."

Eva was a wreck: the doctor had her in the psychiatric ward for all of a week. Hannah had to go up to deal with funeral arrangements. At first, Addie was too broken up to go. But privately deciding she'd find a way to embarrass that lousy little Berg, she said she'd go along. Hannah told her not to make a fuss. Addie said the fuss was all inside. Al had been a brother to her—and more. Shot like a miserable sewer rat. "Nailsmith," outright bastard that he was—too bad Al didn't have steady aim.

That night shortly after midnight, a long wail, as from a lone wolf, sounded in the town square. A hunter rolled over in bed, saying "Turkeys better watch out." Just before dawn next morning, somebody turned on a fire alarm from the box outside corporate headquarters. As their spotlights played over the towering glass doors, clumsy, clad firemen made out the rough letters spray painted in red and mouthed the words "The Man Who Got Shot Was KY'd."

This was repeated on several side windows along with the scrawl "Hate Kills, As KY Wills." The blown-up pictures, taken before the window washer arrived, consumed a good half of the front page of the paper. Management was furious.

Word got out that a reporter from the *Times* had had a mysterious phone call telling him to come up and look into things. The quirky caller was quoted in the paper. "What the company puts out are *lies*. The truth is on the doors and in their deeds, where many a Jew hater breeds." The word about bias went up late day, after the windows had been sparkle-cleaned.

Within a day, the *Times* reporter showed up wanting to talk to unavailable corporate executives. A picture of him approaching KY headquarters appeared in the local paper. The whole town was a-buzz.

CHAPTER 33

"Enter the Whimp"

Having been driven back by DJ, Addie poured herself a generous glass of Dago-red and relaxed. Settled into her cozy little apartment again, she slept a lot and found it difficult to work up much enthusiasm for a stupid course plan knowing she was at her best when she had none. She picked up *The Nation* at the corner drug store and did some desultory reading. It didn't help her state of mind that the wrong guys were winning.

For the time being, she didn't know where to go with what she'd learned in upstate New York. Though the fervor for justice might get sidetracked, her awareness would not as when she and Betsy summed up their attitude toward vulnerable Johnny, champion of the underclass. Betsy saw the guy as an outright bungler, and because of that, they couldn't help loving him (much as he could disappoint). He had a heart to go with that broad back, and unable to see himself as others did, Johnny innocently thought he had an instinct for finding his way in a political world unfriendly to his aims: he intended to do the good thing, and for that, no flame burned brighter. Except that it also flickered, particularly when he was in recovery from the damaging gut shot.

Almost welcoming an interruption, Addie knew she'd once more find herself being drawn into complicated relationships with men. Something, in light of bruised feelings past, she had sworn she would avoid—half-knowing, as she swore, that fate was bound to ambush her. For when it came to matters of the heart, she would ask herself, *How could I have done other than let them unfold as they humanly would?* The new involvement began with Betsy's male callousness toward an obliging friend.

The Whimp showed up one chilly Saturday morning, bringing along bottles of wine and ginger ale, which he mixed for PMC (Poor Man's Champagne); and making himself at home, he poured a couple of glasses and asked her to sit with him for a bit. He wanted comforting. He said he'd been staying in this homey little apartment with Betsy while Addie was gone. But then Betsy got herself a better paying job with the city, and she wanted a place of her own.

Whimpy knew the guy who went with the place, a certified monster feared by all. Just by looking at him, you knew he had to be the enforcer. *Of all people for Betsy to take up with. Typical!* But then, the brute in this guy, which made others edgy, probably made her horny. Anyway she'd given Whimpy the air, and he needed somebody to talk to.

"You're lucky, Addie. You got a place of your own here. A little island where you don't have to take any hmpf from anybody. Me? I'm not particular. Just now I'd settle for any place. But I like it here. I'll be good company for you. Be a friend and let me stay for a while, okay?"

"Stay? You just walked in the door."

Whimpy had known Doctor Boy from high school, where they had been on the track team together; and he was the one who got DB the nurse's aide job. DB had suggested they double-date with him and Betsy the summer that they all worked at the hospital, and the one time Addie consented, it was fun. Betsy, who had picked up all of the current locker room jokes, had them in stitches. Her big mulatto boyfriend had a ready supply though he said he actually preferred the oldies.

Whimpy was just a whisp of a guy, thin as a wafer, with close-cropped hair, all legs, and no torso—the image of his Irish father. He'd be the first to tell you he was a born loser partly, he thought, because of his Puerto Rican mother. She had been an activist and got her skull cracked by a certain mounted policeman during the demonstrations around city hall. Known as Billy Club Bill, The Second—namesake of his legendary father—he swung a mean one and was the guy everybody ran from.

But not Whimpy's stalwart Mama Maria, sign-carrier-in-chief during a weeklong protest against the brutality exemplified by basher Bill, who single-handedly organized a roundup of idle Puerto Ricans whenever there was some brutal shooting or robbery.

So Bill took it personally that these 'spics' should mount a protest against "police brutality." Maria died after having been in a coma for three months, and there was a big demonstration about that. The angry neighbors blamed Whimpy's drunkard father, Sean, for not being there to protect her. He insisted that he told her not to go. The neighbors kept at him, and Sean gave them a piece of his Irish mind. Finally, his hotheaded PR brother-in-law, Gordo, flashed a knife; and Sean flashed back a finger and left town.

Having to find a way to support himself real quick, the Whimp had his sister get him a job doing cleanup at the beauty salon where she did nails. He saw that the men styling hair made a good living at it, and he wanted to learn the trade. But on his way home one night, a bunch of guys hanging out on the corner called to him.

"Hey, Mick, come over here. We wanna talk to you."

One of them threw a jarring punch that bloodied his nose, and another flattened him against a retaining wall. They knocked him down; and the first guy put a switchblade to his groin, saying they'd do something if he didn't quit working there. About that time, he ran into Cowshit Eddy, who needed somebody to clerk his flower shop; however, Whimpy got in trouble with Cousin Bullshit Eddy when he sent a dozen roses to the wrong Rosie—Cow's sleep-in. It was easy to get confused.

After bawling him out and noticing how meekly the Whimp stood there and took it, Cow developed a liking for him and invited him to come live with him and be his housekeeper. They got on fine for a while until Cow found out Whimpy was beating his time.

He was seeing Betsy, wasn't he? It got him kicked out of the flower shop. Whimpy came back next day, acting like nothing had happened, and tried to explain.

"If you're seein' Betsy, you got to know that she gets around. She treats sex like a man does. Why sweat it?"

It was a remark that almost netted him another shot in the mouth.

For a while, he drifted and fell in with a bunch of no-goods, used up all his savings on pot, and wound up sleeping under a bridge until the priest found him and made him a handyman at church. He had cursed the priest at first for interfering but wound up loving him—and not just because he was a supporter of the Puerto Rican cause. More than a padre, Whimpy found him to be a sweet and caring man.

Addie asked why he couldn't go to the padre and tell him about his current troubles, which this self-invited guest wanted to unload on her. He indicated that he really couldn't bring himself to talk frankly to a man of God about how Betsy became so nasty to him. Addie thought it a lame alibi, but he seemed so hurt that she felt obliged to listen.

"You'd never know it—she being so ditsy—but she was real demanding in bed. Not in the ordinary way. More than one guy should have to handle."

Addie held up a hand saying she really didn't want to hear any of that. Whimpy, clever dude that he was, sensed that it was probably more like she did than didn't. It was also important for him to tell somebody that Betsy had done him wrong *big-time*. He said there were times he couldn't get a night's sleep. It could take so much to satisfy her that what at first seemed pretty fulfilling to him was just the opening act to her.

A person wouldn't think it to look at her, but she was a woman you didn't want to frustrate. She'd take him by the nape of the neck, so he had a choice to get with it or to risk suffocation. Sometimes if he didn't go along, she'd take to cuffing him like he was a stuffed animal; and after a few drinks, it got so she seemed to enjoy that about as much as the other—though not quite.

Being a quick learner, he finally had it going so well she had all the satisfaction she needed—which for him was much, but though she got to digging her nails into him, he was glad he adapted. She did his laundry and put food on the table. Seeing how they'd come to understand one another, he thought they had it made. Addie had been curious to know what guys saw in heavy-lidded Betsy—she being straight as a board. Now she knew.

"Whimpy, please."

There was the possibility he was laying it on, thinking it might give her the jollies and get him a home. *But then, maybe not.* He too wanted justice, a victim of screw 'em and leave 'em. *Johnny with a Spanish accent?*

"Anyway, after all I do for her—can you believe it?—she blows me off!"

"She did you a favor."

"Yeah, a super favor. I'm out in the street! Just when I'm shaping up like the priest wants me to."

"And you're here because I could use a housekeeper, and it brings you in out of the cold."

"Right."

CHAPTER 34

"She Acquires Whimpy and Loses Mother"

As Whimpy made his case for a home, he thought that while Addie and Betsy were best friends, it didn't mean they shared their private lives; so he wanted to fill her in. When he had returned to get some of his clothes, Betsy banged the door in his face. When he went to her new place (a deluxe town house) to ask for the relief money he lent her, the *boom, boom* of heavy footsteps sent him flying down the stairs; and Big Meany-Beany, looking twice the giant from below, warned him that he'd bust him in two if he ever caught him bothering his woman again.

Enforcer or not, Meany-Beany was one colossus of a black guy (actually, café au lait), who became bag man for the local numbers racket. He wasn't shy about unwrapping big bills from the wad like it was nothing but a head of lettuce. He took Betsy to nightclubs, bought her real gold jewelry, and got her a cushy job working for the boss of bosses (a resident in city hall); she was living it up with him, wearing the latest in décolletage and giggling when he goosed her in public.

Though he liked to kid around in off-hours—putting on a falsetto laugh at his own raunchy jokes (last year's thigh-slappers) on the job—fat–faced Meany-B, black cap down on his eyebrows, looked all-business mean like the hardened hit man some people said he was. He had never made it out of grade school, having been left back three times in seventh grade. They almost threw him out after he brushed a forearm against the redheaded substitute's ample chest. (How can he help it when she's standing right beside his hook on the coat rack?) And they finally did have to throw him out when he put dog turds on the teacher's chair. He winked and pushed the cap down on his nose when the whole class laughed him out the door.

He was relieved to be out anyway and had no trouble getting himself work as a security guard. When he was assigned to be a bodyguard for an old floozy in a theater company that came to town on tour, the story was (as he told it) that she looked him up and down and asked "Is that a gun you got in your pocket, lieutenant, or are you just happy to see me?"

So when some guys made the mistake of calling him lieutenant, they paid for it. Nobody knew how he got called Meany. It sort of came naturally; and he accepted Beany because somebody in the hierarchy liked to rub his shiny, bald head when he was being paid off. It was okay with him because his real name was something like Marvin though he wasn't sure of that. When friends decided on the floozy's Louey, that was pretty much what stuck. He'd always hated Meany.

Whimpy still wanted to get his money back plus the Swiss watch he'd given Betsy for her birthday, costing all of a week's pay at the flower shop; however, Addie persuaded him it wasn't worth his life. He wanted to talk some more about his troubles with Betsy, but Addie saw it coming and held up both hands.

"You're driving me crazy! You gotta go home now."

"What home?"

"Then you have to find a place. The Y is real cheap."

"That's where I met those guys with the pot."

Even if she did what she would, she couldn't get him out the door. When she tried to physically push him out, he sat down on the doorsill so she couldn't close the door.

"Go ahead and hit me."

It was no use. She thought he was at the point of tears. He untied his bedroll and curled up by the heat vent on the kitchen floor like a pet dog, promising he'd shut up. It turned out he actually didn't have any place to go to. He had stayed with his sister for a couple of weeks since the Puerto Rican in-laws had claimed his father's apartment. But when Sis's boyfriend moved into their two-room flat, he told her Whimpy was in the way.

Addie felt she had to let him stay, and at first, she was glad she did; in fact, she found it rather touching that he was so grateful to her. He was bagging groceries at the A&P and bringing home bread and veggies, occasionally dated chicken and ham. When he was living under the bridge, he used to pick through their garbage bins for something to eat; now he was getting it before it went out, and he was also taking stuff that he thought ought to be going out. So they lived pretty cheaply.

He was also a great housekeeper: he split the cooking with Addie, did the dishes, vacuumed, dusted, and cleaned the toilet. She got a kick out of watching him trot down the street with the Santa Claus bag over his shoulder, whistling off-key to himself on his way to the Laundromat. He liked "Bye, Bye, Blackbird." He liked to repeat the refrain "Make my bed and light the light. I'll arrive late tonight." She threatened, "One more time and . . ." So he shut it off, except when he thought she was out of earshot.

She especially appreciated his help in what became a devastating time for her. Hannah, out of the blue, had come down with a stroke. Addie, in her agitation, didn't know what to do first; and upon seeing it, Whimpy instantly swung into action.

He had the ambulance over and went along to the emergency room, where he got the doctor on duty to think triage and give Hannah immediate attention. He asked a night nurse he knew to keep an eye on her in the hospital. He even got a hard-of-hearing Puerto Rican lady from his mother's family to look after Otto; then when Eva drove down, he said, before disappearing, that Addie could leave a message for him at the church.

"Bless you," Addie whispered. She gave him an endearing hug.
"De nada."

The sisters sobbed as they talked about the years of petty criticism Hannah had taken from Father Otto and said nothing.

She didn't have to do anything particularly grievous. He'd get on her for little, niggling stuff like having misplaced his slippers on a cold morning, forgetting that the only way he'd eat liver was in Braunschweiger, failing to sew a tear in his trousers or to pick up his Sunday suit at the cleaners . . . whatever.

They'd heard from Iris Klagemann that there had been a shoe-throwing episode when Hannah was pregnant with Addie. It was known he didn't want another kid. That part passed, but Hannah secretly wondered if he'd ever gotten over it. She couldn't help being jealous of Addie, who Otts adored. On the other hand, there were so many things he hated that he just needed someone around to spout off to and, more often than not, at. She understood it made him feel better. That was just Otts, and Hannah said she'd gotten used to it; but as they saw it, if Mother was resigned, it wasn't quite cheerfully.

By week's end, the girls found that Hannah wasn't doing very well: she had no movement on her left side and spoke haltingly out of the corner of her mouth. All of their guilt feelings started coming out. Eva recalled that Hannah had suffered through those blinding headaches the time that they saw her home from the hospital after Al's funeral. Eva felt bad that instead of so much as asking why Hannah took all those aspirins, she had just been thinking of her own trouble.

Addie remembered how she too had been so consumed with her own woes over the worthless Doctor Boy that she failed to step in when irritable Otto was running Hannah ragged following his heart attack. And that was shortly after Hannah herself had, had an operation to remove the feared tumor, which was fortunately benign. Though Hannah hadn't fully recovered her strength, all the concern had nonetheless been for poor Otto, who came through remarkably well. Eva said that if he could badger the Puerto Rican housekeeper like he did Hannah, he'd live to be a hundred.

After another week, there seemed to be improvement. The physical therapist even had Hannah taking a few steps with the walker, so they saw her into a nursing home. The doctor having assured them that with continued therapy and medication,

Mother should be recovering movement. Eva decided she had better get back home since part of her therapy had been to take a secretarial job.

Three days after Eva left, Hannah had a sudden relapse. Her left arm hung lifeless again, and she couldn't move her leg; there was no feeling in either. She had, had a cerebral hemorrhage in the night; and by morning, she was gone.

Addie would never forget the agonizing last afternoon she had spent with Mother. It was as if she couldn't wait to talk to her once she knew Eva had left. The words were slurred, and Addie had difficulty understanding much of what she tried to bring out. nor could she get answers to questions (some were stupid) like how come she had caused bad feelings between Mother and Father.

"Happens to all couples." She was alert enough to avoid what she didn't want to touch.

"Dear Child, I should have told you before. Somethin'. Somethin', at least. But . . . I didn't believe . . . didn't believe I should tell things."

"Yes, Mother. Why can't you tell me?" She caught herself stumbling for words just as Mother did.

"Thought there was time. Now gettin' real sick. No, no. Don't cry. Somethin', somethin' I shoulda told. Your father—real father . . . should know. But can't. All my fault."

"Please don't talk that way. Doctor was here this morning and said you were doing better. Can you hear me? You're gonna get better."

"Don't think bad about him. Always a good father to you. Okay, terrible back then. Can't blame him. I did wrong. He forgave. Not easy for a man. And him, not an easy man. Forgive him. You brought out good in him. Says you gave him back a daughter. Remember when you were a little one?"

Hannah paused, took a deep breath, and went on.

"He comes home tired from work, and you can't wait to jump in his arms. Such a joy for him. He's laughing. A different man at supper. Okay, crabby lotsa time, but he loved his Rika from the beginning. You shoulda heard him brag to neighbors. 'Ain't she one tough German kid?'"

Moist-eyed, she gave a crooked smile. She said she was sorry the girls hadn't seen more of his better side; then after a pause, she said quietly, "Be good to him."

"Of course. Don't worry about anything like that."

"You'll forgive me?"

"Forgive? Mom, what are you talking about?"

"Lawyer will tell. Not now. You heard about the baron. Yeah, him. The lawyer knows. He promises to tell."

They sat in silence, holding hands, till Hannah tightened her grip and sat erect.

"Call. Ask the nurse to get me something. My head hurts—Ah, the lawyer's card. Where's my purse?"

"It's not necessary. I'll go for the nurse. Rest. I'll be here all day. You can tell me later."

She slept the rest of the day and into the night. Only it *wasn't* sleep.

Father Johannes gave Hannah a beautiful eulogy; however it got to be lengthy, and the longer it went, the less it resembled Hannah. Still, he meant well. He was thinking of the living; and Otts, who was known to have his sentimental moment, hung on every word, especially as the priest had to talk about what a devoted husband and father he'd been.

Afterward Otts chastised the girls for not going to mass with him. Eva shrugged. She was really down on herself as it was, saying she shouldn't have left; and depressed as she was, all that driving hadn't helped either. She'd decided to stay with Addie, which also bothered Otts.

"How could you!" he shouted on the phone. Eva held the receiver toward the wall, but they could still hear him sounding off. "Shame!" People, he declared, were wondering what kind of daughters he raised. "What would your mother have said?" He paused and his voice dropped. "Don't know what I'm going to do without her. Come and be with me a little."

It was a painful visit: They said they were sorry—they genuinely were—and the three of them had a good cry. Addie had never seen her father looking so lost, so out of it—humble, in fact. She put an arm around him and pulled him close. Eva came in for a three-way hug. They drove out to the grave site, and on their knees, Otts led them in prayer. None of them slept well that night.

CHAPTER 35

"She and Whimp Get To Know One Another"

It was the morning after the burial, and over coffee and donuts, Eva said it had become too much. She'd wait maybe another day to see how Father was doing. Addie could tell she was in one of her impulsive moods, during which no one could divert her from what she was about. She read Otts some poetry (Keats, in fact), and finding him unresponsive, she said she'd be in touch by phone. It went rather quickly.

She accompanied Addie over to her place to pick up the paperwork she had volunteered to take care of, and as quickly as her car disappeared down the street, the Whimp reappeared. Addie greeted him with a wan smile. "My guardian angel."

They talked into the night, drinking his PMC; and when they got tired, they'd lay down together like two little kids that had just been put to bed. He had her in his arms and was softly rubbing her back. He had a consoling touch. When she rolled over for a full back rub, he became amorous and added little kisses to the back of her neck. She knew it would be coming and indeed felt in need of it, a comfort made all the better by the liking they had for one another.

His hands moved gently over her rump. She didn't resist. It felt good. They kissed, and one by one, she slid off her clothes. With the mounting excitement of his touch, she was shivering—partly from her vulnerability and partly from anticipation—which the sensitive Whimp perceived as he moved his kid-glove hands over her with an unrushed, loving caress like he was treasuring fine porcelain. His skilled tongue wove its way slowly over her pulsating tummy, smoothing the goose bumps as it went.

They kissed and soon his tantalizing delicacy took her into the beyond. He too was breathless, but lost in wonderment at her richness, he came roaring back in a frenzy. They fell apart exhausted—both euphorically astonished.

When the alarm went off, she was staring at the ceiling and couldn't recall having slept at all. She was rarely late getting to school, but at the sight of her coming in disheveled, the principal waved off her apology. Her fellow teachers were also concerned, noticing how drawn she looked; the black swatches under her eyes accentuated her pallor.

Obviously, she was taking the death of her mother very hard; and they knew how difficult her father could be. So the first grade teacher volunteered to take the kindergartners in with her kids, and with a nod from the principal, they implored her to take a few days off—for which, lowering her eyes, she solemnly thanked them.

CHAPTER 36

"She Can't Go on with It"

It was as if a haze had settled over her as she sat at the kitchen table several days later, numbly looking out the window at a smokestack nobly thrust into the pale sky. She told Whimpy she couldn't go on with it. She'd go mad. She said that it wasn't his fault but that he'd have to move out: she needed some breathing room. He was shocked.

"How could that be? We have it so right."

"You do. It's getting to me that I don't. I can't explain—it's difficult. What's right is part of what's wrong. It can't go on, and if you're here, it will."

"Can you throw this away?"

"Throw away? I've still got it in here! Only I'm not sure I know what it is I've got, except that I'm uneasy with it. You have to understand."

"Okay, but let me stay. You know how I feel about you. I'm willing to go back to where we were. Like I told you, I have no place to go."

"I know how you feel, and that's one of the reasons. I want to spare you—dunno. Maybe I'll talk to your sister."

"No. Don't. There's no emergency, right? Give me a couple of days, and I'll find something."

When it became a week and was starting on the second, they got into an argument. She said he wasn't even trying to find a place.

And he'd been in the bed with her again after she'd told him no way. He pleaded for her to have a heart; and she retorted that, that was precisely why she was being so insistent. He was down on his knees beside the bed, palms up, trying to calm her down; and for a moment she did.

"Please don't look so sad. I'll do what I can to help you. But you gotta go."

"Addie, baby, how can you be like that? Does all that happened with us mean nothing to you?"

"I want you to *go*, you hear? And *now!*" She paused then more quietly said, "Can't you see what you're doing to me? Go or I'll wind up despising you like I'm despising myself."

"Despising? How can that be?"

"It is. I can say no more. Leave."

Making like he could hear no more, he crawled over to his bedroll and lay down, face to the wall. All of a sudden, a red rage possessed her.

"If you don't move, I am—dammit—going to physically eject you!"

Grabbing him by the belt, she gave it a hard yank and fell over backward as the belt came free. She got up with fire in the eye and, pulling down his pants, started whipping his bare butt.

"Okay, now you gotta go. Please. O-U-T!"

He hadn't so much as flinched. He just lay there and took it, softly crying "Ah, Ah, Ah, Ah," lips drawn back as the strokes landed. She couldn't be sure he was in pain. In profile, he looked like a primitive man. She hit him two more licks and got the same response.

Agonized, she fairly growled, "Will you go now, please!"

He went into the fetal position.

Finally aware that she'd drawn blood, she gasped and drew back. Convulsed in tears, she retreated to the bed, slamming her fist into the pillow.

"Oh, Whimpy, Whimpy, Whimpy!"

"I love you, Addie."

CHAPTER 37

"She Visits Otts"

She got up later than she wanted to. A leaden weariness pulled her back down onto the bed. She ached all over from a bad dream in which she'd gotten herself entangled in a sheet that began to bleed, and the more she tried to free herself, the more it bled. Looking quickly over at Whimpy's corner, she saw he was gone—rucksack, shoes, socks, pants, and all—leaving not a trace but the dust marks that outlined his bedroll.

She ached with guilt and couldn't dislodge a rock from her craw. She had to find him and somehow make it right. *Make it right? How? Wasn't I making it right when I told him to leave? That way?* Her eyes welled up.

For a minute, she thought it might help if she could explain. But there was no explaining. That was the heart of it. *He's perceptive enough*, she thought. *He'd get it. In fact, he probably had.* For the time being though, she couldn't leave him hanging in limbo: he was too good a guy. She would make it up to him for how she threw him out. She'd assume responsibility for his well-being. *Okay, but for now, it would just have to rest.*

Obviously it couldn't. (Darn it!) He had to be reassured. She wrote a note, read it over, and tore it up. So she wrote another note that simply said "I love you too" and stuffed it in her purse. At the right moment, she'd ask the priest to see it got to him.

With the time off they gave her, she thought she should go over and see how Otts was doing, particularly how he was getting on with the deaf housekeeper. Knowing him, she thought he would likely get through to her without words. He would, of course, yell, forgetting that with what little might be heard she still didn't know English.

He lived two flights up in a storefront wood frame tenement that bordered on the poorer neighborhood where the blacks and working class Jews lived, which rankled him, except that the rent was reasonable, which was why he had talked Hannah into moving there. Next to the tenement was an empty block-long lot (the DMZ, Otts would call it), where in summer the older kids played softball while the younger ones chased grasshoppers and put them in glass jars where they croaked. In winter, they'd build a bonfire and roast the potatoes they wouldn't eat at home.

She greeted Otts with her big bear hug that brought forth a smile of reminiscence, and she had him talking nostalgically for a while, recalling happenings when she was a little one. His eyes were at the point of tearing up.

"Oh, Rika, you were one scrappy kid. You even sent the boys home crying."

He went on in this vein until he hit on the contrast with his present emptiness. Whatever their differences, Hannah did love him; and Rika did too. He knew that. But now . . . And he was off.

"She doesn't understand a word I say, and you know how I can holler. I have to show her everything. It doesn't help. Look at the floor! Was she brought up in a stable? Here, look at the dishes. With hand language, she shows me if food spots are left, it's okay to leave something for the towel. Puts them away with food marks. She'll give me another heart attack."

It did no good for Addie to ask that he show some tolerance. Bonita was another of the lost souls the priest had rescued (plucked off the steps of city hall).

"Also, mein Kind, du hast 'n Herz für die Arme, aber . . . [She had a heart for the poor, however] In plain English, tolerance ain't gonna get her to stop tramplin' mud on my bedroom carpet. Okay, she wants to make the bed, but she doesn't wipe her shoes on the mat after takin' the garbage out."

When Addie produced the pad and pencil she had brought, he sullenly shook his head. "I don't know Spanish, and she lets you understand she can't read English. Who knows? Maybe she won't."

He obviously missed the monologues he used to have with Hannah and was starved to talk, so Addie let him rattle on. For one thing, he thought he was overpaying Bonita at $25 a week. When Addie pointed out he might have to pay twice that if she could hear, he countered that at least the dishes would be clean.

Then there was Eva.

"Look at how she slighted me! Saw her mother into the ground and was gone with not the least thought about me being left alone. Okay, she came for a visit. Damit abgefertigt. [With that, she was abruptly finished.] She could have stayed a little, *nicht*?"

When Addie tried to bring him back to reminisce about the four of them on family picnics in the park and their swimming in tubes over at the other river, he scarcely listened. She tried other good memories, mentioning Hannah's festive Christmas dinners with the fat goose he liked so much (guaranteed not to be fish-fed, when it was); but that got her nowhere as well.

He wiped away a tear and blew his nose but would not be otherwise distracted, going on, as he usually did about the blacks coming over the lot to play the numbers with their welfare money at the candy store out front. He knew for a fact that Bonita was putting into Big Louey's bottomless pocket the money he paid her out of his own welfare check. "She may be deaf but claims she ain't dumb. Won twice and kept her money and ran until she got the itch again."

He, on the other hand, had been very prudent with his money. He had squirreled away proceeds from the sale of their house years back, beating out the bank on foreclosure—which, along with Hannah's insurance plus what was saved from decades of thrift, was all secretly stashed in a German bank—allowing him to say, with a deep breath, that he was okay. So long as he could keep the stash out of sight of Social Services (SS!), bandits that they were.

They were the worst people for snooping around to find out where the money went and for figuring everybody must be putting milk money given by SS right into Louey's big paw.

That secret honeypot of his, more than the medicine, did wonders for his frugal German soul. Who knows? With something like that in reserve, he might even find himself another woman so he could get rid of Bonita He'd been taking a good look at some of the ladies who sat in the widows' pew at church. He talked to one, but she smelled like she'd used last year's sample cologne. Of course, it wouldn't do to get one who was too religious. Think of the money she'd want him to donate to the church!

Addie had heard much of this before, but the prospect of a woman was new. With him having all of those empty hours to himself, his mind was apparently filling them up with fantasy bubbles. She was feeling bad that she hadn't come over more often. But it wasn't easy. Talk about money always got him warmed up, and going back to when they had a house of their own, he started in about the revenge he'd gotten on those borders from the old country by selling their belongings when they got behind on the rent.

"They called me a filthy capitalist. Remember? But wait, Rika. I gotta tell you something. You know my friend George Klagemann, who moved in downstairs? He wants to go to our lodge. You know, the German-American Friendship Club. He is not halfway down the block, and these *Neger Kinder*—maybe ten, twelve years old—they stop him. One kid pushes him against a fence. He gives them five dollars and shows an empty wallet."

"Are they hungry? They need shoes?"

"They go right back to the candy store, buy bubble gum, maybe a soda, and put what's left on the numbers. Klagemann calls the police. They say he has to come down to the station and file a complaint."

"Why don't the cops come and arrest these kids?"

"Arrest? Does he know who they are? Klagemann says it's like he's the robber. Just last week, that Stumpfkopf detective Mario, Guipiletti's son, moves in here. George tells him what happened.

He mighta been talking to a wall. I ask why he wants here, and all of a sudden, he's talkin' about the murders years back at the castle. He's got clues that lead him here, he says. Mentions prints. Looks at my shoes and wants to see George's."

Otts frowned. "What's he want with us old bastards? I oughta show him Bonita's shoes. They make a print. If you ask me, what he's lookin' for maybe it's right under his nose. I'm thinkin' his fat papa had something to do with the baron so he wants to find somebody else."

"Anyway, Rika, maybe you got a little pull with the football player. Wants to be mayor. See if he can do something."

She was becoming a little impatient, and upon noticing this, Otts remarked on how poorly she looked. He knew. *First Al and now Hannah*. Himself, he had gone to see Father Johannes and felt much better. He advised her to see him too.

"You'll see. He listens. Lets you get things off your chest. Talk for as long as you want. He takes an interest. And it's free!"

CHAPTER 38

"Louey Weeps for Whimp"

Who, indeed, does she bump into—literally—but Louey, exiting the candy store and (as he was accustomed to saying) *in person*! He held onto her, which was a lot like being embraced by an oak tree, and said he'd been looking for her. She had to help out.

"Me? With what? Help you, of all people?"

He took her aside and told her Whimpy showed up at their place and started bugging Betsy about letting him sleep in their basement locker. All he had was a pillow from Addie's bed and the clothes on his back. He looked so sick that Betsy was afraid he'd die there and that rats might get him.

"So he's curled up like a fishin' worm in our hallway. Betsy wants you to come and get him. It's a 'gotta-do.'"

Addie said the church would take him in. The priest knew him and had already been a helper for him.

Louey said, "Okay, however, somebody would have to carry him there. "But he don't wanna be carried. This guy's a real basket case. Won't eat nothin'. It's like he wants to die, and let me tell you, we don't want no dead man on our hands—me, in particular."

He paused; and with a "By the way," out came his goofy, high-pitched laugh. "Betsy can't figure out how you coulda throwed him out."

"She did."

"But talk about help." His expression changed, and for once, she saw there was a human being underneath that granite exterior. "Poor guy. I see him like that, and I gotta say the bastard gets to me. He will go with you. Do a good thing, Addie, and help him, huh? Please. I'll pay yer carfare."

Was I being the hard one? A thought like that coming from him! Well, then, could I be wrong in thinking that to be soft might make it harder for him?

As she stood there wrinkle-browed, Louey insisted she couldn't just walk away from the guy.

"No, I'm not for walkin' away, but taking him in would put us back to where we were. I think I can help. Just have to find the way."

"Okay, find it. This guy ain't gonna last."

"Right, but hold everything. Gimme a day or two, okay? I got a job, and I want to keep it."

As she stood there drumming her fingers on class notes, Louey said, "For now all you have to do is come and see him. It might tide him over for a day. Hopefully more. 'Cause think about it, our 'super detective' wants to question him about his father, who tried to put a bite on the baron. Needed money to get out of town."

"I want to help, but one couldn't just drop him off at the parish house without the priest's consent. Tell Whimpy I'm goin' ta help. I'll send in sandwiches. If he knows they're from me, I believe he'll eat. Here, give him this note."

"Sorry. He says it's you he needs. Never mind sandwiches."

"Tell him, down the road, I think we can find a way. For now, we've got to cool it. It's not that I ain't gonna look for help. Fact is I'm gonna look high for, let's say, salvation."

"Yeah. Don't we all need apiece o' that?"

PART V

IMPULSE WILL HAVE ITS WAY

CHAPTER 39

"Father Jay a Solution?"

"Your pained look tells me you feel some responsibility. I assume that is why you are here. An emergency mission, I'm told."

She should have known this all-knowing priest would instantly conclude she had something going with Whimpy. With that sexy build of his, why wouldn't he have bedroom thoughts? She felt she might have made a mistake in coming, but she wanted him to know how things stood and even hoped he'd be curious. Anyway, now that he knew, let him—for goodness' sake—help.

"Strange as it may sound, I hardly knew him," she began. "Ditto he me. But we got to liking one another. It became too much and we broke up. To be truthful, I did the breaking. But I had no idea it would get this bad, Father."

She felt really uncomfortable about having that word tumble out of her mouth, especially with the sense she was standing there before him like a naughty child. He wasn't all that much older than she was, and without the collar and black coat, no one would take him for a priest. Broad in the shoulders—thanks to all of his workouts with the weights—he had the rugged look of an athlete, a Clark Gable dimple, black hair, and striking blue eyes. *Yeah, those eyes.*

He was such a dreamboat up close that Addie thought she'd become tongue-tied. She was also intimidated by the empty cavern of a church with its high-groined vaults. Sensing her uneasiness, he took her hand (*unusual*, she thought) and led the way to his wood-paneled office in the rectory next door, where they sat in high-back facing chairs. As she moved forward on the red velvet cushion, her dress came up over her knees; and her fidgeting didn't help matters. She noticed his glance.

"You know, I saved Carlos once, and I told him it was now up to him to save himself. As I recall, he thanked me. I can't keep picking him up. For his sake, it wouldn't be wise. You'd agree, wouldn't you? Since you've had an involvement, I imagine you would be in a better position to help this time."

"Father, please understand I am here because I am helpless to help him on the terms he wants. You know what? I fell in love once with a guy who said he loved me. Those were his words, but it turned out otherwise. I took it hard. Now Carlos . . ."

"Well, he gave a lot of himself in love, and that led him down to where I myself had been with the guy who left me high and dry. I feel rotten about that. But as there were big emotions, I had to stop it before it got worse. So considering where we're at with one another, I can't help him for now. And you can."

"Ah, you had loved Carlos physically. As you know, sex is one thing, love another."

"No. For us, the physical was love. It came from the heart, as deep as anything either of us felt. Real love, I tell you."

"And I tell you not quite real. Now you want to turn it off so you don't do to him what's been done to you. Love doesn't have a spigot. I tell you that you don't know what love is. What you've had was self-indulgence."

What a pain! She saw this wasn't going to get her anywhere. So she bluntly told him what she shouldn't have, saying sex lost them in feelings so intense they came from the soul.

When that got her a frown, she added, "Father, I tell you we worked ourselves into a religious frenzy. Didn't Freud say something about sex and religion?"

"Nonsense! Self-deception is as bad as self-indulgence."

She was getting disgusted. "Father, you and I, we use the same words, but we do not have the same language. Remember, he came to me."

"You accepted him. And not just to stay with you. True?"

Suddenly, this dreamboat was becoming a real pain in the ass. *All he had to do, dammit, was take Whimpy in! Like he'd done before.* She said so, but he kept evading a take-back.

"My problem?" he says.

"Look, he came to live with me because he had no place to go." She spoke deliberately, putting a little bite in her voice. "I didn't want him to stay, but I frankly did the charitable thing and took him in. To you, I am immoral. To him at that time, I was—forgive me—something close to salvation. For that, he should have gone to you! Better still, you can now go to him, if you would. Or best of all, allow him to come here!"

She knew she had taken it too far, but she figured he'd heard worse; and as she took him in, it didn't seem like he was all that upset. *The bastard liked an argument.*

"To accept him, you did not need to go beyond his immediate needs. Bluntly put, there could have been no urgent need to have sex with him. You know as well as I do it was pure hedonism. How then can you speak of love—the saving love you allude to—when the reality of love is precisely that which lies beyond the physical, beyond what you can personally get, in exchange for what you can give? If you love him, it suffices to be loving, nurturing."

"Oh, my gosh! Sex. Is that what bothers you? Honest as it was, if you knew what our intimacy was like, it would probably shock you even more that in the depths of it, darn it, our sex was—to use your word— ethereal!"

"We do indeed speak a different language. What you say is outright nonsense but forgivable. People who have sinned talk all kinds of sacrilege in confession." He paused and a peculiar half smile came over that handsome face, his head cocked slightly to the side. "As for sex, this collar doesn't exactly make me a babe in the woods. I wasn't born in these vestments."

"You will go to him, won't you? Better still, why not take him in here?"

"For now, let him know I'm concerned." Her flicker of hope faded when he added, "I'm expecting a visit from the bishop. He has heard of my activism on behalf of the Puerto Ricans. Bringing Carlos into the parish house now might be a problem."

"Leave him out there, and he'd be preyed upon by this guy who thinks he's that Victor Hugo Inspector. As a kid, Carlos was with his father when he went to ask the baron for money. Our Mario-Javert thinks Carlos was an eyewitness to something."

"Oh, that? Will there be no end to it?"

"I'll tell him you'll accept him here after you've seen the bishop. Pastoral care, Father."

"There is no other. Would that its effect were lasting."

CHAPTER 40

"A Handkerchief Left on the Altar"

"Oh God, Oh God, Oh God!" she'd kept repeating to herself.

She welcomed the cool rain on her face. *Really concerned is he? Had to know what kind of a consolation that was!* There seemed to be such painful constraint in the way he acted that she, for the moment, wondered more about him than the Whimp.

Where was the person, the man, hiding in this priest? Was he afraid of him? Darned if, after all that high-minded talk, he wasn't checking out my ass again as I turned to leave. Well, it showed that underneath he wasn't made of wood. Could be he needed a woman. Might in fact have known one. While he was talking one way, was he actually thinking another, sitting there and looking me in the eye while imagining me naked and jealous of Whimpy? Love! What a good lay wouldn't do for him! How easy to tear those vestments off!

She recalled the ugly rumor that accompanied Jay's arrival—people being almost in shock over his striking, good looks—which had it that fresh out of seminary confinement, he'd been connected with a woman; and the bishop's nuncio, as they alluded to him, had instantly jumped on him and made him do the "cure," which began with the reassertion of his vows.

The woman in question, having gone gaga over him, took it hard. (Had he made a secular vow?) On his own, he supposedly fasted for all of a week. What gossip wouldn't build up? Most church people regarded it as slander, particularly when they got to see him in action as with finding food for the destitute. They remarked on what a caring and honest priest he was. Above all, one who knew life. And could dirty his hands with it.

Addie had dismissed all that, but as she thought about it, it seemed a lot like he was irritating her because he was in need—and frustrated. If it weren't for her having to put Whimpy first, she might have made a play. She could have started with a parting hug to show she understood; and having put her boobs on that solid, manly chest, she'd let this Adonis take it from there.

She was all for going back to put a scented handkerchief on the altar. A blind erotic impulse got stronger with every departing step and finally sent her rushing back to flagrantly do it. When the hanky kept slipping off the polished oak surface, she dug into her purse for a stick of gum and gave it a chew; and downing second thoughts, she had the pungent cloth spread out and stuck tight at diagonal corners. "Ah . . . Sexy," she breathed.

However, on the way home, the unnerving idea of what she'd done hung there in the fresh air and wouldn't go away. *How, dammit, could I be his tormentor?* She stopped, raced back, and found herself breathlessly chugging up the church steps. Leaning her head in the big door, she looked around; and just as she was about to tiptoe in, she thought she heard a low moan coming from somewhere left of the sanctuary then a muffled cough.

Half a black back showed itself from the corner of a recessed chapel, his head bowed against the railing. He was on his knees. It had happened so fast that he must have heard her footsteps and saw what she did.

Crushed, she hurriedly drew back, sat herself down hard on the top step, and gripped her head. The imp had gotten the better of her again. She bit her lip and fought back tears.

CHAPTER 41

"Whimp One Problem, Jay Another"

Pulling herself together, she cursed her vulnerability and his too. Once cold sobriety returned, she went over to see Betsy to let her know it didn't look like they were going to get much help from this priest. It looked like he had troubles of his own. Crudely put, *Did she know this guy could use a good lay? In fact, he might be one.*

"So you want to give him to me?"

"First of all, he needs some love, but he's blocked up so bad he can't have what he needs."

"Bluest of balls, huh?"

"Yeah, but this priest man has got to be treated tenderly. By a woman who can soft cushion him. If done, it might, of course, be a loser—for both. Still, he has an outrageous need. And don't ask me how I know."

"You're thinkin' it might be interesting for me to bust his cherry?"

"To the point, for the time being, he ain't gonna be much help for the Whimp. Jay creates suspicion if he helps the guy, more so if he doesn't—after he once did. Jay has a big thing for the PRs. Seems he ain't big like that for the rest of us. Must think their need is greater than ours. It's like we got a priest who's gonna get screwed either way."

Addie brought them back to the Whimp. Since he was known at the hospital, she said Betsy should be able to check him in for a couple of days. If nothing else, they could get him intervenes nutrition; then, too, since Father Jay does his rounds there, if he sees the shape Whimpy is in, he might just have to step in and do something like offering him a place where he can hole up. Betsy was doubtful that she could get the guy officially registered, but she knew the woman who'd let her sign him in anyway, provided he's her responsibility.

"Whatever is offered, he keeps wantin' you, Addie. If he's gonna be goin' anywhere, I think you're the only one who can get him there. Please do me the favor. Ole Louey keeps leanin' on me. Seeing those pencil arms, he shakes his head. Says he can't look at him. Yeah, last thing we need is a dead man in our basement."

They were sitting on the plush settee in the beautifully appointed suite, which her spendthrift lover had set up for them in their new town house digs. What the numbers traffic wouldn't do. The hardwood floor underfoot reflected a chandelier. There were Monet prints on the walls and a maple dining table with matching sideboard; and all of this was surrounded by piped-in music. The latest. *Ah, the comforts of suburbia!* Out the backdoor, they had a row of tomato cages.

In the midst of their idle chat, in charged Louey himself with the latest. First, they wanted him to take Whimpy home, which the guy must have heard because he went limp. They plied Louey with a bunch of papers and wanted him to sign. He told 'em he had poor eyesight, so paperwork had to be entrusted to Betsy. He tossed a handful onto the coffee table.

And second, he saw Otto in emergency being checked out by a cardiologist. What made him a bundle of nerves was the other day when Mario came over, clipboard in hand, wanting to know point-blank where he had been the night of the "murders at the castle." On top of that, between Bonita's sloppy housekeeping and those kids hitting him up for money, he was getting chest pains and nausea.

Chain-smoking Betsy lit up another and blew some smoke at Louey—reminding him that, for goodness' sake, this poor Whimp has no home. Wasn't "kind Louey" supposed to be checking out the Y? He held up his hands, signifying that he'd had enough.

Betsy, as a last resort, knew of a way to keep Whimpy in the hospital. He used to have a cleanup job there, so he'd knew some nooks where he could be hid—bedding, for example, would be ideal. They remembered him in food service too. All you had to do was mention getting something for nothing, and the Whimp turned on. Meanwhile, Addie said she'd work on the priest to visit the hospital for both patients, which was doable after the bishop's short stay.

Johnny R had insisted on showing "His Holiness" around. (Let there be no question about the Catholic vote.) Addie insisted that what the bishop really had to be shown was the four thirty bus. And while she was insisting, in came her big Pollock himself, on break. He had been scouring the town, looking for her.

She said, "I'm glad to see you . . . I want Mario off Papa's back and the kids out of his wallet. You have got to use your pull—your punch, if need be . . . Yes, what job you want me for, I know but it has to wait."

"Love you, Addie, but—"

"Sorry, Johnny, but 'buts' won't do. Need to find the nonexistent room for Whimpy. He's hurtin'—real bad."

"Okay. But frankly, I hurt too. For you. A lot. Got this scar to prove it. Kin I show it to yah?"

"First the room, lover boy."

"Yeah, I know how you feel for the Whimp. Told him I might get you to put him up again for the time we're gonna be gone."

"You didn't."

"Well, as you'll find out, I'm gonna be takin' you on the road. And we'll need somebody to hold the fort."

"Oh, my God! Then we come home and he is fully ensconced, just waitin' for me."

"Yeah, think of it. You'll have done a good thing. Should make you feel good. Besides, I'm working on Mr. Big to get you set up in one of these classy condos."

"I hate having to do things I don't want to do. Like, tell me what's this business about me supposedly goin' 'on the road'—and with you? Tell Mr. Big I've got my limits."

CHAPTER 42

"Paperwork"

With papers piled to the right of him (and even more to the left and still more into the valley below), you could barely see the guy. And he wasn't small. Not surprisingly, the overflowing papers diminished a not-exactly-oversize office that reeked of cigar smoke and gym socks.

Johnny never got on the line when you called in. He was always in conference, on the phone, or gone for the day. You give your name to the secretary in the outer office, state your business, and leave a phone number. But not this time.

He began by twisting his cigar in the ashtray and chomping on the stub. "I'd open the window a crack but can't have the paperwork blowin' around. Great window though. Lets me see right across the bus terminal to the mayor's office. Mine come November. And yeah, 'His Holiness' made that four thirty on the dot. Breathless as he was, he still took time to bless me—I think.

"You're frowning at the mess. Well, Natalie out there is afraid to go through it. Can't tell yah what half of it is. Some are probably people wantin' jobs that ain't there yet."

"Did you manage to get Mario shipped out?

"Well, not exactly. We did some arm wrestlin', and damned if he's not one tough son of—"

"Dammit! Did you get him onto another assignment?

"Got somethin' cookin'. His twin, Rocco, is runnin' up bills to keep his women entertained. Told him to charge some stuff to Mario. And said 'Already done.'"

"So Mario's workin' on that? Okay, something else. Look here a minute."

She brought him up to the wall map next to his private bathroom and pointed out the stretch of blocks between Otto's apartment and the German-American Club. She was about to pick up a pen and underline it when he swept through the papers to grab her hand and, slipping as he did, almost brought her down on him. Wishful slip.

Since the kids were playing the numbers, Johnny thought a first step might be to have the source removed from the scene—namely, Big Bad Louey. A laugh. "Of course, there's no easy way to be movin' that big black bagman. Does the low-hangin' fruit. Orders are he takes anybody who wants to play."

Stamping her foot, she shouted, "Come to the point! Something's got to be done about the thieving kids."

"Well, I'll have a squad car make the rounds over there. Bring in a couple o' kids, and scare the shit outta them. Word should get out. But you know, we can't get a car out there in the first place unless somebody makes a complaint. Tell this guy Hoffmann or what's his name . . ."

"No. He'd be afraid the kids might get back at him."

"What? Older citizens afraid? I'm big on safe streets, you know. One of my campaign themes. Hoffmann doesn't have to let 'em know he's the one 'cause—"

"'Cause I'll file the complaint. Don't like what these kids are doin'. Now back to Mario. You used to attend his poker parties. What did you tell him?"

"Like I said, twin Rocco would go anywhere for a lay and finagle payment from Mario. Drives him crazy. Remember they're twins. Creditors believe he's Mario. Anyway, I told Mario he'd met a stewardess on the Argentine Airline."

"He did?"

"I made it up. Last seen, Mario was at Newark Airport. He should be checkin' for a while. His brother's costing him money."

He wanted to talk more. She didn't, sensing he might get into something personal. Like "how about lunch tomorrow?" He had some interesting ideas he'd like to run by her. She begged off, saying she had some interesting obligations that were running by her. And she thanked him for getting on the priest to see her father home. She gave him a peck on the cheek as she eased her way to the door.

Calling his attention to lights going on at city hall, she withstood his parting embrace and reminded him to keep Mario looking for a while. "Just mention pot—plenty in the ghetto." She sounded off his campaign slogan: "We'll Get Good Things Done." *Inspired!*

"For you, honey, anything."

She couldn't resist taking in that broad chest, which she knew to be hairy. Dilemma: how does a lady have an affair with him—and no more—without feeling she's exploiting the guy? He's so sweet-natured, but the trouble is this fella could be cloyingly sweet. So immature. Call it naivety. He wouldn't know how to take it lightly and let it go, at that. He'd probably want marriage. A workable compromise? Something to ponder.

CHAPTER 43

"A Ride with Father Jay"

On her way home that evening with her canvas bag of groceries, she watched a white police car come by and stop in front of her apartment building. Two big-gutted officers got out and were looking around to size up the neighborhood. The older one with sergeant stripes ran a finger over something in his notepad then squinted at the house number and nodded to his partner.

Addie dawdled along till they were well inside; then softly entering the hallway, she looked up from the stairwell and could see the sergeant knocking on her door. Taking his cap off, he put an ear to it while the other cop nosed around the other end of the hall. The sergeant called him over to listen, and they exchanged looks. Just as she was easing her way past the newel post to go toward the ground floor apartment, her motion caught the sergeant's attention.

"Say, miss, would you happen to know the person who lives here? A lady called . . . lemme see here"—checking his notepad—"Uh . . . an Adeline. Yeah, Adeline Heiss?"

"No, can't say that I do. Fact is I believe she may have moved out."

"Oh, zat so? Sounds like there's a cat she might be comin' back for. Know anything about her? Like maybe where she moved to?"

"No. Beats me. We mostly keep to ourselves here."

"We'll check back. But if you see her, give us a call, huh?"

"Right away, but I don't see her very often."

With that she glided out the backdoor, putting it noiselessly to, and bounded through a weedy backyard to the street one block over. She had barely reached the corner bus stop when a dark-colored car pulled up to the curb. As she turned her head away, she heard the window roll down; and a kind voice called "Can I give you a lift somewhere?"

"Father Johannes! What a surprise! I'm going over to Dad's. Thought I'd fix a nice cheer-me-up dinner for him. He's not been too pleased with the housekeeper. You know how he is."

"Would you have enough for three? I was thinking of dropping in on him."

"Of course, of course! Yes, please, I was hoping . . . Oh, Dad would really like that."

When she got in, sitting next to him, the first thing she detected was a faint aroma of cologne. Her jasmine, in fact. She was so ill at ease that she tried to think it was his aftershave.

Hmm, she mused, *smells pretty good on him. Had I done the right thing then?* Perhaps, but for the wrong reason. Since she had phoned Otto to tell him she was coming over, he had doubtlessly called the priest.

Jay seemed deep in thought. She sensed they were traveling a mere twenty miles an hour. People were beeping and glaring as they passed. Finally opening up, he told her he could barely wait to let her know how sorry he was. He said that he shouldn't have become argumentative, certainly not judgmental. He had to admit there were times he didn't understand himself. Said there was no excuse even if he was being pressured on a variety of fronts—like the budget, a front he detested. He nervously inquired whether she knew anything about bookkeeping.

Without waiting for an answer, he apologized for rambling on. He should, of course, do something for Carlos, particularly as he'd been there with him before.

"I see you're pleased with that."

She nodded, and he slowly reached over and covered her hand with a reassuring squeeze. She squeezed back. He came on warmly with an offer to deal helpfully with anything that might still be bothering her. She thanked him for that and said she was okay.

"Would you want to do Saturday morning Bible stories with the kids? They at least wouldn't take that out of my budget."

She said maybe and they rode on in silence.

As they lumbered by the candy store, there was Louey, big as life, coming out with the day's collection securely tucked away in that saddlebag of a coat pocket he had. He turned his massive head this way and that before treading off in his casually erect style.

"You know him?" the priest asked, watching for Addie's reaction.

"Doesn't everybody?"

"Yes, and everybody knows his business, but nobody can do anything about it. I tried and it looked like it might cost me."

"Really?"

"I made the mistake of approaching the man he does security for, that Mr. Dimallo, the Party personified, and was told no one was to be mentioning Louey in his presence. When it came to the increase in the church's charity load, Mr. D. was used to asking him how much and having his man with the green eyeshade quietly make up the difference.

"No one asked whether I was putting the church in bed with an unsavory source. For real trouble, the Party had recently hired themselves a Wall Street lawyer who went by the name of Scheisser-Dunneville. People secretly played around with the name, as with 'Dunn-that,' when something was accomplished, but one never fooled with the man. Then there was Moro, Tough Tony's respectable brother-in-law, the city's Director of Public Works and presumed power behind the throne, rarely seen—the spider in the web."

It was a late October day, and dusk was descending on them sooner than they'd realized. He pulled over to the curb and stepped on the brake, and as he leaned her way to open the glove box, she tensed up as if the arm pressed against the back of her seat might come around her.

"Forgot I was wearing these tinted lenses," he explained. His "sorry" was followed by another tender squeeze. Instead of squeezing back, she quizzically turned her face toward him. He looked away.

They rode on in silence, and she sensed that he wanted to say something but held back. When they arrived at Otto's place, that sturdy right arm was finally around her back as she found herself being helped onto the sidewalk. She remarked that the cool breeze felt good. He nodded, noting how the air in the car had been warming up. As they stood there for a moment, looking at one another eye to eye, Addie caught her breath and finally came out with it.

"Where do we take it from here, Jay?"

"We'll think about it tomorrow."

"Regarding omens, I saw a gathering of red-shoulder hawks in the western sky as they prepared for the long journey south. They had mated and hatched their young. Now it was on to a lush feeding ground. Instinct would take care of the rest.

"It wasn't an easy life, but together they were determined to meet it, knowing what was valid for them even if their life span was not great. They had experienced *romance*, and since it must be from the heart, it lasts forever."

CHAPTER 44

"A Celebration Dinner"

"Hah-loo! Rika makes dinner, and Father Johannes eats with us!"

Otts gave them a spirited reception. His eyes fairly twinkled.

"Also, gibts Heute 'n Feiertag?"

And once he got the day's complaint off his chest, it was indeed a festive evening.

"You know the big boss Dimallo from downtown since he bought this building, so nobody can make the candy store move— Gott bewähre!—the heat goes off at nine o'clock like people should be in bed by then. Everything he touches has to make money. Here, feel the radiator. It's already starting to cool down. Ah, but tonight we'll make it warm all by ourselfs, huh?"

He broke out his prized Apfel Schnaps, direct from Klagemann's bathtub, and poured a round of generous double shots in old-fashioned tumblers, calling out "*Prost!*" Downing his in two Schlugs, he clapped the remaining drops into his palms and rubbed them together. Addie, warmed by the Schnaps, gave Jay a hug; and the priest joined them. After pouring another round, Otts got so downright gay that he started trotting out one corny joke after the other, the three of them laughing tears.

"Do you know when God created Adam? A little before Eve . . . Which animals always eat with their tails? All of them! They can't take them off . . . Why did Cleopatra tell Caesar 'No'? Because she was the Queen of de-Nile . . . How come the Indians got here first? They had reservations."

And on it went. Addie made the long beard sign Otts would use for stale jokes by others, and he even laughed at that. He, in fact, laughed so heartily that he went on a coughing jag, which he calmed with a hefty Schlug.

Addie had originally planned to just make herself a couple of hamburgers, but now she needed a stretcher; and finding a head of cabbage in Otto's frig as she expected, she was able to add rice and fix Krautrouladen, one of his favorites.

When she got them out of the oven, the aroma was so appetizing that Otts dug into this delicacy so ravenously that beads of sweat broke out on his forehead. After dinner, he toasted the cook and said they'd have to do it again. To top the evening off, Father Jay announced that he was going to get Otts an English-speaking housekeeper; and he'd have Social Services pick up most of the cost as it would be a form of rehab for the person he had in mind. Otts was beside himself and brought them together for another triple hug.

Addie said she was tired; and Otts, red-cheeked, yawned and said he was getting pretty tired himself. Father Jay pointed out that it was rather late for Addie to be waiting alone at a bus stop, and he'd be glad to drive her home.

When they came to her street, she turned noticeably apprehensive. Thinking the Schnaps was giving her a problem, Father Jay pulled over and asked if she was okay. He said that she needn't be embarrassed. She shook her head and, leaning forward, saw there was an unknown car parked in front of her apartment building. A hulking figure was planted on the passenger side, smoking a cigarette and looking ominously up at the windows.

As they got closer, she saw the car had a city license plate; and the beefy hulk looked a lot like one of the bulls who had been pointed out to her at the Athletic Club.

Not knowing what else to do, she hunched down on the seat and asked Jay to keep going. As they drove on by, she rose up just enough to get a look at the guy. Darned if it wasn't Johnny himself!

When they turned the corner, she told Jay about Klagemann, the call from Johnny, and the cops knocking on her door.

Jay said she could come over to the rectory and rest for an hour or so. It was already close to eleven, and Johnny wouldn't be camped out all night. He, on the other hand, would be up late working on a painful sermon aimed at getting people to appreciate the church's financial pinch. He assured her it would be very quiet. Father Tim, the younger priest who did weekday mass was on loan to St. Patrick's, where the resident priest was recovering from the flu.

CHAPTER 45

"It Happens"

The rectory was one of those old brick, white-columned structures with limestone trim around the windows (Neo-Georgian) and had well-polished wainscoting in all the downstairs rooms. It smelled as old as it looked.

They went upstairs to the second floor living quarters, where Father Jay guided her down a dimly lit hallway to his bedroom. The newly carpeted floor absorbed the sound of their footsteps. He flicked on the floor lamp and motioned her in.

She entered hesitantly with a bit of a tremor. *A woman in the priest's bedroom? Ah, from his attitude, not all that sacrosanct. He was that confident of its being all right?* Tiredness overcame the queasy feeling that she really should be heading downstairs to find herself a couch. But she was wakeful enough to be curious. *How did a priest live privately?*

Pleated brown drapes hung over the windows. In front of one of them was a broad mahogany desk with a large leather blotter and a white shaded lamp. Everything was very Spartan: plain, no frills. Over against the far wall were two well-filled bookshelves, and resting in the corner were a set of weights and a cushioned lifter's bench. There was a glossy brown comforter on the bed and an oversize pillow and, attached to the mahogany bedpost, was a long–necked reading lamp. An open door led to an adjoining bathroom with glistening white tiles.

Hmm . . . Girly mags under the mattress? Well, if caught in a bind, supposedly he can work it off on the weights; and there's always a cold shower. Both quite handy.

He pointed to the bookshelves and told her to help herself. Squeezing her hand again (didn't he do a lot of that?) he said, he'd be in the study next door and would be back for her in about an hour as he softly closed the door behind him.

Evidently quite sure of himself, he didn't mind her being there; so why shouldn't she just make herself at home? Still, she couldn't help wondering about priestly frustration. *What if the weights didn't do it? Could they just pray that it would go away and knot themselves up?*

Telling herself to let up, she quickly dismissed dangerous ideas and felt comforted by the thought that he was turning out to be a really good guy after all. In no time, she had dropped her dress, kicked off her shoes, slipped between the rustling sheets, and was gone.

She jumped at the touch of his hand on her bare shoulder, instinctively threw her arms around him, and pulled him unresistingly down on top of her. She covered his quivering lips with her mouth, forcing her tongue between them. He made an effort to get up, but she brought him back down with a bounce; and running her tongue on his neck, she tumbled him over and went for his belt. She swiftly had him out of his black pants and white boxer shorts, tossing them overboard; and she was swifter yet in disposing of her things, whereupon they lost themselves in an embrace that had him gasping for air.

"Please, no more," he pleaded in a hoarsely anguished voice; but eyes tightly shut, he was powerless to hold back as something suddenly gave way, and he succumbed to a shattering release. For minutes afterward, he was unable to control the shakes despite all of her comforting: words had no effect. Fearing for a moment he might be falling into some kind of internal vortex, she ran calming hands over him. She thought she could make out a briefly whispered monologue, the most audible part of which was "Mother of God."

After they had rested, she expected him to tell her she had to leave. Instead, he kissed her forehead ever so lovingly while absently stroking her hair.

"I have wanted you, ached for you, Addie, for too long a time." Then hardly able to get the words out as he drew her close in, his hushed voice said, "Impossible to hold back anymore. Truth is struggle with it as I have, it only grew. You're good. I admired your strength. I love you, Addie . . . from the heart. You don't know how relieved I am to say it. And I've finally encouraged myself—well, you've actually encouraged me—to find it possible."

Renewed and no longer having to fight inhibition, he came to her with liquid eyes and a gentleness of touch that made her blood race and swept them away in mutual abandon. His breath came in short, rasping bursts that made it seem like he was weeping; and he may have been, but if so, she knew it was from pure joy. Fascinated herself, she felt a great warmth welling up in her chest that spread through her being and carried her aloft on a wave of euphoria that washed over her like she'd been bathed in the all-purifying sea.

"I love you, Jay."

Keyed up as they were and mindful of how rare their golden moments might immediately be, they lay there companionably talking well into the morning, sharing past experience and intimate thoughts—touching on aspirations, also self-doubt—not knowing quite when they dropped off to sleep. Hers was light, however: he had set the alarm for six o'clock, but she was up before that.

She had showered while he was still in bed and came out of the bathroom fluffing her hair. Quickly dressed, she turned on the coffee machine and found he had meanwhile slipped into suspendered trousers and, barefoot, was sorting out some papers on his desk. As he turned, she put her hand to his lips.

"Let's not say anything now. It's too much. But we'll find a way. Meanwhile, nobody will know, and what we have, no one can take away."

He winced and she said she was sorry; she didn't mean it the way it sounded. He said he knew how she meant it—something for him to deal with—and added that he fortunately was going to be extraordinarily busy the next few days. In addition to the bishop, there was this big wedding coming up and a touchy meeting with people from the mayor's office about his least favorite subject, money, and how to share the burden of educating the young. At the moment, however, she had to be out before the new housekeeper arrived. She wanted to test his feelings again but held up, fearful he might raise reality doubts.

It seemed like he knew her thoughts anyway. Hands to her cheeks, he had brought her lips up for an endearing good-bye kiss at the door. She didn't want to let go, but there was consolation in her knowing she would have his touch with her every day thereafter. Indeed, as he drew her back from the door and, on a last minute impulse, pressed her close against him as if he was struggling to let go, she felt she could leave knowing that in the clear light of day, he still meant it.

On the other hand, having seen his sensitive side, she was also concerned about how things might unfold and how, above all, he would handle himself publicly. It stuck in her mind that she'd just have to say something. So when she did, he came back sad-eyed and somber; but as if feeling support from the beyond, he whispered "It cannot be unknown, and that's not to be feared. God may be invisible, but He is not an abstraction."

And seeing her worried look, he added, "Don't you think He understands something about love? The life force, you know. The source of this creation of His and ongoing—so long as He allows it all to last."

Looking about, he raised his outstretched arms. "As for the human and *personal*, let me outright confess it's not until love is allowed to fill a cold heart, that a person—particularly this one—realizes the emptiness that has lain within."

It began to sound like the spillover from a sermon he was preparing. *Poor man.* She felt for him groping for justification. Of course, she could understand that as an intellectual, he had to put words around it to satisfy himself that it was all right. Despite their cloudy prospects—indeed because of them—he craved clarity, being the kind of person who likes ideas clothed in the hard brilliance of a winter moon.

She understood that too but couldn't help thinking, *Oh my, does he leave the priesthood but take the pulpit with him?* She had to let that go. After all, thank goodness he doesn't make love with his head! The fact that he turned out to be so much the man was a lot of what she was counting on to coast them through. His dimpled smile offered reassurance. She gave her own.

"Of course, God is all-comprehending particularly since as we, *women*, have it, He is really a She. And as you know, *women* have to have a lot of understanding in this life. They live the unacknowledged rough side of daily life, the bread we pray for—and sometimes have to earn."

Smiling more broadly yet, he pressed her into an embrace that engulfed them again in sweet sorrow. But when they parted in the parking lot, his face grew taut and seemed to take on a grayish hue. He was obviously preparing himself to go out and brave the world.

"You'll be all right, won't you?"

"I'm sure I will. Same for you?"

Walking away, shoulders squared, he probably didn't hear her say "God bless you."

CHAPTER 46

"From Jay to Johnny"

Left with an incessant hum inside and knowing that tired as she was, she would just lay awake in bed, Addie walked down to the All-Night Diner, took a booth, and ordered scrambled eggs which she scarcely tasted. Half the pleasure of eating there was breathing in the aroma of their freshly ground coffee; but even that was lost on her as she lingered over a second cup, staring blankly out the window and letting events sink in.

What to make of it all . . . Could it really have happened? She had tasted the very sweetness of him. *But where does it go from here?* She thought of the swan that wept for his departed mate and wouldn't leave their favorite pond when winter came and was frozen in it. *No, not that!* Like a butterfly in courtship, her emotions kept flitting up and down from hope to despair and back again.

And how wrong she'd been about Jay. She bitterly chastised herself for having had the stupidity to have imagined a vengeful seduction. For shame. "Dear Jay, how little I knew you. How little I knew myself!" Without realizing it, she had banged her fist on the table.

"You okay?" the waitress asked. "More coffee?"

Wondering why she was so nervous, something struck her.

"Good grief! Am I ovulating?"

The clock tower at city hall struck eight times. She dared not think ahead. Instead, she tried to distract herself by watching the street awaken: an elephant-like garbage truck went lumbering by; the pharmacist, putting a scarf around his neck, took in the bundle of newspapers left at his side door; the postman was adjusting the strap on his mailbag and was sorting its contents; the night watchman on his way out of the bank tipped his cap to the two elderly clerks hustling in a little late; and the street repair crew, wearing thick sweaters under their tar-stained coveralls, slid off the equipment truck.

They had themselves a smoke, looked down the street, shrugged, shuffled through the diner door, and seated themselves heavily at the counter where—looking like so many pumpkin-head dummies for Halloween, out-sized and overstuffed—they leaned over their coffee and donuts and waited, as they said, for the truck with a load of asphalt and gravel patch to arrive. They talked rather loudly and burst into a gust of laughter when the one guy made some crude joke about the upcoming wedding night of boss Moro's hefty daughter with the chubby son of the Don from Scranton— who operated the not-so-classy whorehouses, along with the rest of the franchise east of Harrisburg.

When the straw boss Hank arrived, he had news that they were bidding on the contract for the new airport runway. He'd been there to have a look, and out of nowhere, Friend Mario approached with some questions about the baron's murder.

"Old news, but not for him. Fact is he got himself an industry-strength magnet and found a rusted gun down in the bushes. Traced it to the candy store, sellin 'em out the backdoor. Ground floor of the apartments where some o' you guys used to live."

Hank asked if any of his crew got a gun there. The guy next to him winked. "You think we're gonna tell?"

Her dreamy spell broken, Addie walked out and took several deep breaths. She stopped at the grocery store for a few items, adding a bottle of cheap Dago-red for sleepy time, and rode the bus home. Her pulse picked up as she approached the apartment door, and she did a little jump as she slipped on a blank white envelope going in. She looked about and, finding nothing amiss, opened it and called Schmutzy, who sprang on her for some neglected lap time, as she sat down to read the longish note handwritten on a sheet of foolscap.

"Addie, dear, I meant to talk to you personally about this, but I fell asleep waiting in the car. It seems that somebody informed a member of the school board that you'd recently had an unauthorized absence, and this person thought we oughta be reexaminin' your credentials anyway. [Yeah. Remember that Dimallo girl?]"

There was a knock on her door; and Johnny shuffled in, saying he'd been waiting on the back stoop. And when he heard the opening of her door, he rushed up to give her a personal explanation.

"She claims you weren't actually hired to do teaching in the first place and talked about us needing to have a real professional to do it, especially your kindergarten.

"There's a lot else. BS about credentials, which I won't go into. Now, you and me know that the business about credentials is pure baloney. Of course, it's my fault for how I set you up in civil service. The thing about it is we can't let it come out how I did this dumb thing—for Chrissakes, not in the middle of an election campaign! You understand, of course."

"Do I ever!" she hissed.

But before she could go on, he had another proposition: this one was about a new job, which she might be needing. It would be easier to get that for her if she was part of the team.

"Team! What the hell are you talking about?"

"My campaign manager says—what with the divorce and everything—I need a woman to join the campaign. A woman who gets to the men and shows the women I have their interests at heart. Help us, and it'll be a real step up for you. Has some interesting perks."

"What outrageous bullshit!"

Before she could unload, he said he was going to be leaving the wedding reception early and would send a driver (DJ) around to bring her down to city hall so they could brief her on her role and the goodies that went with it. This would have to do with the thing he had mentioned about their going on the road. She was free to reject it, of course. He could help her and she him.

"Sort of I scratch your back, you scratch mine. Okay?"

Okay, indeed! She rolled her eyes. "If I start scratching, it'll be more than your back."

"Why, for goodness sake," she murmured to herself, "did I ever get myself involved with this pitch man? And damn me anyway! Am I going to be out of work? I'm not far from broke right now."

She and Jay found one another, and away from him, she's worried sick they might *lose* one another. Moreover, they had to see to it that Whimpy wasn't lost. Now *this*. Things were piling in on her.

She needed some distance and asked herself, *How about a counselor?* Yes, of course! There was friend Tom all set up in that business; he could be professional enough. Trouble is how much could she tell him?

CHAPTER 47

"Lots She Didn't Need"

Tom's advertisement said he mostly counseled couples with marital problems. *Well, what about nonmarital, and hadn't he said to call if I needed help with anything?* Of course, she'd previously unloaded some things to him, minus details. Why not have him take it from there?

Tom had initially renovated the first floor of a sturdy old two–family frame house just uptown from what had become Puerto Rican village (aka the Latin ghetto). He had converted the place into an office with several therapy rooms, and as his business grew, he took over the rest of the house. Wanting at the same time to retain his job with the paper, he'd asked a school chum to come and partner with him.

Tom was fuller in the face than he'd been as a grad student—having acquired the portly, tweedy look that showed he felt himself rather well set up in life. He put his pipe down, poured two cups of coffee, and offered a sweet roll. Seating herself on the plump cushioned couch, Addie readied herself to lay it out for him to consider when she caught herself at the passing mention of Father Jay. A light turned on (not exactly needed). Noticing that Tom was being his observant self, she saw she had to tread lightly on that one.

There were voices in the adjacent conference room. Detective Mario-Javert had been holding forth before a group of Tom's reporter friends, and he was in mid-stride. Sticking his head out on hearing Tom was close to the double door, Mario invited both of them to come over and listen in.

"Yes, indeed, Father Johannes," he began in answer to a question, "the great do-gooder who has done a lot of no-good around here. You know about the Puerto Rican invasion, don't you? And you know who helped it along." As he seemed about to go off on a tirade, Addie whispered that she'd just as soon see Tom another time. He took her arm, whispering back "Cops think that the baron brought the PRs in as his favorite scabs. They'd work for less. Supposedly the church helped do the deal. Located boat rentals. Much appreciated."

"Listen"—Mario went on, looking over at Tom—"the PRs were just a block away on this once beautiful residential street named for your father's old Dutch family, Tom, where he had owned several properties. And if those PRs crossed the main north–south thoroughfare, they'd soon have this office surrounded, which would chase away Tom's clients and force him to relocate and start over.'"

Tom asked that Mario leave him out of this. Addie was feeling impatient. She had come to Tom with the feeling she had been struck by impulse lightning and, for reasons she couldn't define, was going to lose control of her fate.

As he went on, Mario said he didn't know how well acquainted these out-of-town reporters were with the local situation; but when the PRs first started filtering into town, they naturally had a hard time finding housing.

"They were loud and dirty and were getting into trouble with the police. Nobody wanted them living next door. So they appealed to Social Services. 'Hey, we American, you know!' And who steps in to help but, yes, charitably minded Father Johannes. He starts what they call a blockbuster just down the street."

Addie was again all for leaving, and Tom had to restrain her whispering, "He might have word about the Whimp—maybe you too."

"Okay," Mario continued, "so the good Father sets up a poor family in a house down this quiet old street of fine one-family wood-frame houses—all well maintained, regularly painted, and spruced up with neat little lawns, clipped shrubbery, flower beds, sparkling windows, and swept sidewalks. Look at it now.

"The family that the priest moved in overnight brings maybe five additional families into that one house. Kids sprawl out onto neighbors' lawns and porches. And the adults are jabbering from dawn to midnight. So when the neighbors sell out at a loss, in move still more PRs. And in less than a year, the place is a total slum. Porches sag, barefoot kids run wild, garbage piles up, shrubs are torn away . . . And where there once were lawns, only dirt, weeds, broken toys, and discarded furniture remain. One sorry sight."

Tom raised his hand. "Doesn't that tell you how sad things are for these people? 'The new downtrodden,' as one of our more generous editors put it."

Mario wouldn't let up. "Listen to this from an essay by a foreign visitor, something our *Messenger* here recently published:

'The neat little, white picket fences were among the first casualties. Occasionally, a fat aproned mother with red hands and a baby on one arm would appear to yell at the kids for breaking a window, and she'd disappear back into the open doorway. Long-faced men in tank-top undershirts lean on upstairs windowsills, looking out with hostile black eyes, indifferent to the racket below.

"Our ever-lovin' priest gets 'em jobs they do not want to hold when they can get more money by having children and staying on welfare. Girls over fourteen regularly get pregnant and are forced into random marriages if they cannot identify the fathers of their offspring. And these people are resentful that they are resented. Some have said that if it weren't for the priest, they would have burned down the town.

"Now how do you like that?"

"I don't," Tom's fellow reporter answered. "You sound like my father. Let's face it, Mario, the Hispanics are here to stay. We've got to learn to get along with them. Them with us too, of course, but most of us don't really know them."

Mario was ready for that. "Fact is, as I see it, we know all we want to know, and it's not been very good."

"You sound like somebody hired one of them to kill the baron."

"Could be, could be. And we have our eye on somebody who may know something about that murder. He is known to Addie here. In a bad way just now and in the hospital. But we plan to have him released once she claims responsibility for him. We're gonna have Tom here calm him down so the guy can be talked to."

Addie was whispering in Tom's ear "Mario thinks I'm going to set him up? Tom, I want outa here."

"Please hold on."

As Mario was about to open up for questions, Tom took the floor.

"The situation is not going to get any better by spreading hate. Have you heard about Mama Perez, the fat lady who runs the All-Night Diner downtown? If she finds a hungry kid in the street, she brings him in and gives him lunch. There are some really good people among them. It might help if that downstate rag you guys work for would write up the good part of this story. Anyway, I must say in the long run, the course Father Jay is taking will prove to be the right one."

Wanting to get in the last word, Mario claimed the baron wasn't all that liberal a guy as people thought he was. "Exploited the PRs, didn't he?"

With that, Tom excused himself. Back in the therapy room, Addie said she didn't know where to start. The room had been freshly painted; and combining that smell with hanging uncertainties, she foresaw a headache, which was not long in coming. What followed made it worse.

She told him from the start that one matter she wasn't going to talk about was Jay. There was something about the way Tom looked her over that she disliked and told him so. As that broke the ice, they had themselves a little back-and-forth. "Back" returned them to Jay. Tom jumped to the conclusion she'd been disreputably having this sordid little affair with a priest.

"Well," she countered, "hadn't I bedded you too, which you didn't think was all that immoral?"

He couldn't give her a very good prognosis regarding this priest, other than to say that if he professed his love, she could a thousand percent rely on it. At the same time, one therefore had to put a kibosh on any hope that she and Jay could run off and find themselves a new beginning somewhere in Brigadoon.

"I'm not feeling very well. Let's get on to this other thing with lover Johnny."

"Sure, sure. Well, you ought to know that his handlers now think they've made a mistake by putting him up for mayor. He's got recognition value but also baggage, such as the slippery deals he'd gotten himself into—some involving gambling, others graft. Businesses see him as a shoe-in for mayor and want to get to the head of the line. He takes advantage of that, the latest being the cut he took for a contract with the asphalt people who do street repair.

"Worst of all, he's making all sorts promises to the PRs, a hundred percent no-go with The Party. Since they're nonetheless stuck with him, they're looking for whatever gimmicks they can muster to make him manageable."

"I'm to be a gimmick!"

"On account of you, he's pulled himself away from grafting. Control impresses The Party. Furthermore, since Johnny goes over as a totally likable guy, your presence will promote that *and* reach the women as well. The men, of course, for their reasons."

"Oh yeah, bein' behind in my rent, I could use somebody to do a little promote for me," she sarcastically intoned. "Sounds like they're lookin' for a certain kind o' woman. And that ain't me!"

"Doesn't matter. They've evidently decided you are the one person they want. If you were to pull out, you'd be bucking city hall and, more than that, offending Scheisser-Dunneville, Johnny's personal manager. Of course, they'll promise you shopping and other perks. Anyway, their high card is that, for you, there ain't no goin' back to the classroom."

"Truth is I've got a card of my own. I can spill details of what took place prior to Johnny's getting shot. Stuff that has never come out and would be eaten up by his ex-wife's lawyer."

"Oh, I'd stay away from that. Hurt him and you hurt yourself. One thing I'm sure you can count on is that however much of a snake this Johnny can be, he'll bust his butt to do good by you. That's your leverage."

"Yes, I know he likes me, but how did you come to know?"

"Remember how Reform talked about the sad state of public education? Well, Johnny took them on. He called a press conference and started trumpeting his accomplishments. It wasn't just that you were his star accomplisher. The light in his eyes when he talked about you . . . well, that told it all. Unfortunately, I wasn't the only one who noticed.

"Mario was there and so was Scheisser-Dunneville [SD], who is swiftly making himself The Party's power. Seeing Johnny knock down his critics, SD decided on the spot that he was looking for the next mayor. And lookin' at you, he sees who's gonna cinch his election. Think about it."

Addie wished she hadn't heard any of this. She wondered if she would survive this crazy political stuff while waiting for Jay. She had felt adrift going in to see Tom and now was coming out minus a life raft.

"Got some aspirin?"

She welcomed Tom's good-bye hug when he drove her home. He put a little gift wrapped item in her hand and wanted her to stay in touch. "Keep in mind, you've got some leverage with these people. It should help."

CHAPTER 48

"Lots She Got Anyway"

At night, the hulking Victorian City Hall rising from a low hill in the center of town looked like a crouching sphinx with a cyclopean eye in the center of its forehead, provided by the light shining from a shaded second floor window. Across the street on the left was the local Savings and Loan with its Greek Revival frontage, a remodeling insisted on by its major stockholders—the sister matriarchs Rosa and Josephine Dimallo—who, now that they had the money, insisted on the style.

Next to it was the *Morning Messenger*, the city's one daily newspaper, run (it was said) by the supposedly anonymous political machine familiarly known as The Party. It printed a generally unflattering picture of matters Puerto Rican and wasn't much better on the Blacks. When the troubles broke out, it would be one of the first buildings to be torched.

Flanking the city hall on the other side was the town's exclusive haberdashery, "Brenerton's," noted for its tailored suits made (they said) from imported fabric; and next door was "Enchanté," the counterpart lady's upscale dress shop, favorite haunt of politicians' mistresses and occasionally of their wives. Looking around at the enameled facades and polished brass doorplates, Addie wondered how she could ever fit in with any of this—even temporarily.

She stopped in the ladies' room to hastily check her makeup and adjust her dress before being ushered into the conference room, where Johnny and three cronies in dark suits and light blue ties got up to greet her with fixed smiles and inclined heads. After the youngest of them left, nodding some whispered instruction from the take-charge fellow at the head of the table, Johnny introduced the other two; but their names flew by her.

Domo Sr., the little guy with the simian build, outsized arms, and puffed–up boxer's face moved his chair over to the door and took out a book, inside which he opened the racing form. Harmless as he might look, he was a person to be reckoned with as she would learn. Desired backup would have been his spitting image of a son, DJ (also not to be trifled with), invisible until needed—supposedly in between bank heists. For Addie, *anything*. Just walking in, she wished that he were here instead of his racetrack papa.

Mr. Take-Charge, obviously the boss turned campaign manager, who waved Domo to his post, reseated himself in the middle of the table; and Johnny eased Addie into a chair directly across from him. Sensing she didn't realize who he was, Johnny told her again that this was Chick Dunneville as if the name in itself should have rung a bell. On the contrary, all she could think of was that with his red brush cut and small-beaked nose mounted on a fleshy face, there was indeed something of the barnyard look about him—an impression instantly dispelled, however, by his commanding tone of voice, spoken from the side of his mouth when emphasis was needed. *So this was the monster*, Addie mused.

Johnny had started out with some pleasantries about how good Addie was looking and how great it was to have her onboard when Chick cut him off.

"Miss Heiss, let me come up front with you. Our opponent has a wife who is a looker, and so far, she's been a big plus for him. Now he's none too subtle about tryin' to make Johnny look bad without a wife, on top of which they're throwin' us a low one about past womanizing and an ex-wife just outta jail. Never mind that the ex is workin' for them behind the scenes. So what we need is an attractive female who's always there smiling up at Johnny and radiating support. You've seen the Norman Rockwell stuff, haven't you?"

"Yes, and I'm definitely not Rockwell stuff. It's corn and pretty stale corn, at that. I know what you mean, but I have to say you're talkin' me out of this deal."

"Frankly, that's just the kind of woman we want—honest, innocent, modest, who doesn't think she's God's gift. Just the opposite of that showboat which Mr. Reform has. We want the neat and pretty type, like yourself, who makes it with shop girls and housewives. Everybody's sister. Corny? Okay, but it works. You'd be surprised how innocence goes over with the men. Just ask Johnny." In whose direction, he gave a little cackle.

"If I can speak frankly too, I can tell you I'm none of that either."

"You don't understand. You don't have to be. You just have to look the part. And lookin' at you, we think you do."

Running on through her, he went on to say "Oh no, it'll be easy. All you have to do is sit on the platform when he's talkin', smile, and cross your legs. Maybe expose a little thigh. The point is, like I said, we need to have somebody who will show up Quickie-Dickie's Hollywood Missus for what she is. A flashy brunette wearing designer clothes who walks around with her nose in the air. Right now, they promote her as class, and she's doin' lotsa good for him. But people ain't all that dumb. When they see you, they'll notice the difference. You're for real. She ain't."

"How come me?" she asked, looking at Johnny. "I'm not an actress, which is what you just described. There have to be others who would do much better at it."

"Point of fact, there was another. She was real eager for the job when she heard what went with it. But then her boyfriend got her pregnant, so she mentioned you. Says it shoulda been you in the first place. And it comes to our attention you and Johnny are . . . uhm . . . friends. He showed us the picture of you in the paper with the kindergarten kids all over you. Good stuff. That fits in with the pitch we wanna make. Let me point out that with this job, you get lotsa goodies. We run a tight ship, you know, not a cheap one."

"Since we're talking frankly, may I ask what you have in mind when you picture me in some kind of devoted relationship to

Johnny? To put it bluntly, I'm not going to be sitting up there looking like I'm his whore—however innocent a one."

Johnny blanched, but Chick came out with a hearty laugh. "What! You come across like a floozy? I doubt it. You'll be exactly what you're supposed to be. An official campaign aide, an ID hanger around your neck, part of our team. It can seem like you have an interest in one another, but that look of yours will show it's good, clean stuff. Leave it to Bozo here to do his part. Or else." This was said with a mean look at Johnny and a mock jab to the ribs.

After a pause and looking around with a sideways smile, he went on. "Hey, on the other hand, should anything personal develop . . . well, that could turn out to be a big plus!" He cast a none-too-subtle wink at Johnny.

"Listen, I didn't volunteer to come here. You're making this less and less interesting to me. I need the money, but forget it if there's supposed to be some kind of phony-baloney romance here." Biting off her words, she let her resentment show.

Johnny was tapping his fingers nervously on a briefcase, but to his surprise, Dunneville was not the least bit annoyed. "You're quite right. Let's stick to business. You know why we lost the city hall twice in a row? We didn't get the women's vote. You know how women think. They—"

Cutting him off, Addie blurted out, "Indeed, I know exactly how women think. Obviously, you don't."

Dunneville's eyebrows went up, and Domo's book hit the floor. They couldn't have been more startled if she had dropped a bag of dog poop on the table.

Not waiting for a response, Addie went on, "Yes, women think differently from men, and thank goodness they do! You can't buy their vote by sweet-talking them. You guys keep treating us like kids. You've got to show you can do things that matter to women. And if you want to know what, I can tell you more than you'll want to hear."

"Wow!" Fake panting, Dunneville acted like he was just getting his breath back. "Hey, you're gonna make one helluva campaigner. By all means, give us your ideas. We'll run 'em by the speech writers." He motioned toward the two nonentities sitting at the back of the room. "You know, on second thought, we might just turn you loose."

"Don't count your chickens."

"I understand, but I'm not sure you do. You're thinking politics is a dirty business, and you—yeah, I mean you, ladies—want things done clean and proper. But, Miss Heiss, it's not just an election. This party against the other . . . That's a side show. Gives the press a circus to amuse the people with. The same with Reform. Reform sounds good, but it ain't practical . . ."

She cut in and the eyebrows went up again. "Please, I don't need a course in civics! Had that in high school. I want to know what you want and what you're gonna pay for it."

"Okay. One more point and I'm finished. Reformers here are fakes. They have these pie-in-the-sky ideas but no idea of what it costs, and our people on city council stymie them. So the public says this stinks. Nothing's getting done. Truth is what it comes down to is business. There are major construction contracts coming up for bids, some long term, to last many years."

He got up and walked around the table in thought, gripping his chin. He motioned Domo to pour her another cup of coffee and continued. "We know how to get things done. So we're talkin' money. And I mean *lots*. Right now Reform has attracted good, clean Republican money. Only nothing gets done. No streets paved. If we recapture city hall, the streets are taken care of, the garbage truck's on schedule, the people are served. And you'd be part of it, understand? After the election, you're on your own—provided, of course, you don't embarrass us. Meanwhile, we're taking care of you *bigtime* like we do all our friends."

"Meaning what?" She couldn't resist. *Could he, for the hell of it, put a figure on what all my play-acting might be worth to them?*

"What?" *He didn't get it?* Taking in that forced incredulous look of his, she thought she'd seen this guy somewhere but couldn't remember where. Maybe in a New Yorker cartoon.

"The payoff. What's in it for me?"

"Well, you are a smart girl. Usually people who work for us don't ask. However, for openers, how about a ritzy Heights town house? A whole new wardrobe—that you keep. A charge account at Enchanté. Use of a car. A chauffeur. Pin money. And a bonus tied to how big he wins. Like I say, we're not playin' nickel-dime poker."

"And if he loses?"

"He won't. And neither will you."

The youngish honcho came in with the pizza cart, and several other dress-alike operatives filed in with him (the Team); but she said she understood all she wanted to for now, wasn't hungry, and asked to be driven home. Johnny gave Dunneville a look and received one and, following an okay, had an arm around her while secretly dropping a slip of paper into her handbag.

Just then, who else appears as the chauffeur but Rocco? *Just returned from Argentina, didn't he?* He explained that sometimes he drove, and sometimes DJ. He was Mario with a French mustache and barber-trimmed beard. Not exactly Rouault's Jesus.

"Perchance, Mario sent you to spy on me?"

"Wouldn't be a bad idea. Careful when you see the Whimp. Have a Psychologist talkin' to him, they say. And my regards to your dad."

Chick called to her as she went out, giving her the zip-up sign and adding "Keep in mind, we gamble in poker, never in elections."

CHAPTER 49

"It Could Not Be"

The Monday _Morning Messenger_ arrived a little later than usual. She was about to toss it onto the table as she left for the bus, but it unfolded; and the screaming headline sent her reeling.

"Oh no! Nooo! It cannot be!"

"'Beloved priest dies. Poisoning suspected. Housekeeper and handyman held for questioning.'"

Her eyes blurred. She read on hastily, catching bits and pieces. "Found by sexton in basement . . . Coroner's initial finding poisoning . . . regurgitation at side of mouth . . . internal hemorrhaging, organs collapsed. Rat's bane bought for newly hired handyman sleeping on cot in basement . . . warfarin base.

"'Poor box emptied. Enriched by priest's appeal . . . bills stuffed in stocking of newly hired housekeeper, partially deaf . . . In Spanish said she was poor, wasn't she? Feared she'd be out of work and back on the city hall steps. Handyman, also Puerto Rican, thought to have been accomplice . . . drifter, no known address . . . had been saved from life of drugs by priest, thought to have poisoned him when found stealing to support habit . . . Suspicious acting, gives incoherent answers.'

"Why poison? . . . 'motive unclear. Priest good to those people, championed their rights. . . . had just done emotional marriage ceremony for influential family, community leaders . . . had asked fellow priest to do Sunday mass on his behalf . . . failed to attend meeting wherein he was to seek help for nondenominational nursery school. City in shock and disbelief . . . people flock to church . . . police line setup. Interrogation of suspects continuing.'"

They republished the photograph of Whimpy embracing Jay, which was captioned "Victory over Drugs: Priest to the Rescue."

Unable to go on with it, she crumpled the paper, threw herself down on the bed, and cried into her pillow. Rocking from side to side, carelessly banging her head against the wall, she wailed out his name, reaching a crescendo of near hysteria in which she tore at the sheets and slammed her face into the mattress.

When at length she sat up, wanting to compose herself, she caught a glimpse of her face in the mirror—shiny, wet, red, and scrunched—and the effort gave way to compulsive sobs that left her short of breath. She would break down again before her head began to clear, and it came over her that the racking pain would fruitlessly perpetuate itself unless she was ready to deal with the agony of guilt.

"How else," she half whispered, "but to find healing within myself."

Her chest still heaving, she began by dropping to her knees, wanting to pray with true intent for the first time in her life. But it didn't go very well. She started with a plea that Jesus would be kind to this good priest—who was himself so kind to others, so great in soul, so loving. She also asked Jesus to ease the pain that burned in her heart, and with that, she choked up. She had additional thoughts but no words for them. A deep sense of futility came over her.

She just stayed down on her knees in silence until opening her blurry eyes, she called out "Jay! Jay, forgive me. Do forgive me, please! Jesus knows there was no evil in our loving. Surely no sin. Whatever wrong there might have been will be counted against me alone."

There was a knock on the door, followed by more insistent knocking; but she didn't move. She decided to take a relaxation pill Tom had given her and drowsed off. On getting up, she rubbed her eyes not knowing for a moment where she was.

Looking out her window in the fading light, she fixated the path running through the overgrown backyard and had a vision of it's becoming a set of labia that opened up into a bottomless chasm with naked women (she among them) clawing helplessly at the walls of raw red earth and trying to lift themselves out. They were weeping blood and crying out "Enough, Genug, Bastante. No more, Nicht Mehr, No más!"

She joined in, and hearing her own voice, she came to with a start. She was biting her bottom lip. "No more." Lying there like a stunned fish, she could neither eat nor sleep. Needing air, she took a walk around the block. People she ran into were wearing black.

Looking for a way to console herself, she tried to silence her envy of people who believed in the conventional End in the Sky. It was as hard for her to conceive it as it was not to. The soul for her was eternal; Jay's certainly. She was down on her knees again, palms clasped, let the tears flow, and gasped for words that would not come.

She babbled incoherent prayers—none of which could stifle the utter sorrow of it all.

CHAPTER 50

"Betsy Reporting"

The funeral would be several days off. She did not want to go; but she knew she wouldn't be able to keep herself from going—particularly when late the next day, Otts called and said they should go together. She assumed he would be broken up, but she should have known better. Before she could get a word in, Otts went on a tear.

"The new housekeeper! A deaf thief. And, Holy Toledo, I get a priest killer. This Jesus-lookin' young man, thin like a noodle, quiet like a ghost. Who would have guessed? Okay at cleaning—anything monotonous—but ruined the food. Stood there absentminded, stirring and stirring and overcooking the stew. Finally burned it to the pot. I was told he would be good and very quiet. Quiet, okay. But good? Good for nothing!

"Imagine . . . I had to cook for him! You saw the picture in the paper. Kills the priest who gave him work and a place to sleep. I didn't like him the first time I saw him. Imagine what he coulda done here—for practice. Donnerwetter noch a Mal. The Puerto Rican lady, she doesn't hear. This PR boy, he doesn't talk.

"I was expecting a nice middle-aged lady who could keep me company. Imagine he wanted to sleep here so he wouldn't have to go back and forth from the church. The nerve of him! He asks do I have a daughter. I told him I have two but none for him. He stinks. I tell him he should take a bath for a change. He says he's afraid of water. He went swimming in the river as a kid and near drowned. I went to mass to tell the priest I was better off alone. Well, we all make mistakes, but . . . look. I'm crossing myself just to think about it."

Addie didn't much mind the chatter. She only half listened, and it was good to hear a voice. He wanted to know about her coming over when there was a knock on the door again. She said she'd call him back.

A key turned in the latch; and in came bumbling Betsy, tripping over the doormat in her stiletto heels and out of breath as usual. She wasn't so much clumsy as always in a hurry. She took in Addie's red eyes and puffy face without comment, saying Johnny was concerned there was no answer when he came by earlier; then, he remembered that Betsy had a key and told her to take Addie shopping.

"Shopping, shopping, honey! On their dough. How about that? Baby, let's go."

Looking her over, Addie said it was plain to see that she'd already done hers. Betsy did a spin to show off her mink-trimmed coat and, taking it off, did another spin to show her frilly maternity dress. She stuck out a leg and flipped her ankle so Addie could get a closer look at her sparkling gold pumps.

"Can't wear these much longer. Shouldn't be wearin' 'em now!" Oh, Addie! You hadn't heard, had you, about my being one of Dunneville's secretaries? He's got one for the politics, another for the law office, and probably still others for whatever. One, I'm sure, to suck him off before he gave an important speech. I'm not quite sure which one I'm supposed to be, except it seemed a lot like the first."

She said that Sonny (keeping her endearment for Louey) got her the job. "They like to keep things in the family, you know."

She'd learned all about the great impression Addie made at her interview. She wished that she could have done the thing with Johnny.

"Be quite a gag, wouldn't it," she continued, "if he gives a talk and I'm standin' there belly out, and they look at him standin' next to me and they go 'Hmm, so he's the one'?

"Hate The Party candidate's stuck-up wife, Laureen. With a name like that, you had to know she was from money—and a bitch besides. Thinks her rear end don't stink. Anyway, even if it wasn't for this [patting her belly], I knew Johnny would still have found a way to bring you in with him. I had insisted you were perfect for it."

Addie thanked her, but she couldn't think about shopping. She hadn't been able to do much thinking about the whole affair, what with Father Jay's passing and her father being unable to cope now that Hannah was gone.

"They want you to get going on this, you know. They have fundraisers set up and rallies all around town. But I guess I can explain to 'em. You're wantin' a little more time. It oughta be okay to wait till after the funeral since that's what everybody's talkin' about anyway. But, hey, isn't it exciting? Doctor says it's gonna be a pretty big kid—a boy, I hope, or Sonny says we'll have to go back to the well till we get one, and you know what that does to the figure . . .

"Heard yours got their attention. Old Dunneville's always has an eye out. Kinda hinted he might have a place for you after the election. Gets a look from Johnny and says he's kiddin'. He's got this bug up his ass that women's vote is gonna make the difference. Of course, you and me know these guys don't give a royal umph for the women. They say swing the wives and yah swing the men. Shows you how much they know . . ."

She rambled on, parroting Dunneville's supposed campaign strategy.

Betsy was in a talking mood as when she wasn't, and once launched, it could cover quite a bit of territory. Annoying as it became, it didn't really annoy Addie, blunting as it did the collapse of her world; then, too, there was the matter of her responsibility with an add-on for the Whimp. *What, for goodness' sake, did I drive him to!* Thinking about it had become intolerable.

She suddenly felt the need to get some fresh air, bleak as it looked outside on an overcast November day. So they had themselves a walk in dismal Westside Park—on other occasions, a refuge. With the trees being bare and the leaves having been piled up in long, brown mounds, it wasn't an inviting landscape but was suitable for her mood. Disregarding the chill, she inhaled deeply as if that would chase correspondingly dismal thoughts. Betsy's empty chatter about available sales downtown flew by her the way an express train would speed through the local station. Finally, she'd had about all she needed of the walk and the chatter.

"Please, Betsy, hold all that. I've got to get in to see poor Whimpy in the lockup. Since you have this in with Dunneville, can't you use his name with somebody to arrange it?"

"Me? No. But I think Sonny can. He knows the chief. Yeah, maybe we could all go . . . Why would that damned fool do such a crazy thing? Awful, huh? He's mad! And I mean *mad* mad too, but at least, that's got him eatin' again.

"And, say, did you know Mario has it figured out that the Whimp knows who killed the baron? His mad father, the typical Irish hothead. That's why he's still on the lamb. Mario's glad they've got Whimp where he can be interrogated. Mario claims you fit into this puzzle. Sonny wants to talk to him about gettin'—"

"Please, first me. The visit, okay?"

"But listen, I wouldn't get too involved with anything like that. Keep in mind, there's this image they're counting on. Not like the little princess in the fairy tale but, you know . . ."

And she was off again. Uneasy as she was, Addie had to ride along.

"If you wanna get an idea of how they set you up, come and see the town house they got for us. Orange drapes so it's always sunny. A pink marble dining room table with chrome molding. Overstuffed couch. TV practically covers the whole wall. A picture of Jesus over the mantle. Currier and Ives winter scenes on the living room walls. Precious Moments figurines on the end tables . . .

"A cute cartoon in the bathroom with a kid on the seat and a German title, *Dukatenscheisser*. The kid squeezes out gold coins. Our bedroom's got a four-poster. And oh my! Did you ever do it on a waterbed? Of course, we got to do some of our own decoratin'!

Like Sonny got a perpetual motion gadget with two piggies doin' it to a burlesque tune. You gotta see the pictures he's got in his study. He's an ass man."

"Good. But just now, be a friend and see if Sonny can't get through to the chief today."

"That ain't gonna be easy. You heard about those rumblin's in the Puerto Rican ghetto, didn't you? They're claimin' Whimpy's one of their own and talkin' protest again. You must've read what their leader said in the paper. That uncle of Whimpy's, Gordo, built like a bowling ball. He never got over what happened to his sister, Whimp's mother. Like they're gettin' blamed again whenever something bad happens.

"Says how could one of them—good Catholics that they are—go and steal from a priest, and then another of them gets mad and poisons him when he finds out. Does that make any sense? And besides, this priest was on their side. Guess the one they call Gordo, his fatso uncle, has a point, you know."

"All the more reason I've got to see the Whimp. Lockup ain't right for him. Do they want pickets at the police station again? Tell Sonny to lean on the chief. I gotta get in."

"You want 'em to interrogate you?"

"The way he's sounding off, it's like he wants 'em to think he's got a piece of poisoning his benefactor. He sure can play crazy. His way of makin' them crazy."

PART VI

WHIMPY IN CHAINS: RIOTS

CHAPTER 51

"Whimpy Holds Forth"

Hobbling in in leg irons, he had the skeletal look of a hostage fresh out of some dank medieval dungeon. His finger bones seemed like they would come through the skin as he gripped the counter to steady himself for sitting. Through the wire mesh, his long face looked a lot like it belonged on one of the apostles in the church windows.

The broad-bellied guard told her that she could stay for no more than fifteen minutes and waddled over to a stool at the far end of the counter where he could watch. Whimpy's eyes looked like two pee holes in the snow, but they suddenly bugged out when he saw Addie. He kept asking how she got there since they said he wasn't even going to see a lawyer yet, let alone his uncle with the temper.

"Guess you don't recognize your lone sister," she said. "What are the leg irons all about and this jump suit? What are they charging you with anyway?"

"Nothin' so far but they're workin' on it. On me, actually, till they can put something together. Right now they're calling it suspicion of murder and a potential danger to society, which means—they say—I can be held without bond pending arraignment. They keep asking the same questions and take notes. First, one guy then another. I give them different stories.

"Like, 'Where's the rest of the rat poison?' 'Oh, I hid it in the attic.' 'There ain't no attic in the church, dammit!' [They forget he was found in the rectory. Ha!] Then I tell the other guy that last time I knew, it was right there under my cot. Er, they didn't find it? "The only time they roughed me up was when I said, 'Him and me . . . We were gettin' it on."

"That's the third degree. They can't do that."

"Oh, can't they? Nothing they can't do, especially now that they've got the whole city riled about me. You know, like they're ready for slivers under the thumbnail, acid on my nuts. They want a neat little confession—three words—and soon, like, tomorrow morning."

"What's the rush? You told them you didn't do it, didn't you?"

"So far, whatever they put to me, I don't say no."

"What!"

"If I agree to everything, it gets 'em screwed up. They can't come up empty on this one, and they want something before the funeral so they can make people feel better—especially about themselves.

"But I don't want 'em to have what they may yet get, so I'm stalling. Think about it. Suppose I'm able to get some legal eagle in here, which is what I'll insist on if I want out now. First thing he'd want me to do is plead innocent, regardless. He checks with the sexton, the coroner, the pharmacist.

"Bingo! He floats the idea it was a suicide. Big sensation. The paper blows it up. You know what the Church would do, don't you? It'd be a second death for Jay and *worse*."

"But tell me you for sure didn't have anything to do with it, right?"

"Of course I did."

"You put that rat poison . . . Where? In his evening tea?"

"No, not that way. There were no rats in the rectory basement. He was depressed and felt a pain in his chest. He'd been taking something for his heart problem, a blood thinner, something they say that also goes into rat poison—warfarin, 30mg pills. Makes the rats bleed internally. Us too if we take too much.

"He probably was able to get himself a refill Saturday morning at the hospital pharmacy without contacting his doctor. You know how it was around town. Anything for Father Jay. The coroner found it in his system, so stupid as he is, all he had to say was that from the level of the stuff that showed up in his blood and what was seen in his stomach, Jay must have OD'd. No one could shove all those pills down his throat. But like the good Catholic he was, the well-meaning coroner figures if people want to think 'poisoning,' it's okay with him."

"Why would Jay do such a thing? I take it you knew about us. The way we were feeling . . . it was so big for both of us. I was sure we'd find an out. You get carried away and your head doesn't matter—it's mush!"

"Why? Yeah, why, for sure, would he? I knew about you and him, but there's something about him and me you don't know."

"No. Please don't tell me that."

"It's true. Remember him coming to my well-advertised rescue? There I was, a prime example of his social involvement. We hugged. He kissed me on both cheeks. I hugged back, and we just hung there in each other's clasp. But he suddenly went rigid, like an electric current had run through him, and he pulled loose. That stopped it.

"It was because of him and only because of him that I kicked that habit. Since I'd straightened myself out, I could see how he wanted to straighten himself out. And there was you. You were his rescue. What he was for me, you were for him. Having found you, the last thing in the world he wanted was to put me up in the rectory. But he did do it. For you."

"I don't believe it. How do you know that?"

"We were close. I read him. Jay felt if I just kept my distance, he'd be all right. So I asked your father couldn't I sleep at his place. I'd get more work done. No travelin' back 'n forth. I could see it was tempting for a minute ['Ah, more work'], but then the thought of it gets him shook up. He looks at me like I'm gonna knife him in his sleep."

"You couldn't have been reading him right."

"Something else you should know. Jay not only played the role of the good and caring priest, he was one. You probably noticed he was an intellectual. He belonged to a group of liberal priests, activists, who had their own little underground. One of them, a friend of Jay's, got married. His ordination meant he could celebrate mass and perform the other sacraments, but obviously his being married meant the opposite.

"He still felt himself like what a good priest should be. Had been to Mexico to help the peasants. When he went back and carried on his priestly duties like he was for real, they said he was talking revolution. Word got out and somebody shot him. The liberals held a mass for him and circulated a statement for a dialogue within the Church on the nature of sexuality and on priests being given a choice of marriage or celibacy. Went over like a rock.

"Jay was pushin' the statement against awesome opposition. There was even talk of ex-communication. So think about what was percolatin' in his head. The Church was a heavy weight on him, made heavier by you. He wanted both and it was rippin' him apart."

"It was because he saw he couldn't have both then . . ."

"Like I say, it tore at him, but that wasn't the whole story. He came back from the wedding shortly before I had returned from your dad's. Knowing how rotten he felt, I went looking for him and found him all alone in the sanctuary, on his knees in front of the altar, his hands clasped, lips moving. He gave a sudden cry like he'd been hit by an arrow and fell facedown on the red carpeting and beat it with his fist."

"Oh, poor, poor Jay!"

"I came to him, called his name, and helped him to his feet. He seemed about to collapse in my arms but came to and hugged me. But I mean hugged. I hugged him back and we stood there like that, clamped together, him holding on for dear life. Talk about agony. He was shivering head to toe. Imagine a monkey in the claws of a lion—better still, Saint Anthony tormented by demons.

"For an instant, he looked upwards trying to pull himself together but then pushed me away and let out a long, drawn-out 'Nooo!'" and called me Satan. I told him it was all right, no one would know. And at that, he howled like the arrow had gone clear through him. 'Beast, beast that you are! We know. And that is enough!' He grabbed me by the neck and dug his nails into my flesh like he meant to choke me on the spot. He threw me down and rushed out the door.'"

Whimpy paused. She was trying to control herself, but the sobs kept coming; and she sat there shaking, her hands covering her face.

"Here, take a look. You can still see the scratch marks. They keep asking did I get into a fight with the Father. I tell 'em 'Yeah, whatta yah think? We loved one another.' 'What!' they yell. 'Lyin' bastard!' 'You people don't know what love is,' I yell back. So they're callin' in a psychologist."

"Why do you tell them such things? You know you don't have to tell them anything. It's the law. Didn't they read you that thing about self-incrimination or whatever it is?"

"I want to talk. I get 'em all screwed up. Like—really—what would they know about love?"

"Do you have to die too?"

"They know my people would blow this town sky-high."

"There's no need for any of that. After the funeral, a decent lawyer could show what the facts are and get you out of here."

"Oh yeah, just like that," he said, snapping his fingers. "Chances are the DA will scare up a don't-give-a-shit public defender who, if he wants to get anywhere in this town, will know how far to take it."

"But the facts . . . Like there were no rats to poison. No question he OD'd, right?"

"Yeah, the facts. It's crazy. They asked the pharmacist, 'Did Jay come in for something Saturday morning?' He says he can't remember. He was pretty busy. Not remember Father Jay? Anyway, a patient's prescription should be confidential, he claims.

"Baloney! He doesn't want it known he was illegally doing the priest a favor when there was no refill on the prescription. The police have already cooked some of the facts. The paper quotes them as saying he was found in the basement. No way. Just before

I got taken in, the sexton told me he found him on his bed—buck naked—arms out in the form of the cross, a black smudge on his forehead. Jay once told me Jesus saw the cross as a sign of human fallibility."

"Why, for goodness' sake, did you kiss him?"

"Yeah, I don't know. It was kinda spontaneous. I felt for him. Maybe, deep down, I did it because . . . because I knew I shouldn't. He was a priest. And . . ."

"That turned you on."

He nodded. His eyes were swimming. "Turned you on too."

"True but not for the same reason. It was me that killed him. I spent the night with him."

"I know. But you're wrong. You sent him to the edge. I pushed him over."

CHAPTER 52

"Tom Gets Involved"

According to Addie's scribbled notes, he lay in state for all of two days. The line outside the church curled around two blocks. It did seem as if the whole town was in mourning. Johnny, who had nominated himself to give the eulogy, remarked that even the atheists wore black. Jay was universally loved but not without reservation by the Church hierarchy, which was sternly at odds with his liberal clique and was about to give him hark from the tomb.

True, there were those among the laity who might find it tempting to become cafeteria Catholics. But a priest? Still, a priest had been murdered. It was decided that an official funeral mass exclusively for the clergy would precede the public ceremony. The big city cardinal, who was outraged by the infamous request for dialogue, declined to attend and asked the bishop from a neighboring diocese to represent him.

As the procession made its way up the church steps, one could see the mitered heads of two bishops, whose purple sashed soutanes flashed in the sun as they turned to bless the assemblage of priests in their train. Bringing up the rear was a group of acolytes in their white surplices. Knowing the delicacy of the situation, people wondered how the ceremony would be handled.

But Father Tim, Jay's baby-faced assistant, later made a point of assuring the congregation that it had been a very moving service done with fitting dignity and compassion—as was the great public mass presided over by their local bishop, reading passages from 1 Cor. 15 ("For as in Adam all die, even so in Christ shall all be made alive.") and emphasizing Jay's humanity and dedication to the Church's mission.

However, through the grapevine, it was learned that the cardinal's representative had had some rather blunt words about deviations from doctrine. He too cited 1 Cor. 15:58, carefully looking over his flock as he gave the concluding verse, "Therefore, my beloved brethren, be ye stedfast, unmoveable, always abounding in the work of the Lord, forasmuch as ye know that your labour is not vain in the Lord."

She couldn't bring herself to get in line. *What if I pass out seeing him there?* It took all she could muster just to accompany Otts when he insisted they couldn't be the only two people in town who didn't show up. She said for him to go by the coffin so long as he spared her the details. She'd wait for him in the library across the street.

She said, "My stomach is misbehaving."

"Really?" he looked at her skeptically.

She sat herself down in a quiet corner of the periodical reading room, staring at the brick wall beside the stacks, undisturbed by the snores of a fragrant tramp resting his head on the table.

She jumped at a tap on the arm. "Tom!"

"I saw you go in."

He'd had his session with Whimpy, who said to tell her he was going to be okay. More than that, Tom said he really shouldn't go into for the time being. Asking him to sit for a minute, she said she had to have a hint of how it went.

"Well, as you know, he's a handful. Not just difficult. He's perverse. Says things like he wants to die to save Jay. Tells me he has no fear of judgment and has none for Jay. Says Jesus will judge them sanely unlike the Church, which he didn't trust to help the down and out."

"I know. Whimp goes on like that, wanting to alienate everybody. Like, 'Do what you want! You can't hurt me any more than I'm already hurting.' If he had such a thing about Jay, I ask point-blank why did he kill him, and he says it's because he loved him. Go figure."

"But you, of course, know he didn't do it. Are you the one who's supposed to assure the court he's not too crazy to stand trial?"

"I'm not ready to assure anything. My report will be strictly professional. But look, I've got to get back in line. Dad's holding my place."

"Why are you being so elusive?"

"Well, it's hard to know who he's protecting."

"Certainly not himself."

"True. And certainly not his people. We've heard from his uncle Gordo about that."

"Surely not the Church though it could use some protecting."

"What makes you say that?"

"Well, Jay was known to have been something of a rebel. At odds with the bishop and the hierarchy. Stuff the Church doesn't want to come out."

"So they're the ones who wanted him out of the way? Great story but this ain't the Church of the Borgias."

"What you've got to think about, Tom, is if you find the Whimp can't go to trial, they'll send him downstate to the funny farm, where he gets lost maybe for life like the baron's daughter. And if you say he's not all that crazy, there's no judge or jury that won't hang a self-confessed priest killer."

"Yes, it's a dilemma. But if I can see what this prisoner is up to—and you too—you're all but telling me the way out makes no sense. Can anybody believe that this priest, who had doctrine in his very blood would—regardless of his social views—deliberately condemn his soul to burn unto eternity?"

"You're making our point all right. Though more likely, it'd be purgatory. But to answer your question, he and Whimpy were two of a kind. Either one would willingly burn for what's true to him. However, it's just as well nobody would believe it. And by the way, Jay was already on the way, and I'll be there with him. Whimpy to join us."

"You lose me."

"But you don't have to lose him, Tom, if, friend that you've always been, you can persuade that awesome father of yours to throw his legal weight around on poor Whimpy's behalf. Particularly since Mario wants a shot at him."

"You know, if I'm reading him right, this creep seems to have been jealous of you."

"I was Jay's last stop."

"Amorous ping-pong! What next? Addie, baby, you never cease to amaze me."

"Stay tuned."

CHAPTER 53

"Post Eulogy Talk:
Otts's Remembrance"

Otts insisted that she come over for the eulogy. It had already been droning on for a bit with Johnny intoning his equivalent of high seriousness. She let it fly by, catching a chance phrase here and there that sounded just short of lugubrious. Still, he did sincerely feel the loss, and though he hit it a little hard, he initially got "Amens" at every pause.

"Everybody's priest . . . a real human being . . . Hand outstretched . . . Oil on troubled race relations . . . Wanted us to make it better . . . Me? . . . I can speak personally . . . Made mistakes, but his heart was always open . . . Richer in spirit for having had him here . . . Great loss but, to our people, never lost . . . Lives with us yet."

Huffin' and puffin', poor ole Johnny didn't miss a cliché. Just when you thought he'd finished, on he went with stories. It wasn't easy sitting there. Otts forgot the cushions. Dunneville, off to the side, tried to give him the cut cue; but invincible Johnny was too much into it. He genuinely liked Jay and had, in fact, played handball with him; and he obviously felt he had to do justice to him, unfortunately to the hilt.

Also unfortunately, he remained oblivious to the sound of rustling in the pews. There was scattered coughing, kids had to be shushed, and heads were turning back toward the doors. Addie looked around. *Wouldn't somebody tell him more is less?*

Those who remained attentive were mainly awed by the banks of flowers that covered the entire sanctuary: there were tiers on tiers of red, white, and pink carnations; large, yellow chrysanthemums; white and purple daisies; red, yellow, pink and white roses; lush orange gladioluses; even pots of red tulips interspersed with Boston ferns and sprigs of baby's breath. A whole row was given to stately white lilies flanked by evergreen fronds and potted palms. People had rushed in their last-minute bouquets, followed by pots of red geraniums. They declared that others were on the way.

The effect was kaleidoscopic: flowers upon flowers cascaded down on the coffin and practically buried it. That ocean of color was all the small talk once the service was over. People seemed to have had about as much solemnity as they could handle for one day.

Their small group was joined by the Klagemanns on the way out, and Iris was dimly heard talking in her most discreet stage whisper (heard by all within earshot) about how beautiful he looked—made up almost like a woman, she thought, with eyeliner, lipstick, and rouge, as well as powder with blush doubled on his cheeks. She figured Niebettler, the be-all and end-all expensive cosmetologist, must have been brought back for emergency assignment from the overload which was waiting for him in Chicago.

"And weren't those fake lashes?" Iris wondered. "Reminds me of those famous people we saw in that wax museum. Where was it, George? Las Vegas? No, I think it was Florida."

Johnny appeared out of nowhere and instantly had a python arm around Otts and Addie as, hunched over, he guided them through the crowd to the parking lot. Crunching down the gravel walk, Addie expected him to have some choice reminders of a business nature but was pleasantly surprised when his only communication was a "doin' good" wink while beckoning Betsy to give them a ride home.

Otts looked over at the Klagemanns, and Johnny—generosity written all over his broad face—motioned them to come along. They wondered if there'd be room, but Betsy assured them.

"Hey, wait'll you see the size of my bus!"

It was the long, black limo in which Louey was to be driving the bishops and their entourage to the cemetery in the morning, and otherwise to be shepherding them around town prior to lunch. At the moment, Louey was making arrangements for the Irish wake that was to be held at the Athletic Club.

"Couldn't count the barrels waitin' to be rolled out."

Louey had silently taken over the driver's seat, freeing Betsy from gossip. So the group made themselves comfortable on those plush velvet seats while Betsy and talkative Iris Klagemann detailed the flowers, which looked as if they had magically dropped out of the sky (courtesy of Tough Tony, the vaunted produce king, and delivered by Cow Eddy, who was promoted to front man, actually wanting front office). The city's gratitude was something Tony nonchalantly shook off like cigar ash.

Duly praised for his philanthropy by the business community, Tony had gotten word out that the tower of flowers was expressly donated by his garden store. On the qt, he let it be known he'd appreciate some small change out of the city's discretionary fund to cover "hipping and shandling"—say, something like five grand. He had to tip the help, and of course, good things don't come cheap these days.

He always insisted that even though flowers were just a sideline, when the call went out, he had Cow put on a more-than-decent show—especially for weddings and funerals, wherein no one wanted to be chintzy. For funerals in particular, Tony made sure that Cow really humped himself, like when Nephew Nick's friend walked into a bullet for stealing cases of whiskey from said nephew's saloon (floral arrangement to be obligingly covered by the nephew).

It was said that on command, Cow could have the flowers there before the body was cold. To keep him from getting bored, Tony had allowed Cow to take on some topiary work in the better neighborhoods, where a fifty-percent markup seemed more than fair.

Anyway, shortly after word broke about Father Jay, Cow contacted his workmen, had them in the church before sunrise, and set up bleachers on which the growing display could be mounted. He had emptied florists' reserves for miles around.

Given more lead time, Tony said he would have had orchids via a friend who flew them in from Florida. He did a lot of big-shot puffing but turned scornful when questioned "How much?" pointing out that what he actually made on flowers was chump change. More like charity. Why else would he have put a clown like Cow in charge?

Otts volunteered that those tons of flowers, while a nice gesture for Jay, were a terrible waste. "For that kind of money, they could have put a week's worth of garlic tortillas in every Puerto Rican kitchen. Would stop all the demonstratin'. Fill their bellies and it shuts their mouths—*Nicht*? Next thing you know, they'll be wanting to come into my cheap rent neighborhood. Jews and PRs. Some mix. But Tony wasting all that money? Hard to believe!"

"Not to worry." Betsy was quick to reassure him. "Truth is this guy always lives up to his reputation as one shrewd dude."

She went on to explain that a day after Jay's burial, Tony would have his crew dismantle these properly cooled flowers in preparation for recycling them to fill orders already on Cow's books. A refrigerated truck from his uncle's firm would probably back up to the church, and like clockwork, everything would be loaded and tagged for delivery to far-flung places throughout the state and beyond.

"So," Betsy added, "like I'm tellin' you, it always works out for Tony. The story is you can't have money dealings with him, but that afterwards you walk away wondering how come you're feelin' that cold breeze on your behind. There are people who admire him for that. You know, if a guy wants a good shave, he goes to a barber with the sharpest razor."

Not a word about Jay, Addie noted. *Had they become so quickly bored over his passing? Had their fill even about the mystery of it?* Maybe Johnny's tiresomeness had drained it out of them, which was fine with her. They'd jump at any distraction, and shortly there was one.

As they drove out onto Main Street, where they sat for a while bottled up in traffic, Iris spotted this large hulk of a woman no one had seen before. There was something strange about her, swinging those long arms in unison with that masculine stride of hers. She, for sure, didn't look like a local. She had a funny kind of rounded back like it was padded out somehow. Iris said it made her look like she'd grown a shell.

"Who is she anyhow?" Iris asked. "Gives me the creeps."

"Dunno," Betsy shrugged. "A lady turning into a turtle. But hey, stick around down here, and you'll see all kinds! Ever seen the Deaf and Dumbs on the city hall steps talkin' with their hands? Anyway, should I see if she wants a lift?"

Suddenly, they saw Mario descending on her. Louey gave Betsy the wheel and joined in the greeting. As they were still halted in traffic, she rolled down the window and heard the turtle enunciate "Sean," Whimpy's dad, who had spent some time at the downstate asylum.

In the car, they chuckled as Betsy blew the horn to make her way through traffic. The talk went back to legendary Tony. Once people got started on him, there was no end of stories that were passed around. Otts wanted to chip in with his, saying there might be legal matters coming up with that guy, at the thought of which everybody moaned. Addie, however, was glad to have her father carry on—a welcome digression—for she didn't want people to be wondering why she seemed so down at the mouth when Johnny had gotten everybody so well over it.

Otts recalled it was not too many years ago that Tony had put together a floral extravaganza for his late lamented competitor, a loony old German, feckless Heinzy Hagelmeister, who had had the bad luck one rainy night to wander out onto Tony's muck farm down by the river. Heinzy, who had been drinking, wasn't too steady on his feet in the first place.

It seems that the cold–eyed security guard with the binocs had spotted Heinzy and chased him along the bank till he stumbled into a swamp, where he supposedly got caught in quicksand and drowned. The guard had been on the lookout for Heinzy since he'd been seen surveying those eighty-something acres of prime bottomland in preparation for his lawsuit laying claim to them.

Disillusioned with flowers, it seems Heinzy wanted a new start in something else. He already had a name for the place, River-Run. It had occurred to him in a dream he'd had about the floods that regularly enriched the soil with new deposits of black humus. And he saw his River-Run as an ever blossoming muck farm Eden with rows of billowing lettuce, fat cabbages, hard-stalked celery, and carrots like knockwursts. He had a vision of displacing Tony as salad provisioner for the major restaurants. A far call, of course, since Heinzy was a more fertile dreamer than farmer.

Before continuing, Otts did a throat-clearing "harumpf" to get Addie's attention and told her she might one day have to pursue this thing with him; so she ought to listen. It was learned, he went on, that ailing Uncle Helmut Stolpermeyer, knowing what a bust this prize nephew had been as a florist, had told his lawyer (that long Dutchman) while he was in the hospital that he wanted the German-American Club to get the land.

However, because of his stroke, Helmut couldn't sign the papers; and before anything could be done, he had another stroke and died. So Helmut was declared intestate and Heinzy being disappointed he hadn't been made the heir was so slow in getting back with lawyer Vander that it gave Tony the opening to put in his bid for the land.

When Otts said some members of the club wanted to get with Helmut's lawyer, Betsy had a word of caution for him.

"Look, Mr. Heiss, you've got two good knees and looks like you can see outta both eyes. Personally, if it was me, I think I'd just as soon let well enough alone. You got yourself a look at the flower show they put on, okay?"

That had Otts talking to himself. He mumbled something about the baron; and George Klagemann picked it up, saying he and Otts remembered the baron wouldn't be bullied by the Big D family (Tony's Dimallo clan) or any other.

"They were eager for that land off North Hill Road—you know, the Heights," Otts added. "When the banks started calling the baron's loans, the Ds saw their chance and made a ridiculous offer. But the baron outsmarted them as he'd already had long Vander put it in a trust, and a trust ain't him. Said he'd die before he'd let them get their dirty hands on that land. And to this day, he's got that land locked up in a trust. In the agreement, he charges the Ds outrageous rent, over which they tear their hair and pass it onto home builders. In effect, the baron is victorious, even in death. Somethin' to chew on."

"How come you know all this about the baron?"

"Lots I don't know." Clearing his throat again, Otts went on, "Lemme just say I once had a big trouble with him. But he settled and it turned out okay. Nothing to talk about. Someday maybe everything comes out. Me . . . I think already I said more than I oughta know."

Betsy agreed: the less he knew the better. She reminded them that when the Puerto Ricans complained that Tony wasn't hiring many Hispanics, he promptly fired the three he had and brought in a bunch of Mexican migrants. He built them ten-by-twelve shacks with outhouses and paid them a generous seventy-five cents an hour—a fortune by Mexican standards for dawn-to-dark work, with, after all, half a bread and diluted wine for lunch. The *Morning Messenger* had a front page picture of Tony with a family of thirteen able-bodied hands, kids and all, captioned "Whatta yah mean no Hispanics!"

Seeing this, Otts fumed and, turning to Addie, whispered that the baron had called Tony's bluff—declaring he was an outright fraud, a straw man who had no connection whatsoever with the Mob. Of course, he liked to give the impression that he did for purposes of intimidation, which worked so well that no one had the courage to check it out. The baron's advice: fear him not. He made the charge to Tony's face, which backed him up, giving the baron a weapon to be used in financial negotiations.

CHAPTER 54

"The Flower Carnage"

Out from under the cover of background chatter, Addie found herself confronting the weighty silence of her little apartment. The more she wondered whether she was going to have another sleepless night, the more the thought of it guaranteed that she would. So after much tossing and turning, she got up and finished the bottle of Dago-red. She tried to read a book and found herself just looking at words; nothing worked.

In despair, she picked up the stack of mail that had accumulated. She tore open some dated store ads and was about to pitch the rest but stopped short. *Could Jay have written me? No, it would have been too painful. But, then again . . .* She hastily spread some envelopes on the floor, and sure enough, there were a couple of first class letters.

"Damnation!"

Both were from Principal Dean Schmertz (three days apart) and she opened the latest.

"I notice you unfortunately have not been checking your mailbox. Trust you will open this red-letter one. I want you to please make an appointment as soon as possible. There are some urgent matters we have to talk over now that it has been decided you will be taking a leave of absence . . ."

She skipped over things about "adequate communication," "administrative regulations," and finally "credentials"; then, she got to his having received a memo that spelled out the terms of her leave, which she should be informed about.

There were papers to be signed. No leave without that. Maybe no leave anyway unless . . .

So that's why Johnny didn't want to talk and instead gave her that toothy grin that spelled satisfaction assured! She had forgotten he dropped a note in her handbag as she left Dunny's interview telling her he would take care of the credentials thing, giving her assurance that he had her back. Yes, as promised, he's been looking out for her and, for proof, has a check waiting.

Nonetheless, she was going to have to sit there before that pompous stone-headed principal peering over his glasses as he tried to be ever so gracious in spelling out terms of her "leave." He was sorry but . . . *Did that mean Johnny had or really hadn't gotten me off the hook on credentials? I have to sign first? Whaat!* She was boiling, so she decided that maybe fresh air would help.

Bundled up against the evening chill, with a babushka over her head, she walked dream-like through the soundless streets, in and out of the misty light from street lamps until she found herself at the steps of the church. Inside, the familiar musty smell of the pews mingling with the sweet aroma of the flowers gave her a queasy feeling; and she thought her stomach was going to act up again.

A good portion of the display remained in place. Aha, the workman had just started packaging when, as she'd learn, somebody came by to give them a high sign for the wake.

"Less go, fellas!"

That's why the truck was gone. As Johnny was steering her and Otts out of church, she'd heard the men buzzing about nothing else. Cow Eddy in particular was making big eyes in anticipation.

"All the beer you can drink!"

Sure enough, a crude note was taped to the altar; and it said "Flower Guys On Brake. Be Rite Back Soon. Maybe sometime late. Don't try an' do a Touch!" *Oh well*, she mused, *just shows what a sixth-grade education will do for you.*

It must have been well after midnight that she sat in the first pew, for a moment taking in all of that floral splendor highlighted by the movers' spotlights, which they forgot to turn off. One gaudy splash of color was piled on top of its ruddy neighbor. Blinding.

She picked up the ruby-reddest multifoliate rose she could find, took it to her nose, and pressed her face tightly into it until she became aware of the thorns stinging her fingers and impetuously threw it down and stamped on it. She pulled the thorns out and pensively sucked the little bubbles of blood. She grabbed one of the potted lilies, yanked, and up it came with roots and clotted soil. But it scarcely had any scent, so she cast it aside.

All of a sudden, her gorge rose and the imp with it. Her face was getting red, and there was an uncomfortable sensation surging through her chest. In an instant, she felt herself possessed by a demonic fury. She pulled out another lily then another and more yet till she had both fists full and began banging them to shreds against the altar.

Next, she picked up whole vases of carnations and tossed them against the brick walls, shouting "Huzzah!" as the shards exploded around her; then she went after the mums, glads, daisies, tulips (all were recently misted) and were thrown this way and that. Potted geranium got slammed against the altar.

She rampaged up and down the bleachers, tearing at petals, kicking over vases and pots, picking up others randomly and heaving them out onto the pews and over the chancel railing while letting out a triumphant war whoop at every plop, crash, and splash. She kept at it—tearing, kicking, throwing, splattering, and scattering—till she had demolished the whole bombastic display.

Torn flowers, shredded petals, stripped ferns, broken palms and fronds, smashed vases, terra-cotta shards, broken glass, dented pots, soil, pebbles, pools of water, and ice cubes were strewn everywhere—on the pews, over the chancel, upon the altar, down the steps, into the aisles, along the walls, over the sanctuary carpet. It was as if a whirlwind had just spiraled through. Only the skeletal bleachers remained somewhat intact, covered as they were with debris.

Having finally spent herself, she kicked her way through the color-drenched carnage—a shredded lily here, stomped-on glads there—and burst out into the chilly night with her head spinning; she was utterly bewildered, shivering, and directionless. Trudging up the hill to the center of town, she felt like she was trying to drag herself to shore through an outgoing tide.

Her legs, in particular, seemed weighed down; and the bad one was about to give way. She ached in her bones. Pulling herself to a bench outside the All-Night Diner, she flopped herself down on it. Not knowing how long she drowsed there, she was awakened by clenched-teeth shivers just as a faint, rosy gleam of the coming day began to brighten the eastern sky.

CHAPTER 55

"The Riot"

On the next day, everyone woke up to the *Morning Messenger*'s headline: "They Slept at the Wake."

Tony was livid. Spitting out words like "desecration" and "sacrilege," he was shown in a front page picture, fist in the air, yelling "They'll pay for this!" Who else could he have meant but the Puerto Ricans, especially the unemployed youths he'd fired who now hung around on street corners and were up to no good? As the *Messenger* had it, they had, in fact, been egged on by outside agitators, like those people who called themselves "Hispanics for Civil Justice." Their local representative had been noted as saying that somebody had killed their priest, and good God, it was being pinned on one of theirs? Great!

"So it's justice they want, huh?" Tony fumed. "So they butchered the flowers and think they can get away with this?"

The following night, a pickup with four, stout gorilla-types roamed the Puerto Rican neighborhood, stopping wherever they saw a group of idle kids hanging out—who they proceeded to jump, knock to the sidewalk, and beat till they're bloody, swinging lengths of hard rubber hose. The rampaging goons were herded by a brass-knuckled coxswain who took a shot at anybody left standing.

Addie was horrified. *This madness has to be stopped! But how?* She called the produce office and told the bitchy secretary it was she, a lone woman, who did it. There was no reason: she just flipped.

"Yes, gone completely batty . . . Why? Couldn't, myself, tell why! Ja, von meine verwirrte Kopf ist kein warum. Ja—In plain English, there ain't no why! . . . "That's right, crazy . . . No, I not talkin' Puerto Rican. But for sure they ain't done it . . . How I knows? Because [back to normal speech] like I told you, it was me and no other, I swear. The Puerto Ricans have not done any harm to Tony. *Please* he must know. Not them. Me!"

Tony scoffed when his secretary told him about the call. A prankster. Scratching his head, he says "Maybe I should put somebody on it. Did you trace the call?"

"Trace it? How?"

"Okay, never mind."

If he had to chase after every prank call, Mama Mia!

"She said they never did me no harm, huh? Before I'd put a stop to it, they were stealin' from my fields for years and got the buckshot in their asses to prove it. Bring the guy with the green eyeshades in here—No, wait. Just tell him to get with the insurance people. Cow will give 'em the estimate. *Where* the hell is Cow! Where was he?"

"Somebody said he left town. I called his wife, and she said she thinks he must be hiding."

"He better! See if he has some idea who did it. That crazy woman. Recognize her voice, did you?"

"Seems to me it was some foreigner. How'd I reckonize her?"

"One of the outsiders. Okay, forget it. If I had to go after every friggin' nut . . ."

He stood there, chin out, thumbs hooked on his ample belt for a moment. Grabbing a cigar in his thick fingers, he rolled it on his tongue, lit up, and blew out a pensive smoke ring.

"So we got a mystery woman out there, huh? What language did you say she was talkin'?"

"Dunno, but it wasn't Ayetalian. Did seem pretty crazy and said so."

"Kinda not when they say so. Okay. Call Louey. Didn't he say he used to do detective work? Yeah, wasn't he the one who told us the PRs were rippin' off our bean fields? Tomatoes and corn too.

Give him a call, will yah? And, Liz, get me my house slippers, will yah? My feet are killin' me."

The second night out, the goons were met with a hail of rocks; and on the third, the pickup caught a Molotov cocktail and burned to the ground. Shots were fired and the police were called out. They too were pelted with rocks; and while they waded into the crowd, cracking every head that flew by, somebody took a baseball bat to their cruisers, bashing in fenders and windows. Others were slashing tires before being tackled and worked over with the bat.

For a while, the fat was really in the fire until the cops called for reinforcements who finally whipped out the teargas canisters, which got the people dispersed. Those that remained exchanged pistol fire with the cops before disappearing into the night, only to join the crowd that had reformed and taken off for downtown, where windows were broken and stores were looted. An explosion outside the newspaper building broke all the windows and started a fire on the ground floor.

A Molotov cocktail landed on the chief's car and set it ablaze. A cruiser was overturned. A heap of discarded tires was set on fire, lighting up city hall square. The down-and-out inhabitants of the steps came out of their cardboard boxes and scattered in all directions.

People were running off with looted goods, which were mostly clothes: nightgowns, dresses, slacks, skirts, coats, furs, bras, boots, hats, leather jackets, sexy panties, women's purses, one dribbling dollar bills. But really, they took anything they could lift. A heavyset woman with flashing eyes was bouncing along with a bejeweled mannequin bust but dropped it and scooted down a dark alley as she was about to be caught.

Kids were scrambling for discarded booty—anything from wigs to three-piece men's suits. In no time, a full-scale riot had broken out with the cops again going club happy. Things eventually quieted down when the fire department's pumper truck arrived, and their pressure hoses started knocking people up against buildings and sweeping them off their feet. Things really quieted down when they brought out the snarling dobermans.

A curfew was put into effect, and the mayor went on the radio appealing for calm; he said he would call in ethnic community leaders and address their problems, which (let them be advised) would not be solved by violence. People said that they'd heard that before. Father Tim, green as he was, showed he had learned something from Jay by asking the Puerto Rican leadership to come and talk to him, after which he arranged a meeting with the police that didn't come off.

Somebody saw a gorilla-type making a second go at the Home Savings Bank. He meanwhile had a stethoscope around his neck and carried a black doctor's bag with its sides bulging. Not exactly one of the usual suspects. But since he was seen exiting the bank, it was thought to have been Domo Jr. In the midst of the tumult, he grabbed Addie by the hand and led her to a vantage point on the rise west of Town Center.

After all the yelling, there was agreement that the violence had to stop; but each side insisted on conditions which left things at a standstill. The curfew didn't go over very well. How about people who worked the night shift and those who worked days and had to shop at night?

Meanwhile, the Blacks wanted in on the talks, saying they'd had grievances long before the Puerto Ricans showed up, and resented being left out. So complaints were aired, tempers finally cooled, and with the police in a one-against-two situation, understanding was finally reached. Police would reduce their presence in the neighborhoods, and the neighborhoods would mainly police themselves. The "law-abiding" folks in the ghettos didn't care for the arrangement, but they were told to live with it. (Better than shootin' and lootin'.) The town heaved a collective sigh of relief.

So there was peace . . . for all of a week until a policeman was shot by a bank robber; and his partner, returning fire, killed a little black girl. (She was a cutie.) Puerto Ricans joined the Blacks in taking to the streets. They marched on to city hall and held a rally, whereupon the mayor came out with a bullhorn and urged them to go home so nobody gets hurt.

"Believe me," he bellowed, "I'm workin' on it, and, trust me. I'll see justice is done for all our people."

He pointed out that the policeman who shot the kid had been suspended and that an investigation was underway. Someone yelled "smoke screen," names were called, tomatoes were thrown, and things began to get ugly. In the midst of the mayor's using his bullhorn to tell the crowd he'd called for the feds to go after a bank robber, out of the crowd came a beefy Puerto Rican pulled at the arm by a young woman with a limp, who hobbled him up to the top of the city hall steps and yelled out, "Bullshit! That ain't the real problem here. People, listen to this guy." There were shouts, a chorus of people chanting "Gordo, Gordo!"

The heavy fellow grabbed the mayor's bullhorn and shouted "You want peace? Justice first for Carlos. You can't kill a man because you hate his people. Look at what—"

He was cut off when several cops penetrated the cordon that had sprung up to surround the speaker. The cop who tried to get the cuffs on him was left with an empty jacket. Things got chaotic up there at the city hall door. In the midst of the pushing and shoving, the shouters got Gordo pushed into the thick of the crowd. The girl who had held up a sign reading "Hate eats up the Hater" ducked free of a noose and also disappeared into the crowd.

The mayor had retreated to his office, and minutes later, a platoon of cops came streaming down the street led by the mounted patrol, who rode their horses into the crowd. There were angry clashes as the mounts pushed the crowd back. Billy clubs were raised, teargas canisters thrown, and stragglers arrested.

At nightfall, just when it seemed order was restored, a gang of young toughs went to the police station and started chanting "*Libertad por* Carlos!"

When the paddy wagon appeared, they took off; and there followed another night of window smashing, looting, and burning. Fire hoses were cut, and teargas canisters were lobbed back at the police. Grown men were silhouetted against the flames, walking off with furniture radios, some carrying turntables complete with speakers. Two guys who were seen trotting off with a showcase of watches turned and threw it at the cop chasing them. Armed with clubs of their own, the toughs for a while seemed to be giving about as much as they took until the mounted patrol started running them down and cracking their heads.

Once the dogs got there, people scattered. By morning, an uneasy calm returned as state troopers were brought in to patrol the streets and to protect the cleanup crew.

Accusations flew: police were said to be no better than Tony's thugs. The chief countered that his men were hard put to protect themselves in a war zone. He came out with the bright idea that they should quarantine the key neighborhoods for a while to contain the troublemakers; then, those people would realize they were only hurting their own.

Even the *Messenger*, normally supportive, found the chief's plan difficult to swallow. Think of the loss of business. The chief said it was just a suggestion and that, after all, somebody had to be concerned about public safety. The cop who killed the kid left the force and quietly left town. Things began to cool down on their own as people got on with trying to make a living.

Resentments, however, continued to simmer; and the town knew it was going to have to live with "occasional disturbances," as the paper put it, and trust that "the majority of citizens would show tolerance and live up to their reputation for decency. Minorities would hopefully respect the law that they look to for their protection."

Somebody sent the editor a sheet of paper containing a prominently etched middle finger extended from a fist. Meanwhile, graffiti artists were painting "Free Carlos" on walls of the city hall; and it kept coming up on mailboxes around town.

By dawn, an uneasy calm had settled over an exhausted city.

CHAPTER 56

"Talking It over with Tom"

A general pause enabled her to address her own problems. The registered letter was there waiting for her. Her position at school had been terminated. As she had indicated, she expected nothing different and actually wanted none, different—or not. But out of a job, things were going to be different. That part she didn't like. Nonetheless, not all was lost.

Having finished packing up her things at school, she put in a call to Johnny. Surprise: Did she want to talk to him? Not really. Just a short message would do for now.

"Tell him sorry I couldn't get back to him sooner. But I think I may be ready to go first of the week. No need for an upscale apartment just now. But do need the use of a car. ASAP, please."

Actually, she had another request. Mario came by, accompanied by Louey, who was putting on his mean business face. Actually, it was like they'd been waiting for her when she returned to vacate her apartment. They showed her a picture of Sean, Whimpy's father, and said that her father knew the guy but wouldn't answer questions about him. They'd ask Otto something, and he started talking in German. He tells them he can't handle the English and knows nothing when it's complicated.

They need Addie as an interpreter. She also says she doesn't know the German when it gets complicated. Well, she didn't want her father taken down to the station for questioning, did she? It got her wondering, *Could Johnny get Dunny to call off the wolves?* She was after all preparing for his riff.

Returning from the grocery store with additional boxes, she expected a call back from Johnny. Instead, there was Tom, knocking on her door. Precisely the guy she wanted to see. She told him the letter said she had as much as resigned by walking out on the principal, which meant they could dock her the bimonthly check. Did she want to think it over for the kids' sake? What trouble could it be to break someone in? Ah, that was the key.

She had half a notion to say okay and then give notice, which technically could have gotten her the check, plus severance pay, with an appropriate assist from Johnny. But working with Johnny, she was told, would get her solid take-home pay. Hopefully, he had enough pull that he could get people with the fangs to lay off Otto; he had to be sheltered and so did she.

She found herself bumping up against the bottom line fact that she could no longer afford this apartment, and she couldn't very well live with Otto. So she needed new digs but not the ritzy ones Johnny had for her. *No.* Her need was for some kind of a hideout, at least for a while.

"You need a hideout?" Tom was taken aback. "Holy smokes! What kind of talk is that? What have you done now?"

"No more than what was morally right. Which usually comes at a price."

Tom had on a typically worried sigh. "Well, truth is I came over to tell you I'd noticed ol' Louey prowling around your place the other day. I wondered whether you might have offended him."

"If I'm givin' offense, he'd not be the guy to start with. But I've got other things on my need list right now. Like, first of all, an out-of-the-way and not-very-well-lighted place."

"I suppose I could put you up in one of the rooms I rent out upstairs from my office. But you know what's going on in the streets. Might be a bit chancy at night. When do you have to be out of that sweet little place you can't afford anymore?"

"I've probably got till the end of the month, but I want out now."

"Now? Listen, if you can hang in for a couple of days, I'll set you up in the office we've got in our finished basement. Right now, my dad and I are up to our eyeballs in talks between Father Tim, city hall, and the PRs. The street people are raising Cain about Carlos again, saying if the police meant it when they talked about goodwill, they could start by releasing him. Naturally, the police are dragging their feet. With the public up in arms about the riots, how can the chief cave in when it comes to a priest killer?"

"If you're lookin' at me for a quick fix, I ain't got one. But I do have something in mind."

"Okay, but don't hide it. Time's of the essence. As you know, Dad carries a lot of weight in town, having been in the role of honest broker before. He's also not a little worried that they might start torching the block with my office, where he also has a number of properties."

"Listen, we need action. I have a notion of what I'm gonna do. What about you?"

"Very uncomfortable. The DA wants me to certify Carlos can stand trial, or he's outta here—down the pike to the loony bin—which, they're saying, might be the best way to settle it. But Dad says he wants to work out a way to spring him clean while he awaits trial, and he can handle it from there. Meanwhile, as he sees it—"

Overriding his "Meanwhile," she interjected, "Hold all that. I'm up to my eyeballs on it. In fact, I'm thinkin' about something concrete. I know how I can save Whimpy."

"Oh sure. This plan of yours. I hope you're not going to make yourself its first casualty. The way he's carrying on, don't believe he realizes how dangerous his situation is. If you can get him to realize that, we'd have something to work with."

"What, set him up? Never!"

"Well, you know the alternative. That morgue for the living downstate. And frankly, there's a lot of sentiment building for that solution, both in city hall and the city in general. It gets everybody off the hook, and the PRs have no comeback. He's alive, released, and—pathetic soul—being cared for. Now that's the way things are tending. If, on the other hand, he shapes up, Dad can begin some legal maneuvers. So unless you're willing to get him turned around—and pretty quickly—the bureaucracy takes over, and he's gone."

"Work on him? I couldn't do that either. It's the town, not Whimpy, that's gone crazy! He physically didn't do it. Where are the cold facts that he did?"

"Fact one, they tell you, is his craziness. Who else but a loony would have done it? You haven't seen him lately. If it's an act, it has gotten out of hand, like he's enjoying it too much. This thing seems to have taken hold of him, and he can't let go. You get the feeling he's going to take it as far as he can, not caring about consequences. Even if I don't say he's outright crazy, I can verify that he's neurotically perverse."

"Oh hell, so are we all! You know, as I listen to you, it's sounding a lot like there's a catch here. If he's crazy, he must have done it because only a madman would kill the priest. And if he's sane, why else would he be playing crazy except to cover up the fact that he did it?"

"Ah, but he did say he killed him. You heard him say so, didn't you?"

"I know. So if he's crazy and confesses he did it, it must be because, in that state, he can't prevent the truth from coming out. But if he's sane and confesses, that shows he's gone crazy for sure, and remember, only a crazy man would kill this good priest. Whichever he is, by virtue of being the confessor, he is simply not crafty enough to hide the truth."

"Stop it! That kind of talk . . . it's . . . well . . . It's full of non sequiturs."

"Never mind, Tom. You're also saying time's running out. Okay. I'm going to come up with a simple solution because, crazy or sane, in this nutso town, he loses either way."

"Addie, baby, please. Don't be a madwoman yourself. The PRs are just itching to hold a rally. Things are getting pretty mean out there. Don't get yourself caught in the middle."

"I know. Nothing stupid. On the contrary, I'll fight the stupidity that has gotten into this town with a dose of the sanity our DA had originally wanted. And talking about 'meanwhile,' could you do me a favor and move what little I have here—bed, chest of drawers, desk—down to your office basement?"

"And where are you gonna hole up?"

"Dunno. I'll deal with that when I have to. Just now, I got somethin' else cookin'."

CHAPTER 57

"She Writes a Letter"

So banking on the notion that a pen is the mightier weapon, she became a letter writer. The first one went to the _Morning Messenger_. She wrote that she was the one who had poisoned the priest. He was a handsome man, and she had a crush on him; but she knew she could never have him. So she flipped. Now her conscience was bothering her.

Addie saw she was on the wrong track the moment she sent it and was glad they wouldn't publish it. Rather, they did a brief story about receiving an anonymous crank letter from an unbalanced woman who claimed she'd poisoned Father Johannes for reasons she was not very clear about. An obvious hoax and sad commentary on the airheads who would like to sensationalize the town's tragedy. They buried the story on page nine, amidst ads for bedding and women's brassieres.

The only way was to tell the simple, unvarnished truth; and she had an idea of where such a letter could be planted to do the most good. But she also realized she was up against a dilemma: could she damage Jay to save Whimpy? She wrote a draft and tore it up; then, she tried another and tore it up. Betrayal stared her in the face. _What to do?_ Surely, Jay would be willing to sacrifice himself; and that would be all right for him to do, but could she do it to him?

Wait. She could put it on herself, show that she did him in; and she did, didn't she? Still, there was his reputation. Except that, for those who would see it for what it was, it would mostly be the Church that would look bad. *Wasn't that group of fellow priests saying that the Church was hurting itself with doctrines that went against nature? Or something to that effect?* Pure heterodoxy, as he was told, in the sternest terms. Best to steer clear of anything which smelled of that.

As far as God was concerned, Jay would surely have earned a place in His heaven. As for herself, it might well be that she was destined for the hot place. She only knew she was sure to wind up there if she didn't try to save an innocent man.

She didn't like the sound of the letter, but she'd made up her mind that it had to go out regardless. Time was short, and it looked like Whimpy was facing a padded cell here or there. She thought about Jay again and hesitated then reminded herself he probably wouldn't want her to stand idly by. Want to or not, she had to do something to salve her own conscience.

Domo Jr. was late with the car and apologized. He said he was supposed to take her down to the station house, where Mario wanted to have a face-to-face with her. He knew she didn't want to go. She gave him a hug and said she had a hot letter to be hand-delivered in the dead of night.

"That hot?"

She dropped DJ off at the Old-Time Saloon and, taking the wheel herself, delivered the first copy of "Hot Stuff" under Gordo's door. She went on from there to make several critical deliveries, making sure a copy went to the Klagemann pew. Like they said, if Iris knew, the whole town would know.

Fat Umberto (known as Gordo), the most notorious of the hotheads, was Whimpy's Uncle—the guy with the knife who had chased his father, Sean, out of town. He had come forward as the lead spokesman for the PRs; and he was the one who was most insistent that, however strange his nephew was, sometimes *estrafalario* ("whacky"), he was not so dumb that he would kill a priest and for sure not this one.

When she returned the car to the saloon, it came back to her that this Domo, unlike his namesake, was a far cry from *the* Domo

244

but could be just as lethal. Fortunately, he had a crush on Addie and could be depended on for a "small change" job, as he called the lesser bank jobs. Nervous as she was, she couldn't dwell on it; but this was a clean-cut young man. Those sharp features of his father had been smoothed out. His hair, though long, was neatly combed; and he looked innocent enough, if the light wasn't too bright.

She was startled on looking at the business card he gave her, on which he had scribbled "Help for the Helpless." *Well, at least he had a sense of humor.* He said that if not otherwise engaged, he'd be her *helpmate.* Except that he had this terrible addiction when it came to banks. He knows a vulnerable one when he sees it, and it turns him on. She dismissed his parting wink, and under-the-breath offer "You need a leetle money, gimme a call."

"Thanks. With what I'm into, you never know. For now, just steer Mario away from me and from my father too."

"I would add flashy Rocco, my alternate. He knows stuff that could be useful to Mario, who won't go near him, his own twin brother. Afraid of him, maybe. Darned if I know. What Mario knows is he spends big bills on the women."

"Remember, my helper, talking about who knows what . . . You, my friend, know nothing about the deliveries I've made."

"Well, dear lady, come to think of it, I'd steer that Rocco guy away from my father too. There's something about him. Your papa eases away when he sees him. Anyway, just now I'm gonna ease with you for special deliveries."

"Remember, we don't need the gun this trip, but it's reassuring you got it. So long's you don't have me in the car as your getaway when the shootin' starts."

She liked DJ's eagerness but knew the story that he could be long on promise but short on performance. So for dependability, she loaded up on salt and decided to take what was offered but remained content to settle for half."

"Talk about a getaway, these deliveries all that tough?" This he whispered with a touch of anxiety. Like it should be fun.

"Toughest."

She wasn't going to let him down.

PART VII

A BOMBSHELL LETTER

CHAPTER 58

"And the Bombshell Letter Is Out"

At eight o'clock in the morning, coffee cup in hand, Thomas Vander Veer Sr. was holding an eleventh hour conference with Dunneville, his former law partner. The two are now separated by politics but mutually concerned about how to bring the city to its senses. Looking out the window of the "war room," the mayor's oak–paneled private chamber, they saw people milling around at the bus terminal below, hoisting their red-lettered placards and cheering the new arrivals as they flowed out of incoming buses. They formed a picket line and, pumping their placards, began to chant in rhythm "No justice, no peace." The notorious Deaf and Dumbs were marching with them, signing the same.

Van said he'd told the mayor to contact the National Guard and motioned Dunneville back to the table, where they peered over the map. Opening his briefcase, Van produced the Martial Law proclamation. The festering strife served neither of their interests. For one thing, no one was paying any attention to the mayoral race. In negotiating sessions, Gordo saw them as the two members of the establishment who were most reachable; but that in itself got him no traction.

He had noticed their open disgust with the intransigence of the DA and police chief, who blocked any concessions, and, in fact, were not opposed to a little bloodshed (if necessary), knowing it would gain support from voters. Others in the administration agreed: going soft on a hoodlum uprising would send the wrong message. Van pointed out that avoiding urban strife would surely send the right one.

There was a sudden clamorous roar from the crowd, over which a single voice rising up in triumph addressed them in Spanish, which was followed by raucous cheers and a volley of the "Libertad" chants. It was like the home team had just scored a winning touchdown. Within minutes, Gordo burst in on the conferees, waving the letter in their faces and slapping it down on the table.

"Read, gentlemen, read! My nephew is out in the streets, or all the rest of us are."

Dunneville's mouth fell open as he read. Van had read along with him. Soberly picking up the letter, he rose to his aristocratic six and a half feet and, towering over Gordo, asked in his deeply measured voice "You can authenticate this letter?"

Gordo extended his arms, palms up. "No comprendo."

"You can certify this is no fake?"

"Si, si. My good son Pepe. In the middle of the night, he hears footsteps on the front porch. He wakes up and he sees a lady with a scarf over her head. She hops into a car with the motor running and drives away in a hurry."

"That lady will have to be found, you understand? How old is your son?"

"Sixteen. He smart. Muy inteligente." He pointed to his head.

"He can testify to what he saw?"

"Si, si. You don't have to pay him, but if he is helpful . . ."

"Help is usually rewarded but, in this instance, not directly and not now. To the point. If your people are clear of the streets tonight, I'll have your man out among them by noon tomorrow."

"You can guarantee that?"

"I do not mince words. You do your part. I'll do mine. By the way, did Pepe happen to get a license plate number?"

Gordo shrugged. "I ask him."

"It's okay. No time for that now. Got enough for openers. But your muy inteligente kid has a good memory, yes?"

The distinguished, white-haired, old-school, bow-tied lawyer was the heir of old money, a Yale graduate, a captain in the infantry (wounded in combat), and an elder in the Dutch Reform Church; he was also known as the gray eminence of the local Republican Caucus. He was widely respected and accustomed to having his way with people.

In the face of the Puerto Rican protests, he thought he ought to see for himself what kind of fellow this Carlos was. As attorney, he asked for permission to talk to him in the interrogation room; and it was instantly granted. After introductory nods, the Whimp went silent on him; and Van bluntly demanded "Speak up, man, and defend yourself!"

At first, Whimpy distrustfully would only give him a meek "I have." Prodded, he went into his mumbling act head down, at which Van slammed a wake-up fist on the table.

"I don't have time for nonsense. You want to help defend yourself or don't you?"

Looking up, Whimpy slowly took in Van's august presence. From his immaculately tailored blue serge suit and wide-knotted bow tie to his steel jaw, azure eyes, and icy-white complexion, his patrician persona was intimidating. Temporarily cowed, Whimpy recovered sufficiently to say "I thought you, sir, were going to do the defending."

"Only if I can get your help."

"Frankly, the way these bastards have been wearing me down . . . I've reached the point where I'm ready for a fight."

"Good. Let's start with the 'where,' the 'when,' and the proof thereof. And, good fellow, we'll take 'em on."

When Van showed up with the letter at the District Attorney's Office, DA Jack Magowan handed him the chief's copy. Van brushed it aside and dropped a Writ of Habeas Corpus on the desk.

"What's this all about, Van?"

"Seems to me the prisoner hasn't been assigned a public defender, nor has he been arraigned yet, Jack."

"Does this mean you want to be his defender?"

"It means, Jack, what it always does. That I expect to see the law very strictly applied in this case as in all others. You've had him in the lockup almost two weeks now, and there's been no formal charge. Just suspicion. Principle, man!"

"You've got yours. I've got mine. To protect society from criminal suspects. In a day or two, I'm expecting your son, Tom, to have him certifiably ready to stand trial. Then we'll take him before the court for arraignment."

"But surely not before you've checked out the letter. With that out there, you know as well as I do you'll get nowhere with my good friend Judge Vreeland. As amicus curiae, I'll have to have my say about the manner of your proceeding, and Vreeland is liable to throw the whole case out on you. I trust you covet your status with the judge."

"You believe what's in this letter? The paper doesn't. There was another one the other day. There may be others. Somebody's playing games with us, Van. You're the last person I'd expect to fall for this sort of thing."

"Yes, the letter. It can be authenticated. This Jezebel exists. She has been seen in connection with its delivery. We have the witness."

"And you're going to deliver her?"

"Don't have to. Not our client. She's yours to find. With a little digging, you'll surely be up to getting a plate number and tracer. But let's face the critical issue, Jack. The PRs say they know the letter is for real, and there's nothing to show it isn't. To ignore it while you move ahead against their man raises a red flag. Since you'd have to reject an ultimatum, the trouble will be on your head. So stand back and allow me to oblige you. The writ will take effect as you'll learn from the court. I filed yesterday."

CHAPTER 59

"The Letter Is Out and So Is Whimpy"

As city hall's tower clock clanged out the hour, Whimpy was blinking in the light of day at high noon, arms raised to a chorus of cheers from the victory crowd that had been gathering practically since daybreak. Gordo jumped up the steps of the station house, hoisting a red flag, and led a chant—which, amidst the general commotion, sounded out "Gringos No, Carlos Si." They carried Whimpy off on their shoulders, car horns blaring.

Police redirected traffic as the swelling crowd spilled onto Main Street, where people snaked their way around halted cars in a conga line, beating out the syncopated accents as they went "Tah-dah, tah-dah, tah-dah!" Some went over to embrace astonished onlookers; others threw kisses at the iron-faced police spaced along the curb. Skinny-limbed kiddies in white tights were spinning cartwheels and Gordo, trying one himself, came down hard on his rump; but his grimace faded before the ensuing hilarity, in which he finally laughed the loudest. The circus atmosphere prevailed well into the night, highlighted by firecrackers and a rumba band.

A copy of the letter had found its way to the church pew where the Klagemanns sit; and Iris, who had lately been in every day working on the rummage sale, gasped when she spied it. Whoever put it there must have understood that for her to know what it said was not only like telling the whole town, but it would also be considerably elaborated in the transmission and would gain general acceptance besides.

Except for the vindicated Puerto Ricans, most of the congregation—particularly the more conservative members—were shocked that anyone could do, no less write, such things (or so much as think of them). The outrage gathered steam and got rather heated.

Iris put the message out. The only refuge for some was to have Iris declare it an outright hoax. Around town, one heard talk of hypocrisy and the usual rancid remarks about PRs and defamation. Some couldn't resist a joke or two, like "A hard priest was good to find," etc.

The publicity forced the *Morning Messenger* to do a lead story on the letter; but out of decency, the text, they declared, would find no place on their pages. And they said they remained skeptical anyway. On the other hand, Protestants and various nonchurchgoers tended to think it was true: it did seem to make sense.

The DA obviously had very little to support his pinning it on the poor, deranged Puerto Rican, from whom it should not have been all that difficult to extract a confession. Hadn't the respected psychiatrist shown that you could get him to agree to anything, like what he really wanted was to assassinate the Pope? And when the pharmacist came clean about refilling the prescription, even those who didn't want to believe it thought the suicide part was probably true. Some pointed to biblical precedent, as with the disgraced Judas hanging himself.

So the speculation soon turned to who this mystery woman might be, and at one point, it became somewhat wild. The night watchman at the bank reported having seen a weary old lady with a babushka hobble past the bank in the early hours of the morning after the night of the flower massacre. She might have come from the church, and he thought there was something kind of strange about her. She might have been homeless since she fell asleep on the sidewalk bench. Iris wanted to go after that watchman with a rolling pin.

"What? Our handsome priest had it with some old hag!"

Like other middle-aged women in the congregation, she had, had a crush on Jay herself.

For the benefit of the curious, who were clamoring to see the damned letter, some Puerto Rican wag had it blown up and posted on the kiosk in front of city hall. But people were so used to ignoring the quickly dated stuff put up there that nobody noticed until the Deaf and Dumbs started jumping up and down and drew a pushcart peddler over to see it. Word spread and soon there was a crowd ten deep pushing and shoving for a look. Women walked away talking to themselves.

Word got to Tom, out on the fringe of the crowd. He was brought forward and urged to read it out loud to the assemblage. Reluctant, he was goaded by Gordo to do it.

"Fellow townspeople, "I am not an angel of truth, but I must tell you a truth that will save you from doing what is *false*. I remember a Saint Anthony who helps people find things. Honor the truth about the priest and the prisoner, and with Anthony's help, you will find your souls.

"The man you have imprisoned did not kill our priest. There were no rats in the rectory. Sad to say, good Father Jay took the poison himself because he had spent the night with a woman. I know. I am that woman. I may have his child in my womb.

"I am to blame. I could have avoided it, and for that, you may despise me. But what happened between us was honest. It was love, and he suffered for the good it brought him. I am doomed to suffer for its consequences, as I do now, and will yet in the Hereafter. But I have no regrets. He enjoyed the only earthly love he would know in this life.

"The man in prison loved his priest, who had rescued him from despair. Father Jay showed his love for him, and I think he would say to you 'By condemning this man, you will condemn yourselves. Deliver yourselves from perdition and from injustice in the 'here and now.' Yours is far from being a bad town. Some good will come of this sad event if you but open your hearts to forgiveness.' You will honor your priest if you but honor the hard truth I give you.

"You ask for *proof.* Here is my thumbprint. It matches the one on Father Jay's bedroom desk. Have a look."

As the crowd dispersed, Tom caught sight of Addie sitting on the cold steps among the Deaf and Dumbs; and he went over to her.

"I did okay?"

She nodded and he went on, "You've got yourself another dilemma, don't you?"

"Maybe."

"You need the money, but with baggage from the letter and fronting for Johnny, you're gonna be living dangerously."

"Yes on the money. No on the rest."

"But you can't risk identity."

"Not to worry."

Turning to leave, he stopped to look back for a moment; and shaking his head, he asked, "This cardboard box your bedroom?"

"The Whimp is free, and I'm gonna get decent lodgings. I've got Domo Jr. for help."

"I'd watch that. He's not on good standing with the authorities. And I told you about his dependability."

"The way he's standing with me couldn't be better."

"With others, I think it could. Anyway, watch out. There may be a price to pay. Obviously, he's got a crush on you."

"And obviously, he hasn't done any crushin'."

PART VIII

POLITICS & JOHNNY

CHAPTER 60

"She Finds Herself a Car and a Home"

The bus chugged up the long, winding North Hill Road and let her off at the last stop, where it swung around at the intersection leading into the "Heights." A sign featured several model interiors obviously laid out by professional decorators. The newly paved road was also flanked by a row of luxury town houses with a view. On evenings, their bay windows are typically aglow with sunsets that painted the clouds a royal red.

These units had been put in, it was learned, with a federal subsidy obtained for low-income housing, which optimists said might yet be built (elsewhere) supported by a percent of the income from town house rentals. And this is all done within terms of the Federal Housing Administration. As it was publicized in town, Tony's agent would be putting their tax dollars to work—the site, optional.

The previous evening, Addie had driven up this treacherous North Hill Road in the car Domo Jr. had brought her direct from Rent-A-Wreck. Noticing a problem with the brakes, she had to turn around and go back down in low gear using the emergency brake at stop streets. Even in low gear, the thing had picked up sufficient momentum to give her a scare going around curves where there was a drop-off from the outside lane.

She wanted another car, but the mechanic at the rental agency said she was supposed to have this one; so he'd fix it. Addie called the number on Rocco's card, and an answering service told her that he was presently out of town and that she could leave a message. She blurted out the Bronx cheer and went on to say the car just didn't live up to his looks.

Following speedy service, she was able to claim her fixed car; but, distrustful, she said she'd leave it with the mechanic to be picked up at her convenience. This rental agency was part of what was called Tony's "Enterprise Octopus." You could rent anything from a wreck to a funeral limo. Rent the one and they'd save the other for you. She wanted to put Domo Jr. on this agency, but he was busy and couldn't say with what. There's mystery about him too—which, of course, she'd been told to expect.

Next day, on getting off the bus, Addie checked out the fork in the road and headed for the branch that veered up and to the left beyond the town houses. The location she was looking for necessitated a precipitous climb through an overgrown road. Having to go through a patch of brambles, she wished she had a machete.

At a precipitous swing upward, there was a break in the trees; and crouching there like a giant prehistoric bird, the moldering castle, shrouded in morning mist, suddenly rose up before her eyes. About fifty yards from the wrought iron gate, a heavy-duty loggers' chain was strung across the road and attached to metal posts that displayed "Private Road, No Trespassing" signs—all of recent installation.

Okay . . . She stopped to catch her breath, ducked under the chain, and went the rest of the way to the hulk, which she assumed was deserted. A light drizzle began to fall, which was nice. The climb had made her feel pretty warm.

With the squeak of the gate, she was startled to hear a second floor window crack open, from which a black gun muzzle snaked its way through the ivy; and a husky voice yelled down "Hey, you! Can't you read? What cha want?"

"Hi. I'm a woman in need. Can I talk to you for a minute?"

Even more startling: who else was materializing out of the gloom behind the massive oak door but the big turtle-back lady, looking bigger yet up close, and not a little scary as she scrutinized Addie with narrowing pig eyes sunk into that moon face of hers?

"Sorry if I'm intruding, but I'm in a bit of a fix. Had to give up my apartment and need to find a place to stay till I figure out what to do."

"Oh. Why did you come here?"

"I thought it was deserted. You're just holing up here yourself?"

"I guess it looks that way, but it's supposed to belong to me— finally— and will, free and clear, when that high-priced lawyer completes the paperwork."

"And you are? . . . Uh, the daughter?"

"Yeah, Peggy, the lost daughter, in person. As you probably know, like everybody else does, I was supposed to be long gone. And I was. None of the pills did much good, so they drilled into my head, pronounced me cured, and told me to go home. 'Where's that?' I asked. They looked at my chart, found an address, and gave me a bus ticket.

"Oh yeah, what helped a lot to get me out was a test visit they gave me with a couple of elderly sisters in town, who put in a word for me. That said, I was fully rehabilitated. But frankly, the nurses down there mostly wanted to have a success posted on their records.

"Once I got here and looked around, sure enough, there was home up on the mountain. We had a cat that once got lost. Was gone for a year. And one bright day, she found her way home. It just took me a little longer. You need a place too, huh? Well, I need somebody to help me make this atrocity livable. You can help me clean and put it in shape, can you?"

"Sure, sure! Will work for bed."

"This 'fix' you mention . . . What's that all about? From the looks of you, I'd say you couldn't have left more than five or six corpses down there."

"Fact is I may be needing somebody who can shoot. Shot anybody lately?"

"None, so far. But you never know. I'm on the lookout."

"Are you saying I can stay if I help?"

"Could be me needin' the help. See where they drilled into my scalp? They said most of the time, the operation works. Cut out a piece of my brain, but said they left most of the good stuff. We'll find out. Can't be sure the seizures won't come back. They said it oughta be a good idea to have somebody around. I put in at Social Services but so far no benevolent takers. You still want to help?"

"Sometimes I think it's my middle name. Have been scheduled to help people I'd just as soon not help. Why not you?"

"You probably haven't seen a person in seizure. First, you check that the tongue doesn't block the windpipe. Then pile pillows around me so I don't bang into anything hard and wait me out. When I come to, give me a couple of these phenobarbs, and I should be able to sleep it off."

"I can move in?"

"Yeah, come inside and pick up a paintbrush. I'd have a bigger welcome for you if you could latch onto a car. With this condition of mine, there's no way I could get a driver's license."

Addie explained about the Rent-a-Wreck—which Peggy, rubbing her palms together, found reassuring. The first thing that struck Addie as they clonked over the slate flooring in the entry hall was the heavy smell of mold as from some long unvisited basement. *Probably a good place to grow mushrooms*, she thought. Since there wasn't much light coming in from the narrow casement windows, Peggy noticed her groping along and guided her up the creaky staircase by flashlight. She also noticed Addie taking in the spiderwebs strung between the balusters and said not to let it scare her.

"This ain't Halloween."

She added that it showed all the work that lay head of them. Addie said she could handle the work and the spiders.

"But what about the ghosts?"

"You'll know about them when you hear the mousetraps going off in the night."

"Then I'm the companion for you. I've got a cat."

"Whoopee!"

CHAPTER 61

"Peggy Tells the Story about a German"

The dank smell of the ground floor gave way to the sharp scent of fresh paint, and in the glare of an unshaded lamp, they spent the rest of the afternoon doing her bedroom in a soft pink. Peggy gabbed away like she hadn't talked to another human being in ages—and likely hadn't, except for the bad time they gave her downtown about getting the utilities hooked up (especially the phone) so she could stay on the lawyer's tail, and also have access to a doctor if need be.

"Funny town. If they don't know you to look at, they think you're from outer space. That's what the gal at the phone company looked like to me. You asked about ghosts. I might as well tell you it can get kind of spooky in here at night. Kids from those fancy town houses down there come prowling around. I suspect they might have been playin' in here before I arrived. I picked up this old air horn to scare 'em. Might get me a dog yet."

"I notice you have a shotgun."

"Yeah. There are people I may be stirring up a bit once I get more information out of the lawyer. You probably know about my mother and father. The police have it down as a murder-suicide, which nobody believes.

"Now this lawyer's brother, Bob, the reporter, thinks there very likely was foul play. The DA says 'Ain't no play, foul or fair.' According to Bob, there were some people putting pressure on Dad regarding a land deal. He thinks it's that and maybe something else too—both involving money, of course. But what, he won't say. A typical buttoned-up lawyer. Won't be comin' out with anything until he's got his ducks in a row.

"You saw all those posh town houses over on the hillside on your way up. Dad owned that land. Payment is still in dispute. The Tony people say 'No way.' They grab first then tell you the rest is negotiable. Anyway, I may in time have some accounts to settle, which means this place may yet become the hold-em-off fortress Daddy had in mind, with us pouring molten lead down on them when they come for us. You still wanna stay here?"

"Planned to camp out here anyway on the QT."

"Good. Yah won't need a tent. My situation ain't very sunshiny. For one thing, there's the matter of a trust that's got quite a bit of dough comin' to me, but it's tied up in the secret legal deal. So all I get for now is living expenses. I'm told there's another beneficiary out there. Seems it's written in the trust that who she is can't be disclosed till her father dies. Bob had been looking into all that messy stuff. It's interesting but confidential, I'm told. Wanna hear? You can keep it dark, can't you?"

"Down a well."

They had taken a break, and Peggy said she had just the other day asked for some information about her dad. She couldn't wait to share it with someone: it was a relief to talk to a non-professional.

She asked, "How about some wine?"

Addie said, "Anything but Port."

"Brother Bob, as a curious reporter looking into the murder-suicide thing, came upon a lockbox up here that the sloppy police never looked at, figurin' why dust it off if the case is closed.

"In the lockbox was Dad's private journal. It tells about a mad German guy who comes up and accuses Dad of having slept with the guy's housekeeper wife. Dad is able to cool him off but not before he takes a shot to the jaw, which helps the German's disposition. Anyway, he pours the guy some whiskey and puts several big bills on the table. That brings the German to his senses. They start talking settlement.

"The German gets a payoff and Dad's promise to provide for the kid in the same trust he's going to set up for me—which, for the German, is a guarantee that Dad will see that the terms of the trust are legally protected.

"The German loves the kid so much he claims he's the legitimate father. He gives Dad an old German saying, 'Vater werden ist nicht schwer, Vater sein dagegen sehr.' A cliché, I'm told, meaning something like 'it's not as difficult to make the child as it is to bring her up.'

"Picking it up from where Dad leaves off, Bob fills in subsequent events. The German's wife dies, so he's even more stubborn about keeping the secret, especially because, like he says, no chance he'll have another kid. 'It's okay,' he says, 'this kid lights up my life.' The lawyer speaks with the German, and he's able to loosen up a chunk of cash for me.

"But on one thing, it's still no-go. The German insists the girl is not to know about their true relationship, not before he dies. He's her dad and that's it. But that ties up the trust for me and the other one. You say you want to help. Would you mind killing a German?"

"I believe I'm one myself."

"Anyway, there's more to the story. Bob got to see the German. Seems the guy thinks there were people who might see him as a person of interest. If those people ever find out what he knows, he's gone. Bob took it as typical German paranoia and told him to play dumb, evidently not all that difficult for him to do.

"The point is the German had worked in one of Dad's mills, and when he was laid off, he had asked Dad for assistance. His daughter needed to have her tonsils out, and he was already up to his eyeballs in doctor bills for the other daughter. So Dad said to send him the bill.

"Later on, the kid broke her leg, and the German needed help with that. When it came to kids, Dad could be an easy touch. He had a heart and felt especially bad about me, his true daughter. Would come down to see me and call when he couldn't.

"Early on, Dad told the German when he came for his check to have the kid wait in his outer office so he could have a look at her without her seeing him. He looked and had to turn away. Couldn't hold back tears.

"I told you about trouble. Well, there are these relatives on my mother's side. I wanted to have a little visit with them, but they don't want no part of me. Fact is they resent me. I stand in the way of their suing the estate for what they call their 'fair share.' Probably mine."

She stopped to wet her tongue, giving Addie the chance to interject. "So there's no way around the problem of the mystery heir? The relatives know about the heir?"

"Know about it? The very idea of it drives them up a wall. Me . . . I'm not very comfortable with it either. I'd like to get with that quirky German and give him a piece of my mind. But he's as much a mystery as the heir. Those who know much about him— maybe just the lawyer and his brother, Bob—seem sworn to secrecy. 'Cause the German says there are people who shouldn't know about him. Silence was part of the bargain when he evidently okayed additional cash for me."

"Okay. When it comes down to it, can I find the German?"

"Whoa! There's a whole pack of 'em in town. Got themselves what they call a *bund*. Try crackin' it."

Peggy poured some more wine and looked at her watch. "Hey, it's getting late. Can you cook?"

CHAPTER 62

"Thoughts about Papa Otts and Johnny"

As with everything else, showtime with Johnny was not exactly as advertised. Arriving in the war room promptly at nine in the morning, Addie was greeted by the secretary with word that Johnny was running late but running. *Ah, at last! A face behind the whining voice.* In the flesh, there she was. The pock marked, frizzy-haired, and incomparably ugly Lady Collins, said to have been chosen from above by design.

Lady set out the coffee and donuts and brought out of the closet a couple of rustling bags emblazoned with the logo of the Discount Dress Mart, from one of which she slid out several boxes of costume jewelry, inviting Addie to have a look. She said they had to guess at her size but were assured the dresses were exchangeable.

Addie said nothing. Lost in thought, she sat there with her arms folded across her chest, staring vacantly out the window and taking in the buses coming and going. It gave her time to try to digest all that Peggy had unloaded on her.

She'd gone to bed with her head smoking. Another dilemma and a knottier one, at that! How could she tell Otts she knew and rob him of his heart-held secret? What a stinging hurt it would give him to know that she knew! Would the shock throw him into a downer, send him back to the hospital, and maybe (God forbid) bring back his heart trouble?

Well, maybe that was taking it a tad far; but however she turned it, she felt nothing good could come of letting him know. She was certain he'd never believe her if she told him she loved him just as much as before. He'd think she was simply trying to make him feel good and would be insulted that she could think he was so dumb as not to realize it. She could live without the money.

It was better to go along with the illusion. It was no illusion that Otts loved her and none surely that she loved him. Okay, there were things about him she didn't like, especially his treatment of her mother. He nonetheless had been her father in the real sense, and there was no illusion about that. She recalled his sleeping on a cot in her hospital room the night of the tonsillectomy.

At some point, in some way, she felt she might have to come out with it that she'd been told his secret; and it didn't affect her love. But try as she would, she couldn't picture how that might be done. How sad for him to have the cherished secret torn from his heart! How touching that he, above all, wanted her to believe he was her true father when in a real sense, he in fact was!

She spun around at the grip of Johnny's big paw on her shoulder. Practically lifting her out of the chair, he gave out with a roaring "Hah-lo, Addie honey!" His tie was loose, his hair windblown. (They'd told him he had to let his hair grow out and get a conventional haircut, in reaction to the *Morning Messenger*'s cartoons that depicted him as a mug-faced street fighter.) He apologized for his appearance (the new consciousness), saying he had run all the way from his office at the boardroom.

Brimming with joviality, he hoped he hadn't kept her waiting too long; but there were exciting developments. He'd just landed a campaign contribution from the Office Products people—big bucks that he planned to put into his stash. He'd tell her about that later. It pained him to see her looking so glum. *What could I do to make her happy? Dinner at the Rooftop Café?*

She turned the bag upside down and shook out the cheap, frilly dresses. Not exactly her style and not the Enchanté elegance that was promised. Angrily clawing them with one hand, he wound up and threw them into the trash basket. "Schmattes!" he yelled, imitating his Jewish handball partner who ran the Mart.

Further venting his disgust, he swept the jewelry boxes off the table and crunched them underfoot like he was rubbing out a colony of ants. He said she had to know it was not his doing. As she'd probably noticed, Enchanté had been burned and looted. He wouldn't go so far as to say the fire sale dresses might have been Dunneville's way of punishing her for showing up late.

Nonetheless, he'd see to it she got the clothes worthy of her—and him. He'd put Betsy on it. Before he could go on, she told him about the car, which was greeted by an expression that looked like he'd just had heartburn. Of course, those rental people are contributors; but if it isn't fixed right, he'd certainly take care of it. In any case, the rental was intended as a temporary thing.

"Didn't Domo Junior tell you?"

"Oh yeah, Junior. Seems he had some problems with board, and they with him."

The one perk that approximated the sugarplums that had been promised was the town house suite. Either he'd forgotten her message rejecting it, or he wanted to show it off anyway. He insisted that she had to see what he had in mind for her.

It was in one of the separate parcels at the Heights, the luxury complex called Castle Estates, in the same building where Betsy and Louey had their unit. It was a swank affair with deep-pile carpeting—powder blue, which set off the French Provincial furniture—and flower boxes on a balcony that looked out into the pine woods beyond.

There were sparkling new kitchen appliances, a jacuzzi, and a huge radio console with speakers in the bathroom. Everything was really posh. But she later learned from Betsy that she would have been sharing it with Dunneville's mistress and co-hosting Friday night poker for the cigar–smoking inner circle, which interestingly excluded Johnny—who, she soon began to realize, was looked upon as the stooge they'd use to rubber-stamp their high-stakes patronage.

For all his bluster, she found there were times when she could feel sorry for the big guy. He lived in a world of hard characters, which he was not. Her dropping some remark about the tough world he moved in gave him the opening to admit, with a bashful twist of the head, there was no secret about his being soft on her, which made her wonder how she could damp that down without hurting the guy. He meant well, and for the time being, she needed him.

When Betsy took her shopping, Addie got the word that her job was not just to stand on the platform and look admiringly at Johnny but also to make sure he stayed sober and didn't get too handy with the women—at least not in public. He seemed to know about these admonitions as he assured her *believably* he was changed, adding that his feelings for her hadn't.

She told him to stop it; theirs was supposed to be a business relationship, and if he had any other thoughts, she was gone. But no sooner had she said this than she saw him cringe with that stupid heartburn look. He said sorry. She reflexively put a soft hand to his cheek, and he brought it to his lips. As things worked out, he had a protective, dog-like devotion to her; and she could see he was not about to impose himself. With that settled, she felt more comfortable. He wanted her but would wait her out. Out of a growing affection, she had to tell him not to.

Still, she was troubled by what role Johnny might have had in getting her sacked at school. Not knowing quite how to take it up with him between trying on dresses, she quizzed Betsy about the debacle at school. She said she figured the situation had been manipulated to compel a walkout on her part.

Betsy concurred, "What else? . . . Dunneville would have been behind that. You hadn't hopped-to fast enough. Besides, he wanted you insecure. It would make you anxious to please."

Addie had herself a little laugh. "Oh, really? Wait till he finds out he's not the only one who can pull surprises."

Betsy heard that Johnny was furious when he found out about the forced walkout at school, and he and Dunneville got themselves into a yelling match. What with pressures of the campaign, they'd been doing a lot of that lately (sort of like an old married couple who accepted it as part of the relationship and went on from there) although it seemed to have become a little more than a farting contest of late, particularly where Addie was concerned.

Betsy noted there was something about this Dunneville that in addition to the anxiety tactic, he just had to have women under his thumb; and as she'd mentioned before, it looked to her like he also wanted to make it tough on Addie because he realized no way Johnny would let him make a play.

As Betsy appraised the situation, she said, "Of course, Dunny's single-minded enough that he won't lose sight of the fact that you are his ace in the hole to keep Johnny happy enough to get along and go along and secure the win that was wanted of him."

"So I'm a pacifier, am I? I swear once I get some money out of these people . . ."

Betsy told her to hold it. "I wouldn't get riled at this point. You're too far into it now. Consider it a job. Who likes work? A strange guy, all right, this Dunneville. Also relentless. But do you know what his mistress calls him? . . . Bunny. Ain't that cute?"

CHAPTER 63

On the Campaign Trail

It took a while, though a short one, for Addie to have the sudden realization that she was none too subtly being subject to restrictions. They wanted her in that town house, or she'd have no house at all. Socially, they wanted her isolated. Louey, Betsy's sweet Sonny, had overnight turned sour, walking out on her, and was being posted to keep an eye on Addie. She was to be locked out of any other job than the one assigned to her.

What it practically came down to was that Johnny would be her sole companion though with restrictions there too. On the plus side, she began to have a new appreciation for him, seeing him as a welcome refuge. He was observant, noticing what was happening; and she had the sense he was looking out for her. "Fear nothing," she told herself. "They'll find out what they could do with their restrictions." For one thing, she decidedly wasn't moving in with Dunny's mistress.

During Addie's first week on the job, they were working fundraisers and talks with focus groups (unions, teachers, small businessmen, and the like); and Johnny had gotten his canned speech down to a trim ten minutes. To her surprise, Addie found herself becoming more than an appealing ornament that pumped up Johnny's confidence. She was making an impression on her own and got good vibes from the fact that she seemed to go over with the public, which was something new in her life. Manna for the ego.

She was being told in the reception line what a great couple she and Johnny made. People instinctively liked how they looked together, and she found she wasn't as bothered as she thought she would be in looking like she was attached to him. Even when he had an arm around her, he couldn't be more respectful. Maybe ragged at the edges, but a gentleman.

Meanwhile, Dunneville, observing from the back of the room, was giving them a thumbs- up. So she was proving him right, after all, and indeed proving herself—which felt good, contrary to the prior distaste she'd had for this stupid "job"; however she was also becoming aware that she had better watch herself, lest she enjoy her night in the limelight to the point that she lost sight of the fact that she was sure to be butting heads with this foul crowd.

That would come upon her unasked during the unpleasantness she shortly had to handle on being pushed to get out there and mingle with the public—which meant making small talk, smiling, listening to the people's woes, enduring their garlicky hugs, and obliging the smelly old men who wanted to dance with her. The night they held their long overdue rally for the Blacks, things started off rather well (what with the generous helpings of barbecued ribs, chicken, cornbread, and the ever-flowing barrels of cold beer).

But she could tell that the women standing there, arms akimbo and heads canted, were not exactly enthralled by the sight of their men dancing with this sickly-looking white chick. Despite her making friends with the wallflowers before the evening was out, she took an unkind elbow from a chunky lady, whose wobbly husband had steadied himself by sliding an arm over her shoulders and going cheek to cheek.

The following night, it was the poles at the church's tightly packed bingo hall, where Johnny's home folks were greeting him with all the boisterous acclaim due their conquering hero. Making his rounds of the tables, laughing, drinking, hugging the fat mamas, back-slapping and glad handing the jowlly Papas, all the while chomping on a fat sausage, he barely made it back to the platform in time for Father Tim's blessing.

Once things settled down, Johnny gave them his rousing get-out-the-vote talk while people were stuffing themselves with kielbasa, pierogi, dumplings, meatballs, stuffed cabbage, potato salad, hot peppers, pickles, and sauerkraut, swilled down with brimming schooners of beer, which some of the men were using as vodka chasers that had them reeling well before Domo brought in the guy with the accordion.

"Hey, c'mon, you lazy Pollocks!" Johnny yelled. "Listen to this snappy stuff Polka Mike is puttin' out! Yeah, c'mon. Let's shake a leg and get with the music."

After he'd taken Addie out on the floor for a couple of clumsy whirls, she sat down to nurse her bruised toes, only to be hauled out again by one of Johnny's old beer-gutted football buddies who was so far gone that as he picked it up on the second turn, he went down with a plop pulling her down onto his pillowy stomach. Luckily, she came away with no more than a sprained wrist. Everyone had a big laugh, and the accordion player brought it up real loud with "Roll out the Barrel" that sent the couples off on their high-stepping whirl again.

Before the evening was out, Addie found herself cornered by a couple of belching drunks competing for the honor of teaching her Polish. It wound up with them going at one another in what must have been something less than the King's Polish. *Dobrze*, (*dobzha*, good) the only word that got through to her, was her unfortunate response to whatever they said.

Johnny came to the rescue and complimented her on being a great sport. He told her to take the following day off. She thanked him and said she'd rather have the weekend with a little extra in her paycheck.

She thought she had been through the roughest part of the week, but she had no idea of what it would be like to party with the volatile Italians, especially on being given the once-over by those yeasty young bucks with slicked down black hair who fancied themselves lady killers. Tough Tony took over the rostrum and laid out his idea of how their ward was going to produce the big win.

Shooting his fists out for emphasis like he was shadowboxing, he even got the old folks revved up for the fight. They would vote the young and the old, the kiddies and the grannies, the sick and the well, the living and the dead; but above all, they had to make sure of the women's vote. He wanted the men to go right into the booth with them to see that they didn't on the sly vote for the good-looking Reform candidate, that aristocratic judge's son who never worked a day in his life and sported a white-gloved wife beside.

The line had formed for those wanting to dance with Addie, and the heavyset guy who pushed to the head of it caught her off guard with his exaggerated deep dips that rolled her disgustingly up on his thigh. The next time he did it, she pushed herself off and caught him by surprise with a swift knee that landed just shy of its target. He was about to give her the back of his hand, but the guy next in line intervened.

A near fistfight ensued, and in the course of the shoving, Addie got knocked back against the wall. She shook off the apologies and danced with her rescuer, Carmine, who made it a point to be extra courteous. He told her not to mind the aggressive guy: he was Tony Jr. and thought he could get away with anything, but people had his number. With a laugh, he told her he had almost become his brother-in-law; and there'd been quite a to-do over that.

It seems that Carmine, who was Mario the detective's son, had been dating Tough Tony's buxom daughter; and when it started to get serious, Tony voiced a doubt. Being a substitute teacher, Carmine didn't have a steady job and had turned down the offer to supervise Tony's Mexican field hands.

"How's this guy gonna make a livin'?" Tony asked. "Offa me? I don't care if he's pickin' shit outta cuckoo clocks, but he's gotta be able to support my daughter!" The daughter turned rebellious and got her revenge by running off with a married man.

Addie looked in vain for Johnny, who was making his rounds and was going from table to table; then out of the corner of her eye, she caught sight of Domo yanking on Johnny's tie for him to bend down and have something whispered in his ear. Upon hearing it, Johnny wheeled about and, finding Tony Jr. over by the bar, grabbed him by the collar and, giving him a head-bobbing shake, spat some harsh words in his face.

The crowd was steaming up the packed dance hall to the point that Addie and Carmine took their spaghetti and meatballs outside to the picnic table by the side door, where they were joined by several other couples. Tony Jr. suddenly appeared out of the dark, and picking up Carmine's plate, he twisted it in his face. Arms flailing, they went at one another. At one point, two of Tony's henchmen pinned Carmine's arms back, allowing Tony to get in a quick one-two. Carmine tore himself free, and they were rolling on the turf when Addie got Johnny out to pull them apart.

Not her idea of fun, she told Johnny as he hustled her out to the car. They stopped at the diner for coffee, and she was all for telling him adios; but before she could get it out, he was plying her with apologies and promises.

"This is never going to happen again."

"Who was the genius," she asked, "who wanted me out there dancing with these bozos? Didn't they know it would bring trouble if they put a woman into a mix like that?"

"Well," he said, shyly rubbing his chin, "truth is it goes over. The mayor-to-be sharing his fiancée means votes."

"What!" she practically howled.

Insisting he'd see to it that there was no more of that, he took both of her hands in his and, all but down on his knees, pleaded with her to hang on for just one more ethnic party, the most important one of all—with the PRs—because the Reformer had made some inroads there, pointing to the oppressive police force and a DA who was all for filling the jails with their people, whereas it was Mr. Reform himself—none other than princely Van—who had been behind the effort to get Whimpy out of jail.

"It's a gotta-do thing, Addie. I'll keep a close lookout. Depend on it. No more rough stuff. We're gonna move on to better things, the country club crowd. Money doesn't have to fight for what it wants. And talk about better things, we got a big shindig comin' up over the weekend. A retreat up in the Jew Mountains, where we lay out the plan for the rest of the campaign and divvy up the patronage. But mostly, it'll be party time."

"Johnny you're a sweet guy, but I've got to level with you. Partying with this bunch you're in with ain't exactly a day at the beach for me. I look around and all I see is dishonesty! Unscrupulous men abusing the public trust and corrupting government to enrich themselves . . . They get caught and the first thing out of their mouths is 'We did nothing wrong.'

"Do they for Chrissakes know what *wrong* is? I'm no saint, but I ask myself 'where do I fit in with any of this?' I'm here because I've been done out of my job, which I think you know something about. And I frankly need the money, which was handsomely promised, most of which I have yet to see."

"You're right. I have to admit I'm not liking it like I thought I would. But I'm in so far now it's as tough to go back as to go forward. I gotta level with you too. Yeah, you're doin' good things for the campaign, but that's not why you're here. It's me. Told 'em I needed you. The truth? Just having you near me . . . Well, I can't tell you how it warms me. I'm a new man. I put up with their crap in hopes I can do some good—like you want. Stay with me."

"Johnny, please. You're getting yourself worked up. Not good for either of us."

"I know I made some stupid mistakes—terrible ones! And you've been good enough to understand. It hurts to this day. I think you're telling me it's no-go. And that's okay. Except the feeling won't go away. But I'll make it." He got out his handkerchief and blew his nose. He wanted to say more but couldn't.

"Now it's my turn to say I'm sorry. I'm more than sorry. I wish it were different. I like you. But as I've told you, *like* is as far as it goes for me."

"S'okay. I got it big enough. If you want out, I'll help you get whatever you want."

He was doing his best to hold on, clenching and unclenching his fists. A stray tear escaped the handkerchief. *Had I been taking his feelings too lightly?* She moved over to his side of the booth and leaned on his shoulder. Bringing his head over, she kissed his wet cheek. He seemed to have read it as a kiss-off. Reaching into his wallet, he stripped out the bills and stuffed them in her purse.

"Sorry about the pay thing. But like everything else, this bunch is pretty sloppy about bookkeeping. Come, I'll drive you to your car."

CHAPTER 64

Talking It over with Betsy, also Johnny

She got together with Betsy for lunch, wanting to unload.

"I've had it up to here," she began. "Despite what you tell me about a stranglehold, I want out. But I mean <u>out.</u> As distant as I can get out!"

Betsy was sympathetic and shook her head in agreement as Addie ranted on then interrupted her. "I myself was lookin' to go 'over the hill' on them, but I was told nobody could beat these guys. Nobody ever had! Then I hear a rumor that there was one guy who has—so far."

"Really? Who the hell is that Braveheart?"

"You remember Domo's son, Junior, the guy who dropped off that car for you? He unloaded on them for slappin' you with a wreck. They told him to get lost and he did."

"Just like that? How? Where'd he go?"

"Not for you, dearie. We got word he wanted to join the Dillinger Gang. And he meant it. But he can talk big then do what he wants to. He'll be around for you."

"Hmm . . . Good to know. But there are obligations of the heart. Johnny. It hurts to see that poor guy so wounded. I had thought it would be best all around if I just let him get over it. Then, it began to eat at me that I couldn't be so miserable a bitch as to leave him in that shape. I called to tell him I'd stay and help him. I knew in my gut it was the better thing to do."

"And how'd he take it?"

"His thank-you was sort of slow and thick-tongued, like he wasn't sure it was for real that I called. He paused, swallowed, thanked me again, and I heard him hit his glass against the bottle. There was another pause, another swallow. Then he said, 'You're kind. I love you for that too.'"

Betsy squeezed her hands. "Don't you think you could get to . . . uh, really like this guy?"

"Betsy, I like him more than I thought I would. But I'm not up to what he wants. And I don't mean getting in bed. I think you give your heart only once . . . in the big way. True, that situation soured, but I haven't got over the bad taste. For anything to happen, I gotta feel the true sweetness is back. In a way, I wish . . . Well, I'm not sure what I wish just now."

"What are you trying to say?"

"Oh, nothing. You know I've been in a similar fix with Whimpy, and look at what happened! Wasn't good for either of us. Maybe something down the road. A homeostasis, like they call it."

"Pity. A pity for sure. Johnny's a good guy. The way he's been gone on you has made a difference. I wish Sonny might have felt a little like that for me . . . I think I can say it now. Johnny has some character. If you're around him a little more, you never can tell. He has already changed—a lot! Anyway, what did you mean when you said you were gonna help him?"

"I have some thoughts. How they work out remains to be seen. Since I'm stuck with this damned business, cashwise—at least for now—I figure I might as well take advantage of what I can do with it. He says he wants to do good, and I'm going to see to it he makes good on that."

The lunch they were having was in the hospital cafeteria. Having made up her mind, Addie needed particulars about the PR rally, like where and when. Johnny had been busy working on a presentation, and she had no interest in calling Dunneville.

Addie hadn't seen Betsy since the shopping venture, and it was quite unlike her to be away from the campaign for over a week.

Addie had called, and the cleaning lady said she could look Betsy up at the hospital, as she'd gone in for a checkup. Turns out she'd had a miscarriage, and there had been quite a bit of bleeding.

They'd had an argument over Sonny's keeping late hours. He had taken off, come back, and wasn't so sure he wanted to stay. *Was he getting it elsewhere?* She frankly wanted to know since he thought she was looking so unappealing with that bulging belly. The inquiry got him mad, and he started slapping her around.

She locked herself in the bathroom and had a good cry. He thought the miscarriage was revenge. Thankfully, he had found himself another woman and moved out. She was ready to get back to work now—in fact, welcomed it.

Dunneville brought everybody together for a staff pep talk. He said the PRs were known to be block voters, so if his personnel could swing a core constituency, they'd get 'em all. Addie got a nudge and Betsy breathed in her ear. "Pure bullshit! It's what he says about all 'constituencies.'"

"Besides," he went on, "by marching right into the heart of the dreaded Fourth Ward, we'd show the rest of the city that we could handle these unruly people and keep the peace. No more riots. And the timing couldn't be better. With infamous Carlos out of jail, and he along with other PRs given decent jobs—like at the country club, where none of them would have been taken on before—we ought to be ripe for a celebration!"

Domo and Louey got orders to grab a couple of trucks from the Public Works' car pool (duly checked out with Eddy, the BS one) and had them round up hot bands from the city's jumpingest bars and drove them to the hub of the ward, where they set up the beer barrels and put on one big rollicking block party. They trotted out their high school cheerleaders, and the bands blared away till midnight and beyond.

As Dunneville reported, "We danced those kids till they fell over. They couldn't have thrown a bottle if their lives depended on it. I mean we had 'em!"

Betsy had joined Addie and Johnny on the platform, and except for waving on cue, they were able to stay pretty much in the background and take in the wild scene. Heads jerked and fingers snapped in rhythm with the beat of a fired-up drummer as sweaty olive faces moved in and out of the rays of the street lamps.

Addie reminded Johnny that while Dunneville might advise him on the campaign, if he wanted her to be with him, she was going to be his personal advisor. She gave him chapter and verse and got an indication that he was going to be receptive when he agreed to her nixing the stump speech.

After Dunneville had Johnny and Addie stand beside him, things got interesting as some of the Latin females began making eyes at Johnny, who was for them the obvious Alpha male, and asked him to come down and dance. Addie's tug at his sleeve stopped that, which produced yet another Dunneville frown. "Hey, Buster, whatta yah think we're here for? A show 'n go? Get with it!"

Following a look from Big D, Betsy gave Addie a tug, adding, "Don't know about you, baby, but I want a paycheck. Gotta dance."

It seems they were having a buffet for the older crowd at the Union Hall down the street. Betsy took her into the lady's room there and said orders were for them to change into these sexy dresses. Addie's was a tight-fitting, low-cut red knit that was really snug across the breasts and butt. When she went to the mirror, they both broke out laughing.

"So Dunny's up to his old tricks again. I thought Johnny talked to him about this kind of thing."

"Yeah, but he insists on calling the shots, especially if he thinks he's being challenged. And you saw what happened at the dance. Can't recall seein' him look that mean."

"I saw. But no way I'm going to wear this stupid thing! We're supposed to be teasing these hot Latinos, are we?"

"Johnny said something like that to Dunny, but he was told to wise up. The way Dunny puts it, the people is an idiot. And plain and simple, girls' asses mean votes."

"And you're going along with it?"

"Honey, I'm the guy's secretary. Remember? They're not payin' us to be standin' around back like we're wallpaper."

"Hey, so far they haven't paid me a cent for not standing against the wall. What I got so far has come out of Johnny's wallet. Have you seen any money for this gig of ours?"

"It'll all be taken care of. I know how they operate. Nothing for a while then you do something good, and there's a fat envelope."

"So we gotta keep jumping through hoops if we want to get the carrot eventually?"

"Yeah, it's stupid, but right now we gotta show."

"Maybe you gotta. I'll show when Dunny shows me the envelope."

"I'll cover for you. Tell 'im you've got a headache. Menstrual."

"Thanks! Dunny's gonna share my headache. I told Johnny he's got to come through, or I'm through. I've got other ideas about what I'd like to do with my life."

She unzipped, stepped out of the fire engine dress and back into her basic black sheath. She did a mock curtsy and was out the door, where she jumped at the shock of finding herself up against Johnny's chest. It was like running into a wall.

He had his arms around her and said there was no way he would have allowed it.

"Not to worry."

She comes as she is and sits at the head table with him.

"No mingling, no dancing. No nonsense of any kind if I have my say about it. And just watch—a say I'm going to have!"

"Whatever, don't walk out *please*. There'll be ups and downs. I need you more than ever now. I swear I'm turnin' myself around."

She was quite aware of her own ups and downs. Unaccountably, just as his enthusiasm for the fight began to build, she found herself becoming heavy with doubt.

Reading her dispirited look, Johnny gave her a little shake. "Remember, you said we could do some good. Let's—Let's do it together! Leave me now and I go bust. I want you to marry me."

"Oh no!" She feared having to deal with that again.

"I mean it. My life would be empty without you. It is now."

"Cut it out." Actually, his innocence was appealing. He didn't even know how to propose.

CHAPTER 65

Johnny Gives a Speech

She shook her head and breathed. She should have known their prior agreement wouldn't hold; it was folly to think it had been settled simply because it was done to suit her. What use was there to remind him that the two things couldn't be mixed? She'd never given a thought to marrying anyone, and there had been a couple of men she'd been close with. Yes, they could work together; but romance had to be stowed somewhere in grandma's attic, if they were going make a go of it.

Jobwise, stowed was good enough for him. He said their situation was having the same effect on him that it was having on her. In fact, "more so." He could no longer ignore the fact that this crowd looked upon him as a mere pawn, a messenger boy for the Dunny game of power and money. Not once did they consult him about the campaign or the policy. They never included him in their high-level meetings wherein they talked about divvying up the spoils.

They even wanted to cut him out of the upcoming dinner with the lieutenant governor, and he practically had to threaten a walkout if they didn't let him go on the retreat. The only time they talked seriously to him was to give him the schedule and to tell him what to say and, above all, what not to say. So if it was a matter of ammunition, he was loaded.

Reality had a way of settling in on her. Looking out over the Union Hall and seeing these poor bronze-faced people dressed in their modest Sunday's best—here and there a necktie on a plaid shirt—smiling up so hopefully, she wondered if Johnny could put himself in the position of deceiving them. *What good could he, for goodness' sake, do them?*

While she was trying to think of a way to restrain him, he, as if determined to instantly prove himself, abruptly got up before dinner and, clinking his fork on the water glass, fumbled his way into an impromptu talk.

"Er . . . it's great . . . uh . . . bein' here with all you, good people. As you can see . . . uh, we got food for the stomach. Well . . . I wanna give you food for thought. Eh, hope so anyway." He grinned and looked down amidst whispering out on the floor. "Hold it, please. I do have something to say." After an awkward pause, he caught his breath and readied himself to try again. Dunneville looked up at the ceiling as if to say "Has this chump been drinking again?"

"You know my name, but what you really want to know is who am I an' where am I comin' from. Well, lemme begin by givin' you an example of what's wrong in this city. You know about the people livin' on the steps of city hall. The politicians go by them at least twice a day. Those people can't hear them and that's sad, but sadder still is the fact that the politicians can't see them . . . Except to cart 'em away when a VIP comes to town. That's the kinda situation I'd like to do something about. And lots more, like where the people are ignored."

Greeted with polite applause and a "Yeah, yeah!" here and there, Johnny saw that if he was going to get anywhere with these hot-blooded people, he'd better throw some raw meat out there—and quickly—or he was done for. So he mentioned the police, a sure-fire starter.

"How come they only show up to nab or shoot somebody? Ever seen them walk a beat in your ward?"

The crowd instantly perked up with a raucous "Hell no!"

And Johnny knew he had them. Moving on to the streets (a moonscape, last resurfaced ages ago), he began to pick up momentum, giving them more of the same (beginning with run–down public housing) above all, addressing the people in a one-on-one tone and making eye contact from person to person as he went along.

When he promised to replace their dilapidated school with a new one—something he'd been warned was taboo—he spoke with concern, and people could tell he meant it. He drew unanimous "Yeah, yeahs," and a great approving hum went through the hall.

Bewildered, Dunneville was pulling at his sleeve, trying to get him back down in his seat. Addie tugged on the other sleeve, and he took off his jacket and rolled up his shirt sleeves. Continuing with a ripping demagogic twang in his voice and making critical pauses for the pumped-up response, he blistered away at their neglected needs.

He said they should have a recreation center to get the idle kids off the street. He exclaimed "No wonder they got in trouble," at which Dunneville rolled his eyes.

"You should have increased presence on the police force, wherein you have two token officers, and in city hall, where you have nobody. Who better to represent you on Social Services, for goodness' sake, but your own? How come the federal money for low-income housing never found its way into the low-income neighborhood?

"What about all the red tape you have to plow through to get food vouchers, rent allowance, admittance to free clinic, basic dental care for your kids?"

Dunny looked over at Louey, standing in the far doorway, wearing a tank top and flexing his muscles. He waved him off. Obviously, a brawl would be counterproductive.

Johnny rolled on. "You people are sittin' in a union hall, but how many of you get union wages? What about workmen's compensation for people injured on the job? What about police brutality, prison reform, scumbag guards, strip searches, lying snitches, planted evidence, indifferent lawyers, biased juries, hanging judges? What about it, folks!"

On and on he churned, citing injustices—real and imagined—and wrapping it up with a shrill rallying cry. "Hey, are you, folks, bona fide citizens of the U.S. of A.?"

This brought out a rousing "Yeah!"

"Then, ain't it time the goddam politicians in this town started treating you like you are!"

"Yeah, yeah! Yeah, yeah! Give 'em hell, Johnny!"

"An' I'll tell yah somethin' else. I'm gonna open a special nursery school for your little ones, and I've got the greatest teacher in the whole country to run it. She's right here! Let's give her a hand! Stand up, Addie."

He pulled her up, and there was riotous applause.

"And you know what else? How many of you ladies get prenatal care? That ain't free. Well, all that's gonna change when our Addie manages the Women's Free Clinic."

Addie's protest was drowned out by the women stamping their feet and clapping in approval.

"You know what? From the moment I take office, you're gonna see a difference. Why should human necessities be reserved for Gringos only!"

Gordo had the people on their feet chanting "Johnny, Johnny, Johnny!" He beamed back at them, arms held high as if signaling a touchdown; and they thundered up to the platform. He was getting embraced, kissed on both cheeks, high-fived, and backslapped from all sides.

"Olé!" he triumphantly shouted, circling somebody's cap; and they shouted it back to him. They stormed around Addie, hugging her and chattering away in words she couldn't understand. Polka Mike materialized out of nowhere and was cranking out "Happy Days Are Here Again" on his accordion.

The crowd had completely forgotten about the food. Partly to rescue himself and Addie, Johnny waved them over to the ample steam table—where the people exuding feel-good smiles started heaping their trays with assorted tacos, enchiladas, tortillas, and burritos; it was a feast for which Johnny had defiantly gone over budget. Dunneville was nowhere to be seen.

CHAPTER 66

Aftereffect: Dunny Gets Congrats

Next morning, it was all over the front page of the *Morning Messenger*. Tom had seen to that. He did it up right and for good journalistic reason. Johnny's performance was sensational news, a vital twist in the boring mayoral campaign. Deleste had been on hand to take pictures; and Tom had come up to Johnny for an interview as he relaxed, feet up, with his after-dinner cigar. Word was all over town about what a dynamic speaker the mayor-to-be was turning out to be. If Johnny was the toast of the town—and great newspaper copy—Dunneville found himself the toast of the political establishment.

The inner circle was huddled in the war room over ten o'clock coffee, and everybody was shaking Dunneville's hand and showering him with complements. Wide-eyed with amazement, he managed a half smile. When word got around city hall that their grim, behind-the-scene boss turned overnight popular sensation was in the building, people that Dunneville had never seen before were dropping by to congratulate him—obscure operatives from the Zoning Board, Weights and Measurements, Sewer Maintenance, the Utilities Billing Department, the Welfare Office, Social Services, Engineering, Community Development, the Clerk of Courts—and before long, the party Faithful from near and far were calling in.

In the midst of holding court to all the well-wishers wanting to be onboard with him, Dunny got a call from the lieutenant governor himself. Flabbergasted, he breathed, "My God, I thought only bad news traveled this fast."

People couldn't contain themselves, for the polls had been showing some slippage for the party's slate. This tide was lifting everybody's dinghy. He was hearing things like "Bombastic strategy move" from the LG and "Yeah, promise 'em anything. Give 'em what they want to hear, and after you win, give 'em what you want to give."

From others, he was hearing, "Stroke of political genius," and on it went with the verbal confetti falling all around him. As Magowan put it, "Bottom line is Reform could never win without the Fourth Ward."

Even the poker-faced chief, Tony's man, was excited. "Boy-oh-boy, have we got a lock or what!"

He came over to Dunneville and gave him a kiss on the forehead—adding, in high spirits, that it wasn't what it used to mean.

When the dust cleared, Dunny was left with his right hand friend, Magowan, who was pouring the Jameson's for their Irish Cream. Magowan had narrowly lost the nomination to Johnny and shared Dunny's contempt for the clown. He wanted to know what it was really like down there.

Dunny said there was no way to describe it and burst out with a giggle that mounted into the wildest laugh. It was so infectious that Magowan couldn't help joining in. The hilarity grew, and soon they were hacking away and all but rolling on the floor. Finally recovered, Magowan wanted to know "What now?"

"Plenty," Dunny replied, reaching for the Jameson's. "We humor him. Let 'im say what he wants. He wins the race. We win the city. Talk about red meat . . . We get a direct line to the state house, and the Lieutenant Governor is joining us on the retreat. Wait'll you see where we go from there."

CHAPTER 67

Country Club Affair and
Trouble with Louey

To his credit, Johnny knew how to work a room, regardless of what his inner mood might have been—up or down. But he could really turn it up a notch when given the posh setting of the country club ballroom, where every place you looked something glistened—from the crystal chandeliers reflected in the room-length Versailles mirrors to the sparkling bone china, the long-necked wineglasses, and the newly polished oak floor that gave an expensive click to the two-hundred-dollar patent leather shoes.

There was even a glisten to the well-heeled clientele coming off the bald heads of men with Florida tans shared by their diamond necklaced wives—mostly dyed blondes in low-cut black evening dresses, looking like they had just stepped out of the whiskey ad, but actually just Lord & Taylor. If they were rich enough, they might have acquired the young mistress with an hourglass figure.

Addie had been thinking that what she most had to fear was that Johnny might be getting a little cocky. Not a good thing when he had to stay on his toes. But as she watched him ease his good-natured way from table to table, pressing the flesh and bowing to the women, here and there bestowing a kiss on the cheek, she could tell it was somehow forced and not up to the level of his usual bonhomie. Even the patented toothy laugh of his that responsively lit up faces seemed a touch exaggerated.

At first, she thought he was simply adjusting to the more conservative crowd; but when he edged her out into the foyer, cocktail in hand, she found out otherwise. He'd been thinking they were there to raise money for his campaign, but then without the customary by-your-leave, he's all of a sudden told it's going to support the gubernatorial race. His race was in the bag so no sweat there.

Now they had to be thinking ahead, like about the state chairmanship for Dunneville and all the sweetmeats they'd be getting from that. *Johnny did want to be a part of it, didn't he?* As for that lousy table at the back of the room, Dunneville had no idea why they hadn't set up a place for Johnny at the head table, right up there on the dais next to W.C. (as in Fields), the moniker they'd given the bulbous-nosed lieutenant governor. Anyway, it shouldn't be a problem to get Johnny an introduction. Johnny said he didn't care to meet W.C.; it was him, his pal Dunny, that he wanted to meet with.

"Well, there are some things we do have to talk over, like where the money's coming from to cover the PR shindig, but not now. I gotta stay with this guy. Like I was tellin' you, it means big things for us, so we gotta show the kinda resources we can tap into up here. This place . . . Well, look at it! Makes an impression, doesn't it? Appreciate your help. Keep it up, and we'll all be in clover."

Johnny blocked his way, and Dunneville got impatient. "Didn't I tell you later, man?" Johnny said he wasn't going to be put off. His campaign fund was in deficit. The fund was him, so he owed people a bunch of dough. And that wasn't all.

"Ease up, man. Sit down and enjoy the evening. Can't you see what's at stake here? Why make a pain in the ass of yourself? Everything's gonna get taken care of. Even you." Dunny said with a toothy smile. "Confidence, man. We're sittin' pretty."

Dunneville spent a good part of the rest of the evening evading Johnny. Every time Johnny approached, he either ducked into a circle of his well-heeled guests (preferably with women present) or he put W.C. between himself and Johnny as he walked the "Gov" over to meet another deep-pockets baldy. Whenever Johnny got too close, Dunny had the annoying habit of snapping his thumb at him.

Johnny finally corralled him as he was weaving his way to the men's room. Inside, he backed him against the far urinal, saying he wanted some information. How come, he wanted to know, they cut his budget and high-handedly latched onto his special bank account—campaign money he'd personally raised!—while Dunneville and Sammy (his new assistant) were spending money like drunken sailors?

Also, what about Domo Sr. telling him they had commandeered all the official cars, including his Buick, to show W.C. around so he'd have to get along with Addie's car for a while? Then, Johnny just got this note from Magowan, saying it would probably be best if he went on the next retreat since they were fixing W.C. up with a broad at the resort; and he wouldn't feel comfortable if there were too many people around.

Dunneville listened patiently, and sliding out his bottom lip to show concern, he said "There must have been a misunderstanding somewhere along the line. But all of that would be set to right—no question. And now how about letting me take a decent leak?"

Johnny waited for Dunneville just outside the door. He motioned Addie away, and when Dunneville emerged, Johnny put an arm around the guy and walked him out into the foyer— where Dunneville, angrily twisting free, had a few choice words for Johnny, spoken to the beat of his forefinger.

Fearful that she might have to intervene to save the situation, Addie watched the scene in pantomime from the glass in the door window. His face tomato-red, Johnny started pumping out his points with supporting arm motion.

Straightening his tie, Dunneville unflappably let him get it out; then he came back at him with that forefinger to the chest and, rocking from side to side, told him how things were going to be— period. He ended with a dismissive wave of the hand as Johnny began to open his mouth again, followed by a quickie pat on the back; and he slithered away to catch hold of Domo, who had been pacing in the entryway waiting for instructions, one part of which evidently was to get hold of Louey.

Addie had never seen Johnny so worked up. "Well," he said, "I'd never been so royally screwed, and I just wasn't going to take it!" Addie tried to remind him of what they'd talked about. He had perfect leverage now to get things his way. He was going to be able to do the campaign on his terms, or he'd walk. As for the money, he could tell them, in the first place, he wasn't going to do anything further on the campaign unless they coughed it up—his own money first! Could they afford to lose their winning candidate?

Meanwhile, on trying to pushing it with Dunneville, he had to back off with the approach of an obvious Industrialist dressed in a tux. Didn't he notice, as Addie pointed out, how much in command Dunneville was by the manner of his calmly avoiding confrontation?

Seeing he only half listened, she drew him back to the table and had the waiter bring him a double Scotch. Downing it, he slammed his fist down, ordered another, and had some testy words for the waiter when it was slow in coming. Deciding that for the moment it was the lesser evil, she told the waiter to keep the Scotch coming until she said "Whoa." And it did seem to slow the big fella down a bit.

Usually an impressive eater of *anything* in his sullenness, he had barely touched his juicy broiled salmon. *He doesn't like fish now?* However, recalling how he liked the atmosphere of the diner, Addie seated him off in a dark corner of the anteroom and told the waiter to bring him a plate of his favorite steak and eggs, hoping it might perk him up a bit. Knowing they'd do breakfast any time at the club, she asked for a side of home fries made with bacon chips, onions, and green peppers.

"What do you think of that?" His brief mumble suggested indifference.

Seeing that the bear in him was dug in, she knew she'd have to go easy. So she snuggled up and, putting a warm hand inside his jacket, rubbed his well-muscled back, which brought an appreciative smile. A kiss loosened him up even further.

"You're a honey."

"Well, I want the best for you."

"You are the best."

She'd been wanting to know what had happened out in the foyer. With that, she had an opening.

"Had you told Dunneville if they expected you to stay with it, you are going to have to be your own man?"

"Well, yes, I'd said something like that, but Dunneville didn't seem much interested. It was last week's newspaper. He thought the mayoral campaign could just sort of coast along for a while."

"And what about them shafting you?"

"He'd heard all he wanted to about that. Gave me the same old snake oil. Trust him. Everything was going to come out right. There's no getting through to this guy. I'd have needed a swift two-by-four."

"Any concessions?"

"Yeah, we're re-invited to the retreat. Goin' in your car."

"Are you up to telling him you've had it?"

No answer.

"Well?"

"You know, I got the feeling in or out wouldn't much faze him just now. He's got a bug up his ass about state, and that's it."

"Is it that you really don't want out in case he says 'Okay, go?'"

"I don't know."

"Didn't we agree if it came to crunch time, you'd be just as well off out of it? Instead of us trying to do good, we prevent him from doing bad. Why don't I put it to him we're thinkin' about pulling out? State may be great, but it ain't there if he doesn't come through locally. He'll listen to that, especially from me."

No answer.

"Well, what are we waiting for?"

"The money, baby. Yours and mine. First that. They owe me a good chunk o' dough, and I'm determined to get it out of them, come what may. That's what I was hammerin' away at him for. He said to give him a little time. I told him he had till the weekend at the resort."

"And?"

"And that I'd make a helluva stink before W.C. if we came up empty."

They made their way past the groups of three and four men in black-tie tuxes clustered in the entryway, waiting for their wives to get their fur wraps. Outside where the parking valets were bringing up their Cadillacs, W.C. was surrounded by a circle of big-business types.

Dunneville called to Johnny to come over and to meet the next governor, but he brushed on by. Out of curiosity, Addie lingered long enough for Dunneville to see she wanted a word with him. He came over and gave her a surprise squeeze on the shoulder, asking in a low whisper that she try to get Johnny straightened out. Not good for him, the way he's going.

"Myself, I told Johnny he's playin' a dangerous game."

"He thinks you are. You could lose city hall."

"What? He can't be that stupid. He has to know what it would cost him."

"I think he's smart enough to do some damage. Lots. Beginning with do-re-*me*, like money embezzled from his bank account." *A risky bluff but worth trying*, she thought, *if it would hasten Johnny's exit.* Dunneville responded with a sneering "We'll have to see about that, won't we?" Whereupon he did a curt about-face.

They forgot where she'd parked and had to wander about. One of the caddies strangely seemed to be following them. *A valet lost his way?* She finally remembered, her car being a jalopy, it was sent to the end of the lot down by the fence. She had just turned her key in the lock when they heard a car door opening behind them. It was the prowling caddy; and out into the lamplight stepped a very large figure, his shadow the size of a church door.

"Well, if it ain't my old friend Louey," Johnny said. "What are you doing out here?"

"I want to give you a friendly message."

"Zat so."

"You gotta fall in line or there's gonna be trouble."

"You know, Louey, I faced many a tough defense in my time, and I always found a way to run through 'em."

"No jokin', fella. The reason I'm here is I follow orders. Like you're supposed to. So listen up for what I'm tellin' you. Lay off Dunneville and shape up. Or you can get hurt."

"And you're supposed to do the hurtin'?"

"Better me than Domo. Take it as a warnin', okay? I'm gonna be up there at the Jew Resort. And if you ain't careful . . ."

Ignoring him, Johnny motioned to Addie that they ought to be taking off. He grasped the door handle and stopped as if to say something. There was a tense pause; then Louey, wheezing through his teeth, came out with a barely audible "This is a sample of what it's gonna be like, buddy."

There was a hefty "oomph," as he cat-like lunged at Johnny, who ducked a roundhouse right only to be positioned for a cannonball left that made a resounding flesh-on-flesh smack on the side of his jaw and staggered him back against the lamppost.

Just as Louey was about to move in for a finishing shot, Addie swung her long-strapped purse like a lariat and gave him a surprise bash to the back of the neck. Startled, he turned to see what that was; and in that second, Johnny, catching him off-balance, dug his shoulder into Louey's gut. And with those pile driving legs of his digging dirt, he shoved his giant adversary back like he was a blocking dummy, banging him into the side of the caddy, where the protruding side-view mirror knifed into the soft kidney area of Louey's back. He yelled like a stuck pig and went down clutching his lower back and spitting out expletives. He started to get up but a leg buckled under him.

As they drove off, tires squealing, Johnny lowered the window and hollered "See you in the mountains, Louey boy! Remember, the Jews like their comfort. They get annoyed by rough stuff."

CHAPTER 68

Arrival in the Catskills

Sipping on their cool drinks, they sat through the floor show that featured a line of long-legged chorus girls with big headdresses parading topless behind a crooner who was followed by a plate juggler and then a stand-up comic, formerly a rabbi, making jokes about the Jews, who had a good laugh at themselves. The auditorium was a large, white shell with terraced rows of tables projecting out twenty deep, with the first three occupied by a group of Japanese businessmen brought in by tour bus. The comic bowed to them and said "Welcome to your country!"

Everybody but the two of them seemed to be having a good time. People were laughing; but they, in themselves, were totally mirthless, which wasn't just a matter of nervous anticipation. They were at odds over how best to handle things with Dunneville. As Addie had suspected, Johnny no longer seemed very keen about the idea of taking the money and running out on them. Darned if in his heart of hearts he didn't really want to be mayor. On the way up, he'd been spouting off on being free to work for the good of the city.

Look at all I'd promised to do for people. Could I make suckers of them? Talk them into voting for The Party and run out on them? Hell no! I'd be a new kind of mayor, a guy who could—like I'd been saying—"Make the city work for the people." After thinking it over, he'd even come up with a plan to play it smart and whip Dunny at his own game—meaning he'd be a smoothie, letting on that he planned to be a good boy.

Then once he got in, he'd turn the tables on Dunny and his people and clean up the patronage racket, the kickbacks, the fat contracts, the extortion and clear away all that humbuggery with which they'd covered it all up. He'd get the people behind him. Hell, state would be looking to him and not to them for the future!

"Oh my God," Addie moaned. "Thinks he's back at the Union Hall."

She tells him that it's clever but that he's dreaming.

"Look at why the present Reform mayor is getting out. He tries to bring in new people, professionals to handle building code enforcement, for example. And the Civil Service Commission, being dominated by The Party, blocks your appointments. Party people own the ghetto apartments and don't want any outsiders snooping around.

"You want their problems? Listen up. This Reform mayor wants to appoint a much needed additional judge, and he's stymied by the state legislature, also in the hands of The Party. He wants money to clean up pollution in the river, but either he hires their thieves who come up with an inflated estimate, or he can wait till the damned water turns to apple butter. He finally gives up. Wild horses couldn't make him run again. He advises these new Reform people they better be careful of what they wish for."

When Johnny insists it would be different for him, she gives him a cross-eyed smile. But he won't let go. He believes it is still worth a try.

"Better than doing nothing. Didn't you once say something like that?"

"Sounds great," she tells him. *Goodness, how to bring this big boy back down to earth?* Wanting him to reconsider the run, she tells him to think about having a Louey-type watchdogging him all the time, his life in constant jeopardy.

"Besides, hadn't you pretty much poisoned the well by openly bucking Dunny? You might be thinking you're the boss, and they gotta kowtow to you or else, but that won't wash. Like Louey said, you've had your warning. What it comes down to now is that you're going to have to get them before they get you."

"Really?"

"Yes, really." It's war, and whether he realizes it or not, the first shot has already been fired. "You better put that ice pack back on your jaw."

When his blood was up, Johnny would have jumped at the thought of locking horns with the bastards. Somehow the fighting spirit had ebbed, and the old snarl seemed about to give way to a smile. *So he's going to soft-soap them? Goodness! Didn't he realize they'd see weakness?* She wondered what it would take to give this sometime bear the backbone to pull out and leave those crooks candidate-less five weeks before the election. "Now that would be what fightin' looks like."

Not knowing what else to do, she tried to set things to rest for the time being saying, "Okay, then, let's get our clammy mitts on the money first. Then, we'll know where to go from there."

That's the way it had gone on the ride up. They had gotten a late start to begin with since when she came by to pick him up, he told her his swollen jaw hurt so bad that he couldn't get to sleep. So she dragged him to the hospital for x-rays. Fortunately, they were negative. It took up quite a bit of time, but that was about how they wanted it anyway. The others had caravanned up right after lunch, and there was little joy to be had in joining them. She wanted to come in late on the poolside party so they could get to Dunny when the gathering would have thinned out.

Addie saw the need to have Johnny in a spunkier mood and hoped the floor show would at least loosen him up. But, it had made him feel worse. And she had even more depressing news for him. It was intermission. They were standing at their table, idly people-watching.

What the heck, I might as well come out with it, she thought. There was no good time to bring up a delicate subject. So she said she didn't know whether he'd noticed, but her belly had begun to show. Strangely, that not only gave him an up; but also in the blink of an eye, he was radiating sunshine. Of all things!

"Oh, Addie, honey. I'll be the kid's godfather—No. Dammit, you seem to be livin' alone. *I'll* be a father to him. Or her. Have twins. One of each. Me, your kids' daddy. Gee, that would be a big up for me!"

"Well, one thing it means is that after this gets settled, I'm going to be out of circulation for a while. In fact, out of town. My sister and I have it planned. I'm going to be staying with her. It means win or lose here, I'm gone, Johnny."

"Gone? No way! Where you go, I go. I mean, you don't have to marry me. It'd be enough if I could be near you and watch over you. Support you and little Addie, make sure no harm comes. I'd love it."

"Johnny you're not making any sense."

"I know. But you're bringing me to my senses. If it's between you and politics, no contest."

"Oh my. I don't know what to make of this. Let's—please, step back a bit. I haven't even thought about what kind of life I'd be having as a mother."

"You're lookin' at me like you think I'm crazy."

"No. I'm touched. Really."

She was impressed that he didn't ask the obvious question. Her vision blurred. She found herself nuzzled up against his rugged chest, drawn in by those enveloping arms, and held as she'd never been held before with an adoring tenderness that all but wafted her away. It was a sacred moment, her turn to be speechless.

She had sat down, elbows on the table, her head resting on upturned hands, lost in bewildering thought. He gave her a shake, and she came out of it and nuzzled up again. It felt good and she told him so, which pepped him up. With the audience starting to file back in, he looked at his watch and said, "Come on. Let's go get 'em."

As they were leaving, the crooner came back; and when the band started giving the intro to his song, Johnny asked her to hear the first few lines.

Say, it's only a paper moon,
Sailing over a cardboard sea,
But it wouldn't be make-believe
If you believed in me.

"Great," she said, "but I seem to remember there was also something about its being 'a Barnum & Bailey world.'"

"Well, yeah."

As they were pacing down the hallway, he stopped her in mid-stride.

"Hey, you do believe, don't you?"

"Yes. More than I ever have."

"Oh, Addie, you're beautiful. The world may be a circus, but not ours."

"You're sweet."

"Love you."

"Oh, Johnny. Save it."

CHAPTER 69

A Fatal Poolside Party

Unexpectedly, the poolside party was still going strong when they arrived. This pool (one of two) had been reserved for them, and a buffet table lavishly laid out with all manner of delicacies, had been wheeled in. Johnny's chin dropped when he looked over at the groaning board with its assortment of cold cuts and cheeses, shrimp, Nova Scotia lox, sturgeon, chopped liver, caviar, deviled eggs, smoked oysters, crab meat dip, roast beef, stuffed peppers, pizza slices, ribs, chicken breast, potato salad, coleslaw, olives, pickles, freshly baked bagels, and salads galore—the whole shebang flanked by a wet bar with a gamut of bottled whiskeys, wines, and beer.

Upon being greeted by Dunneville, Johnny remarked "My campaign funds at work, huh?" which got a big laugh. In keeping with his high spirits, Dunneville facetiously took Addie's hand and raised it in a victory gesture.

"State is practically in the bag," he whispered. "No fuck-ups, please."

And this was supposed to be a small private party. It looked like he'd invited every two-bit ward heeler in town. A bartender kept the drinks flowing, and Addie urged Johnny to participate—moderately—wanting him to keep enough edge to see it through. Committed to not turning back, she was—if need be—prepared to do something provocative. But as she counseled Johnny, they should also be committed to biding their time. A botch would be disastrous, regarding which she pointed to problem one.

Perched on the high-dive at the far end of the pool, feeding his face, was none other than their friend Louey, grinning like a gargoyle. He was sporting a wide-brimmed sombrero and blazing orange trunks. When he bent over the food plate, his open flower-print shirt exposed a back brace; and noticing they had detected him, he pointed to the ace bandage on his knee, apparently also injured in the scuffle. Johnny grinned back and gave him the Italian forearm salute.

Not to be outdone, Louey shook his cane at them. He pointed a finger, motioning from Johnny to himself and then outside, mouthing "See you later" with another shake of the cane. He'd been drinking and was chasing his shot with a beer. Dunneville had sent him up there (despite the bad knee) when he tried getting it on with one of the women. Johnny knew how much better it would be to contend with a Louey than a Domo, the Terrible Turk—who, innocuous as he seemed, could get pretty volatile and had been fired for roughing up W.C.'s advance man, not knowing the guy was supposed to stay close to his lieutenant governor boss.

At a signal from Dunneville, all the women disappeared into the ladies' locker room and reappeared in skimpy bathing suits: W.C.'s companion came back in a more-than-skimpy bikini that had nothing in front but a strip of nipple covers and a triangle patch. Dunneville whistled all the men to change; and when they reappeared in a flash of color, ready to frolic the women, he rolled out the tape player for some Latin tango music—to which his mistress, Mary (her real name), did a hip-wiggling cha-cha.

As things heated up, there was more grabbing than dancing; and the men were throwing the women into the pool, and the women them. W.C. was pretty much in his cups, and upon his insistence, the triangle floozy jumped up on the billiard table to do a stripper's bump and grind, which ended with her taking her thin top off and tying it around W.C.'s head. He wanted an encore; and as she shimmied up to him, off came the triangle, which she snugged over his nose. Everybody roared, including W.C.

One of the loudest laughs came from the high-dive, observing which W.C. abruptly stopped laughing. He called Dunneville over, wanting to know what that oversize Black was doing up there.

"Oh him! One of our boys. A good ol' guy."

"Good guy! How come he was shakin' that cane at us?"

"Oh that. He's a big kidder."

"A kidder, huh? What's he doin', lookin' at our naked white women?"

"Sir, he's got a white wife. Nice girl. One of us."

"I don't care if she's purple. Where is she?"

"They're separated."

"Ah-ha! I don't want no Black lookin' at our white women. Didn't you notice how he was makin' a play for that little blonde? I want him the hell outta here! And tell him to stop shakin' that cane. I coulda sworn he was lookin' at me."

"Yes, sir. He's leaving. Right now."

After giving Louey the high sign, Dunny motioned the bartender to bring W.C. a stiff drink; and wrapping a towel around Miss Triangle, he sat her down on his lap. Taking a hint from Louey's exit, the couples started saying their goodnights. Some of the lights were being turned off; then, Johnny looked at Addie for the high sign and took a deep breath.

PART IX

DEALINGS WITH DUNNY

CHAPTER 70

The Disaster

Impatient as he was, Johnny had to hold it. As the clock ticked on, he was all for them making their move; but as Addie coolly surveyed the scene, she thought it was still premature. There were still too many people around—some going back for seconds on food, the men crowding the bar.

Johnny heaved a sigh and was glad for the pause. He'd actually been wanting to take in the sauna ever since they'd walked in (a great relaxer). Having some time to kill, they changed into their swimsuits.

Addie told Johnny they could do the sauna only if Dunneville joined them, which he did, wanting somebody—even Johnny—to reassure him that Louey hadn't spoiled the party. By the time they'd had themselves a refreshing swim, Addie observed the rest of the couples were finally beginning to drift off; and she nudged Johnny to approach Dunneville, who had just sent the bartender over to package the leftovers.

"It's time, Johnny. Catch him now *before* he takes off."

Dunneville had just put on his beach coat, and laying down his empty glass, he was looking around for Mary when Addie jolted an astonished Johnny into him.

"Hey, Johnny. Easy does it, man! Liked the Johnny Walker, did yah? Er . . . you okay?"

Johnny took a deep breath and spoke up. "No, I'm not. You said you'd have those envelopes for us."

"What's this now! Not, fur Chrissakes, here. Relax, will yah?"

"When we get the envelopes. You said you'd have 'em. I ain't gonna be put off anymore."

Johnny's voice was getting louder, and he was shuffling Dunneville back against the sauna when the noise got Mary up from the lounge chair where she'd been drowsing. She yawned and excused herself, saying she was going up to the room.

"Hey, cut it out, will yah! You'll get the fuckin' money when I'm good and—"

Johnny put a hand around his throat. "No, Dunny. It's when I'm ready. Like now! Or I'm gonna shove your ass into this goddamned sweatbox, and you don't come out till you're ready to cough it up. Get me!"

"B—Eddy! Hey, where's strong-arm Eddy? Somebody get Louey!" Dunneville looked around and suddenly realized they were alone. "Where the hell is everybody!" He made a panicked effort to break loose, but with an iron hand on his chest, Johnny waltzed him over to the sauna door.

"Get your fuckin' hand off me, stupid!"

"The money."

"Tell you what. I don't have anything much here. Best if I get hold of Eddy. You know everything financial has to go through him. Lemme put through a call. Get you big bucks."

"Stop the bullshit! What you got in that fat clip of yours ought to be big enough for now."

"Wait here. I'll be back in ten minutes."

Johnny laughed. "*You're* gonna do the waitin'."

Opening the sauna door with one hand while clamping down on Dunneville's neck with the other, Johnny motioned Addie to hold the door open; after which, he lifted the guy and bodily heaved him against the wooden bench where he landed with a thump and an "Ow! . . . You, bastard!"

Johnny edged out, slammed the door shut, and left Dunny sputtering away. He shook his fist at the window. Johnny mopped his brow with a stray towel and, turning up the thermostat, held the door tight.

After several minutes of frantic hammering on the door, Dunneville had to drop his tired arm. He started to go at it again but the effort weakened. Drooling and utterly exhausted, he called out "Okay, enough!" and seemed to mean it. His eyes had rolled up, and with the poor guy looking like he might pass out, Johnny thought he could trust his promise.

A quick dialogue ensued.

"The money, right?"

"Yes."

"Now and here, right?"

"Yes. And where is here?"

"In my jacket in the locker."

"Keys to my Buick, too?"

"Yes."

Johnny moved back from the door, and Dunneville burst out huffing obscenities. He was wet as a fish, and his whole body was lobster-red. He flew at Johnny, hands outstretched, going for the throat; but Johnny flicked the bony hands off as if they were chopsticks. He instantly twisted Dunneville's arm around, behind his back and hop-stepped him to the locker room, telling Addie meanwhile that he was going to get dressed and that she should do the same.

While dressing, she heard all the commotion next door, a clatter of locker metal punctuated by shrill "Ows"; and shortly after she emerged, straightening her dress, out came Johnny pushing a badly shaken Dunneville ahead of him with an armload of clothes that he heaped onto a lounge chair. Johnny was bleeding from a slash on the neck, where Dunneville had keyed him as he leaned over to tie his shoes; and Dunneville was bleeding from the nose and lips.

After he'd been bashed for the keying, Dunneville had tried to throw the key down the shower drain and had gotten his face shoved into the locker door for that. Bleary-eyed and bloody-beaked, he looked more than ever like the bird that lost the cockfight.

Addie quickly searched the jacket pockets and produced two envelopes each with their respective initials. Short of breath,

Dunneville moved over to the diving board to steady himself as he struggled to slip his trousers on over the bathing suit. He gave Johnny a squint-eyed look and, talking from the side of his mouth, warned "You know this is going to cost you, don't you? Big-time!"

"Not as much as it's going to cost you."

Ripping the envelopes out of Addie's hand, Dunneville pitched the heavy one over to Johnny, and holding out the other, he taunted Addie to come and get it then waggled it in her face. Opening it, she found three slim bills—two twenties and a ten. In disbelief, she ran a finger inside to see if she'd missed additional bills.

"Fifty for me? You got to be kidding!"

"You think you deserve any more than the other whores?"

She was ready to take him apart. She crunched the envelope into a ball and mashed it against his sensitive beak, eliciting an "Ow! You lousy bitch!" She was moving in to deliver a knee, but he got ahead of her and reflexively threw her back against the sauna. Stunned, she was about to make a rush at him but was eased aside by Johnny as his sledgehammer fist crashed into Dunneville's face with a ferocious shot that sent him flying back against the diving board—where his head hit the metal railing with a loud, hollow thonk. He sank to the deck and lay motionless.

"Oh, my gosh!" Addie gasped.

"Let's get outta here," Johnny said, taking her arm.

"What? We gotta get a doctor."

"You think I hurt him bad?"

A small pool of blood was forming under his head. Addie kneeled down to check. The blood was seeping through his hair. *What else could it be but a crack in the skull?* She felt for a pulse.

"Still there—thank goodness! But ain't strong. I think you better take off."

"You're not comin' with? Whatta you gonna do?

"We got two cars. Remember? Divided, they won't know which one to follow. Leave together and we're leavin' one-way footprints. I'll get back to you. Depend on it."

"I love you, Addie. Kills me to be without you."

"Love you too, Johnny. Want yah to play it smart."

"Wish I could put 'em on Louey. He had a reason. Left in a huff, threw his hat at the women, and the darned thing is still down there."

"That ain't gonna fly. Call the desk on the house phone, and tell 'em there's a drunk zonked out at the side o' the pool."

"I don't like it that you say we gotta separate—over *this*."

"Johnny, good fella, his troubles are over. Ours are just beginning."

"That bad, huh?"

"That bad."

She couldn't wait to get this now helpless hunk packed into his Buick and on his way. He kept insisting she had to go with him. She said that she knew better but that she'd stay in touch.

"Wait!" he called from the car.

"What?"

"The money."

"In your shirt pocket, remember? Don't count it till you hit Chicago."

"I should have checked the pants pockets. I've seen him pull out that fat clip."

"Go, Johnny, now!"

"Here," handing her his envelope. "Take it. I didn't mean to put you through so much trouble. I'm sorry as I can be. Because . . ." As before, words were giving him trouble. "Because, you know, Addie, I love you with my life . . . I need you."

She tried to push the envelope back, but he just rolled her fingers around it and held them tight.

"I can get money elsewhere. But it's not what I want. What counts . . . is . . . what I'm feeling . . ." He choked. Brushing away tears, he got out and gave her a bear hug. Throwing her arms around his muscular back, she gave him a full-mouthed kiss. He pressed his firm body hard against hers. The kiss he returned was like white lightning, a flash that spread and spread again through a wet summer night and all but drowned her in its moist air. For a flickering instant, she had the wayward desire to tangle herself around him and make them crazy with passion and pain.

"Come with me."

"Can't now. Save it."

Of all times. Sex hunger. No way. Bathed in the surreal brightness of the fluorescent light standard, his dimpled profile looked like it had been sculpted by one of the great ones. And there was a for–real human being inside, a feeling person. And did she ever yearn! *Yeah, of all times. The Imp. What else? Was I supposed to laugh or cry?*

Hands to his chest and head down, she finally had to go and push him back into the car; and once there, she tried to put the fear of Eddy in him.

"Okay, but what about you?"

"Not to worry." She gave him her sister's phone number.

Secretly fearing it could be a last good-bye, she let the tears roll. There was goodness in the man. She'd have to find a way back as soon as he called. He leaned out the window to blow her a kiss and kept waving all the way down the blue-lit driveway and onto the road, where his car disappeared into the blackness of the night.

She suddenly wished she'd gone with him, and she cursed herself that she didn't. He'd need protecting, caring for, and (dear man) loving. She'd promised she'd find a way. "Lord God, help me. I've got to."

As she looked out at the pool of blackness enveloping the spot where she last saw his car, she let the tears roll down afresh. Her chest heaved. "Ooh," she cried in pain. "The hell of it is you don't know you're in love when it stares you in the face. The saddest part . . ."

PART X

THE LIFE BEYOND JOHNNY

CHAPTER 71

Needs To Find Him: Where To Begin?

Her recovery wasn't swift. With the love they had found, she instinctively knew they'd find one another. But first, where to look? In fact, how? She had pointed him to the West, and the West was *large*. As easterners envisioned it, the West was a great, big, wide open prairie that was very flat, with Chicagos here and there, surrounded by cornfields stretching out to a thin-lined horizon that kept evaporating. She cursed her idiocy. "Fuck this stupid head! Fuck, fuck, fuck, it!"

In the next instant, she found herself looking into the car's rearview mirror and slammed the image with her fist. Looking backward wasn't much help. She unexpectedly found she was laughing at herself, a low rolling laugh that sounded like running water. She paused to tilt the wine bottle again.

The West is a big place on the map, where people carry guns and shoot one another. Johnny fortunately is big. She started humming "Lover Come Back to Me." And feeling it spin around in her head, she rolled the window down. She had found love with Johnny, but where was she supposed to find him? *The darned West*, she agonized, *is so big*; it's where you naturally get lost.

She took another slug of wine. She had picked up the bottle to celebrate; but instead it was making her dizzy, dizzy with futility. All the more so that her love retained its glow, a virginal sweetness that wouldn't let go of her. So when all of a sudden the lover of a lifetime isn't there, it leaves an emptiness as big as the sky.

Ironically, she didn't know she had the special feeling; it somehow wasn't really there until she was about to part from him. She kept repeating how she hated her stupidity. *If you find a man and the love so genuine, you bind yourself to him, don't you? You don't let him go off alone!* But of course, the time was short. Rush, rush. That's just how she knew it. Thinking narrowly of protection, she has to send him off *alone*. It makes no sense. She took another slug from the wine bottle, and the eternal embrace came swirling back to her.

Then, seemingly out of nowhere, she became aware of a new something she had to confront: there was pain in her lower gut. She saw she couldn't afford the luxury of dreaming. Her problem was nothing less than getting involved with the pregnancy of a past life, a real-life child soon to be at her breast—her second self, plus Jay. The tears started streamed again. The windshield was fogging up. She had to steer for the side of the road—where, as she went, she kept pulling out Kleenexes.

Where am I? Her head was spinning. She had scooted out of the resort right after seeing Johnny off and planned to drive through the night to her sister's and start making phone calls. Things were closing in on her (matters of a prior world), and they wouldn't let her forget it. She figured she probably was more than halfway through to having Jay's child. The last thing her doctor wanted her to do was to go on long trips, least of all by car. But obviously, the first thing to do was to keep going.

So there she was driving westward from the Catskills over heavily rutted back roads. She got herself a really good jostling that simultaneously produced a worry about her jalopy falling apart and a bigger one over low abdominal cramps (her falling apart). She stopped for gas and asked the mechanic to check her tires while she used the restroom, where she discovered bloodstains.

She used the phone to call worrywart Eva and explained her situation. She learned there had been a Western Union money order and a couple of phone calls. Neither was evidently from Johnny. On her arrival, Eva got her in to see the gynecologist in time for him to offset a possible miscarriage. She was given pills, told to apply a heating pad and to rest. Another laugh.

She clued Eva in on the situation with Johnny.

"When he calls, I'd have no choice. Where he was, I'd have to be . . . Could I borrow your car?"

"Yes, you could. In fact, I would drive you!"

The craziness was infectious. But Addie would have to rest first.

"Got a good book?" she asked. There was still no call from Johnny. *Of course, he'd have had a long trip.*

A call from Peggy at the mansion got her up off the couch. Louey had been looking for her. She said he'd come up twice. The second time, she outright warned him that if he showed his face again, it would look a little different after her Doberman got finished with it. She told him to have a look in the kennel run. He gave her the arm pump and said he'd be back.

Peggy felt the situation was getting precarious. She cleaned the bore of her rifle in case she had to hit him at the gate. Louey had been insisting he wanted that car. (Dammit, things he needed to check out with the driver.)

"Oh, yeah!" She shot off a practice round when he slid under the chain-link fence, and before leaving, he told her what she could do with the rifle.

An hour later, she had a call from Otts, who was worried that he hadn't heard from his daughter. He said that Louey had been at his door, and as he tried to wedge his way in, the two of them were going at it jaw to jaw when Iris Klagemann came down to intervene. Iris vowed that if he came up close to her, she'd hit him with a steam iron.

Addie wanted to know how her father was.

"Is Otts okay?"

"Yes and no."

Iris had called the ambulance, and she reported, "The emergency doctor said he had the old boy stabilized. Otts had kept asking for his Rika, and looking up, the doctor asked me, 'That's you, huh?'"

Next day, a Western Union money order arrived—a hefty twenty thousand dollars, with love. Johnny said he wanted to cover her medical expenses, plus a little change, in case he couldn't be there when she had the kid he had pre-adopted.

But immediately there was Otts. Addie called Tom to ask if he could put her up in that house office where he saw clients. He said he'd be glad to, and she explained why. Eva was up in arms. Addie would be putting herself at the edge of the PR ghetto, a risk that made no sense, especially since Eva couldn't lend her the caddy (sure to be stolen there), leaving Addie with the fall-apart Wreck. Eva was also put out that Otts didn't ask to see her too.

Tom was most obliging. Addie arrived in the dark of night, dead tired, and needing a drink to steady herself. Two shots of Tom's prime scotch did the trick. She was eager to find out what had happened in town once the news got out. But he first wanted to know what had previously happened up in the Catskills.

So she told him. It was a far cry from what he'd heard. It sounded so fishy—Dunneville dead and Johnny gone—that no one believed the story that was passed on. On her part, Addie said she had Johnny promise to point the nose of that car into the setting sun and to keep going till he found a city big enough to get lost in, though she secretly feared it might not happen.

As Tom was able to piece things together, Johnny had made the mistake of driving back home to pick up clothes and stuff but mainly to empty his bank account and land as big a loan as he could swing, putting the equity in his house up for collateral. He kept half and sent half to Addie, saying more would come.

In any case, they spotted him, of course, and had him trailed by the goon squad who, once he was well out in the country, forced him off the road where they jumped him. He fought them with all he had, strangling the one he grabbed for a shield; but with the other three guys on him, one of them with an ax handle, he never had a chance.

Hearing this in Tom's private office, Addie burst out with a scream. Tears rolling down as she fell back on the clients' divan, she cried out "Why, oh why did I ever let him get away without me? I would have steered clear of town and saved him!"

After calming down, she explained how things had stood between them. "Tom, I loved the man! Never thought I ever could. We were so different. Strange as this sounds, that's why it came home to me that I was in love with him without knowing it." Choked up, she went on. "Seeing that car vanish—how it hurt! I just get to know my feelings, and he's gone." She went through another handkerchief. "Oh, oh! Tom, it hurts."

When Tom asked if she would like to hear how the situation was reported in town, she nodded with a wan smile.

"Well, the way Dunny's people gave it to the paper, Johnny was so depressed by the loss of his campaign manager that he fell asleep at the wheel. His car swerved into a ditch and got wrapped around a tree."

Tom couldn't find anyone who would go for a tale like that, least of all Johnny's relatives. The whole Polish community was up in arms. How could Johnny have fallen asleep, driven into a tree, and then shot himself in the back of the head? They wanted to hire a detective but couldn't get any takers.

As for Dunneville himself, they tried dressing it up this way and that before settling on him being a devoted public servant who had worked himself to the point of exhaustion; and then when he at last got the chance to take a day off, he was so beat that he fell asleep in the sauna, dropped off the bench, and cracked his skull on the cement floor. Originally, they'd had him falling into the pool half asleep and drowning; but that had to be dropped once the coroner's inquest leaked out.

The funeral was just short of Father Jay's in extravagance, and fat Angie Sr. somehow came forth to give the eulogy. He never missed a chance to curry favor, of course. Father Tim hid his reluctance and was at his dignified best. Tony had Cowshit Eddy put up a floral display that had a red carnation profile of Dunneville in the middle, his notorious beak done to a rosebud tee. The tearful family was impressed. Mary fainted and had to be carried out. Tony had a guy with an Uzi guarding the flowers after everybody had filed out, and Eddy had to account for every last petal.

Johnny was to be buried in a small-town cemetery out in the western part of the state, where he had an uncle. Heartsick that she couldn't go to the funeral, Addie decided to attend the burial service and had asked Eva to come down and bring some clothes that she could disguise herself in. That would also make it possible for both to visit Otts. No need for him to think ill of his "other" daughter. They both wore babushkas tied under the chin.

The cemetery was set on a windswept hill, where between the headstones there were tall arborvitae bent over by clumps of snow; and here and there a stout beach tree was showering down the snow that coated its branches. The sky was a sight of leaden barrenness, the sun a bleached lemon circle that was barely visible. The priest did the traditional invocation in Latin and then, at the request of the relatives, had a few words in Polish, followed in English by a canned eulogy—obviously put together by the relatives, who spiked it with variations on *Duzha* (good)—all of which Addie and Eva shivered through.

Back in Eva's car, they cried together. Addie was glad to have Eva there with her, to have someone to confide in over how close she had grown to Johnny. Eva gave her a good ear. What haunted Addie most was that she had never actually told Johnny she loved him, which damnably she herself had been too late to recognize. She tried to convince herself that with Johnny having finally stood up for his convictions before these crooks, he had come to realization. He'd shown such promise, having acted on principle, and experienced love. In that last hectic week, he had enjoyed a short but happy life.

Eva brought up the irony of how things had played out with men who had become important to her, a divorced neighbor. They were nowhere close to Al but a sort of consort she could go to the movies with. That got Addie started on her love for Jay, which was so impulsive; she was overcome—as much as *he* had been.

With Johnny, it had been different, totally unexpected; it had grown on her and expanded her heart. Here was a guy she had at first detested. At the end, she would have stopped a bullet for him. Johnny and Jay. What should appropriately have been carnal became a matter of character; what should have been a matter of character became carnal then both at once.

"Life is strange."

She felt she had learned a lot from love. On reflection, it was surely the right thing with both men. It had put her in touch with her humanity and theirs. Still, could she love two dead men? Memories did not go into the grave with them. Eyes wet, she took in the tired smile reflected in the mirror.

CHAPTER 72

Difficulty Exiting Hospital

It was past time for them to see Otts. Eager as Addie was, they were brought up short by Tom, who reminded her that the people who had owned Dunneville were intent on finding her. They were not amused by the hoax Johnny had pulled on them. They wanted vengeance on whomever they could find.

"It was best to cool it for a bit."

"Yes, wait, but where?"

Tom said his office house couldn't be more than an overnight stop. His first client next day was Tough Tony's fat daughter. Her husband had taken off with the bridesmaid just weeks after their million-dollar wedding. Nothing would give the daughter greater pleasure than to put the goons on him. Tony's message was brief: husband's father has the Scranton connection.

After calling the hospital to get a report on Otts, which was the meaningless "He's resting comfortably," Addie called Peggy for a haven and was invited.

"Come ahead. I've got news for you. First, young Domo drove by and gave me a thumbs-up."

"He didn't care for Dunny?"

"Dunno."

After having been away for a while, people often come back to surprises. Upon arriving at the castle, Addie saw a station wagon parked on the driveway that wound around to the unused garage.

Peggy told her that when those newspaper articles about the "murder in the mountains" came out, someone appeared at her door right after Louey left. This guy had in fact been hiding in the bushes—from where, knife in hand, he had kept a suspicious eye on Louey.

Peggy's apprehensions eased when Whimpy told her who he was. Not only hungry for somebody to talk to, she was also badly in need of a driver she could depend on. So before they'd finished talking, Whimpy had been hired as her official chauffeur.

Upon getting herself this secondhand wagon, she thought, *To hell with the driver's license!* (It was likely to be denied.) There was a need to swing downtown for groceries from time to time, so she'd drive it and—considering her seizures—hope for the best. Whimpy, in exchange for services rendered, had himself a room. Here he was getting a roof over his head, food for free, and company too—the whole shot. That was Whimpy all over.

Addie recalled how she happened to have found a room for Whimpy after he'd been freed when no one took the trouble to think of a place for him to stay. Addie, being likewise bereft, had Betsy get her a key to the empty town house being reserved for her; and she and homeless Whimpy were able to put in several comfortable nights there, feasting on prepared meals in the fridge that had been set up for Mary, Dunny's mistress. It had been a delight, like they were a married couple on honeymoon. Whimpy was nothing less than Mr. Accommodation.

Peggy called for him to come on downstairs; and following warm hugs, Addie learned why, in addition to his other virtues, Peggy called him a walking newspaper. Scrounging around in the hospital where he'd gotten himself hired as part-time janitor, he had found out what the sisters were eager to know: what had happened to Otts that put him there?

Angered, Louey had returned to see Otts and had pushed him around, trying to get him to say where Addie was. Otts gave him a proper cussing out and got jammed against the pantry door with some hot words. When Otts spat out a German curse and showed Louey the door, that got him jammed harder, his head striking the knob on the cupboard as he went down.

The loud voices brought Iris to the door again. She screamed at Louey "What are you doing to this poor old man!" and when she went for the phone, he left. Otts made a feint to go after him and collapsed. In the hospital, they had a machine monitoring his heart; and it said he seemed to be in decent enough shape. Not so much for Otts's personally.

Hastily taking in Eva's caddy, Whimpy suggested they play it smart with Louey. Since with the Chevy they had two cars, they'd just leave the albatross for Louey. He was welcome to it and, for spite, was bound to take it, showing his bosses he'd been on the case.

Being a realist, Addie bought herself a little twenty-two-caliber pistol that hid itself very neatly in her purse. Skittish Eva had a fit but had to go along with it. When Addie clued her in that as they faced serious business, she meant to keep it simple, for immediate fears, she alluded only to Louey.

Eva downed her phobia about hospitals, out of curiosity to see how Otts was doing; and Addie was glad to have her along. It also helped that Whimpy, having taken the night shift, would go down with them and stick around as a lookout.

Peggy, on being briefed, hemmed up one of her moo-moos for Addie to wear and sat a broad-brimmed flower hat on her head. She oversized the lipstick, amplified her bosom, gave her a pair of sunglasses, and finished the picture off with a pair of worn tennis shoes. A try-on for Halloween. Addie looked in the mirror and asked "Where's the bag?"

Having looked left and right as she entered the hospital waiting room, Addie still felt a little suspicious about the person she saw approaching in the corridor. As he passed, she saw it wasn't Louey in disguise, but—surprise!—a genuine white-coated intern with a stethoscope in his side pocket.

Holy smokes! Could it be? She called to him by name but got no answer. She called again louder, but he just walked on and, before turning a corner, gave a quick over-the-shoulder look. Puzzled, he kept going. For sure, it was Doctor Boy. Snubbing her! Eva told her to hush and pulled her back to the receptionist desk, where they got Otts's room number.

"It was him. I know it was!" *Did he purposely ignore me? Didn't want to have anything to do with me?* "Damnation!"

Then, looking down at her hemmed moo-moo, she laughed. But of course, it was this ridiculous getup. He must have thought she was some disgruntled charity patient.

As a favor to Tom (and Otts, as she later learned), Van persuaded the police chief to have a patrolman walk the cardiac ward during visiting hours. Nonetheless, Whimpy posted himself at the door to Otts's room.

Otts was asleep when they went in. He might have had a little trouble recognizing Addie, but—another surprise—neither would she have recognized him right away. No longer the ruddy-complected father she had known, with the broad chest and sinewy arms, Otts seemed to have shrunk. Sickly white in the face with a tinge of blue at the lips and around the eyes and lying there with his limp head to the side, he resembled a puppet some kid had thrown in the corner.

She was touched to see him like this. Hand to her mouth, Eva wondered what could have happened to him. Their poor, dear, bigoted father had come to this. Addie very softly kissed him on the forehead, and he woke with a start. She quickly explained, and seeing his daughters, his eyes moistened; and he held out his arms to them.

They cranked up the back of his bed, and frail as he was, it didn't take long for the old Otts to come to the fore. It took no time for him to get started on this Black buck, this no-good Black bastard. Circling his fists, he said "You should have seen me make that big lunk back off. Wasn't he lucky to get out the door before I bashed a chair over his black head!"

Addie's big hug calmed him down. He'd shortly become fully alert and told them there was some important business coming up that he wanted them to take care of.

"You remember, don't you, that the German-American Club was taking Tough Tony to court over the bottomland he had stolen from the Hagelmeister estate when that land had rightfully been willed to the club? I have been leading the fight. I have a folder on the case, and in a couple of days, the club is going to have a strategic meeting with the lawyer."

The girls assured him they would go to the meeting.

"But wait. Did you say a couple of days?"

"No, the meeting is tomorrow and I'm counting on you."

They sat by him till the nurse came in with his pills. On the way out, Addie asked Whimpy what he knew about this darned suit.

He said, "Not a great deal, but from what was said in the paper, Tony was sending a lawyer over to see if something couldn't be worked out with the club, which means the Germans probably have a case."

Whimpy had to say it wouldn't be all that great an idea for them to exit just then: there were serious goings on right there in front of them. Having seen Tony Jr. prowling around, Whimpy said they had better go out the back way. He ushered them over to the door marked Stairway, and at ground level, he barely opened the door enough to look around when two shots rang out from a bordering privet hedge, followed by another and the whine of a slug ricocheting off the brick siding. Whimpy had fallen to the floor but wasn't hit.

They rushed back up the stairs hoping to find the policeman. But he was gone. Whimpy said he'd seen young Tony talking to him. He wouldn't be surprised if the cop was asked to tip him off, making them out to be suspicious characters. The cop did have a walkie-talkie, and Tony had probably slipped him a bill.

"What now?" Eva wanted to know, her voice rising. "I hope you're not saying all this is just to keep us entertained."

Whimpy said he'd heard about some weirdo who had found an empty room in the hospital, got in, turned the key, and stayed for all of a month. He even made out with one of the night nurses who had brought him food. He thought they ought to be able to find themselves a nook and overnight it. In fact, he recalled from the time he'd worked in the hospital laundry that they'd have it made if they could get into the linen room.

"Gosh, with a little luck, they could stay a week, get meals, and who knows what all else! People he knew still worked there."

"Something I've always wanted to do," Addie interrupted. "I can just picture them finding the three of us fast asleep on a pile of sheets. Me in this stupid costume. They'd have us down to the station in nothin' flat."

"Better'n gettin' shot."

Eva was up in arms. "No way I can stay in a hospital! I've already had more than I can take of the smell. I'm going right out the front door like we came in. They don't know me. I'll call the police, tell them we've been shot at, and they'll come and see you guys out."

"Hold everything," Addie said, lowering her voice to a whisper. "Police are the last people I need to see. Look at this phony getup. Don't you know they'd be suspicious? With them having me down as an accomplice—maybe the murderess herself—if they so much as knew I was around, they could get a bench warrant out for me."

Realizing how suspicious they looked already, with no one else around but the nurses down the hall, Whimpy suggested they make their way to the lobby and see what they could figure out from there. He led them down the front steps to an oblong waiting room that had recently been refurbished with flower-print wallpaper and indirect lighting panels mounted on the walls to give the place a comforting glow.

At a desk up front, facing the entryway sat a volunteer wearing a pink jacket with an ID tag: a white-haired woman who looked over at them owl-eyed through post-cataract glasses. She offered the polite reminder that visiting hours were over.

Eva took it as an overture to go for the door, but Whimpy held her back and gently pushing her into a cushiony seat, said he'd get a wheelchair. She was incensed. "Addie was the one who got us into this pickle. Put *her* in the wheelchair!"

Whimpy took the volunteer aside, telling her in a stage whisper that Eva was exhausted from the long trip she'd taken to see her sick father. Slipping the girls a wink, he asked if she could get them a wheelchair so they might take his exhausted daughter to her car. And incidentally, if security could help with the lifting. The lady shrugged and pointed to an office next to the elevators. He knocked and, getting no answer, looked back at the lady, who signaled him to go in.

CHAPTER 73

The Escape

And who else did they find raising his head from the desk and blinking at them but good old Uncle Gordo, looking like Smokey the Bear in that tight-fitting blue uniform?

"Great!" Whimpy exclaimed. "Gordo to the rescue!"

There was a big embrace and an exchange of explanations. Spanish salutations floated between them, rolled out so fast it was like they were late for a train. Gordo was moonlighting after putting in some ten sweaty hours in Mama Perez's kitchen. He had a host of immigrant relatives to support, so he needed the extra income but couldn't make it through the night without a little catnap. He really came awake with a snap upon hearing about the shots, particularly when Whimpy breathed the name of Tony Jr., who he thought wanted to exact his father's vengeance. Young Domo had breezed by and lured Jr. (plus friends) away, but the plus group were back in an instant.

Oh, did Gordo ever know the guy! Tony Jr. was in the cab of the pickup that brought the thugs into the neighborhood. Come to think of it, he thought he'd seen him in the lobby a while ago and wondered what that guy was doing with a walkie-talkie. But then again, he'd been getting sleepy.

"Aha!" he exclaimed. "From what you tell me, I think I see what's going on here. Junior was probably acting on his own. If Tony wanted you put away—inconvenient now with the lawsuit coming up—he would have hired a pro, and it would not have been done in a public place. Of course, the boy would know enough not to assassinate you where there might be witnesses. You saw, didn't you, what an open space there was beyond the hedges out back, with all those office windows looking right out on it?

"I could be wrong, but more than likely, they have a car in the parking lot out front, and it will cause an accident that does you in. So when somebody informs them you're going out back, they fire a couple of rounds out there to make you turn around and exit from the front. That must be where they're set up for you. Of course, it could be they just want to give you a good ole pee-yur-pants scare."

"You're giving us a pretty good scare as is," said Addie. "But if scarin' is all they want, you can tell 'em they've done it, and we go home. Better we think about how to make a getaway if they're lookin' to put a hit on us. What do you think they might do?"

"Any number of things, depending on what opportunities you give 'em. Like, if you happened to be driving down North Hill Road, for example, they'd just crowd you over and ram you off the cliff. Real easy."

Eva asked if he knew where the nearest linen room was.

"What? You want to wrap yourself in sheets? A *ghost*. Ha ha ha! Hey, it *is* getting close to Halloween." He came out with that gurgly laugh of his like he was crediting her with a sense of humor. "Confuse 'em good, eh? Well, it's a thought. But you know the simplest thing would be for me to call the station and tell 'em there's been a shootin' out here. The cops pull in, the boys see them sniffing around, and you're home free."

Addie objected, "Oh, I don't want the shooting thing reported, okay?"

"Just as well. It might reflect on me."

"We just want out any way it can be done."

"Sure. I could escort you to the car, if we'd put a little pep in our step. But that might just give these goons a chance to run all four of us over. Ha, ha! Well, maybe I stand there flashing my police '38, which guards us as we make a run for Eva's car?"

Addie broke in to say that there'll be no way she'd be able to run in her outfit. She slid along the wall of the entryway to where she could see what it was like on the half-moon drive leading up to the front doors. A car was parked at the curb some twenty feet back from the doors, and Junior's notorious pickup was parked like a distance forward. She had a vision of them having Eva's caddy sandwiched and taken out on the nearby expressway—where the goons would have them at their mercy, force them up to top speed, and nudge them into a ditch. She'd heard truckers bragging about doing that to highway patrol cars.

Addie huddled them around Gordo's desk, and with some quick fingering on a napkin, she roughed out a plan. Their vehicles were parked counterclockwise. Her idea was to have Gordo wheel Eva out to the car and put her in; and she would drive it up to the entrance clockwise, but outside of those vehicles of theirs, where Addie and Whimpy would jump in and take off. Gordo standing at the curb and pistol at the ready would give the blocking car a palm-up stop sign. If the other goons in the pickup started after Eva, he could shoot out their tires. Addie would have her gun at the ready, in case he missed.

Eva looked like she was about to cry. She didn't care for these shenanigans one bit and wanted out. She kept dabbing at her eyes and blowing her nose, which Gordo said was good. She was to keep the handkerchief to her face as he rolled her out to the car at a leisurely pace, which he did. He collapsed the wheelchair and put it in the trunk, and the first part of the operation came off just fine.

Eva drove in to the double-door entrance as instructed but, contrary to instructions, put the steering wheel curbside. She waited for Gordo to get out and slipped herself over to the passenger side; however not till then did she become aware, with a gasp, that in her nervousness, she had brought herself head-on to the trailing car, which thus blocked their way.

Nonetheless, Addie gave everybody a reassuring nod to proceed as planned. So Whimpy pulled the hat down hard on her face and wheeled her out, carefully helping her onto the backseat, whereupon he quickly threw himself in behind the steering wheel.

With a go tap from Addie, he gunned the motor and swerved right to get around the blocking car. In that instant, shots cracked out from the bushes behind them—one bullet zinging by Eva's ear and through the windshield, another chipping the steering wheel while others slammed into the trunk, sounding like the car had taken so many whacks from a hammer. Addie meanwhile returned aimless fire, recalling just in time to hit a tire on the blocking car.

Amidst the screech of tires, there were back-and-forth shots as they pulled away, followed by a shrill "Ow!" from Gordo as he careened backward into the open doorway holding his stomach.

Through it all, Eva was hysterically screaming despite the shaking she took from Addie. Whimpy meanwhile noticed in the rearview mirror that the pickup was doing a hairpin turn to come after them. He had gone left while it had gone right. So he floored it and turned onto the main road; and before the truck could spin around and close in on them, he pulled their car into the first opening he saw, which was a carwash.

But what's he blowing the horn for? Addie wondered. *Service? For goodness' sake, fella! Oh my gosh! He's passed out on the steering wheel.* There was blood on his shoulder. They'd winged him. And bless him, he'd driven away one-armed in *pain.*

CHAPTER 74

Old Farts vs. Young Turks

It was the last place Addie wanted them to be in; and as George Klagemann droned on in that adenoidal voice of his, intoning how the club had been wrongly denied its right to the bottomland—very old news indeed—she was all for leaving and would have had Otts not insisted that they vote his proxy and stay to find out how the vote went; besides, she felt relaxed now that she could be comfortably attired in sports slacks and a turtleneck.

What preoccupied them was that just as they were getting ready to drive down, Tom had called to give them the distressing news that Gordo had mysteriously died sometime in the night when the plugs had been pulled from his life support machines. To boot, his roommate, Carlos (the Whimp), had disappeared.

Gordo had reported the presence of the goons and also, when pressed, that, yes, he was quite certain they were the ones he'd exchanged fire with. The goons, who were unemployed high school graduates, Nick Dimallo in the lead, claimed otherwise. When they pointed out there was a dead wino in the bushes and next to him a pistol smeared with blood, sure enough, it checked out, which left the police scratching their heads and asking for leads. As for who did Gordo in, the boys said to look no further than Carlos's empty bed.

But hazy as they were, the two cops called to the scene decided to put that one on hold for lack of a motive.

"What does Tony's son stand to gain? Why would a guy with a fever and a bum shoulder just encased in plaster have taken off?"

"Furthermore," as Nick reminded the cops, "Gordo didn't say he actually saw us shooting, did he?"

Tom, on the other hand, really got them in a tizzy when he asked "If one witness had been silenced, why would the silencers leave another—if they did leave him?"

The cops looked at one another then told him to take a hike and to let the professionals work this thing out.

The meeting was being held at Faith Lutheran Church, an expensively architected modernistic structure where the suburban Young Turks (YT) of the Rotary Club worshipped, and a site opposed by tradition-minded Old Farts (OF), the faction led by Klagemann and Otts.

The girls were greeted by the scent of freshly stained redwood siding as they walked up to the arched doorway and, once inside, were awed by the polished poplar ceiling canted to arrive at the spired point over an altar backed by a pseudo-cubist mosaic of Jesus, and paralleled east and west by huge glass panels that allowed the sun to light up the entire sanctuary (which their fresh-out-of-the-seminary minister apparently was not very good at doing). Having made their way around knots of men locked in animated argument out in the red carpeted vestibule—voices raised, hands and arms in motion—they slumped themselves down in a back pew and looked around for Klagemann.

Eva was in one of her Nervous Nelly moods again.

Since they were prime witnesses themselves, wasn't it pretty stupid for them to be appearing in public? Yes, Addie noted, she'd be of the same mind if they were in public; besides, knowing Gordo and Whimpy as she did, she could assure Eva that neither of them would have breathed a word about their presence at the hospital. *As for the bullet holes in the car . . . It was dark, wasn't it?*

"Darn it! This is a have-to-do thing for Father."

She didn't want to upset him, did she, considering the delicate shape he was in? Eva grumbled that he'd be in worse shape if they were hauled in as accessories to a crime. Addie gave her a look.

"So, we did someone in, did we, and you supplied the gun?"

"Well, what'll the cops think when they see those bullet holes in my car?"

"That it did some shooting, and there was return fire."

"Oh, stop it! All of this . . . this shooting, this being chased by people who want to kill us, Whimpy getting shot, his uncle killed, me nearly getting one in the ear, and insurance won't pay a cent . . . Well, damnation, I'm scared! And I've had all the scarin' I can take."

"Hell, I'm scared too! But if you let it get to you, you make mistakes, which just now we can't afford. We oughta do to the scarers what they're doin' to us."

"You like trouble that much? Wish I had your guts, Addie, but sorry, I don't. It bothers the dickens out of me that somebody may still be coming for us. Maybe even the cops. You yourself said they wanted to question you. They'd haul me in too! Wasn't I, like . . . harboring a fugitive?"

"Listen, for now, if you want to be somewhere safe, you're there. The last place cops are going to be looking for anybody is in a rich man's church full of Germans. Who do you think are their most faithful supporters?"

"The things you think of, how you can take it so calmly . . . I don't know."

"I'm calm, am I?"

"Anyways, I envy you."

"Don't. And don't get intimidated. Get riled."

Bringing out her hanky again, Eva apologized for getting Addie so upset with her. Addie said to forget it and started to tell her how helpful she'd been, but their talk had to rest there as the meeting was being called to order.

Otts had stressed what a problem Klagemann had on his hands, made worse by the bait Tony's lawyer was dangling in a last-minute effort at conciliation. It was not that Tony feared losing the case outright; but as a head's-up businessman, he wanted to avoid the adverse publicity their suit would bring, with him going against descendants of old-time German settlers.

So Tony was prepared to settle with them if they'd accept a parcel of land an uncle had long back bartered from the baron—namely, some twenty-five acres on which the ever enterprising baron had once planted mulberry trees in hopes of cultivating silkworms, unfortunately without checking out their winter survival rate.

The club could carve out so many family plots for the well-known Schreber Gardens that had been set up in the old country to promote the health of German city dwellers surrounded by foul-aired factories. When Klagemann came by to inquire about Otts, Eva asked what the yakking at the back of the church was all about.

"Politics," he said, pausing to blow his nose and wipe the snot off his mustache with a railroad man's bandanna. "What else? They're trying to take us over, these Young Turks. Prussians, I call them. Typical Prussian blockheads. They have no respect for Saxon culture. No idea that the club started out as just a *Kammerchor*, a group of singers who liked Bach."

He went on to explain that in a way, the OFs had done it to themselves; for in an effort to assure the club's future, they had insisted on their sons joining—as an afterthought, daughters too. And once in, these Turks began raising all sorts of irrelevancies—like how about making a show of the club's patriotism by honoring German war vets, which their elders said was precisely the thing that would raise questions about their patriotism.

The OFs accused the YTs of lacking common sense, and before long, they were at one another on almost every issue but none so contentiously as Tony's offer, which the YTs found very appealing, a bird-in-the-hand good deal compared to the expense of a losing effort to get land of dubious use to them.

Otts had insisted on the principle of the thing and had told Klagemann the club had to hear from Mad Herman Stolpermeyer, the fireman said to suffer from a morbid acuteness of smell (best smoke alarm in town), last of the legendary Hagelmeisters, and also known as Lost Cause Herman for his obsession with those mucky acres which became the grave of his late lamented cousin Heinzy.

Noticing how nervous Eva was, Klagemann ushered the girls up to the first pew, where they'd be seated next to him—which turned out to be a critical mistake. He told the assemblage that the girls had a message from their father, one of the original founders of the club. When Addie said they had no such message, Klaggy told her to give them one anyway. Amidst their whispering, catcalls arose from the YT section.

"We ain't got no women in this club!" a truculent voice rang out.

"They got no standin' here," said another.

Eva saw that as a perfect excuse to slip out the backdoor. She tugged at Addie to get up; but Klaggy tugged back, saying that it would be the worst thing for them if they should leave, a sign of defeat. They had to hear what their heritage was; they owed it to Otts.

"Do we really have to listen to all of this heritage stuff? We'll be bored," Eva complained.

"Enjoy it and you won't."

PART XI

HISTORY, FIRE, MURDERS RESOLVED

CHAPTER 75

History from Herman

To quiet the hubbub, Klaggy banged his gavel and had Herman rise to take the floor. Holding up the family Bible, he traced the Hagelmeisters back to an obscure seventeenth-century Mennonite from the Rhineland, who became an investor in the William Penn Proprietary. The son of that original Hagelmeister, having prospered from the subsequent sale of those Pennsylvania holdings, reinvested the proceeds at a lower unit cost in much larger North Jersey acreage, where he had to withstand the disdain of the local Dutchers when he stupidly (as they saw it) incorporated in his domain a good portion of the swampland bordering the river—the very property now in dispute.

This brought forth a groan from Tony in the center pew—where, as Klaggy described him, "Er hat sich ganz breit gemacht" (He really spread himself out). Sitting there gorilla-like, knees apart to accommodate his overhanging paunch, he had his lawyer on one side and his medical consultant on the other, both of whom are YTs. The latter, with a languid arm hung across the back of the pew, was shockingly familiar to Addie.

She'd know him by the back, as they used to say. In believably unbelievable cahoots with Tony, Doctor Boy was probably going to extol the benefits of fresh air gardening for workers doing cotton dust shifts in the unventilated textile mills. But as Herman put it,

"Trouble is we ain't got no cotton mills up here anymore, but we got cars that pollute."

Klaggy rapped his gavel to quell additional groans, and his appeal for "a little respect" only begat further groans and louder ones. Tony's lawyer wanted to know what a land purchase two hundred years ago had to do with the proposed settlement at hand. Klaggy insisted Herman was not going to yield the floor.

"Dammit, we got a point to make! Like it or not, you have to know the history to know why this God-given land should belong to the club. Its members descended from original settlers, mind you."

He went on to say that those who had no interest in the club's history *and* future were free to leave. That brought Tony to his feet, flapping his hands to dampen any motion toward the doors. The last thing he wanted was a walkout, allowing the OFs to go forward as they wished.

Beyond a desire to show fairness, Tony seemed interested in hearing things he didn't know about this land of his. Klaggy, for his part, wanting to avoid boredom, asked Herman to condense the history and get on with more recent stuff; however, after nodding agreement, plodding Herman was like a fifty-mile-an-hour freight train that after braking had to trundle along for five additional miles before it could be brought to a stop. Klaggy looked over at dependable Iris, who was the recording secretary. He wanted to make sure everything was being taken down, regardless of length; and by and large, she did get the gist of it.

"Since water was the best means of transporting bulk cargo in those days of the early Hagelmeisters," Herman went on, "they had visions of a barge port on the river. Only trouble was they hadn't taken the waterfall into account, so the land was sold to some dumb Dutchers who had visions of doing only the short-haul, downstream business.

"The land was repurchased dirt-cheap by later Hagelmeisters who got it from the flooded-out Dutcher heirs glad to get out from under [joke-joke]. The Haggies, meanwhile, were so broken up with laughter over having sold land that wasn't there that they hoisted their glasses high. Triumphant, what those cagey Haggies saw was periodically enriched soil and endless truck farm riches. Those guys thrived but only until the returning floods got the better of them. Then—"

Before Herman could go any further, Klaggy felt he had to interrupt. He had been watching out for reactions from the membership and, impatient himself, told Herman he was losing the people. They'd never get to a vote if he didn't, for goodness' sake, move on and bring it up to date.

"Come on, do the important part about Herman, the wizard."

"Oh yeah, the wizard! I was just gettin' to that."

Iris summarized what she could get of the rest of his history lesson.

"While negotiations were going on with the Dutchers, it rained for ten straight days, and in the ensuing flood, the Haggies lost their little twin girls, swept away in their baby buggy, never to be seen again. And the oldest boy, Helmut, was also thought to have drowned, but an alert fireman who saw a head bobbing in the current pulled him out and revived him.

"Well, this Helmut, still a little lightheaded from his ordeal, had a dream in which he saw a ghost of the original Hagelmeister, who was shaking a crooked finger at him and giving him 'what for.' He said the reason the twins were lost was that his father was at the point of selling the land, and the ghost prophesied that tragedy was sure to befall any Hagelmeister who dared to part with the land that had been so good to generations of their family.

"'The wrath of the river god,' the ghost called it. Indeed, the boy wizard said that even for the thought of bargaining with the Dutchers, a blight would fall on the land, and that was exactly what happened till there appeared on the scene Herman's great uncle, another Helmut who by hard work and dedication to the land redeemed it. And so the land was returned to fruitfulness.

"Uncle Helmut took over shortly after he was mustered out of the army following World War I. Where his despairing father—a weaver in the mills—had seen only impenetrable weeds and swamp, Helmut saw flourishing rows of celery, lettuce, and carrots.

After he had sawed down the big willows, he got himself a horse to pull out the tree trunks. He grubbed out the smaller ones, got rid of the cat tails, iron weed, wild rosebushes, swamp grass, and the rest of the brush.

"He filled in the swampy places and had his horse drag a single-bottom plow to carve out drainage ditches, and by late spring, the warm sun and black earth rewarded him with his first crop of celery and lettuce. He ran irrigation pipes in from the river, built a washhouse where the celery would be bleached, washed, and trimmed. And as soon as one crop was brought out, another went in.

"Not only did Helmut become the celery king, he was doing so well he decided to expand. So one fine spring, he hitched his faithful old mare to the plow and put in rows of sweet corn, straight as an arrow, forty inches apart—according to custom, that being the width of Sadie's rump. But expansion meant he needed to hire more help. In addition to the blacks who worked his fields, he took on some Italian immigrants, whose day was, as in the old country, sunup to sundown with a break at noon for half a loaf of bread and a bottle of wine."

Hearing that, Tony jumped to his feet. "You see, it was my people! Us, Dagoes. We're the ones who made that land prosper. That's how come it's right we should have it now. You, Germans, you had your turn, and in the end, it didn't turn out too good."

"Not so fast," said Klaggy, rapping his gavel again. "Let Herman *finish*, and you'll know what really happened."

Herman picked it up again. "The major load of the work still fell on Helmut, of course. And his wife, seeing he'd overextended himself, made the crucial mistake of telling him he had to sell the farm while things were going good and before it ruined his health. So he tells the lawyer to look for a buyer, and you know what happens. The river god sends a flood. His pregnant wife is carried downstream and gets banged against a rock. Helmut gets her out, half-alive. She goes into premature labor and dies in childbirth, along with the child.

"Helmut is so depressed at losing his wife, his kid, and his crop that he has a stroke. Not wanting the curse to go any further, he consents to having the land turned over to crazy Heinzy, but on a temporary basis to see how he does with it. Well, you know how Heinzy did with the flowers . . . Not so good. Wanted prize acreage and, as known, got himself stuck in it and drowned."

There was some hubbub, and Klaggie interrupted, "Okay, that's enough." But he couldn't sit Herman down without his shouting out "Whoever gets this land will have to remember Helmut's last words, 'Beware the curse!'"

The hubbub came up louder. Once it died down, Tony's lawyer got up and explained that while the club might get some sentimental mileage out of its suit, legally it was an absolute loser. He doubted if any lawyer who had the club's interests at heart would take the case.

As he understood the situation, Helmut's letter saying he wanted the land deeded to the club had never been notarized; and when Helmut's estate was unable to cover the tax delinquency (you know how Helmut was about taxes), the city put the land up for auction. And by an error in posting the date of said auction, they had to take Tony's lone bid, which included a proviso that he pay back taxes.

"So," the lawyer went on, "don't get the idea this was some landgrab by a thief in the night." He put up a map showing that the mulberry tree land was well up from the floodplain, prime real estate just across the road from Tony's place. Topsoil would be shipped in, along with fencing, walkways, flats of seedlings, whatever. The offer, which Tony was in no way obliged to make, was more than generous. But of course, it would come off the table should the club's suit be filed.

Calls for a vote went up even before Doctor Boy got up to make his presentation; so at the lawyer's urging, he made it brief, limiting himself to slides of happy German families sunning themselves in their private little Edens. There were the happy mamas churning sauerkraut while smiling papas, beer in hand, grilled the bratwursts; and fat, little *knaben* in suspendered lederhosen were stuffing their red faces with freshly plucked strawberries.

The vote wasn't even close. The Young Turks were on their feet, cheering well before it was over, anticipating a landslide which they got. Over the din came Herman's shouted warning. "Beware the curse, good people. Beware the curse!"

CHAPTER 76

The Aftermath

Shocking. No one so much as blinked. Even the OF's had had enough. Nonetheless, Herman continued to hold forth from the pulpit.

Through it all, Herman's wife, Cass, kept pulling at him but couldn't get him to stop the ranting. She emphasized that nobody was listening, and he said that's why he had to let them know; he had foreboding thoughts for Tony about fire and flood—which were called out in a deep, oracular baritone that for a moment, gave the big fellow pause. Herman, however, far from being ready to pause, remained wound up in his inspiration.

"Someone must warn of the doom. A spring will come and no flowers will bloom. It may not come this year, it may not next, but it's there. Waiting. The curse will come out at its own sweet time. Beware, good people, beware! Fire and flood await us."

Occasionally somebody would look up, smile, shake his head, and continue out the door. Even Klaggy was embarrassed. He came over to console the girls, telling them to let Otts know he and Herman had fought the good fight; and Herman put a scare into them with word of the curse.

Midway, Herman decided to change course; to make people feel better, he decided it might not be a bad idea to play up the good deal they'd be getting with the Schreber Gardens. In fact, he was kind of looking forward to one himself.

His chat detained the girls just long enough for Tony and Doctor Boy (DB) to mosey over to say "No hard feelings." Tony asked the girls if they would care to join them for a drink at the ritzy Centre Hotel.

Her back up, Addie asked, "To celebrate what our side didn't want?"

"We have an idea you're going to enjoy the gardens. They can be inherited, you know."

"Father's in the hospital, as you well know. But he's far from dead, thank you."

"I've ordered flowers. You'll give him my best, won't you? That should never have happened."

"And it won't again, I trust. That would be good to know. Father needs looking after."

"Like it should be." After several jowly nods, for ceremonial emphasis, Tony continued, "Children look after their fathers, fathers after their children. I understand you had a nice, quiet visit yesterday."

"The visit? Yes. That was quiet."

"And quiet is how we want to keep it, of course. Peaceful."

"True. Peaceful. The kind where there's no shooting."

"All a big mistake, I learn."

"Hopefully, *everybody* has learned."

It was the first time she'd gotten a close-up look at Tony—all three hundred neckless pounds of him—and surprisingly enough, the face of evil looked very ordinary, like that of one of those day laborers who was satisfied with his bread and wine. Big-jowled, double-chinned, and sweating around the collar, he had those large, brown, bovine eyes that had an untroubled—one might even say sympathetic—look about them. Toward her, his attitude was that of a kindly papa.

They learned that Tony could well afford the generosity he was showering on the club. It gave him a huge tax write-off which would help offset proceeds from the exclusive contract he had wangled to supply the Centre Hotel and its various catering subsidiaries with salad from now to Kingdom Come, his object being to eventually become a partner in that hotel company by encouraging them to be strung out on credit, which would make cash available to them for expansion. And Tony available for ownership.

He claimed he had long since learned from Brother Francesco to dispense with the dirty street fighter stuff, and while it was better to be feared than loved, he'd also learned one must avoid being hated. Behind the scenes, enemies were to be caressed or annihilated; but publicly, he would be known to embrace all of the community virtues. He would not say a bad word about others, and they should not say a bad one about him.

As Tony pulled away to do some handshaking, there were things Addie would have wanted to say to DB—particularly since DB looked like he knew what she might have had in mind and, embarrassed, he looked aside. Avoiding his half-extended hand, she couldn't resist asking "Why?" which brought him up short.

"Well, it was just sort of a summer fling, wasn't it?"

"I never saw it that way, but one of us did get flung. So painfully did an innocent little soul."

"I'm sorry for that. I really am." Then looking down, he added softly, "You know, my father has specialized in GYN. Fact is I'll be going in with him, and we'd like to uh . . ."

"God forbid!"

CHAPTER 77

A Chase and Fatal Accident

On the drive back, Eva said she wished Addie hadn't been so bitter with the doctor guy. He seemed like such a nice fellow. "That was the trouble," Addie said. She hadn't confided to Eva (or to anyone else) that having lost the nice fellow's child, she thought a compensating event had taken place when she and Whimpy celebrated his release from jail. She'd vowed to keep it a secret, particularly from Peggy, until she couldn't.

She indicated it was a lot more important to think about what kind of report they would give Father. How were they to put the best face on what had happened at the meeting? Stubborn as Father could be, it might backfire if they tried to reconcile him to accepting Tony's settlement after all that he had done to fight it. They drove on in silence for a while with Addie at the wheel.

Eva asked, "Wasn't it a little scary with Tony?"

"That's why I've been driving around the block. Don't mean to scare you, but help me check whether that black car is following us."

They pulled over at the diner and waited. The car drove by. They went in for a cup of coffee; and when they came out and headed toward North Hill Road, they hadn't driven two blocks, before, sure enough, the car pulled out of a side street and stayed with them. Addie thought she had given Tony the understanding he wanted. But then there was still the undigested matter of the resort episode, Tom's articles, the lost election, and loss of Dunneville.

Would there have to be a payback awaiting me before Tony was satisfied? It was a reason to be on her toes. While at the diner, Mama Perez overheard her airing the question; and coming over to the booth where the sisters sat, she took Addie's hand. She related what most Puerto Ricans knew about Tony's need for revenge, something they kept a secret about.

The morning following the flower massacre, in the dim light of a misty dawn, Mama had seen a suspicious figure hunched over on the diner bench. She saw flower petals on her back and, looking closer, thought she recognized Addie.

Somehow Tony got wind of it from one of his workmen and savored his revenge; it was said to involve a gang rape and occurred in a way that kept him clean though he wouldn't mind taking his turn, necessarily first. No doubt baited by Bull Eddy of the big ears, the same gossip wind blew this back to Addie, who felt her purse for the little revolver and gave a half smile.

"No way, José," she said, her voice barely audible.

Evidently, Tony kept putting off his plot, knowing it could be ruinous if word got out. Now as things were developing, Addie surmised that opportunist that he was, it seemed like he'd take pleasure in vengeance any way he could get it so long as he didn't dirty his public hands in getting it. Just now, it seemed that he was going to have these kid goons force her onto a certain side street where she could be boxed in and become easy prey, incentive for kids to get rewarded. Her counter revenge? Pathetic. If it came to it, an unprovable accusation would only mean public embarrassment.

The hint of trouble ahead had been drifting Addie's way for some time and became saturated with the physical. The hush-hush revealed as much, confirmed by her sixth sense. Speculation that had to be put out of mind kept coming back as hard fact. There being a new police chief, she drove over to the station. Its bright lights lit up the steps, presumably as a show that they were in business and *mean* business regardless of the hour. As Eva hopped up the steps (if need be, to ask directions), the car suddenly whizzed by. *Oh, well. Amateurs, no doubt.*

Nettled by those sisters, more so by how to get clean revenge, Tony suggested to those who had ears for it that the girls should be efficiently done in, in a way for which the boys were encouraged to improvise. Tony's assertions about making peace when paired with his violent alternative appealed to the young ears that pricked up when he talked. His game plan: be publically agreeable, privately nasty.

She recalled that the threat of rape might have been paired with her dismissing his extortion threat as being mafia-backed. She simply resented his using the Connection to have his way with people who were too intimidated to check it out. A lot of his putting out the idea of a gang rape had to do with her public dismissal of mafia backing, which reduced his power of intimidation, hence his use of credulous kids to do his retaliation, as now.

Addie thought the stalkers might yet have another try at them, but what with their police stop, it seemed the amateur goons were ready to call it a night. Anyway, she took a back route unfollowed to North Hill Road.

About midway up the climb, they saw the light of what looked like a crazy motorcycle racing down toward them perilously close to the center line. *Well, isn't this a new one?* Weaving unsteadily, it was picking up speed when it should have been braking. The next instant, as it was bearing on down, the thing revealed itself to be Addie's one-eyed Wreck. The brakes were obviously failing again.

Addie instinctively veered to the right, but before they knew what was happening, the Wreck was upon them. They were rocked by a smashing whomp, a cry of screeching metal and a shower of sparks as the Wreck sideswiped them then careened over to the far shoulder on two wheels, where it cracked into the flimsy wood barrier at the curve in the road. And there the Wreck hung halfway through the barrier, its front end teetering precariously over the cliff.

Getting out to check, the girls heard Louey's gravelly curses as he pitched himself fruitlessly against the jammed door. A wild eye being cast at them, he yelled "Bitches! Get me out!"

Panicked, he summoned all his strength for one mighty backward thrust; but the very force of it produced a reverse slippage, which tipped the car further over yet till it hung by the proverbial thread, barely held by the back tires caught against the groaning barrier.

One last desperate thrust loosened the grip of the tires, and over the Wreck tumbled into the yawning abyss with Louey's frantic "Bitches, get me out!" receding to an "Oh nooo!" as down he plunged to the rocks below where the car exploded in flames.

The thought of fate exacting justice crossed Addie's mind, but there was no time to linger over moral niceties. Cars were stopping, and people were getting out to have a look and spoon some blood. Notice was sure to be taken of the telltale indentation and bare metal on Eva's car (to say nothing of bullet holes); and there'd be questions from the police, wanting to know why Louey had been pushed over *intentionally*.

They couldn't take the car up to the castle-mansion, where the police were bound to find it and make trouble for Peggy. Addie spun the car around, saying she was going to take the thing downtown by way of the back road and park it on some dark alley. From there, they'd walk to the bus terminal and get a ride up (by cab, if need be) to the pathway leading to the mansion.

What they later learned from young Domo was that the Tony gang had a really nefarious plan to grab and assault Addie: They'd make like they were saving her. Louey was to block her way uphill, and goons in the black car were to box her in from below. From there, she was to be plucked out and taken to the back of a station wagon, where Tony and friends would be waiting. Having learned of this, Addie could feel her anger rise to the roots of her hair. *Would there ever be a payback in spades?*

CHAPTER 78

Louey Took Advantage of Peggy

They were met at the door by Whimpy—who brushed aside questions about his shoulder and about poor Gordo, whose family he'd just come back from visiting. Very sad but, right now, his worry was about Peggy. In the midst of a crying jag, she had gone into a seizure. He had followed instructions about her tongue and padded her head with pillows.

But when she came to, she screamed for him to get out. He said he wouldn't leave until she told him what had happened. Finally exhausted, she calmed down and wiped the froth from her mouth. She took his hand and tearfully said she was glad he was back. But telling him what had happened got her so boiling mad that she lost it and ran for her room.

It seems Louey had, had a friend drop him off to get the Wreck; and he thought he could sweet-talk her into providing him with the key when, victimized by his charm, she forgot she had already given him one. His entrancing smile was getting her prurient; but she figured, *Why not make him work for it?* He produced a bottle of Southern Comfort; and they kept trading slugs till they got themselves pretty happy, and he proceeded to undress her.

Under his hot kisses, she let it happen. While she was still catching her breath, he got up to look for that other key; and she found herself being left there on the floor, shivering in her pathetic nakedness. Cold, wet, and clammy, she was consumed by a burning nausea and went into dry heaves.

In a fit of explosive wrath, she got up; and still in the raw, her flesh aquiver, she started to throw things; she was emptying her dressing table of bottles, brushes, jars, tubes, ashtrays, makeup mirror, lamp, music box. And with a final pitch, she let go with the whole of her open cosmetics case. Between shots, Louey managed to fish the other key out of her jeans to give her the sense she was at his mercy. Wreck that it was, she was still responsible for it—a financial debt.

Upon leaving, he stuck his head back in the door and said he'd spiked her drink with a passion potion. He broke into a horse laugh and taunted her with the neat little tale that on the way in, he'd bribed her doberman with a chunk of raw hamburger and wished he'd stuck some poison in it. It turned out that, that was exactly what he'd done. She had opened the window, yelled after Louey till her voice gave out, and collapsed into a heap.

And that was the sight that greeted Whimpy on his return. One-armed, he was barely able to get a robe around her; but his attentiveness made her cry all the more, which then climaxed into a seizure. When she finally told him what had happened, bringing it out haltingly, her wrath was re-aroused to the point that she was banging both fists on the wall. Unable to coax her out of her room, he called for an ambulance.

By the time it got there, she had passed out; and the medics took her down to emergency. They wouldn't let him go along, saying he could come down in the morning. He'd called, but they couldn't tell him anything other than that she'd been sedated and that he does not have to be worried. She'd be fine.

Addie thought she might alleviate the downer mood with the news about Louey—a bummer to witness, which nonetheless would give the Whimp and Peggy a lift. Whimpy barely managed a smile. "Good riddance! But there's a bigger fish to be fried."

Before Addie could go any further, Whimpy had fixed a pot of coffee and said for Addie and Eva to hold on. It was important for them to know what took place at the hospital with him and

Gordo. He said that he wasn't sure; but it looked to him like the powers that be (Tony's crowd) were finding them an unnecessary annoyance and thought it wouldn't hurt to put a more lethal enforcer on them, certainly a slicker one.

Anyway, Gordo, when last seen, had been serene, being completely out of it. The pain pills made Whimpy drowse off, but he awoke with a start when he heard Gordo hoarsely gasping for breath. As his head cleared, he saw that the guy dressed in the orderly's smock had to be none other than one of Tony's more experienced thugs who must have tiptoed into the room. Having disconnected Gordo from the machines, the thug quickly shoved a thick wad of cotton down his throat to finish the suffocation.

Just as he turned his attention to Whimpy, stretching out a short lanyard, there came the noise of a medicine cart stopping outside the door. Hearing nurses' voices, the thug assumed a business-like posture and slid out into the corridor. Whimpy jumped out of bed and, going over to Gordo, instantly saw he was gone.

He knew it would be no use ringing for the nurse: they'd think he was telling a story to cover his having killed Gordo since they could never admit they had allowed an unauthorized person to get into the room and kill their patient. Having had his fill of accusations and certain that the thug would be back for him, Whimpy quickly slipped into his clothes; and as they were on the ground floor, waiting for a third floor room, it was no sweat for him to roll out through the window.

The intriguing part of it all was that he saw who the thug was, and indeed, the thug had recognized him too; but with a roll of the shoulders, he seemed resigned that a job was a job. It was none other than that same fellow known around town as the aforementioned Bullshit Eddy, supposedly big in talk but small in action. Which was just a cover for his assignments.

"Yup, none other," he snapped. Everybody knew he sold cemetery lots and took commissions from that undertaker buddy of his. But only the insiders knew that for a price, he would produce the requisite corpse for you. Some people spoke of slogans like

"One-stop Shopping for Those Aggrieved." Except for ordering the hit (his client's call), Bull took care of all preliminaries and everything else that followed, the embalming as well—and in some cases, even the clergy and church service, choir included, which he rehearsed. Those big ears of Bull's took in a lot.

Finishing touches, like makeup, were supplied by his cousin who also came along with the flowers. Smooth as a snake's belly, Cousin Cow could do a hit one evening and next day hold a love-in prayer meeting with the victim's family.

"I swear," Whimpy went on, "if I saw him on the street tomorrow, he'd shake my hand, say 'No hard feelings, pal,' and ask me over to the Centre's executive bar for a shot and a beer."

"And later that evening," Addie suggested, "he'd jump out of some dark alley to give you the necktie party you missed at the hospital. I once knew that guy—knew him rather well, I thought. But then, what did I know back when?

"As I recall, he used to send me orchid corsages—exotic beauties, a specialty of his—for which his cousin charged a mint. And he made such an impression that if I'm not mistaken, we were—he was, anyway—at one time considering marriage. Me and the assassin. A *couple*. Think about that! A friend gave me an earful about him, but where did you come up with this stuff?"

"You remember that series of articles Tom did on the Jew Mountain thing?" Whimpy asked. "I believe you were out of town. In any case, Tom did a lot of digging and discovered his dad, Big Van, had secretly hired a bodyguard for him. And shrewd dude that he is, Van wanted the best. The kind who, for sweets, would tell you to suck on a fireball."

"And he got him, 'Cow'? A guy Tom exposed as leader of the notorious all-purpose hit team? Really?"

"The same. More than glad to oblige. Had the pride of the pro. And like they say, a whore takes all comers."

Whimpy winced and continued, "I hate to prolong the metaphor, but the latest I get from Cow is they're once again wantin' to set Addie up. And Tony keeps chiming in with 'first in line.'"

Out of nowhere came Eva's high-pitched pronouncement. "Then it's *war*! Yeah, all out!" She reached into Addie's purse and brandished her pistol.

Even Whimpy, who had seen it all, was taken aback. "Okay then, lemme me show you, girls, the plan. You know that complex of Tony's greenhouses on the long rise above the truck farm? Well, lethal Cow takes a page from Tony's book on the road to success and asks to be paid off in equity for the hits he'd done—like the biggie on Johnny.

"So he gets himself a partnership in the greenhouse enterprise, where they grow those profitable wintertime veggies. And Cow incidentally had a special row set aside for orchids, his big moneymaker. We target the greenhouses and you get a twofer. The guy who did the dirty work and the guy who ordered it. And as a bonus, we put an end to all talk of gang rape."

"Eva," Addie asked, "didn't we hear Herman call over to Tony as he was filing out and warn him with that funny little ditty of his?

'For you this curse,
Will only get worse.
By Fire or Flood,
The wrath of our blood,
Will rise from the mud.'"

Whimpy couldn't help giggling. "Just what I myself was thinkin', girls. Justice for Johnny and Gordo. And a little leftover for all the suckers Tony ruined, to say nothin' about those drooling over a gang bang."

"Ah-ha" Addie added, "there'll be payment—in advance. But first maybe you'd like to know what happened to Louey."

When Addie filled him in, Whimpy sprang up and did a midair somersault. He said it would be the best medicine Peggy ever had. Next morning, he was at her bedside giving her the news and had her checked out before breakfast. She was so exuberant that she told him to liberate the champagne that the lawyer had optimistically stowed in the baron's wine cellar.

After the third bottle, Whimpy said he had a sobering word regarding Tony's threatening remarks about Addie. It was known that she'd had a hand in the hit on Boss Dunny, which had yet to be paid for. In connection with which, sometimes Tony would speak his mind in the presence of his lowly PR help people who passed it on to Whimpy.

Well, Tony was once again talking up revenge on Addie and pointed to her having had a pretty reckless love life (some particulars derived from Bullshit Eddy). "Since she was so big for that kind of lovin', it could be made available. And the line would form after me!"

Eva pumped her fist and again cried out, "Okay, then it's a war to the end!"

Addie breathed, "Amen."

CHAPTER 79

The Gypsies Set a Fire

The following evening, as people were putting their garbage out for the next day's collection, a tawny brood of gypsy rag pickers pushing a baby buggy showed up in the "Gold Coast" area extending along the rise back from the river. The brood carefully rummaged through trash barrels for paper, rags, and metal.

With their baggy pants and long coats, along with knit hats pulled down on their foreheads, one couldn't tell whether they were men or women, boys or girls. Indulging in a common practice, they, along with the regulars, were scarcely noticed as they picked through the barrel contents with quick, efficient hands. There was always a decent harvest in the garbage of the rich.

The gypsies spent a good deal of time going through the numerous plastic barrels set out beside the field of elongated greenhouses. There was no objection from the caretaker as the garbage company charged by weight.

The old gent looked at his watch and had a few choice remarks about his rotten luck in being last on the garbage truck's route. That was bad enough; but those tired old trucks were forever breaking down, which left him with the disagreeable chore of having to stay on, "past quittin'," and burn the darned stuff himself. The gypsies joked with him about the unreliability of the garbage company, next outfit to be taken over by the truck farmer.

Sadly, they had to tell him they had in fact seen that late truck pulled over by the side of the road with a couple of punctured tires. Since his shift was already up, they told him they'd drop back after they'd finished their route; and if the truck hadn't come by then, they'd be glad to take care of the burning for him. He showed them the pit where they could dump the combustibles, pointed to the trestled eighty-gallon drum of tractor gas—they'd need some as a starter—and he gratefully took off.

The gypsies broke out their sandwiches, garnishing them with discarded lettuce, tomatoes, and olives—thanks to Mr. Caretaker—and had themselves a little picnic. As darkness began to fall, they sorted out their pickings and stuffed wads of gas-soaked paper up against the wood siding of the greenhouses; and the four of them became a lighting brigade, relaying around each of the five buildings before disappearing into the neighboring mulberry grove, from where they could watch the show.

With the wind acting as bellows, the show was not long in getting underway. Indeed, several of the lit wads, looking like so much tumbleweed, were blown over against the gleaming new warehouse.

As smoke curled up from the first of the greenhouses, no one in the large modernized farmhouse beyond the barn seemed to pay much attention. Evidently they were assuming it was yet another annoying instance of the caretaker's being stuck with burning the garbage when the truck failed to show up.

Somebody popped a head out to see what was up when smoke began to rise from around the other greenhouses; then, apparently the order was given to close all the windows as it looked like the lazy old caretaker had neglected to take the garbage down to the fire pit to be burned.

By the time people inside realized that the burning was more than unusual, flames were licking up the sides of all five greenhouses—as well as the warehouse close by them, a huge structure almost a city block long. The barn was also starting to go, flames spiking through its roof. Tony Jr. got busy driving the family's cars out on the road, lest they become part of the carnage.

Tony, looking this way and that in horror, paused to pat him on the back .

The whole Dimallo spread shortly became a raging inferno lighting up the night sky for miles around; hell's great furnace flamed. Here and there, glass panes were popping, the big ones atop the greenhouses exploding. By the time the fire trucks arrived, there was little they could do but glumly watch and try to keep the family and curious neighbors back out of harm's way.

They were unable to catch a sprinting figure who had bolted out of his still-running car and shot past them, screaming something about prize orchids. Fireman Herman said, "With those ears, if he went any faster, he'd lift off." When they caught up to him, his clothes were afire; and they were trying to smother the flames with a blanket. The captain radioed for an ambulance.

Meanwhile, frantic Tony had rushed out in his stocking feet, his pajama top tucked halfway into his trousers and his suspenders hanging loose behind. He was trying to get the firemen to wet down the propane tank beside the barn; but he only succeeded in getting in their way, several times tripping over the hose that was trained on his house.

Also slowing things down were his two sons who were at the same time pushing the firemen to get water on the other propane tank which fed the greenhouse heaters. Just as the captain had finally moved the pumper truck close enough to get at the tank next to the house, the roof of the warehouse came down with a resounding *whoosh*; and a flaming wall fell on the far tank—which exploded with the sound of a five-hundred-pound bomb and sent arcing streaks of flame and metal cascading in every direction, accelerating the carnage and propelling the crowd of onlookers pell-mell back across the road, children shrieking.

It was all of three hours before the firemen were able to get the flames out and the ashes damped down, leaving a devastated Tony in tears, running a towel over his sweat-streaked face as he surveyed the charred and still smoldering wreckage.

"I'm ruined!" he cried. "Ruined! Mama Mia, I am done—finished!" He roared in pain like a wounded lion.

The greenhouses had been practically new, as was the warehouse—the whole complex being less than two years old—and heavily mortgaged, on top of which Tony had leveraged other assets for loans with which to buy machinery and greenhouse equipment.

He was running a big-time operation, as he liked to boast; but he never let on that it required a sizable debt. The flames having originated in certain fixed places that the adjusters said smelled of gas, the insurance company made an immediate determination of arson, which meant they had to delay any consideration of a payoff until it could be ascertained that the insured was not involved.

The adjusters were particularly suspicious as they had evidence that Tony had burned down the previous smaller warehouse in order to get a down payment on the new one. It didn't help matters that as Tony was out the following morning, gloomily surveying the charred wreckage, some joker driving by yelled out "Hey, Tony, the curse!" When he inquired about the previous night's whereabouts of Mad Herman, the response he got from the firehouse was "What's a matter. He ain't satisfied we saved his house?"

Friends said that Tony never came so close to suicide. Those trying to console him (no one had been killed, by the way) recalled the image of his tomato-red head titled upward and his rubber lips spitting out curses of empty vengeance. "Somebody's gonna pay!"

The hunt was on for the aged caretaker—who, it was learned after reading about the catastrophe in the morning newspaper, had left town. The same source reported that knowing Tony's temper, the old fella realized he was as good as dead. It was no different than if he'd been the torch himself.

He wrote a letter to the *Morning Messenger* saying it troubled him to think that because he left town, people believed he must have set the fires. Speculation had been made of his doing it out of revenge because Tony had refused to give him a raise after many dry years of faithful service. He went on to say that the fire had likely been the work of a group of gypsy rag pickers; and he accurately described what had transpired, including the non-arrival of the garbage truck—stuck by the roadside with flat tires—and the instructions he'd given for burning the garbage in preference to letting it rot and stink.

One part of the story was instantly dismissed, casting doubt on the rest, as no one could recall having ever seen a single gypsy in town, much less four. Or did he say five? Maybe a pack. People could as readily believe in the curse, which was all around town, and got a satisfying laugh out of those who had felt the sting of Tony's hardball business practices.

Tony, on the other hand, was so desperate to find the caretaker and to bring him back—in order to clear himself with the insurance people—that he posted a reward emphasizing that he, at all costs, wanted the bastard of a caretaker back alive. The caretaker could claim the reward himself, if he would but return.

However, since no one believed the caretaker—gypsies indeed!—he, upon hearing about the reward, didn't believe Tony either. He would *pay* the caretaker with whom he'd been so stingy when *he* was holding the man clearly responsible for the fires? Oh yeah, Tony would put the money in his hand and get himself cleared of arson; then, having to take it out on somebody, he'd turn around and strangle the guy who had cleared him.

His face going redder yet and fists literally tearing at his thin hair, Tony called for his goon squad to get busy and find that son of a bitch caretaker and to come back with him in one hand and his balls in the other.

CHAPTER 80

Fascination of the Flame

Whereas Whimpy and Peggy said they'd had their fill once the conflagration had massively peaked, sparks flying and flames leaping sky-high, Addie had stood there transfixed. Eva, disbelieving her eyes, had whispered to no one in particular "Is this what we wanted?" Addie, herself somewhat stunned, had wondered aloud "If everybody got what they wanted, who would get what they deserved?"

They several times nudged Addie and told her it was time to go—indeed, *past* time—but spellbound like a child agog over a new toy, she paid no attention. Eva was caught between staying and going. Unable to move Addie and with Peggy pulling at her, Eva finally relented and said she'd leave with the other two. She let Addie know that they'd be waiting for her at the car and told her not to stay too long.

Addie stood there lost in reverie: even Tom's sudden appearance had no effect on her. Papa Van, fearing the rumblings he'd heard from members of Tony's troupe, dispatched Tom to keep an eye on Addie, fearing she might do something stupid. Van let it be known that she was going to be shielded by Domo. That should let the air out of a plot. Van already had his hands full in trying to keep the wolves (Mario, in particular) who wanted to bring her in for questioning from the door.

Deaf to all entreaties, Addie couldn't be moved. After ditching the gypsy clothes and smearing the fake tan off her caramelized face, she had edged her way forward zombie-like, drawn to the flames like a moth to the light. She proceeded through the crowd of gawkers that had bulged out onto the road. As she looked around, their tense features, highlighted in the glare, gave the scene a phantasmagoric effect, which was pretty much in keeping with her own sense of things.

Standing close enough to feel the great heat wrapping itself around her, she was fascinated by the deep yellow, ever rising phantoms that chased back the night. Figuratively heated as well, her thoughts swarmed. She felt she was looking at the secret of life itself, the mothering warmth that permeates the seed and makes it sprout, the light that makes it flower. Both life-giving and death-dealing. The flame in which we live and die and have our being. Gifted from Prometheus, dreaded in the firedrake's tongue.

She thought of the renewing effect of a forest fire that enriched the soil in burning away the old and stimulating growth in the new. So in the burning, there was healing. All things die in nature but to live. The very flesh we live in simultaneously regrows itself as it expires. Before one's eyes and invisibly within oneself, nature reproduces endlessly, makes love defiantly, refuses to be destroyed, and promotes a universal urge to procreate. Within the fire are the seeds of reproduction.

She initially found it strange that in the aftermath, she should have no thought of material consequences arising from the ashes of this very material ruin. But she quickly realized it didn't make a whole lot of difference whether anything beyond self-pity would get through to those she had hoped would be chastened by their loss because for them, there would be no chastening. *Did they ever feel they'd done anything wrong?*

"Tony, you bastard, listen up! The heat, man! There'd come a day when the books could no longer be cooked."

Neither was she particularly hung up on the plea for simple justice that had taken her there. Rather, she was consumed with the feeling that some things had to be done in pursuit of a "call" that wouldn't go away, an urge—a questioning urge—from within.

Thankfully, she could not know what yet awaited her. But she felt it was destined that she would bring forth a child whose awakening would make a fresh morning of the night.

Suddenly, there was Tom, who had to virtually drag her out of there.

CHAPTER 81

Addie Will Have To Hide, Otts and Iris Pair Up

Interrupting Addie's train of thought, Tom had the message that she was to get out of town—a good distance out—and to stay distanced until she was told otherwise. Slipping from Tom's grip, she made a break for it, wanting to catch the dying remnant of the fire.

As she tried to shuffle her way past Fireman Herman, he instinctively grabbed her arm; but in pulling her back, he slipped on the wet grass. And the two of them fell backward, with Addie striking the back of her head on the door of Tony's car, with a resounding *kablonk!* She came to in the back of an ambulance, and the next thing she remembered was streaking out of ER when she saw Domo Jr. revving up the waiting caddy.

From there, her history revved up. Orders were to take her to the western end of the state beyond Buffalo and deposit her at the Chautauqua Institution, where a job awaited her with the grounds crew. The outdoors work helped clear her of headaches. She stayed toward the last of the nine-week programs when young Domo arrived to take her to Sister Eva's place, which had gained clearance after a court-warranted search.

Eva knew of a school where she'd be a natural for kindergarten. Without inquiring about credentials, the principal trusted Eva's word and took Addie on to fill the kindergarten vacancy. It put

Addie back in her element with the old enthusiasm, which as before made an enormous hit with the kids and an even bigger one with the parents. Within a week, she was down on all fours with the little ones, enclosing herself in a world she'd made with them. The lettered blocks were lined up to produce words—which, with the joy of discovery, were sung out in chorus.

As before, Addie was hearing things like "sensational" from disbelieving mothers whose kids didn't want to go home. Sent onto first grade, her kids routinely outperformed those in any other school countywide. So there were hugs all around.

The thoughts she had of recruiting other women to take the overflow of attendees was scotched when word came to her from back home, contained in a message young Domo brought her about keeping a low profile. She suspected why: she'd gone too far. Tony wanted her picked up for arson, and he let it be known he was out to get her personally.

She needed to find a job, and she wanted to move on from kindergarten; there'd be a time to look into other possibilities, but that was not now. For one thing, though Otts needed more looking after than he wanted, he had at the same time been asking "Where are my daughters? Meine kinder, bitte." So there was an effort to negotiate a move back to the mansion with him, where a little apartment had secretly been set up for one of his *kinder*. But after physically checking it out, the thought of being there gave him the shivers. For one thing, it made him feel all too isolated and bereft of independence. So the daughters agreed that it had to be a temporary arrangement until a better one could be arrived at (maybe his home digs in the old apartment, with Klaggy and Iris one flight up).

On the other hand, Otts had to admit it was helpful to be looked after by his daughters for a while; and he was cheered when reminded of Louey's fate. It showed that God did care about what was going on in this cockeyed world of His, after all.

In any event, he lost none of his spirit. Upon leaving the hospital, he had asked Eva to find out where Louey's grave was. He wanted to dance on it. Well, at least piss. And speaking of

Louey, when Peggy came by for a visit, they dared not tell him the paternity of her little brown daughter, who Otts couldn't look at. At least, it did him good to feed a cherished prejudice.

"The big one here . . . She adopted this pickaninny? They look so cute when they're little, but steal from you when they grow up." He never did think well of Peggy and resisted inquiries.

Though he finally succumbed to the happy family atmosphere, they knew that, that in itself would not be enough to satisfy Otts. He had no friends on this isolated mountaintop, out in Nowheresville. To begin with, there probably wasn't a soul within a hundred miles who spoke German. He just missed the sense of home, his club, his old friends. Still, with this heart condition, he had to concede he probably shouldn't be living alone. *What to do?* Again, the winds of fate would blow their way though not without a saddening event.

Irascible Klaggy had gotten himself into a terrible argument with one of the more aggressive Young Turks, who said the OFs weren't helping the club to move on Tony's offer. Klaggy, of course, saw red and countered by pointing out the offer had gone up in the smoke of Tony's disaster; and besides, there would have been no club in the first place without his generation, who went through lots when to be German wasn't the biggest compliment in town.

Insults followed, and slamming his hand down on the table with a plate-rattling shot, Klaggy blew a cerebral blood vessel and fell dead on the spot. Within a month, friends in the club decided to bring Iris and Otts together. They'd known one another for ages and, better still, knew one another well enough to look the other way regarding what Iris called their respective "idiotsyncrasies."

Still, it was a hard sell to get them to think about cohabiting. For one thing, Iris was no Hannah. At his stage in life, Otts wondered how advisable it would be to be saddled with a fishwife whose sharp tongue might send him back to the hospital. And Iris, for her part, didn't particularly enjoy the thought of having to put up with familiarity—maybe even physical importunity—at her stage in life.

It was hard enough to think of sleeping. *Well, where? Surely not together! No, the whole thing would be too awkward.* What finally settled the matter was that they would in the first place not be getting married, for that would reduce their income from Social Services. Secondly, they had to think of the economy of their sharing expenses. But the consequence then would be that they'd be living in sin, which is unthinkable. George and Hannah would be turning over in their graves.

On second thought, since everyone would know there was no sin between them and since they would both be living better financially—and they had the blessing of their friends and children, even Father Tim—well, maybe it should be done. As Otts finally put it, "Kom ich über 'n Hund kom ich über 'n Schwanz." (If he could handle living with an Iris, he might as well accept the whole package.) So out came the Schnaps.

The three of them—Addie, Eva, and Peggy—visited on weekends and were gratified to see how the couple got on together. Iris had insisted that decorum required Otts to move in with her, rather than she with him. Also she'd been used to ruling the roost, and in her place, none of that was going to change. Should her cohabitor get crabby, she could legitimately show him the door.

Otts meanwhile was not unhappy to be bossed around, as Iris—on her best behavior—did it with some affection, relieved as she was of Klaggy's endless irritation with everything in sight, not unlike Otts with Hannah. She seemed to fall into the role of hostess—at first, anyway. The decision to keep their money separate certainly helped a lot.

Then, after about a month, an interesting phenomenon occurred: it seems that Otts was waking up in the middle of the night, and confused, he'd wonder "Where was Hannah?" At length, he took to wandering, which wound him up in Iris's warm bed, where he snuggled up; and before she knew it, things became physical. Amazed, she was also shyly delighted. While Klaggy, after all, had been shut off for years, he still had smooth hands.

Since Otts made nothing of it the next day, neither did she, assuming he wanted to be a gentleman and keep quiet about it.

After the third time, however, she thought she should probably say something. So as he was getting up to go back to his bedroom, she detained him by the pajama collar and said "Since it's been so nice these past several nights, why leave?" Maybe they should reconsider the business of separate bedrooms—to which, taken by surprise, Otts asked "Oh, have I been here before?"

PART XII

CLIMAX

CHAPTER 82

The Kiddies Cause a Confrontation

During the process of getting Otts resettled, the sisters were staying in a newly refurbished bedroom in the mansion that had been converted into an apartment for visitors. This put them next to the master bedroom (also refurbished) that Peggy had set up for herself and Whimpy. As part of a colossally mismatched couple, she was more than twice of him and then some. "Ever see a loggerhead embrace a needlefish?" Eva asked in a low whisper. Actually, she quite agreed that one forgot about looks on seeing how, hand in hand, they were so naturally affectionate with one another.

The relationship would get a little shaky from time to time—as when he volunteered to panel the oversize living room, and she woke up one morning to find he was doing it in knotty pine. Shaking her head, she sighed "For goodness' sake, hon, this ain't no huntin' lodge."

He obligingly took it down; and the next day, humming as he hammered, he started over with the wormy chestnut she wanted. There seemed to be a spirit of give-and-take between them that Addie thought ought to bode well, considering how strange the one could be and how volatile the other.

Addie tried not to imagine what their intimacy might be like, knowing Whimpy was no slouch when he lost himself. Indeed as she well recalled, given the proper circumstances, he could be a woman's dream; however, the very intrusiveness of the thought quickly put it out of mind. Addie had a notion that the relationship might not survive a real crisis. But she as quickly put that out of mind too and learned how wrong she was to think it in the first place when Peggy, exulting, broke the news that she was pregnant.

Throwing caution to the wind, Peggy was so taken with Whimpy that she ignored the doctor's warning that another pregnancy would be extremely risky since she'd have to be taken off the epilepsy medication. She had really gotten away with a lot in having Ginette; however, as she saw it, having borne a child conceived in hate, she couldn't believe she'd be denied one conceived in love.

Seeking encouragement, she went to the top of the tower to pray to the moon, Lucina, goddess of childbirth, hoping she would steer her through. As Lucina responded with a smile, Peggy came down patting her belly, convinced it was going to be all right. So euphoria ruled. Nonetheless—indeed because of it—Addie had a kind of sixth sense that ever-brewing trouble would one day hover over the baron's castle again, doomed as it was certain to be.

A considerable trouble had already lurked in the arrival of unpredictable little Ginette, built along the lines of her mother and hefty grandmother before her, plus an even heftier father. Elf child that she turned out to be, she early on bedeviled Peggy with questions: Who was her father? How come she was brown and Peggy was white? Who made her, and how come she came out differently? How could she—so pale—be her mother? If God could give her to Peggy, who ain't like her, how come He wouldn't give her a father who is?

Then there was the issue of Whimpy. "If he's here and my father isn't, what did he do to father?"

Watching Whimpy broil a couple of steaks out on the patio grill and seeing them turn brown, Genie got angry and punched him in the stomach. When Peggy cut her portion into small pieces, Genie went into a red-eyed rage; and clenching those pieces in a stubby little fist, she pitched them back at her like so many marbles. Another time, she put a July fourth cherry bomb on the coals;

and the steaks exploded up into the dogwood tree. No amount of reassurance could reach her.

However, when she started a fire in the basement with pieces of scrap paneling, they sat down and had a serious chat with her. She wouldn't be quieted until they told her about her father and what happened to him—which they did by way of describing his impressive stature and telling her he was a first-rate bodyguard, the kind of man no one would dare to mess with. Skipping details, they commiserated with her over his demise in a tragic car accident. "Would it help if we went and placed some flowers by his grave?"

They realized this was not a kid you tried to hide things from, and you certainly didn't try to put anything over on her. So when she wanted further information and, all tears, wouldn't stop screaming till she got it, they filled her in as best they could. Come another fit and they were stumped. Despairing, they finally had her in for therapy with Tom Vander Veer, who helped bring her around. Somewhat. Lifting an eyebrow, he suggested that there unfortunately were some aspects of temperament that were not easily changed in *anybody.*

Tom suggested that Peggy adopt a Puerto Rican lady's orphan child who she could no longer afford. He was a very adaptable kid, having been switched from one foster home to another before being put up for adoption. Named Josè, they called him Jay for short; and he liked that. Initially, his adapting to Peggy's daughter went smoother than had been thought. For starters, when she swung a punch at Jay, the sturdy little guy pushed her over backward. She tickled him, and they had themselves a laugh. Genie had actually been wanting somebody her size to play with.

Mystified as Peggy had been over how Jay might substantiate Tom's idea that the boy would help quiet down her unruly daughter, Peggy didn't expect it to happen so fast. She had an instant fondness for the boy, who responded so well to her mothering. She was able to convince Genie that Jay was there to stay. She played games with the two of them, like hide and seek; and the kids did indeed become playmates. It had helped that they were both brown-skinned.

Thick in the chest, Genie was a chunky little thing with lots of wild energy and determined to get at her new brother, who wasn't going to be pushed around. Genie wanted the boy to put up a fight, which he was compelled to do—infuriated at last when she pinned him down on the floor, sat on his face, and gave out a war whoop. For good measure, she did a somersault, lifted her skirt to him, pulled her panties down, and showed herself, leaving him utterly bewildered and madder still.

So the kids went at one another, and a couple of black eyes later, they were joining forces to go after kids from the Heights town houses, kids whose curiosity brought them up for a look-see.

Unbeknownst to Addie, that would be the beginning of the change of fortunes she'd sensed was in the offing as it landed an irate Tony Jr. on Peggy's doorstep, full of threats about her damned kids who were responsible for his twins' broken noses. If his twins had broken noses, she told him, maybe it was because they put them where they were not supposed to be.

It seems that the twins had gone into a foot stomper of a laughing jag when told that Genie and Jay were siblings. So the battlers went at them in a fury. Momentarily nonplused, Tony Jr., who had begun to take on the beefy build of his father, stood there in his sweaty tank top and looked Peggy up and down, his hands resting on a pair of love handles. It looked for a minute like he was about to give her a belly bump. Slanting his head, he let go at her.

"Lady, I get the shit beat outta people for less than what you're sayin' to me."

"And I've put the cops on people for less than what you're sayin' to me."

As Tony Jr. hissed a volley of Italian obscenities, the exchange got louder, bringing Genie to the door. She stuck her tongue out at Tony Jr., who was about to make a stab at her when Whimpy appeared out of the darkness of the open door and fended him off with the barrel of Peggy's twelve-gauge shotgun, telling him to get lost—which was an enormous mistake.

"You . . . You! . . . You! You, bastard! So here you are. You're the one who fried our business. The greenhouses. The warehouse. Jesus,

Mary, and Joseph. You near killed my old man, yah hear? Oh, man a' you gonna pay!"

"Keep this up an' you pay first!"

"Because o' you, Papa's in a nursing home, sittin' in a stinkin' diaper. You, bastard! You die!"

As he reached for the shotgun, it went off with a boom; and Tony Jr. fell back thinking he'd been hit. Whimpy fired the other barrel into the air shouting "Leave! Leave now or you die!"

CHAPTER 83

Peggy Returns to a Novel Situation

So they were on the move again. Addie said they had no time to lose. They'd better be out before nightfall. She called the firehouse and told them to expect somebody wanting to set the baron's castle on fire. They wanted information: Who was she? How did she know? Was <u>she</u> preparing to set the fire?

She hung up and called Tom, filling him in on the encounter with young Tony Jr. and what she said to the fireman. He agreed they probably should clear out. He'd see if he couldn't persuade a cop to cruise up there with him. If he could find young Domo, that would help.

Beating a hasty retreat, they had themselves a pretty anxious ride back to Eva's place. She had gotten herself a roomy station wagon; and they packed it full of suitcases, clothes, and bedding that were piled this way and that, leaving just enough space to sandwich Peggy and Jay in a backseat loaded with blankets. Genie had burrowed herself into the heap of mostly of towels and pajamas behind them. Whimpy insisted he couldn't go along as he'd only be bringing the wolves down on to them. He did have an obscure job at the hospital and needed the income.

Off work, he'd be losing himself among his PR cousins for the time being till he could find out what, in addition to arson, they might be after him for. He said he'd stay in touch and not to worry; he'd be there well before Peggy's time came. The two of them had an emotional parting; and Peggy came away red in the face, unashamedly crying. Genie rolled forward and, moving Jay aside, wrapped her fat little arms around Peggy's waist and pressed her head against Mama's belly.

Addie asked to drive, needing a diversion. With them having to stupidly run for their lives like this over a payback for skullduggery she had initiated, she was sullenly berating herself. *Didn't it sometimes seem like I was making myself part of things I hated?* The ruinous bonfire was more than a year back, but Jr.'s threat aside, the aftereffect in itself bothered her still. Innocently unaware that fate might play tricks on her (particularly in the form of a fire), she failed to consider whether this kind of payback might well go beyond what was intended—considering which alone, she checked to make sure the slick little pistol had a round in its chamber.

She thought about how she hated people getting away with things, the kind who cut in line ahead of you. You look around; and nobody is saying anything even if they're fuming, which grinds away at you to the point of ruining the day.

She, for her part, had been for going after Tony because along with Cow Eddy, he was a guy who did wrong and got away with it, building up a whole empire of error. *But bad as it was, wouldn't I have felt worse if I hadn't gone after them? Nobody else was going to do anything. Do you go along with the people who know it's rotten and don't want to get involved, so long as none of it touches them, and give in when it does? Oh, well. Didn't the Big Game Hunter say you always paid for anything that was good?* She tried it on Whimpy and he laughed. "If you find 'real life,' isn't it free for the finders?"

Tom phoned them to report that on the night they had all decamped, he was able to persuade a cop friend to drive up to the castle with him and have a look-see. A car came by, but when its headlights landed on the cruiser, it did a U-turn and disappeared. The following night, however, there was an explosion and fire, which the forewarned firemen had been able to contain to the first floor living room. The paneling was roundly charred, and windows were shattered. Typically, the firemen, who seemed to be practicing ax drill, did about as much damage as the fire. The police roped the area off, considering it a crime scene; but no criminal was found.

She also learned from Tom how come they had found Whimpy out. The new chief wanted his detectives to smoke out the old caretaker, and Mario found him in the Rest Home for Veterans. When Mario pushed him for an ID, the old guy said he thought one of those raggedy gypsies looked a lot like the thin guy whose picture was in the paper after the priest's murder. He was asked if he couldn't identify anybody else. He shrugged and Mario said he'd like to bring him in for a look at some pictures.

The guy says no. "Who would protect me from Tony, a guy that had every right to come and kill me?"

"From the grave?" Mario slyly asks. "What you have to worry about is not cooperating." Mario tells the old codger he can be subpoenaed, and the poor guy gets the shakes.

What happens? Next morning, he is found dead by the side of the road. He was so scared that he got up out of bed in the middle of the night and went out on the road in his pajamas and slippers to hitch a ride. A drunk reported that he'd hit a deer.

Addie appealed to Tom for info. She wanted to know if they have Tony—or Tony Jr.—to worry about. "Neither immediately" was the response. Tony's nervous breakdown had brought on a stroke that left him paralyzed on one side and barely able to speak. Unable to care for him, his wife put him in a nursing home, from where his futile attempts to run his remaining businesses were turning out to be expensive failures—as when he was ripped off by petty thieves, one of whom was recruited to pick up the numbers racket.

Tony Jr., who had bitterly resented Papa's dominance, set out to show what he could do once out from under, with the result that Cow Eddy had to save the flower business—which Tony Jr., allowing himself to get pushed into a price war, had brought to the brink of bankruptcy. Worst of all, a neighboring family, aware that Tony's empire was falling apart, began to move in on the pretense of rescue; and piece by piece, they were taking over. That made Tony Jr. all the madder and all the more unpredictable.

It was a terrible blow for him to learn that the usurping family was the one that his fat cousin had married into. So resolved that he'd look out for himself, Tony Jr. decided to go back to what he does best: man the gaming tables in the backroom of the Athletic Club. On the side, he'd run an exclusive escort service for the middle-aged rich wanting a piece of something young.

Above all, he had to get away from the old man, who wouldn't believe he was no longer a capo and saw red when told that Tony Jr. was taking over for him. Whenever he came to visit, Tony found enough voice to scold him for this, that, and, the other thing.

In the latest such halting outburst, Tony Jr. was blamed—on top of everything else—for losing the asphalt contract to those same out-of-town friends who claimed they were conferring a favor. "Don't you want to join them? Ha, as a soldier, no doubt!"

Insulted whichever way he turned, the irate young capo manqué refused to visit his poor father anymore, which got him a first class scolding from his mother.

"Bottom line." Addie wondered, "Since he is to be feared, how are we to deal with a man that is capricious, particularly when angry?"

"By avoidance," Tom advised, "and if confronted, do anything to placate the guy unless you are prepared to duke it out with him."

"Ah, good to know! Me placate him? Failing which, ain't I exactly the one to be duking it out?"

As before, work was Addie's salvation; and this time, she had Jay and Genie in class. They were really blossoming and learning to get along with the other kids. But it wasn't long before complications set in: Peggy wanted to go back. She didn't feel quite at home, nice as Eva and Addie made it for her in the mother-in-law suite. Above all, it broke her up every time she talked with Whimpy on the phone.

So along about her sixth month, she said she couldn't stand it anymore. She packed up and said she and Genie were taking the bus home. (Jay had developed a close relationship with Addie.) Nothing she could say or do would detain Peggy, not even the reminder of how risky it was. She kept waving off warnings and finally confessed that she knew of something confidential that would make it safe for her to go back. They guessed it had to do with the mysterious phone calls she'd been getting from lawyer Van.

In a strange development, it seems that Van, who was handling the remnant of the baron's estate and Peggy's interest therein, had been negotiating with a certain person (fire victim, aka, Bullshit Eddy, but not so named) who wanted to rent out space in the castle. For a one-year lease, he'd have the damage repaired and the downstairs fully renovated, saying he wanted an impressive place to meet his classiest clients.

His business was unspecified, but Van nonetheless thought there'd be no harm in taking him up on it once things were spelled out contractually; besides, that would make it easier for Peggy and Genie to come back home: there'd be no fires, no nonsense of any kind once Van installed Domo as his on-scene agent. Eddy, of course, had his own security personnel that consisted of well-paid professionals. Business dealings were to be confined to a couple of unvisited rooms in the tower.

Van had been wanting ironclad assurances regarding Eddy's activities, and after several trial runs that were duly paid for, he was getting the paperwork drawn up before leaving town for business in Washington. Peggy wasn't very comfortable with the idea of having this Eddy as a near neighbor. In truth, he scared her; but trusting Van, she said she'd go along. Aware of her anxiety, he pointed out that money clears the head of irrelevant thoughts like vengeance. This was especially true, he said, for single-minded Eddy—who, by his calculation, had barely recouped his losses from the big fire.

Ideally, she wouldn't know Eddy was there, and neither would anyone else (save the clients he did business with) since it would be an exclusively after-dark situation. Eddy and company would have a separate, secluded entrance; and as far as Peggy and the children were concerned, affairs in his adjacent precinct would be noiseless.

CHAPTER 84

Not Quite as Good It Seemed

But complications ensued. Since the new Gleam Team in city hall would continence no irregularities from its associates, that had doomed the high-stakes games played in the backroom of the Downtown Athletic Club. So to the enormous gratitude of the regulars, that's when friend BS Eddy stepped in with the plan to set them up in the castle tower, a place lots more commodious than it seemed from the outside. He'd have a paperboy posted on the tower with a walkie-talkie so they could relax and play in comfort. Nobody could possibly know.

At any rate, that had seemed much better to Van than having Rocco and the widow come back with their crazy idea of buying out the woman owner at a discount (the damage having made the place unlivable) and converting the castle into a tourist attraction—a Rhineland replica outfitted with suits of mailed armor bearing armorial shields, appropriately embossed, and stuffed horses encased in genuine leather. Properly advertised, it would be seen as a throwback to the baron's original inspiration to build this great pile.

Manager Eddy would, of course, take the house's customary ten-percent cut; and players would be provisioned with drinks, cigars, and munchies, maybe even pizza, at DAC prices. Suddenly, this seemingly ideal situation looked like it might blow up. That was what Mario had warned. Gaming was not in the contract; it was illegal anyway, and Van would be ready to have it shut down on his return. That's why Domo was at the ready and awaiting orders. Eddy, on the other hand, possessed a notoriously efficient tongue (even outside the bedroom). "Had Van envisioned Rotary meetings?"

Certain he could talk money sense to Van, Eddy proceeded to take advantage of the lawyer's two-week absence, moving quickly to install a fait accompli setup that was not easy to dismantle, given his clientele. A Wednesday night game was set up to capture the Friday waiting list; and by discreet invitation, another exclusive party was recruited for Monday nights as well. A contractor was busily outfitting additional rooms.

However, Eddy's boldest move was to set up a lower floor craps table for an entrepreneurial investor from the Heights town house complex who, by means of a substantial down payment, asserted his entitlement to a piece of the action. Though Eddy still looked down on craps as a lowbrow thing, there seemed to be enough demand for it to provide a tidy increase in cash flow; besides, the investor had previously proven himself in a successful venture at the Athletic Club.

In attention to detail, the whole enterprise was so impeccably professional—no need was ever neglected—that it would seemingly be difficult to dismantle. One need only consider the clientele that this enterprise appealed to. Wouldn't they have a voice in its continuance—the old money rich, some of them Van's clients?

It was probably because of that very situation that when Van returned, he was livid, kicking over wastebaskets, slamming file drawers, hectically thrusting aside drapes, and—heatedly on the phone to Eddy—using language that almost never passed from his Reform lips.

Even with his well-oiled tongue, how in hell did Eddy think he could run that kind of a circus and keep things under wraps? People could be ruined. Indeed, how could he have imagined he could pull off that kind of an expansion without having had it first cleared with Van?

Eddy's claim that there was nothing against it in the contract was instantly dismissed. There was also no provision for it. Moreover, Eddy apparently hadn't read that portion of the fine print which stated that Van had veto power over innovations.

After a session of obnoxious haggling, Eddy produced a list of important names of people who wouldn't want to be disappointed. "Oh yeah!" Van countered. "They wouldn't volunteer to be arrested either." The shutdown was to be immediate, if not, sooner.

Compromise? It was not in his High Dutch vocabulary any more than it was in Domo's, a guy who could clear the place on the blink of an eye—the other guy's blink. In short, Van swiftly cleaned house, saying it would be true to its purpose if turned into the residence it was intended to be—namely, a home.

CHAPTER 85

Peggy and Whimpy Settle In

The castle had already become a flourishing, professional operation by the time of Peggy's re-arrival, following her gold-bordered invitation delivered three weeks earlier. She could only assume from the fancy lettering that it had Van's silent approval. He operated that way.

The whole downstairs area had been plushly decorated and, though not quite to her taste, at least consistent as with the dark mahogany and regally massive Victorian furniture. Oversized though it was, its style did fit in with somebody's idea of an appropriate castle decor—complete with heavy brocade drapes and tapestry-backed armchairs, over-sized eiderdown pillows, and even decorative wrought-iron sconces. From an assumedly Old World perspective, it was not totally unappealing, depending on one's taste (or lack thereof). Genie made straight for the monumental sofa and, with one boisterous bounce, claimed it as her trampoline.

The break-in period was short: it, for example, didn't take long before Peggy figured out what was going on, and she had a nervous laugh over it. When Eddy phoned to provide assurance and, in his most oily locution, told her to relax, she did. To her greater delight, it meant that Whimpy could comfortably move back in. It took some doing to convince him he had to ignore the guy next door—he being as unseen to them as they were to him. The presence of her beloved Whimp was like a breath of pure oxygen for Peggy, who prevailed on him to stay put (and much else, punctuated by a huge hug).

Preoccupied with serving a clientele used to the good things in life (there'd been inquiries about women), entrepreneurial Eddy indeed had no idea about comings and goings next door and no interest. Since the clientele entered by secret passageway, invisible to the unknowing, it was the smoothest operation since whipped cream.

Things were going so swimmingly, Eddy claimed. This being the surest of sure things—subscribed to by the old-money elite—it was a no-miss situation. For Peggy, accommodation was a piece of cake. Eddy met all requests. Extra money was coming in, and the Crown of North Hill hadn't been so happy a place since the days of the baron.

After a month of busy weeks, the games suddenly ceased without explanation. *Well,* she thought, *the income wasn't all that important after all since the trust was providing me with enough to cover a bit more than subsistence; and above all, there was what money couldn't buy . . . the three of us setup comfortably together as a family.* She hadn't inherited her father's gene for making money, but neither had she inherited her mother's for spending it. Nonetheless, curiosity prompted a call to Tom at the *Morning Messenger* to find out if he knew what had happened next door. He said to just be glad they were gone, something less to worry about.

Frugality, she said, would do the trick for them. She wouldn't let Whimpy return to work. Having him was a revelation. True, they had their fingers crossed about the baby; but Peggy was on pills to prevent a miscarriage. Happiness, she claimed, was all that would be needed to keep the seizures at bay. Soothing sleep music was nightly piped in, a gift from next door. Energetic Genie slept through the night. Addie had left word to call to keep her abreast of things. Every phone call included some variation on their "smooth accommodation" made smoother yet when traffic next door ceased. The happy couple simply shrugged.

Then came those fateful late-night knocks on the door just as she and Whimpy were cozily enjoying their nightcap. Appropriately enough, it came in the midst of a wind-driven rain storm. Addie, who was averse to the whole enterprise, had warned them that having the gaming people next door would put them next to Mount Etna, making gamers of them.

"Tell Van," she had advised, "that you wanted a way out before trouble strikes."

Peggy cringed at the reminder that she had been told.

CHAPTER 86

Out of the Blue, BS-Eddy Threatens

With his olive eyes flashing this way and that and his signature ears flapping, Eddy applied the pistol to Peggy's belly as he backed them up to the sofa. Whimpy, catching his breath, gently turned the pistol aside from Peggy and asked in as steady a voice as he could muster "What's this all about?" Peggy joined in, asking whether they couldn't help him with something.

"You? Help? Ha ha! Good cover. You bein' the guys who did it. You read the paper, don't you? The front page article tells the whole damn story. I ask the cops, and they say the call musta come from here. One time, I wanna know why. It interests me. 'Cause stupid things like that don't happen to me. You guys may be dumb, but you're not supposed to be *stupid*."

Whimpy wanted to know what he wanted of them.

"You're gonna sign something here," Eddy rasped, waving a sheet of small-print paper in their faces. "Like the lawyer says, it's to 'indemnify' me for loss of income. You gonna help? Yeah, for sure. You good people. You're gonna sign before I'm finished with you."

Irritated by their blank faces, he began ranting about their stupidity.

"Most people I unnerstand. Simpletons, I don't. Why? I wanna fucking know why! Nobody—and I mean nobody—would try to screw me. People with half a brain unnerstand somethin' will happen to them. So how come? Out with it!"

He was waving the gun wildly and prancing about like he had just gotten out of the loony bin. There was a corona of whiskey breath around him, and quite unlike himself, he looked an absolute mess—hair down on his forehead, tieless, shirt and suit coat unbuttoned, trousers slung low on his hips, fly not fully zipped. There was some dribble at the corner of his mouth, which he wiped off with the back of his hand before taking another pull on his hip flask.

"Easy, friend," Whimpy interjected. "We'd for sure do something you want of us, if we knew what this was all about."

"Tell?" he shrieked. "Let me tell you something. Playin' dumb don't work wid me. Cops say the call definitely came from here. From *you*. Who else up here? The high flyin' birdies? You screw yourselfes an think nothin' of it!"

He paused for another pull on the hip flask and, wide-eyed, asked where the smart lady happened to be. When Whimpy said they had no idea who he meant, he roared "Call her anyway."

"Did you know," he went on, "what it meant for eight of the city's most prominent citizens—a judge, doctor, lawyer, banker, minister, industrialist, undertaker, and rabbi—to be huddled in that dank sewer of a tower basement like they were sweating out an air raid while cops were out in the parking lot taking down license plate numbers? Millionaires! Some, who for the life of them would never come to a secret gambling joint. A fun thing fer guys who knew one another in town. A kind of fellowship of the rich.

"The kid on the roof fell asleep. That's kids for yah. But you guys! Holy smokes. Wide awake. Can't tell me you didn't know what was goin' on." He said he'd checked out everybody in the know, and it came down to who else could know to call except his sweet neighbors. Nobody else.

"Simple. You told because we made you nervous. Who else, for goodness' sake? So don't horseshit me! You're gonna make good." Again, he brandished the small-print paper, saying it would put a lien on Peggy's estate.

"Make good on what?" Peggy said she had no idea of what was going on; then in the face of his sardonic stare, she admitted that Van had told her she wasn't supposed to know.

"Yeah. Where did yah think the extra money was coming from? Was yer kid poopin' gold pieces?"

Irritation was beginning to show in Peggy's tone of voice, particularly as he kept circling them. "Well, like I'm telling you," she said as she suppressed her anxiety, "believe it or not, I wasn't supposed to know and actually *didn't* know any particulars. And frankly didn't care."

"Not supposed to knooow," he mimicked. Infuriated, he went on about how much money he stood to lose (and also had already lost) just when things were going good. Frothing at the mouth, Eddy was coming apart at the seams—his jacket, literally—spitting out words that made no sense. He finally sat himself down in the overstuffed armchair with his hand over his eyes. Motionless for a moment, he showed how much this was getting to him.

The phone rang; and as Whimpy described him to Addie, ears above all, she confirmed who he was. Now, however, he is a shadow of the former calmly menacing self he'd uncharacteristically been, rocking as he spoke, while still being none other than the formerly self-confident, fetishistic, necrophiliac, copra nominal, agi-labial, coital-shuttlecock, ketchup-faced, bipolar, manic-hyperthyroid madman—seething, as he was, with words he couldn't have gotten out fast enough—immanently implodable Bullshit Eddy himself.

Addie said they should hold him off as well as they could, give him a beer chaser, and see if they couldn't get themselves locked in the upstairs bedroom. She'd try to drive through the night to get there and see if she couldn't get a call through to Domo Jr.

Coming back awake, Eddy rubbed his eyes and, looking piercingly at Peggy, picked up where he left off. "Yeah, wouldn't you know? Van points to a clause in the contract that says I was supposed to stand the risk of discovery. He sweet-talks me but won't refund the balance on my lease. Says the show's over now. Likes to remind me I'm a gambler.

"Think o' how much it cost my big shots to pay off the police. Just when everything's goin' so good . . . No good brainless sons o' bitches!" Jumping up and down, he brought up dust from the oriental rug and let out a string of obscenities.

"Well," Whimpy dared to intercede, "if you were catering to all those powerful people, who in his right mind would think of telling on them?"

"That's right. Who else but you? Do-gooders. Too late now, but you musta known there are people that characters like you are not supposed to mess with. Look at yourselves! Now, ain't you a pair on the make?" Turning his head to the side, and taking in all of Peggy, he muttered half to himself "So this is the plump turkey that got money comin'. Mama Mia!"

"What you say is true," Peggy interjected. "Who are we to mess with big-time people like you? Doesn't make any sense. Now how about leavin' us alone?"

Up he jumped again, knees bent, and came down hard, stamping his feet for punctuation. With that, two telltale, hand-wrapped Havana Honeys popped out of his shirt pocket. Aha! So he had come from a session of whiskey talk with Tony Sr.—who, by way of reminder, likely got him properly worked up, a last ditch effort at revenge by the fading pseudo-Don.

"No. Cause you dingies are do-gooders. Your kind o' people don't like our kind. You wanna do good even if you get screwed for doin' it. And sometimes you do a little screwin' yourselves, which is okay because it's you. Like that do-gooder priest who was dickin' the women." Pausing to catch his breath, he pointed an ominous finger at Whimpy. "You! You're the one who got the good Father whinin' about the stinkin' PRs. Doin' good don't work, man!"

"Well, yeah, does anything?" Whimpy chimed in, thinking maybe he could get on the same page with this guy. "Like they say, God's in His heaven. That's why all's wrong with this fuckin' world! Even He won't have anything to do with it. And incidentally, I'm broke. How about some ready cash?"

"Incidentally," he went on, "we've got no ready money. Something else we, idiots, can do for you? Like a beer chaser?"

"Nothin'. That's why I'm here."

Peggy and Whimpy looked at one another.

"After you sign, you pray 'cause you're gonna pay with yourselves anyways."

He slapped the paper down on the coffee table and motioned Peggy to come forward. She just sat there incredulous—whereupon he shoved the table over to her, banging it against her knees, causing her to wince.

He was laughing. "S'okay, Sister. I'll sign for you. Just gimme your fucking name." He cupped his hands over his face and started talking to himself. "Actually, this is gettin' pretty funny. Am I—ha ha ha!—gonna screw myself now? I drop bodies here, and they close the joint down for good. I climb on Van and make him reopen."

Looking up, he addressed them again, making a wry face. "Don't think I could carry you, lady? You'll have to bump your ass down the steps. Where you guys wanna be planted? Got a prime side-by-side. Estate pays me off."

"What if we just sell you this place? Name your price. Take it and leave us alone."

"I'm gonna take it, all right, and a chunk o' this lady's dough besides. Leave you alone? You shoulda left *me* alone. Didn't need no Mario nobody with the big smarts to put it together for me. Take down the building instead of the people? No. Cut off the tail that rattles and leave the head that bites?"

"Listen, my wife ain't up to this kind of thing. Can't you see—"

Pulling Whimpy up by the arm, in mid-sentence Eddy had him airborne and swung him toward the door. "Listen, bullshit! Come on, you folks are goin' for a ride."

"You stop it!" Peggy yelled, her voice suddenly cutting the tense air like a whistle. "Stop it, you hear? We have had enough!"

"No, you haven't."

With that, hand raised, he was about to pistol-whip Peggy when Whimpy threw himself at him with just enough force to deflect the blow, so it glanced off her humped shoulder, which jarred the pistol free. With Eddy being spun around, Whimpy, quick as a monkey, jumped on his back; and in the next instant, they were down on the floor, kicking over chairs and end tables.

Down went a lamp, darkening the room. The hallway lamp still threw some light on the scene.

They locked arms around each other in a fierce grapple that suddenly came apart when, out of nowhere, a black cat fell on Eddy's face and sprang off before he could react, leaving him scratched and momentarily bewildered.

He quickly recovered and struck out at Whimpy, gripping him by the shirt collar and ratcheting a fist tight under his chin as if to hoist him up bodily for a throw, at the sight of which Peggy burst forth with a hysterically drawn-out "Staaahp iiit!" accompanied by a shot from her pistol that shattered a low-light table lamp, which sent shards clinking in every direction. Breaking the stunned silence that followed, Eddy let go with muted obscenities and froze.

"Don't shoot! Don't shoot!" he cried, his variable voice rising an octave. Peggy had the pistol in front of her nose and aimed at Eddy and fired another shot that just about parted his hair. Wobbly as he'd been, he swiftly got himself together and, in a mad scramble, hurled himself out the door.

Her legs apart on the diagonal, Peggy labored to brace herself and, aiming at the doorway, was preparing to fire off another round when her huge frame started teetering. And in a deadweight fall, she went over like a sack of potatoes, hitting the floor with a resounding jolt. As Whimpy tenderly patted her cheeks, she came to and crawled about for a minute like a person looking for her glasses before settling against the wall, where she began banging her head in a violent seizure.

And that was it. She'd already had a bad reaction to the injection they gave her in the emergency room. No one had bothered to check prior medications. Her liver started to shut down, and she was moving toward coma. The ambulance came for her, and an hour after she was admitted to the emergency room, she was pronounced dead. Efforts to save the baby failed.

CHAPTER 87

Addie's Return and Whimpy's Revenge

Having thrown themselves into Eva's station wagon in haste, Addie and Jay returned to chaos. Filling her in, Whimpy described how Genie had gone berserk at the sight of her mother in a seizure and had started kicking Whimpy when he said he couldn't stop Peggy's convulsions. He went on about how the commotion in the living room had roused the little one out of a deep sleep and brought her down to the bottom step of the staircase—where she sat hugging Schmutzy, her black cat and bed companion.

Utterly perplexed by it all, she was particularly irritated at the folly of grown men—one of them, a stranger—rolling around on the floor; and when they wouldn't cut it out, she got up and threw the cat at them, aiming mostly at the stranger.

The worst of it occurred on her realizing that the ambulance would be taking her mother away. When protests got her nowhere, she went on a tear with a knife—slashing sofa, chairs, drapes, rugs, her bed—and menaced the paramedics, from whom Whimpy had asked for help. Between them, they finally distracted Genie enough to wrench the knife free; and she was deposited in the psychiatric ward, where she was tied to a bed.

Tom was summoned, and he managed to get her sufficiently under control so they could remove the restraints. They had her doped up with tranquilizers, and it was not until Addie brought Jay in to see her that she showed signs of coming out from under. The kids held one another tightly, cheek to wet cheek. Genie insisted on Jay's staying overnight with her, so they gladly moved another bed in.

Meanwhile, having arranged for a modest funeral and cremation, Addie had to find Whimpy but had no idea of where he might have disappeared to. She called Betsy, who knew his most likely points of contact in the Puerto Rican neighborhood, but even she came up empty. The best she could do was leave word with Gordo's kids.

Addie wanted Betsy to come over and stay for a couple of days; but wholly unlike her, she said, on account of her boyfriend, that wouldn't be very practical. He wasn't fit to live with just now, which was why she had to hang in.

"Really?" Addie asked.

"I know I should have left some time back. I'd told him nobody was a loser all the time, and he slugged me. See these stitches over my eye? Can't say I've had the best of luck with the men in my life."

"The twins . . . Yours?"

"No. From the marriage he got annulled when he caught his wife dippin' into the stash of hash he was pushin'. Turned out to be coke, of course."

"And now?"

She shrugged. "Gimme a hug, hon." They held one another and swayed for a minute.

"How come you're in with him?"

"A bit of a story. I'm livin' in Louey's town house, you know. When he got killed, I thought I didn't have to worry about gettin' booted out. Well, over comes Tony Jr. and tells me he owns it and wants in. I told him I didn't have no place to go. So he said why not stay on as housekeeper for decent pay. He specially needs somebody for the kids. But you know how it is. Of course, that arrangement didn't last very long."

"Now he gets mad and takes it out on you, huh?"

"Well, he apologizes and says it's pressure. That Eddy guy kept promisin' things and had him on a short leash. Begs me 'don't leave.' Needs me. Says, 'I know the kids do.'"

"So you're stuck. You can't stay and you can't leave."

"Listen, it's not all that bad I stayed. I've stopped him from stormin' up here a couple of times. In fact, I actually decided to reform him. I asked him to do something useful, so he joined the auxiliary police—you know, the humpty-dumpties who direct traffic in emergencies—but, as a trade-off, he hangs on to the rackets.

"I tell him if the trouble follows him home, I'm gone. Of course, he's got himself covered. He gives the cops a piece of the action, so he's in real good with them, and they've got him in training to become a regular on the force. I fear for how he's gonna use the badge."

"Never mind. Remember, if it doesn't work for you, we could take you in. Of course, we're gonna want outta this thing, but it won't be tomorrow."

"Yeah. Picture it. Then he'd make sure the place got burned down. Oh, by the way, I found out about the call that got you in the trouble with BS Eddy. Junior here was at headquarters when it came through."

"Who made the call?"

"Ol' Domo, of course. In plain sight, from the tower phone. Right beside him, two high–stakes poker games are goin' on at once. Players are in another world. Five-grand nerves. Domo had instructions for it to be shut down once a police cruiser came sniffin' around."

"So that's how come we got terrorized."

"Well, talk about nerve. Eddy was wanting dough outta you when he'd already made a ten-percent mint on the games."

"Anyway, we have the Whimp to worry about again. Try to find a guy who's invisible as air. Hard enough to track him down when he's hoofin' it. Now that he's got Peggy's wheels, all you'll find is the patch he leaves on the road."

Addie had told Tom to brief her on whatever, and just as Betsy gave her a parting hug, he called to let her know it just came into the newsroom that BS Eddy had been brutally knifed to death in broad daylight on Main Street in front of the Vander Veer Office

Building. His assailant calmly got himself back in his car and sped away. Bystanders were so horrified that no one could describe the guy or the car. Police themselves were dumbfounded.

Whimpy phoned Addie that night from an unknown location and told her they wouldn't take him alive. Until something bad happened, she should know that wherever people were being crapped on, that's where he'd be.

"Oh, Whimpy. None of this had to be."

"Seems like it did."

"Anyway, wherever you are, know that you're loved."

"Love you too, Addie. Nothing else lasts. Give Genie a huggy for me."

"You'll call me, won't you? Got to hear."

"Put a candle in the window. Who knows? I may show up one day."

"Have to."

CHAPTER 88

Otts and Iris at Odds,
Buyer of Castle Slain

In the midst of it all, she got an earful from Iris, who Betsy had contacted on her behalf. The situation had become a little edgy with Otts. Originally, Iris had called to say she'd rethought things and figured it might work out for her and Otts after all, so long as he didn't "critimize." And at first he didn't. In fact, they had settled some things and were getting along "real good," as she put it. Some bedtime Schnaps and he was "a regular doll."

But that was her word last month. Now all of a sudden, there is a change; and everything irritates him. It's like he had an awful shock of some kind. He begins to sound a lot like George. They quarrel and he gets short of breath. She doesn't want a problem on her hands.

She asked if Addie could come over and talk to him. What with the shock, he was also becoming forgetful. They spent all of a morning trying to find his false teeth, which finally turned up under his bed. Lord only knows how it got there. "He blames me," Iris recounts. "If this sort of thing can't be straightened out, the party is over."

Addie said he'd have no place to go; in fact, she pointed out she wasn't certain she herself would have a place. All the more reason, Iris countered, that he'd have to shape up or . . . well, something else would have to be done.

Addie said she'd make a point of that with him. She'd come over as soon as she could. In the meantime, it would help if Iris could be a little patient. Dissatisfied, Iris rattled on about how terrible it was to put up with a grumpy old man at her time of life. He had caught sight of Rocco and it unsettled him. Such a change over some guy just looking at the names on the mailboxes like he had a letter to deliver.

"I'm sorry, but . . ."

"Go easy, Iris, *please*. He may be losing it. A little understanding will go a long way."

"Losing it, you think? Then for sure, I'm going to have to find a home for this guy."

"I'm just guessing, but Rocco was not on the best terms with the baron's family. The baron was very good to Otts, so you can see how he felt about that Rocco guy. In any event, I'm not in a very good frame of mind myself. Hold everything till I can get away. And please, this guy is my father."

Looking out the window, Addie saw Tom drive up and said she'd get back to Iris, who was still talking as she hung up. Tom said he had to take her down to see his father. There was legal business to be attended to.

"Now?" she asked. "Can it wait?"

"Not if you want to avoid any challenges to your estate. And not if you want a place to stay."

"I have an *estate*?"

As Van laid it out for her, it looked like she was going to be coming into a rather substantial amount of money—stock in large corporations that survived the crash very handsomely and had grown enormously in value, plus the quarterly dividends, which, till Peggy asked that they be paid out, had been reinvested.

The baron had invested very wisely for his wife and daughter, setting up model portfolios. And with Peggy gone, Addie now became the beneficiary of both estates, in addition to coming into a trust of her own; then, of course, a little paperwork would also give her the castle. She said she'd never been very much about money. Teary-eyed, she said she'd rather have Peggy back.

"I mean it," she said. "I know it sounds stupid, and I'm so overwhelmed I *feel* stupid. But you know, I never got to tell her we were sisters. I should have, but I just got so used to keeping it dark on account of my father, Otto, as you know."

Rubbing his chin, Van confided, "I think she might have known. I had to go over legal papers with her too, and in doing so, I had to elucidate the provision the baron had put in her trust that on her death, you would automatically become first beneficiary.

"She wanted to know how you could come before her offspring. I told her you didn't know that. She asked that you be the child's godmother, which you do know, and she also made it part of her will that you be asked to adopt Genie in case health got the better of her."

"Oh . . . I'm glad if she knew. And of course, Jay and I want Genie. Truth is she's ours already . . . There's something else. We won't want to stay in the drafty old castle. I want it put up for sale. Looks like I'll have to relocate my dad. Then, the three of us would be moving up to my sister's place. She's got a mother-in-law suite we can make a home of. I want us out of this place as soon as we can get out."

She made this point with Tom, who had been waiting for her in the parking lot. He'd been on the lookout for buyers and thought he'd had one for sure with BS Eddy.

"I have to tell you a sad story regarding that Eddy guy, the man who got stabbed to death outside our building here. Well, the reason he was coming to see me was to put in a bid for the place. He was known for a lot of bluster, of course. And in fact, claimed he had the backing of an obscure millionaire. But I took him at his word. He was really eager to set up shop in the tower again. As he put it, 'True gamblers are addicts.' Of course, he wasn't addicted himself."

"Yes, I'd known him well some time ago. In a different connection, which, to a point, was interesting. The guy who bothers me is this Rocco. Like they say, 'Hard on the men, soft on the women.'"

"Yeah, and suspicious with everyone else."

CHAPTER 89

Remembrances and Dandy Buyer Appears

Addie tried to mediate the disputes Otts was having with Iris but to no avail. The two of them were going at it even as Addie stood there between them. It got no better when Iris's daughter, Elsa-Lore, arrived from California. Her solution was easy: Otto simply had to be removed from proximity to her mother, and the sooner the better—like tomorrow, if possible.

"You're gonna put me out in the street?"

"No. You go to your daughter. She's got plenty room."

"I don't wanna go there. You owe me for the furniture. I don't leave till you pay."

"Pay? I'm the one who should be paid for putting up with this!"

"Ja, bezahlen. Eher ein Pumps aus 'n toten Pferd." (Real tight.)

Iris went to her bedroom and slammed the door. Addie told Otts he had to get himself away from this aggravation: it was bad for his blood pressure. And packing up his daily belongings, she drove him over to the castle, saying she'd take care of payment for his furniture. He was all for calling a used furniture dealer, Honiglecker, a sweet guy and fellow club member, to pick up his furniture. She said that for now, that would be the wrong thing to do. Though she could use that fella when she pulled out of the castle.

They sat quietly for a while, and she got him started on reminiscing. As a child, she had been his "Little Bear," he her

"Bamsa Bear." He never tired of telling how she had those big bear hugs for him when he came home from work and how her face lit up when he promised her bedtime stories; she was such a joy to him.

He recalled taking her to the dentist for the first time. The dentist tried to impress on her the need to brush twice a day, saying that she might not realize it but that the mouth was the dirtiest part of a person's body. There was a pause, and little Rika turned to him with those big, brown eyes and said "No, it isn't."

Still vivid in her memory, she recalled, were those summer days when they made their excursions to the other river (supposedly the clean one)—where, though unable to swim, they nonetheless gripped those inner tubes, plunged in, and paddled around as if they could. She liked to sound out with an exaggerated trilling of the Rs his inimitable fanfare on arrival, "Vell, here vee are again. Jeder Frosch ins Wasser!" (Every frog in the water.)

In time, he taught her how to swim. (Or was it she teaching him?) He became her good old pal, and she his. They went on that way, trading stories well into the early hours of the morning, and fell asleep side by side on the love seat where they sat. She could not know that, that was the last really peaceful moment she would enjoy before her world darkened over.

Next day, she was roused from her much needed nap by the kids calling "Hey, Mom, there's an actor who wants to see you!"

Coming somewhat drowsily to the door, she was taken aback by the sight of a European- looking dandy on the steps, tipping his Panama hat to her. He trailed a whiff of Parisian cologne that had the kids holding their noses, ignoring what he explained with a comely smile that he'd been living in Hollywood, Florida.

Immaculately groomed, he was evenly graying at the temples; and in addition to sporting a handlebar mustache that had been waxed at the tips, he had a pastel-peach ascot tucked in his navy-blue blazer that gave him an air of distinction—something which, with appropriate savoir faire, he tried to downplay. Dandy that he was, he smoked a fragrant brand of cigarillo that was delicately held between index and middle fingers.

Addie scrutinized him for a moment and gasped. This, for goodness' sake, was none other than Rocco himself, dressed up in his lady-killer attire. His latest "date" sat in car.

Before Addie fully came to, he had eased his way into the front hall and, as he looked around, said that he represented a group of investors who were interested in her castle. He asked if she would mind if he looked it over, particularly the picturesque tower.

Would she mind? Suddenly very wide awake, she hastily escorted him to the private entrance, almost tripping over her feet as they went. She wanted to ask him why he assumed she owned the castle; but instead she told him that as he would see, the tower was an ideal place for confidential business meetings, which was how it had been used by the previous tenants who rather enjoyed their privacy.

He could live in the castle proper and rent out the tower as she had done. She babbled on about various possibilities open to him but stopped in mid-sentence on noticing by his perfunctory nods that he was either consumed with his own plans, or was already well aware of what had gone on there. She said no more, dropped the key into his palm, and rushed back, telling the kids to go upstairs and to pick up their rooms and to send Grandpa down to help her deal with the clutter in the living room. He too had been napping, but her excited chatter about a prospective buyer brought him to in a hurry.

"Heavenly days," she breathed while fluffing pillows on the new sofa, gathering up newspapers, straightening rugs, and running the feather duster over lampshades, tables, drapes, and everything else in sight. "We've got to pull it off, Dad. I forgot to ask who sent him up here. Maybe the lawyer, huh? He gets a commission. No matter. Good for him."

Otto frowned, uncertain of where he would fit in and particularly concerned about a move away from his hometown.

"Oh, Dad, think about it. We'll be able to scout out a house for you. Or maybe you could stay with us. I'll tell this buyer we want out, and for a quick sale, we'll—Well, no, maybe that wouldn't be a good idea. Might think we're trying to unload. Gotta be cool. Can't play hard to get, though.

"Kids! You guys up there getting your beds made? Got some ice cream in the freezer."

With a faint knock on the front door, he was back—all congeniality as before—only to be greeted by a gasp of astonishment from Otto, who, trembling, grabbed Addie and all but deafened her ear with a wet whisper "It's *him*! Rika, it's *him*! Um Gottes willen. It's *him*!"

No amount of shushing could quiet him. Hustling him into the kitchen, she shut the door and turned the key, while he stood there perseverating. She led her guest into the dining room and closed the big french doors behind them.

"Your father?"

"Yes. You'll have to forgive him. He's not well. Can I fix you a drink?"

"How come he knows me?"

"I don't think he does. He must be mistaking you for someone else. I've had to move him out of his apartment. He feels uprooted. Didn't get much sleep last night. Neither did I . . . You're interested, are you?"

"What are you asking?"

"You know, I really haven't given it a thought. My lawyer handles all of that. But if price will facilitate matters, I'll tell him to be flexible. How did you find out I might want to sell?"

"I didn't. I'd been thinking about this place for some time. A rather long while ago, it was in the family. You see, I'm originally from here. You may know the family. Guipiletti. The lady who last owned this place was my niece."

"Ah, Peggy. And you are?"

"Angie fils—er, Junior, that is."

"Excuse me, then haven't you been going by Rocco?"

"Yes. My street name. Usually in casual duds, never dress-up."

She thought to ask why he needed two names but let it go. "Like I said, Dad's not been himself lately. But I do know he'd be a very happy man if we could get this place sold, and with your family connection, how fitting that you should be the one to take over! I think that, by itself, should discount the price. Let me give you the lawyer's name and phone number. I happen to have one of his cards."

"Oh, it's him, is it?" With that, briefcase in hand, he got up and bowed; and looking at his watch, he said he was late for an appointment. But he asked if he could take a quick look upstairs before he left and said that he had slept in the kids' bedroom.

"How nice," she said. "My father reads the kids bedtime stories there."

Peering out at his car, Addie saw a person at the wheel who looked familiar. For a minute, she couldn't place him; then, apparently aware he was being noticed, he turned toward her. Why, it was Domo, the Terrible Turk, Dunneville's ex-bodyguard and chauffeur! The dolled-up woman, a bottle blond, sat very serenely in the back and held a long, thin cigarette holder.

Addie was shocked by the sight of Domo, insurance against trouble: He was known to take on men twice his size and flatten them. It was said he'd been with a band of Kurds back in his homeland; and when nabbed by police and flogged for not saying who blew up a train, they brought him to the scene, where he hoisted a weighty axle over his head and tossed it at his stupefied tormentors. Louey, she recalled, had given him a wide berth. *Well, the dandy needs that level of protection, does he?*

Otto had just hung up the phone when she came into the kitchen. His hands were still trembling. All of her "Whys" went for naught. She couldn't get any satisfactory answer out of him; he would only tell her that Vander Veer was going to send a car up for him in the morning and wanted him to pack some things in an overnight bag, just in case."

"Dad, you have to tell me what's going on. And you've got something to tell me about Rocco, this Angie Junior."

"The lawyer. He will tell you." He paused. His hands were shaking, and his voice was unnaturally hoarse. "I'm not sure myself what's goin' on. Except I'm obligated to say something what I know."

CHAPTER 90

The Murder Solved

Unable to get through to lawyer Van, she tried Tom; and he said he couldn't tell her anything just then—nothing over the phone, anyway—though there was lots to be told. He was working on an important story—the biggie—which had him tied to the rewrite desk. But his father needed to talk to her, also to her father; him first, probably in the morning.

Yes, lots to tell and lots that can't be told. There were unspecified doings with Big Van, the most of which involved Otto *solo*. An early morning call briefly said "Breakfast waiting." A car had arrived for him. *Why am I being kept in the dark?*

Nervous as she was, she had to put on a brave face before the kids. She played cards with them and, to their cheers, ordered pizza when Tom arrived. She told the kids to be good for Grandpa when he came back as she might be tied up for the rest of the afternoon. Otto had said not to worry and that to get the kids ready for bed time, he was going to read them more of *Call of the Wild*. That got another cheer.

While driving, Tom put off her questions, insisting she wait. She got the feeling this was to be an afternoon of high-stakes revelations, a hint of which showed in Tom's eye-on-the-road, tight-lipped attitude. She gulped as he ran a red light. Once parked and at the lobby table, he took a deep breath, opened his briefcase, and spread out a dummy of the special edition's front page as it would

411

appear in the morning, flagged by an unprecedented screaming headline, "Baron's Murder Solved," all of twenty picas high—also unprecedented—with a smaller subhead, "Key Witness to Testify."

Anxious as she was to find out how her father figured in this, Tom said it would be best to give her the gist of the story, omitting details. As he closed the office door behind them, she volunteered that she had already heard some things about the murder and also knew of some things she hadn't heard.

"Like?" His head in a whirl, he was supposed to be calming her but was in need of much the same for himself.

Tom said, "Hear me out. You want to know about your father's role, don't you?"

Well, a lot of what went into his story came from what her father had told his father, Big Van, while some over the phone; and once written up and signed, that is what would be offered as testimony in a trial. In fact, Van would be taking Otto before a grand jury, from whom he'd be aiming for an indictment.

"What! That has to be a mistake. Papa Otts won't survive it! He's coming apart as is right before my eyes—totally out of it."

"Hold on, please, and listen. It all went back to the baron's buying Guipiletti out and turning a profit, where his former partner, Papa G, had been nursing a loss.

"The instance came up over which G was still pulling his hair. The baron had paid a handsome premium for his woven label shop, a small-time business G was glad to be rid of. No nose for it in the first place. However, what with the high-speed looms the baron installed, he turned out the same product with a reduced labor force and was able to undersell the competition and make a virtual monopoly in those specialty labels. Insignificant as they might seem, they were artistically done and became big-time stuff when they sported the Lord & Taylor name.

"Naturally, Guipiletti was envious and sorry he'd sold then outright angry. Sam was making money hand over fist, of all things, in labels, along with everything else he had going. Shouldn't there have been something in the separation clause about appreciation, a rise in equity value? Well, Guipiletti had to admit he'd sold because under him, the luxury label business had been slipping and had no great prospects.

"What, then, was the immediate provocation for his wanting to kill the guy? The baron was an enormously helpful guy. He'd even help people who disliked him. Since labels had thrived in his hands during the fall season, friend Guipiletti bought it back. And talk about bad luck, there followed an extended strike, and G, after combined losses, had to file for bankruptcy."

On the other hand, Addie, getting impatient with that sort of detail, was ready to crown Tom, who kept rolling with it.

"Temporarily calmed by his son Mario, Papa G consoled himself with the thought that 'With Gina there, I guess we still do have a chance at getting a piece of the action.' Wanting to rid his father of a desire to waylay his nemesis, Mario offered the further assurance that, 'Should the baron die'—and the guy is a risk-taker—'we'll have it all back, and then some.'

"Good enough. For now, anyway. Papa G seemed glad to have been talked out of violence—"

"Please!" Addie begged. But this was Tom's day for running through stop signs.

"Sullen resignation," he continued, "unfortunately, was not the attitude of rambunctious young Angie Jr., the young buck called Rocco. He was all for a swift necktie solution. But he got shushed by his papa, who was heard wondering out loud to no one in particular whether there wasn't an easier way to get what they wanted. It came down to Papa's appraisal that the more success the baron had, the more he risked—"

Growing more irritated by the minute, Addie shouted for Tom to get on with it, which finally did bring him back to the dude.

"Having heard enough of his father's lament over loses, Rocco finally jumped into action, claiming there'd been enough lost time. He latched onto Domo, and having paid off the baron's security man—ex-cop Billy-club Bill—the two of them went up to see the baron, hoping a gun could encourage him to take the Guipilettis back into the business.

"The baron seemed amused, telling them in time they'd be amply rewarded for their patience. They insisted on having some of the reward now, to which the baron tried to put Rocco off with an indulgent smile, saying that through Gina, the family already had its partnership. Rocco's retort was that once his sister got all of that money to spend, she became a snooty bitch who disowned her family. It made his blood boil. He wanted money on the barrelhead. A piece of the business carved out for himself, and '*now*!'

"The baron hunched his shoulders, and Rocco looked back at Domo, who was standing in the doorway, one-handing a baseball bat. With a headshake, Rocco motioned for Domo to come forward and show himself, which he did, with a self-conscious bow. Rocco smiled saying something about Domo being a pedigreed assassin, and his point made, he went on to note that by tradition, it was the Guipiletti men who should be the baron's active partners—a much saner course than the alternative. In short, did the baron think the status quo was worth his life?

"Wanting to be finished with this nonsense, the baron made another call down to Bill. 'These gentlemen want to leave. Please come up and escort them.'

"That brought a tightly robed Gina out of the bathroom. She had been feeling chump and thought a relaxing bath would help. Quickly sizing up the situation, she nervously wanted to give Bill another call. However, butting up against her, rock-hard Domo wouldn't let her pass."

As Tom described the rest, she yelled at him to move out of the way; but he told her to shut up and pushed her back.

"That incited the lioness in her, wanting to get in there and protect her man. On being pummeled again by Domo, her temper flared. And snatching the bat, she swatted him across the impervious chest.

Before Rocco could intervene, Domo chased her down the hall and into the bathroom, she screaming all the way. Hearing the bathroom door slam shut, the baron saw the chance to gain an advantage and went for Rocco. Hands were quickly clasped around his neck, but Rocco knifed the knuckles. And following through, he suddenly thrust the bewildered baron back against the wall, where, in a fury, Rocco yelled 'You die!' and instantly shot him point-blank. At the same moment, Domo had burst in on Gina, hitting her in the back of the head with the bat.

"'Jesus,' Rocco yelled, 'What the hell did you do, you idiot? That was my sister!'

"'You never told me. I thought you didn't want her to reckonize you. I made sure.'"

Tom continued, "Rocco was cursing all the way out the great oaken door."

CHAPTER 91

The Man in the Closet

"But that's not all. Bear with me," Tom declared.

"After the assassins had sped away, a person emerged from the double-door closet, where, watching the scene from a slit in those louvered doors, he was its lone witness. That man it turned out was none other than Otto Heiss, who, having been laid off due to introduction of the high-speed looms, had come to the baron seeking payment of a doctor's bill for setting the daughter's broken leg. When Otto heard people coming up the steps, he looked at Sam, and Sam shoved him into the closet.

"Now, Mario, who had been looking into the case, had had a ballistic study done on the bullet lodged in Sam's head. Since it happened to match those he'd found in his brother's desk drawer, he couldn't take it any further. A sister had been lost, over which his father's sorrow was deepened by the fact that her demise deprived the family of an assured piece of the baron's businesses.

"Quite unremorseful about the loss of his sister, beyond the practical inconvenience of it, Rocco, having transformed himself into a sophisticated man about town, needed the ready cash to sustain it. He insisted more than others that the family couldn't be entirely cut out of funds assumed to have been jointly held. Gina owned a full half of the baron's fortune, didn't she? A pity she died so unnecessarily, but how come that meant her claim on the baron's estate perished with her?

"When lawyer Van showed them that the baron's testamentary maneuvers blew their suit away, the family came up with their own maneuvers, determined to keep the litigation pot boiling, assured by lawyers that some red-hot sausage was bound to surface. But there followed one rebuff after the other, and unable to swallow defeat, the Guipilettis kept batting their collective heads against a wall of constraints. Lawyer Van advised them to resign themselves to reality while he looked for loopholes on their behalf. Sadly, resignation was not Papa G's style. Domo felt for him. Even he would not make a practice of meeting the wall with his head.

"On-going, Papa in one case charged that their lien on investments entitled them to money the baron had made on sale of Heights land to Tony D for those exclusive 'town houses with a view.' But the baron had gotten ahead of them on that one too as proceeds were tucked into trusts for unspecified offspring, which thereby took that money out of the baron's estate.

"Hence, thwarted on a variety of legal challenges, the unforgiving Gs continued to sulk and share their paranoia with whoever would listen. After a lull, the death of Gina's daughter, Peggy, brought them back to the fray, Papa G thundering it was time to go for the jugular. Absent a lightning follow-through, Papa's mouth hung open in disbelief on being told the one certified beneficiary of the baron's estate was some unknown stranger, said to be the baron's illegitimate daughter. Not to be identified and, worse yet, not to be found.

"Old Guipiletti saw blue. Ailing as he was, he cried foul from his sickbed. There was just no way he was going to accept that state of affairs. It got more complicated when the court ruled that Gina's grandchild could legitimately be placed in line for a portion of the total estate. Euerka was premature. For unbeknownst to the Guipiletti clan, that child had been surreptitiously adopted by the bastard daughter, something they were suing to undo. Yet another fiasco.

"Papa G had insisted that blood would speak eloquently for their side, even though the Guipilettis were not exactly taken with the idea of welcoming a Negroid child into the bosom of their family. [The old man joked, 'In the shape we're in, the family could use a Sicilian.']

"Therefore, feeling that the child gave them a fairly respectable case, they assumed that despite denials, there was no reason to settle for anything less than a total win. Papa, striking his forehead, decided 'why not go for it? What's to lose?' That is, until Van, my legal eagle papa, showed them how a court ruling on the family status of the little Sicilian would cut them off at the pass, the child having been legally adopted."

Tom went on that Papa G, in looking for a sympathetic ear from Papa Van, revealed that what he most disliked about the bad deal was being screwed by a Jew. A big-hearted man in all other respects, Papa G was narrow on that one, compounding his own bitterness—which, in turn, heightened that of his sons. All three shouted a chorus of "Outrageous, outrageous!"

It reminded them that there was an illegitimate offspring yet to be located, the supposed heir to the baron's fortune, upon whom they might have the satisfaction of venting their spleen—if need be by professional assassination in order to finally see the liquid green they had been thirsting for; a stack of money kept waltzing around in their collective imagination.

"For his part, Dad received an essential break on convincing Otto that he might become a suspect unless he agreed to give his eyewitness account. However, he rethought the agreement and reneged. It would amount to a public admission that he wasn't Addie's true father, which would destroy the bond he cherished and jeopardize continuance of their father-daughter relationship. Outright intolerable.

"It was only when Dad finally got it across to him that said daughter stood to lose a portion—indeed maybe all—of her inheritance that Otto was willing to swallow his pride and come forward, only to pull back at the last minute. Dad recalled that Uncle Bob had those details about the baron's unknown daughter, and Dad insisted Bob should pass the details onto me so I would write up the story for the *Messenger*, which left your father no choice.

"Knowing what it would mean to Magowan for him—as returned DA—to be the one who cracked the cold case, my dad, Van, filled your Dad in on your potential inheritance. And with a shot of lager Schnaps, I got Otto to spill the story to him. Post-haste, a Grand Jury was convened.

"Dad wants Magowan to proceed quickly on the indictment."

"And what's the business of having my father overnight it downtown?"

"Your father's testimony will probably be given over two days. Dad has to have him very carefully prepared, point by point, so he doesn't stumble. More importantly, they had, had Rocco cuffed and were to have him held overnight and charged next day, based on Otto's Grand Jury testimony. But lacking a next-day order, the deputy jailor, faced with habeas, accepted cold cash instead. And jailbird Rocco was on the loose, as we spoke."

"Who do you suppose he's looking for?"

"We've got to hope he values freedom more than vengeance."

CHAPTER 92

Trouble Catches up to Her

Did she dare ask what it was? Okay, supposedly a charge. But of what? And for what? One look told her that it would be best if she didn't ask for particulars—at least, not of Van and not then. Let him spell it out.

They had been sitting in Tom's car in the parking lot behind the Vander Veer Building. The pale shadows cast by the ruddy smudge of a setting October sun had given way to dusk, which shrouded the red-tile roof and peaked dormers of the pseudo-Tudor Centre Hotel, visible just beyond the dome of the courthouse. A quaint little glimpse of Europe in the town's modest skyline, another part of the baron's legacy. He had a quaintly romantic side. She was almost inclined to smile. *Why not ask the Centre people to buy the castle and turn it into a classy resort hotel? Great location atop the high point of the entire county.*

She could feel the lead weight of a depression coming over her. *A separate matter, huh? So there's more?* And poker faced Tom is sitting there Sphinx-like, acting as if he's said all he can when he knows damned well what the new stuff is about, and knows too it ain't a chocolate sundae. How do you keep a clear head in the face of bad things that are waiting to come at you from the third circle of hell? What an ugly business this rubbish of the law is.

Unable to ignore her upset, Tom gave her a hug and, with a supporting arm around her shoulders, saw her to the elevator, saying he was sure things were going to turn out all right. Whatever it was, once defined, not just his lawyer father, but he too would see it through with her.

"Thanks. I think I'll need you. The other party has to deal with a new twist, and it looks like I do too. I trust your father makes a pot of strong coffee?"

With all the solemn congeniality of a hangman, Big Van had ushered her into the comfy sitting room, where he puts his clients at ease. They sat across from one another in overstuffed chairs, between them a coffee table with a carafe of freshly brewed gourmet Colombian Sublime, which he very neatly poured. He asked "Would she like a pastry?" and moved the silver tray over to her side of the low table. She declined. And not a guy to beat around the bush, after one sip, pursed-lipped, Van came out with it.

"DA tells me there's a good chance that he'll shortly be having to come forth with a charge that you've committed arson. True?"

"Where? What?"

"I like that response. Lawyer-ly. It's Tony's place. The big bonfire out there."

"That. And who says I did it?"

"Mario asked for negatives of the pictures Deleste took of the crowd. He blew them up on the enlarger and put them under a glass. Says he picked somebody out who looked a lot like you, with partially smeared–off tanning lotion on your face spotlighted by the fire. From what the caretaker said, Magowan knows Whimpy Carlos was there. He also knows the two of you were together a lot."

"And didn't the caretaker say there were all of four gypsies?"

"Addie, you can tell me about it. You do want to be defended, don't you?"

"Yes. And yes."

"Okay. We'll plead not guilty."

"I'm naive, of course. But how am I not guilty if I did it?"

"They have to prove you're guilty. Until then, you're not."

"The law. Oh. Of course."

"Give me some details. First, who were the others, what time was it, and where were you observed to have been that day other than there?"

"Gosh, let me think."

PART XIII

EXPLOSION AND SHOWDOWN

CHAPTER 93

Loving Tom

Tom had been dutifully waiting in the parking lot. Stressed out, he was slumped over the steering wheel. She roused him with a shake and said she appreciated his being there.

"Good of you. I forgot to ask your dad if I could get myself a jalopy courtesy of the trust."

"Well, how did it go?"

"Your dad seemed to be put out with me."

"Did you think you could do something like that and get away with it? People could have been killed! What did happen was bad enough."

"For me, it was a matter of doing, not thinking. And what thinking I did do was different from yours. As for getting away with it, isn't that what Tony and his people had been doing all along? And not just *him*. Isn't the world full of unproven crooks?"

"Good Christ. So you were going to set things to rights?"

"Nobody else was. It got to be too much. People get hurt and nothing happens to those who do the hurting. I had a brother-in-law whose boss did him dirt and rubbed his nose in it. He wanted to retaliate but couldn't go through with it. The cops shot him anyway. And nothing was done about that. They blamed Al. That changed me."

"Happens all the time. We do our best to go after the perpetrators. Some we miss. We can't be a feuding society, can we?"

"What a question. People commit all kinds of crimes and hide behind law and order. I'm talkin' about what's right. *Justice*, not law. The fire seemed to have brought a halt to some bad things. One that was destined to take it out on me. Worst thing for a woman. Now, thanks to the law, they want to prosecute somebody for doing what the police and courts should have done."

"And you're ready to go to jail for it?"

"Not if your dad is as good as everybody says he is. By the way, regarding justice, I got it from your dad that friend Rocco is gone, probably to the Bahamas with his moneybags widow. Domo will probably get the whole thing pinned on him, provided they can find him to do the pinning. Did you get that into your story?"

"No. Something else."

"Additional revelations?"

"That long-gone flight to the Bahamas was the story Rocco put out to stop the cops in their tracks. He wanted to leave in peace. What really happened is what I did the rewrite on. When Domo asked where his plane ticket was, Rocco said he couldn't find it, but not to worry. So Domo got him out of his motel bed at four in the morning and said he was worried. Shivering, Rocco coughed up tickets—also blood by the time Domo was finished with him.

"In any case, it seems that Domo finished him off with a karate chop to the back of the neck, stuffed him back in bed, put the Don't Disturb sign on the doorknob, locked up, and disappeared. But I've yet to check out that story. The mayhem he's done has sprouted all kinds of crazy stories"

"Oh my gosh! Domo's mad and at large now?"

"Don't know. The night clerk caught sight of him leaving and was asked if he could identify him. 'Identify?' he asks. 'Me? Not on my life! Ever see how the guy walks swingin' those ape-like arms of his?' And him, that's just to get the racing form."

"I take it they're looking for him."

"Not very hard, I hear. The story is he worked his way over here as a deckhand on a tramp steamer. And chances are, he might be trying to catch one going the other way. Over there, he might join the Kurdish rebellion. Or he could get himself recruited by the

Turkish Secret Police to go after the Kurds. That fighting's been going on for a long time and has centuries yet to go. Whoever he kills for, it shouldn't make a difference."

"That dangerous, huh?"

"Legendary. You've got to be careful of what you tell him. He's got a strange sense of humor. People in the know say he's the one that Luigi, in a fit of impatience, had asked to dispose of the wayward cousins who turned up with a claim on the baron's estate. Actually, he was instructed to usher them out of town but not hurt them. Luigi blew a fuse when he learned what happened. In classic Domo style, the response was he didn't hurt them. He *killed* them. He said, 'Only way to make sure they got out of town? On a slab.'"

"Scary. You know, he was always very nice to me. His son, even nicer. Think about it. Lookin' at the guy, he's so ungainly I sorta felt sorry for him. I knew the Terrible Turk story but not this one or what he did to Gina. Who is he anyway?"

"Nobody knows his real name. He says he doesn't know himself. The kind of fella they say who, if the mood is on him, could kill somebody for breakfast. Did it in the old country, somebody said.

"As I've heard it, he happens to like delicacies and likes 'em fresh. For instance, brains for breakfast. Not particular whose. Will have them properly sautéed in olive oil, adding a dash of salt, garlic, and oregano. Breaks a couple of eggs over the decoction, pours on the A-1, adds buttered toast, washes it down with fresh brewed double strength coffee, and—like the French—would say 'Voila.' He sort of redefines tough. Hope I haven't upset you."

"Not quite but good try. Where was this guy when I needed him? You know Domo's son has been helpful to me when he's not out there robbing banks."

"What you need is peace—a good stretch of it. I have a feeling all of this stuff will pass. Dad will get the arson case tossed, your father will give key evidence on the double murder and go back to living a normal life. As will you, doing what you do best for each new generation of kids, enjoying your own, making a good future for them and yourself, looking forward to the good things that each new day will bring, including—probably—a new love waiting right now for the time to come into your brave new life."

"Thanks. But if you want the truth, I have the feeling I've been lucky enough having come this far, close as I've been to outright disaster. Right now, I'm feeling my luck is gonna run out. Yeah, I was the one behind the big blaze. Magowan thinks he can prove it. Killer Domo goes one way. I'll be goin' another. Fact is I deserve bein' convicted."

"Oh, Addie, why so sour? You've got to trust my dad. Judges and juries do. Now Domo is hardwired for death. He was born for it. You, for *life*."

"Thanks. But remember, I like to judge matters on the basis of *justice*. I did wrong and really I should pay up. I wanted payment for what was plotted for me. About arson, for the time being, uncertainty will be heavy on me. Nerves a kind of pre-payment."

"There's one certainty you'll be knowing and fairly soon."

"Yes? Something additional?"

"My wife and I . . . We're headed for quitsville."

"Sorry. How come?"

"Don't be sorry. I'm not. Her point is well taken. I've been spending too much time with other things, other people."

"I see but let's not anticipate. It may come for us but not yet."

CHAPTER 94

Reason To Wait, Reason Love Can't

It was a mild Indian summer evening. The leaves were decked out in their richest colors: Lots of maple reds interspersed with oak browns, tulip tree yellows, among assorted others of the same and spruce blue-greens. Tourists drove up to New England to take in their fabled riot of colors when they could take in much of the same from their front porch.

Addie suggested they take a bench in Eastside Park, where they could look out on the splendor of the multicolored hillside that looked out on the baseball field.

Tom picked it up from where they'd left off, awkward as it was. "You've missed out with a couple of other men. Hopefully not with me."

"Wow! With so much smoke in my head just now, I still do think about that. Of course, we have been through quite a bit together. And you may just be the guy to make a new life with me. Would that just now . . . really, you think we could swing it, knowing what you do about me?"

"Yes. What I know . . . that's a large part of how I feel. No way I could push it, but I've had it for you for a long time. It began with amazement. Admiration was not long in coming. Now it's . . . it's in here."

"You didn't do much to disguise it. Trouble is we got off the train a while back, and it's a matter of whether we can get back on.

Actually, whether *I* can. I have to be honest. It's tough for me to say, but good as you'd be for me, I may not be good for you. That's a big one to figure in. I have moods, and I get myself into trouble. Stuff you don't deserve. You've been so faithful, so good to me, and you do know how much I like you. I wish I could go further than that. But all I can say is I'm willing to see what happens."

They slipped into one another's arms, him smothering his face in her hair. There was a tremor in his voice as he whispered her name. It was as if he feared saying any more.

He had driven them over to Main Street and parked the car at the curb next to Mama Perez's All-Night Diner. Her western omelet, browned and spiced just so, was exactly the thing you'd need—even if you weren't particularly hungry.

Between bites, they sat there in silence, absently looking out at passing cars and watching them stop and go at the light while both of them were lost in thoughts of what had just transpired. She didn't have the heart to tell him then and there that she wasn't ready for another relationship. He would have been able to see that for himself even if he wouldn't acknowledge it. She could see that having opened up as he did, he was clearly hoping that things might yet work out, that he could at least nudge her along. As she thought about it, she could indeed picture herself moving his way—given time; however, *How not to hurt him in the meantime?*

Having witnessed her prior affairs of the heart, he'd probably been hurting in silence for quite a while; and dear, dear fella with nothing to gain for himself, he was still devotedly hanging on for her. Following his feelings at the cost of his marriage. Wanting what he knew was not there and helpless to do other than help. She went all soft inside.

"Oh Tom," she softly exclaimed as if to herself, "how you have loved. You are so much more than good."

His was a love that would attract love. *Damn it, then why wouldn't I just let go?* Much as she was moved, something was telling her it shouldn't be rushed. On the other hand, it also told her she had to be some kind of a person—a human being, for goodness' sake—and let him know how deeply she was moved.

"Hell, out with it!," she scolded herself, and taking up his words, she said, "Tom, you have made a difference for me. I've experienced everything but love with you. I now feel that will come."

She let go and they were drowning one another in kisses.

CHAPTER 95

Explosion at the Castle

Strange as it seemed, coming off their high point, the uncertainty reasserted itself. She brought Tom back to what he knew about the arson charge, which he answered with a shrug. Since for the time being, he could be no more enlightening than his father had been—except to say that she could be assured of delays and, in time, a dismissal—she let out an unintentional sigh. What she knew for the moment was that she wanted some air, and she got it from the volatile falls. As they got out of the car, a piercing wind struck them full in the face. A light rain was falling, and the sidewalks glistened in the street lights.

"Never mind the wet, Tom. We'll walk between the drops. Let's take it round the block here and come back to these falls, who will go on to eternity."

They had a brisk, head-clearing walk back to the diner for some of that aroma-rich coffee.

"I've got something to tell you," she began. "It's been on my mind for some time. You've given me your revelations. I've got one for you. You seem to think I'm pretty negative. Actually, I'm not."

"Later." He obviously didn't want to break their mood and tried to inch her down the alley as a shortcut back to the car, but she resisted. But wanting to follow through on their romantic mood, he favored a return to his office.

"No. It's something you should know." They had stopped. She turned his head and held it so they were eye to eye.

"What?"

"I'm going to run for mayor."

His jaw dropped. "Run for—for what? Baby, you're crazy! A *lady* mayor? Not even the women will go for that."

"That's what's wrong. They'll hear from me about that *big-time*. And much else."

"Can you think you're going to accomplish anything? Anything good? If you want to compound uncertainty, politics will do it for you. Just what you need, of course!"

"Yeah, make politics work for the good. That's what Johnny wanted to do. Jay, more so. Remember? . . . Well, I'm thinking about a very special good. After all the bad I've seen in this short life of mine, I want good for women—Don't laugh. Really. I'd like to have an official department that finally looks out for *women*. All volunteers and all women. If we don't start helping one another, who will?"

"Let's get real. And let's get back to the car before we get soaked." He tugged her into a trot that got them over to the diner.

"I'm really real on this. You'll join me, won't you?"

They had barely taken a bite of their second Danish when there was a rush of siren—howling police cars going by, followed by an ambulance, tires screeching, and the roar of a fire engine—all apparently rumbling toward North Hill Road. The two of them spun around on their barstools and went out into the street where they could follow the blinking cherries snake their way up until they got lost in the dark foliage, but from the sustained sound of receding sirens, it seemed a lot like they were destined for the top.

"Tom, the castle! Let's go!"

After a hair-raising drive on a slick road, almost two wheeling it around curves, they found themselves blocked off by police at the turn–around bus stop and were told it was too dangerous up ahead. All the more reason for her to go, she said. Her father and two kids were there.

The head cop said a bomb had gone off, and the firemen were putting out the fire. They had demolition experts checking for other explosives. The wet air smelled of burnt cloth.

Asking Addie to wait, Tom told the cop to watch her; and showing his press badge, he got an okay to go up for a look. But Addie was not to be restrained.

She broke free of the cop's grasp and ran for it, only to be intercepted by another, at whom she shouted her identity. "I'm the mother! Don't you understand?" It took both cops to finally corral her, and despite the kicking and scratching, they got her thrown into the back of a cruiser and locked her in.

Unable to find her when he came back, Tom looked about wild with apprehension until he heard her scream "Lemme out!" and saw she was about to kick at the cruiser window. He told her to hold it, but by the time he caught the attention of one of the cops, frustration had gotten the best of her. She had taken a shoe off and was banging it against the window. The door was hastily unlocked amidst hectic apologies. As it was opened, she flew out, carried by her own momentum, and fell facedown on the cement pavement, knocked out cold.

Tom latched onto one of the paramedics, asking him to come and look her over. The guy managed to bring her to, bandaged her bloody forehead, and told her to sit still for a bit. Replacing her shoe, she jumped to her feet, frantic to learn what had happened, and was quietly told that the three of them were gone.

"*All*? All *three*!" Turning this way and that, she tore at her hair. "*No!*" Her yowl came out as from a wounded animal. Writhing and swinging her arms, she once more freed herself and ran like mad. Tom trailed after her but lost her when she took a shortcut through the trees.

She lost her balance, slipped on the wet grass, tripped on a root, fell, got up, and (wet-faced and runny-nosed) cried out "Kiddies! Father!" as she stumbled onto the brick driveway in time to see the paramedics roll out a stretcher with a sheet covering the lumpy figure of a small body. At the sight of it, restrained by a cop on each arm, she broke down in a fit of delirious sobbing. Her head bobbed with each blubbering outburst. When the sobbing finally ebbed, all the strength went out of her. The cops let go and she collapsed into Tom's arms.

After carrying her back to the car, he returned to the driveway and, again dangling his press badge, learned from the demolition chief that it was a pressure device—something like the Bouncing Betty anti-personnel mine—and it went off when the old man sat on his bed. It got the kids as they were just then coming toward him for a continuation of his nightly reading.

"Suspects?"

"One, for sure. Also, *gone* for sure."

"But you are gonna check into this. We gotta find out *who* and *why*. Yes?"

"We'll be starting with motive. Who wanted the old man gone and why?

CHAPTER 96

Addie's out of It, Tom Takes Over

When Tom found her coming out of sedation, his spirits rose as she called his name, only to be dashed when she looked up and, her vision evidently blurred, said she couldn't find him. The nurse drew back, mumbling about how irritable she was. The intern told Tom not to worry; she'd had a similar reaction to them. Tom countered, "What kind of consolation is that?"

The muscular psychiatric nurses swished in bright and early in their starched uniforms, singing out a cheerful "Rise and shine," ready to take on their unruly patient for the tussle over rebinding. They rolled her over for the needle in the buttocks and laughed about her comments regarding their prior assignment at Alcatraz.

For their extracting a vial of blood one morning, Addie called them vampires and told them to drink it and feed on her misery. Lips drawn, one of them made a motion toward her throat; and Addie signed the cross at them with her free forearm. The vial got jarred and some of the blood spilled. Delighted, Addie said it showed that like everybody else, they had blood on their hands and got away with it, which drew a mirthful rise out of those scheduled for brain surgery and a tightening of the restraints.

Addie said they were *demons*, and next day, one of them came in wearing papier-mâché horns and long black witches' nails. Getting looks from the resident, they said they just wanted to cheer her up.

On entry, the nurses expected to find Addie babbling to herself; but at week's end, they came into a silent room. The bed was empty and so was her locker. Gone too were the flowers Tom had sent along with the little suitcase. Responding to her ring, the quiet-mannered night nurse had untied her so she could go to the bathroom, about which the nurse would keep mum.

The volunteer at the information desk described someone like a nurse's aide quick-stepping it out the front door. She looked like an aide who had just come off the night shift and was eager to get home. Tom was anxious and angrily growled "How in the world!"

Not knowing where to go, she had let instinct carry her to a group of people who, strange as they were, got habitually ignored— sitting unnoticed under the noses of authority, a scant half block from the police station. She being the unique whisperer, her voice was finally noticed; and next day, the orderlies were told to check it out.

They found her amidst the city hall Deaf and Dumbs, snugged on either side by fellow down-and-outs; and she was to be rushed back via police cruiser for vigorous rebinding. But the woman they selected told them the equivalent of "Get lost" in pseudo sign language.

The doctors, meanwhile, checking her chart were thoroughly baffled. They had called her their Enigma Case. When Tom and Eva got her admitted, a doctor taking the customary medical history, happened to ask—regarding the banging—whether there had been instances of epilepsy in the family; and Tom mentioned Peggy.

"Hmm . . . But hers seemed to be epilepsy with a difference." The doctor gave it some thought and said to forget the Dilantin as she'd had no outright seizure, and he instead administered a sedative that was to prevent her from injuring herself in the night.

"You know, when they wake up in darkness and are disoriented by their surroundings, there can be a problem."

Needing to forestall further injury, they, on Tom's insistence, called in a famed neurologist from one of the top research hospitals, a place that sought out arcane illnesses—ideally, patients who were hopeless, the status that was emerging for Addie. A tall, lean, busy-handed fellow given to flexing his Groucho Marx eyebrows when asked anything was a top neurologist and acted like one: he was loath to visit patients. He couldn't understand why in hell they would drag him away from his federally funded research project in order to "deal with this."

But *where* was the patient? Having been sufficiently stabilized by her new medication, she had asked to be taken down to physical therapy; and Tom urged them to go along with it. After all that binding, it would be good for the circulation, hopefully for the head too. As for the drugs, Tom said, "With all due respect, I think you are going at it the wrong way. What I would recommend is a psychiatrist."

Groucho gave him a patronizing smile. *Better the physical therapist for now.* Eager as he was to get back to the lab where he was slicing up the brains of those who had died in various stages of dementia, Groucho paused to take another look at Addie's chart and asked her age.

Then he announced his revelation. "Oh. This sort of thing could be hard on a person so young."

Tom was fed up. "A lot of help *that* is!" he breathed. Deciding it was time to pull rank, he declared that he was a registered psychiatrist and wanted to take over her case. He had, had quiet conversations with Addie and thought she seemed to be coming out of it. The last time, after her stint on the bike, the PT said she had been in an up mood.

What no one was able to make out was the symbol that had been etched on the tachometer. It depicted a tramp who had a stick tilted over his shoulder with a bundle of rags tied at the end. "Oh, Charley Chaplin!" the PT laughed.

From the door to the bathroom, Addie shouted an enthusiastic "Whimpy!"

Hearing this, the PT looked for Addie and recalled that when last seen, the patient had upped her speed, contentedly pumping away on the stationary bike.

An hour later, his colleague asked the PT whether he had come to work on her new twelve-speed bike that morning.

"Yes, and chained it to the fence post."

"Which one?"

"Oh my gosh, it was over there on that end one, dammit!"

CHAPTER 97

Seeking Addie

Addie was nowhere to be found. She'd been gone for two weeks—going on three—and Tom, coming up empty, was at his wits' end. Going street by street, he had even scoured the rentals in attractive suburbia and was starting on the unattractive ones when he ran into Betsy, who was equally perplexed. Between them, they had checked acquaintances in neighboring towns and had come up with surprise and "Sorry." At best, "Can we help?" from people knowing they couldn't.

The two of them proceeded to pitch in with what they had respectively come to know. It occurred to Tom that Addie had told him up front why she needed to disappear hereabouts. "For one thing, try to leave town, and they have you out in the open." Betsy thought the hideout complex had something to do with her behavior in the hospital. "Let's face it. This lady is paranoid."

"Right," Tom countered, "but think for a minute. Wasn't she laying it on thick?"

Betsy came back slowly. "Well, yeah, now that you mention it. But listen, the shock was for real. No getting around that."

They continued batting around her crazy spells, only to be reminded that it didn't matter. Dogged Mario let everybody know he was determined to have her arraigned on arson, come what may; and he would wait her out till it froze over.

Betsy had had a chance to sound Addie out before the kids got blown up; and she'd heard her speak of conscience. She'd been going through a period of self-distrust and was glad to have somebody she could tell it to. She felt there should have been some forethought about what kind of damage they could do before setting that bonfire. In short, it was weighing on her that she should just legitimately face what awaited her in a court of law and let lawyer Van take it from there. Which she simultaneously preferred not to face. "Would a rape threat carry any weight? . . . Well, no matter."

In any event, self-distrust compounded by fear of what the law held in store meant she wanted a place where she could take short-term cover while she considered possibilities—among them, something desperate, like making a break for it. She had talked to Betsy about making a new start elsewhere. What this boiled down to was to ask friends—people she knew—to look for such a place, and that finally meant what else but to consult the dean of legality?

"Lots to see him about again. And lots that will be forgotten when I do."

"What then is the place where she is least likely to be found?" Tom ventured.

Tom couldn't resist adding, with a touch of sarcasm, "The well-patrolled castle, of course. Where else? And if she can do a disappearing act in that cavern, she oughta be able to do it swiftly without being taken into custody."

"Of course. But you need to remember who posted the patrollers. It being thought an impossible refuge since she'd be cornered. That's exactly why she found herself a dark-night entry."

Scratching his chin, he added, "The unambiguous problem that remains is how we might take it from there."

They'd asked Van for advice, but for the time being, it seemed like he preferred to be ambiguous while seeming to be candid. Like he said, "Mario knows his way. I know mine. He can't poach on my ground. I can't poach on his. The only caveat for now is not to get impatient. And that applies to the two of you, as well."

As they pondered the patience they were not good at, it was enforced upon them when they heard that the major stone-throwing kid spotted a ghost traversing the Long Hall. The kid had friends and a bunch of them whooped it up.

For the latest, Tom would ask to be briefed by Van's secretary.

A neighbor mother complained that when her kid called the woman a witch, the "ghost" poked a small pistol out the window. The mother had to be assured it was neither aimed nor fired, but she still didn't like it. The police ought to go in and take it away from her.

On orders, Guard Jonesy pointed out it just seemed to be a way of telling the kids to keep their distance. They were trespassing, after all. Better for them to play elsewhere rather than annoy a sick lady.

Not to be silenced, the kids naturally returned aiming to make merry with the loony; and occasionally they were joined by adults. Farber's Folly now inhabited by the town eccentric. *So this is the illegitimate daughter, is she? Well, it just goes to show.*

Tom joined Betsy, who was waiting in his parked car. "The kids are there now," he reported, "and we'll be there when they have to go home. Dad has an off-duty cop posted to do evenings at the castle, but he probably takes himself an off-duty snooze from time to time. What do yah say we have us a look?"

Tom sped up North Hill Road and showed his press card to the guard, good old Jonesy, the school janitor. Obviously overcome with boredom, he joined them in trying the corroded latch and found it immovable. Together, all three put their collective shoulders to the door but couldn't budge it.

The guard told of his hearing some heavy Victorian furniture being lodged up against it, done no doubt with help. He'd asked what she was doing and who was helping but got no answer. There was no answer from downtown either, except that she owned the place after all.

Betsy tried to console Tom. "If we go easy, we should be able to get to her. She knows us."

City hall was unsure of how to handle the matter. If a trained professional like Tom Vander Veer couldn't get through to her, something else had to be tried. The police chief had his idea of how to handle the situation, which was to be used when all else failed. Meanwhile, neighbors said the lady needed special help—preferably institutionalizing.

Mario shortly complicated the situation. Armed with a Grand Jury indictment, he wanted her hauled out of there to face outstanding charges. He could bring in federal marshals to do the hauling.

It went back and forth for a while until someone in the Law Department, having heard from Lawyer Van, pointed out that you couldn't just go into a lady's house and lug her out minus a warrant that first had been duly served—like put in her unavailable hand.

"But isn't she a public nuisance?" Mario asked. Tom, taking over from his father, wanted to know what harm she'd done the public by being in her own home, away from everybody. Even the chief wouldn't buy the nuisance thing. What law had she broken? For now, there didn't seem to be anything wrong with just letting her be. The chief told people to calm down. "And no more o' that damned harassing."

Mario finally came forth with a solution: They'd make sure the lady got no food. The safest way to get to her was to starve her out.

Next evening, Tom going up to her Long Hall window, heard her mumbling something about guilt; and saying he'd had enough, he decided it was time to be unprofessionally blunt.

"Enough, Addie. Enough of this obsession with past guilt! It's me, your friend. I want you to come away with me. I'll care for you. Give you happiness. I want to marry you!"

"Marry? I have managed so far not to fall into that trap. After such luck, am I to make myself someone's property, the prisoner of a man?"

"You are a prisoner right now."

"Ah, but a *willing* prisoner. With a purpose."

"Still a prisoner and, of yourself, the worse kind. I will free you. I'm the friend you have confided in. I've been standing by you. Let me come to you. I love you!"

"Don't."

She broke down in tears and moved away from the window. *Well,* he mused, *I'd given it my best shot.* Dejected, he started folding his poncho and getting his things together when her thin voice came out to him. "Save yourself."

"Save? How save?"

"From me. Don't you see what you see? I love you enough to warn you. Dearest friend, don't go here. I'd wind up breaking your heart. I have an aim all of my own."

"Listen, I'll embrace both. You and it."

She retorted with a stamp of the foot and an inaudible mumbling followed by an emphatic "No! I've been listening. Now it's your turn. You plain don't understand. I'm for checking out. You're for checking in."

So she showed her love in telling him not to love her. Obviously, it went beyond—in fact, lots beyond the folly of loving a mad woman who wasn't really mad, giving him the advice a counselor like him might give. And there was more to it. How could a man (this man) go where a woman (this woman) wouldn't go? It made him look like the innocent he thought she was.

It didn't take much for her to shift back to her other self, the one who had her obsessions. "I cried as a child and my mother asked me 'What's wrong?' I said I didn't know. Since then, without so much as trying, I've found it, my own included, thanks to the in-wit that smarts.

"Wouldn't it take a rare spirit to contemplate the source of the universal wrong that wraps itself around us in this fallible world and brings the note of eternal sadness in? Saints and mystics seclude themselves for a lifetime to arrive at what it means to come to life. They say, for the rest of us, life is *incomplete.* As it's said, God only knows. He alone knows the depth of what's wrong. I pray that He enlightens me."

"Don't we all?" He joshed, trying to lighten it up a bit.

"And haven't *all* been notoriously wrong?"

CHAPTER 98

Focus on Food

The night was coal-dark; and a drizzle made it dismal, as well, as a wafer–thin phantom figure made his way through the taxus yews bordering the pathway up to the castle. He was carrying a laundry bag full of groceries he had scavenged from the supermarket waste barrels, and suddenly pursued by a guard three times his size, he dropped the bag to trip the purser about to make a grab for him. Ah, gallant Whimpy! So another day with nothing to eat.

As it looked like there might be a showdown in prospect, people feared there would be violence; and that's what kept them there, a prospect that rather titillated the sporting element who brought beach chairs and came to be entertained. Someone said Addie had told the kids out front to stay away because she had a dynamite charge tied around the latch to the front door. They backed off with a big "Oooh!" She said there was more where that came from stored in a room in the tower.

Meanwhile, Papa Van felt he had to step in and tell Tom the hard truth once again that everything seemed to indicate there was nowhere to go with Addie. She was herself nowhere. "Give it up, Tom, and spare yourself. This thing will have to run its course, best without you."

So reassuring his dad he was okay on this thing, Tom pulled away for three whole days but couldn't stand it; so like a moth, he went back to the flame. Some of the kids rushed him and said they couldn't wait to tell him of a remarkable change. They'd heard a male voice, and sure enough, a for-real man appeared at the Long Hall window. He had winked at them when they asked if he was the guy she kept lighting the candle for.

Addie nuzzled up beside him, and they sported a really tight clinch. She was totally changed, talked to them very sanely and seemed a new person. They asked the lover's name, and spreading his pencil arms, he shouted out triumphantly "Have a look, folks, and guess!"

A kid called out for people to come and see the one and only "Whimpy!"

"Well," said the chief, "there's a warrant out for him and should be one out for her. Right now, she's got a pack of explosives that could endanger people in the nearby condos, plus causing a fire that spreads to the trees, and pretty soon, the whole damned mountaintop is burnin'. Folks'll be runnin' for their lives."

Van saw it was time to intervene. He got a court order for people to depart the legal premises belonging to the owner of the castle's grounds.

"Of course, should the owner and her companion exit the building, the chief could exercise his warrants. Meanwhile, as it is best to avoid violence, since the inhabitants couldn't have much food laid by, they could shortly be caught in a weakened condition, and Tom could take over from there."

Overhearing this, Whimpy wanted to sneak out in the dead of night yet again to find food as only he could find it. Addie restrained him, however, figuring the guard would be waiting for him. She reminded him they weren't completely destitute. Not yet anyway.

As the starvation siege progressed, what nobody knew was that Addie wandered noiselessly about and was regularly getting midnight visits from Betsy, her angel, who handed her up warm dinners for two. Betsy suggested that if she'd let her in, the three of them could eat together.

"Wouldn't it be nice to have company?"

"Ah, wouldn't it be nice to think so. You can't open the front door."

"What about the back?"

"Also nailed shut."

"A real fortress, huh?"

"Not a mighty fortress. But all we've got."

"Is that a way to live?"

"We live in here."

"How long can you just live inside?"

"Long? I know no long. I know no short."

"Nothing matters?"

"No, not nothing. We're concerned to the hilt with what matters."

"You sound like maybe you're preparing to die."

"No. To *live*."

Betsy saw she could make no progress with her. Having learned how things went with Tom, she decided not to take it any further.

She was somewhat heartened when Addie said that she had missed her on those several nights that she'd been unable to make it. She said she had looked in vain for the pocket flashlight that bobbed in the dark, beating time with Betsy's hurried footsteps.

She also went so far as to say Betsy seemed rather nervous when she reappeared and, taking in her moonlit face, asked how come she was flushed. Addie said that she feared she was putting a strain on her. Betsy marveled. Obviously, she was coming out of it when she wanted to.

"Dear Addie, don't worry about me."

Just as Betsy was about to hand up the basket with casserole in it, a figure in blue serge wearing an orange vest ghoulishly emerged from the shadows and was on her in a flash, viciously tossing the basket aside with the one hand while seizing Betsy by the neck with the other and menacing her with a fist.

"So this is what you been up too, huh? You're gonna get yours too."

He glared over at Addie, panting and spewing out obscenities. Knocking Betsy back against the stone facing, he spouted "I

447

shoulda known you were in on it, you loony bitch! I shoulda known!"

Betsy cowered as Tony Jr. continued to spit out obscenities. Shaking a fist at Addie, he continued. "You realize what the fuck you did to us? Look at me, bitch! Look at what I got for yah."

As he brought out his forty-five, Betsy grabbed at his arm, shouting a hysterical "Tony, *no!*" He cursed her through his teeth and struck her across the mouth with a head-rattling blow that knocked her to the ground.

"What the fuck a yah doin', you rat, you?"

Hearing Addie yell "Stop that! How can you do such a thing?" Tony hastily reset himself to fire; however, being unfamiliar with the weapon—particularly its kick—though he aimed at Addie's chest, his shot went high and wide, the slug burying itself in the window frame.

"See what da fuck yah made me do!" he snarled at shivering Betsy.

"Beast!" Addie yelled.

Tony turned and hastily fired a second shot with the same fruitless result, and as Addie ducked out of sight, he vented his boiling rage on Betsy again. Wrapping his palm around her face, he started bashing her head against the notched limestone wall.

In the midst of Betsy's spasmodic cries, Addie got to her feet; and with the little pistol held fast in both hands, she shouted at Tony to stop and pay attention—whereupon when he looked up in helpless amazement at what he saw, the bullet met him in the wrinkle between the eyes.

As he fell back, an arm vainly clawing the air, she leaned out and, clench-lipped, put another bullet in his blood-starred forehead. Waiting for a moment to detect movement as he lay there face up in the spooky moonlight, she became aware that under the strain, her vision seemed to blur, through which she nonetheless felt herself taking in Tony's features as if for the first time. And what came out to her from those high cheekbones and stringy hair was the image of a huge, hairy ape.

She felt she'd seen that simian build before. As the image progressively filled itself out, she also saw the beady eyes and flattened nose. "The Great Wrong," she declared. "Eureka! It was there before us, in the blood, waiting to implant!" With that, her vision cleared; and she took aim at the pooling blood that overflowed his open mouth, into which she splashed a final victorious round. "Huzzah!"

CHAPTER 99

Showdown

Next day, a phalanx of the city's finest, six abreast, advanced on the castle in formation with rifles at the ready. Midway, they were stopped by a horror-show laugh from within, followed by an aspirated taunt. "Hey, guys! Who told you you're going to get me?"

Fearing she might be harmed, Tom had asked the paper's star photographer, Deleste, to be on hand, hoping the camera might forestall misdeeds on the part of the police. In his inner consciousness, Tom knew he was facing an end—which was okay, so long as it marked a new beginning for Addie. Despite his personal preferences, he could read her well enough to know that as she perceived it, her future wouldn't align with his. No matter. He was committed.

The photographer's presence was, of course, wholly ignored when he captured the police chief's wild-eyed reaction to a warning shot that grazed one of his own. Having just found out from Janitor Jonesy that there were explosives behind the front door, chief pulled the phalanx back and called for his sharpshooter to blow up that door with some well-placed shots; then, they'd go in for this omni-dangerous person.

Deleste kept taking pictures of interest—one being of the reporter taking a stand in front of the police assault, palms up, and shouting "Hold it! She's sick!" Hustled aside by the police captain, he came back; and making a feint toward the front door, he was met by two cops who cast him into the bushes with a warning to stay put, "Fer Chrissake!"

It seems the lady had prepared herself for the swat team, who, as they fired, were met by a surprise burst of firecrackers—small arms aimlessly fired, they thought. With a swoosh, there followed an explosion and a wall of flame. The team was hastily backed up, stumbling as they went. The torching soon engulfed the entire downstairs area. Like ants milling at a sidewalk crack, out of nowhere came the curious. Some said she must have begun spreading the gasoline as soon as she saw the police cruisers roll up.

From the trail of a blazing torch, the chief assumed she was swooping her way up the spiral stairway leading to the roof. Once there, she shouted down defiance on the crowd that had gathered on the courtyard. They jeered back; and she returned the compliment, adding "Come and get me. If you can!"

By the time the hook and ladder arrived, flames were forking out of the upper story windows. Black smoke was billowing up from the back of the building, and the fire had spread to the tower. Tom simultaneously put a wet blanket over his head, hoping that in the confusion, he could make his way in there for a rescue; but as he inched forward toward what was left of the doorway, the forbidding heat propelled him back. Tears rolling down his cheeks, he ran over to the driveway and leaned against the ambulance, shaking his head. "This *never* should have happened. Never, never ever!"

Up came the laugh again, and the chief impatiently motioned his men to regroup and to move forward. Just as they were about to fire a volley, Deleste snapped Madman Tom dangling a press badge as he charged out in front of the formation, arms thrashing overhead, yelling "Halt! Don't shoot! Don't shoot!"—the last drawn out as a detective rushed the madman and whomped him down with a head tackle seconds before the bullets went zinging over their heads.

Having sprung up on his feet again, the madman stormed at the milling firemen. "Dammit, ain't somebody gonna go up and get her!"

Two of them finally started to warily make their way up the extended ladder when she mounted the battlements. Her reddened face seemingly aflame itself, she stood there legs apart; and lifting her skirt, she thrust her hips forward and raged "Lost two. But I'll get more!"

An electric murmur ran through the astonished onlookers broken by a howl as the lady arced a charred flambeau at them. Tom, spreading his arms, helped to disperse them. The sense of finality arose again and more emphatically sank in as he took a moment to ponder what her next step might be. One thing was for sure: she was determined not to be caught.

Naïve, of course, but having reserved place for her naivety, Tom finally felt that the folly was his. He'd come to realize that with her, the less thinking one did, the better. What thoughts he did have at the moment were on how to save her. Looking around at the growing inferno, he was beside himself.

"Dammit! Ain't you guys supposed to do something? Do it and save her!" he stormed yet again at the firemen, who were debating their next precarious move. A hose had been playing on the charred facade, and two of them finally started to make their way up the extended ladder. Once more an electric murmur ran through the astonished onlookers broken by a lone catcall and a kid crying out "The wicked witch of the west," after which there were awed whispers that rose to a general hubbub amidst the gibbering of the clumsy, coated firemen who motioned for people to back up.

One fireman finally managed to hoist himself up onto the roof. He clomped around in his lead-heavy boots then, bug-eyed, yelled down to his partner, Elmer, "She's gone!"

"Gone? Herman, fer Chrissake, find the trapdoor!"

"Ain't got one."

Elmer, down below, clomped his way to the rear of the fortress; and tripping over a rock back there, he fell and struck his head on it. As he got up, he thought he saw a lady on a bicycle, arms outspread like she was flying, as she calmly allowed gravity to speed her down the mountain path, trailing a flowing white scarf in her wake. When he called for Herman to quickly have a look, she was gone, scarf and all. He shook his head in disbelief.

Then, it got to be creepier yet as he saw a thin spike of a guy on another bike coming out through the smoke and riding shotgun behind her. He blew a farewell kiss to those who were rushing around back there to take in a last look.

But they were gone—and, as they wanted it to be, gone *forever*. And in this town, satisfied with ordinariness despite which Alexander Hamilton had seen such promise, they were never to be heard from again; and they were satisfied with that. A future lay who knows where—except that for the seeker, it will be found.

It was said that Domo Jr. was waiting for them, and rumor had it that they told him "We'll go *far away*. Free to find what's beckoning out there. There in the West."

He said, "That's what I've been waiting to do all along."

"Yes," Addie pitched in, "and find the 'new self' that awaits us."

"And what's that?" her alter ego asked, only to get the answer "We'll know it when we see it."

Embracing him, Addie said, "Let's do what we didn't know we wanted to do and find the way to a new beginning. What Hamilton had sought for the nation's future was found. Not readily found, what we want will mostly be ambiguous. Ours will always be becoming, an open horizon that beckons us to embrace what we dream of. In the dynamic of history, something more often missed than found. Ah, humanity."

THE END